LOST VOICES

CHRISTOPHER KOCH

FOURTH ESTATE

Grateful acknowledgement is made for permission to reprint
the following copyright work:

'*Voices*' by C. P. Cavafy, translated by Edmund Keely and
Philip Sherrard, from *Collected Poems* published by Hogarth Press.
Reprinted by permission of the Random House Group Limited.

Fourth Estate
An imprint of HarperCollins*Publishers*
First published in Australia in 2012
by HarperCollins*Publishers* Australia Pty Limited
ABN 36 009 913 517
harpercollins.com.au

HarperCollins*Publishers*
Level 13, 201 Elizabeth Street, Sydney NSW 2000, Australia
31 View Road, Glenfield, Auckland 0627, New Zealand
A 53, Sector 57, Noida, UP, India
77–85 Fulham Palace Road, London, W6 8JB, United Kingdom
2 Bloor Street East, 20th floor, Toronto, Ontario M4W 1A8, Canada
10 East 53rd Street, New York NY 10022, USA

Koch, C. J. (Christopher John)
Lost voices / Christopher Koch.
978 0 7322 9463 2 (pbk)
978 0 7322 9627 8 (hbk)
A823.3

Cover design by Natalie Winter
Cover image: *Bushrangers, Victoria, Australia 1852* by William Strutt. The University of
Melbourne Art Collection. Gift of the Russell and Mab Grimwade Bequest 1973
Typeset in Adobe Garamond Regular by Kirby Jones
Printed and bound in Australia by Griffin Press
The papers used by HarperCollins in the manufacture of this book are a natural, recyclable
product made from wood grown in sustainable plantation forests. The fibre source and
manufacturing processes meet recognised international environmental standards, and carry
certification.

5 4 3 2 1 12 13 14 15

To the memory of Frank Devine,
joyous spirit, great friend.

Contents

Loved, idealized voices
Of those who have died, or those
Lost for us like the dead.

Sometimes they speak to us in dreams;
Sometimes deep in thought the mind hears them.

And, with their sound, for a moment return
Sounds from our life's first poetry –
Like distant music fading away at night.

C.P. CAVAFY, *'Voices', translated*
by Edmund Keeley & Philip Sherrard

BOOK ONE

*

Hugh Dixon

1

Late in life, I've come to the view that everything in our lives is part of a pre-ordained pattern. Unfortunately it's a pattern to which we're not given a key. It contains our joys and miseries; our good actions and our crimes; our strivings and defeats. Certain links in this pattern connect the present to the past. These form the lattice of history, both personal and public; and this is why the past refuses to be dismissed. It waits to involve us in new variations; and its dead wait for their time to reappear.

God or destiny (whichever you prefer) drops each of us into a location and a time whose meaning we either inherit without thought, or else must struggle to discover. I was given the second kind: an island state on the southernmost rim of the British Empire, minding its own business and remote from the main roads of history. I left it in early adulthood; now I've come home on a visit, and I find myself moving through a series of vignettes from my earliest years. Yesterday, I walked through the suburb where my life began.

A bright, still morning in Tower Road. All very much how it used to be, over fifty years ago. Silence, except for an occasional passing car. A woman weeding a flower bed by her gate. The small prim houses from 1910 and 1928 and 1935 still hiding their secrets, behind tight front porches and lead-light windows. A sense of waiting, and a wide, wide emptiness, under an overwhelming sky. All how it used to be, bringing back that vast desolation and yearning that had baffled me as a child, and which I found baffled me still.

Here was the little bridge that carried Tower Road across the railway cutting: the bridge I'd haunted as a boy. The train tracks were running as always between high, steep banks where the sun lay in dozing yellow patches, and ranks of wild fennel grew. On top of the bank on the western side, the old rambling house with the green roof was still there, the ash tree still in its garden. Still there as well, running north above the cutting, the rickety line of paling fences that hid the little mysteries of back gardens. Over on the eastern side stood the sinister building I once knew as The Orphanage, its sombre brick turrets unchanged. Far off, houses swarmed on a hill on the edge of Moonah, and farther off still, in the utmost distance, lay the looming, grey-blue ranges where Wilson and Dalton once rode.

I stood at the centre of the bridge. This was where the now-extinct steam train would pound through below me as I hung on the railing, sending out a long, high whistle that saluted the world, and leaving behind a thrilling reek of coal. When it had gone, the emptiness and silence would enclose me again under the intolerably high sky, and I'd be filled with a hunger that made my throat ache. The hunger was for nothing I could identify – except to say that it was for the world the train had summoned up, far beyond this suburb that was the only home I knew, here on the border of the district of Glenorchy.

My parents' house was a little over halfway down Tower Road before you came to the bridge. Tower Road took its name from a stone-built, ivy-grown Irish tower-house on the corner of Main Road which had survived from the 1830s. Otherwise, the street was lined with small, decent, solid brick bungalows built between the Edwardian era and the 1940s, set close together and staring at each other in silence. Our house was one of these.

It had been built in the 1920s, in the American bungalow style of that period. It had a central gable over the small front porch, whose canopy was supported by fat brick pylons. On each side of the porch were pairs of wooden-framed sash windows, with lead-lights in their upper sections. There were also lead-lights in a window in the top half of the front door. These were of stained glass, and their reds and blues and greens were reflected on the walls and polished floorboards of the hall. When I was small I would sometimes linger alone there on late, sunny afternoons, and the lead-lights and their reflections would seem part of a mysterious suspension of Time: a place where everything had stopped, and where I found myself in a vacuum.

It was pleasant at first, this vacuum. It smelled eternally of floor polish and clean carpet and the flowers my mother put on the hall table. But then I would sense in it a gathering expectation: the imminent arrival of something vast. Yet whatever it was never seemed to come; and at this, a hollow fear would seize me, and a feeling of abandonment. I was trapped in the hallway's bland afternoon, where nothing finally happened, and the coloured lights shimmered on the wall; and I didn't know what to do. I was only freed by the melodious chiming of the mantel clock in the sitting-room: a sound that told me that Time was continuing after all, and that I was free to go: to escape.

This little hallway would eventually be the setting for the first serious crisis in my life. When it took place, I had the irrational notion that the hallway had always been waiting for it.

An ordinary Saturday evening in November, 1950: close to the end of my final year at High School, when I was eighteen. I'd just arrived home for tea, so it must have been close to six o'clock. I no longer recall what I'd been doing that day; visiting one of my friends, perhaps. I came into the house through the back door as I always did, passing through the kitchen and entering the hallway that ran through the centre of the house. The doorway to the dining-room, where I was headed, was immediately on my right. At the end of the hallway, next to the front door, was my parents' bedroom. Its door was open, and their voices were raised in tones that I'd not heard before.

This brought me to a halt, and a wave of cold went through me. The radiance of the late spring sun was striking through the coloured lead-lights, and their reflections lay across the floorboards in the way they'd always done. But now those ancient, reflected colours seemed to glow with a kind of warning.

I tell you, it was a *certainty*, Jean! Don't you understand?

My father's voice had a note of wild pleading in it, as though he not only implored my mother, but fate.

A certainty! Oh, Jim.

My mother's voice. It had a contempt in it that I'd never heard before: that note of transcendental judgement which a woman can employ with more devastating effect than a man, and which withers any hope of evasion. A pause of some seconds followed; it seemed much longer, as though Time itself had faltered. Then she said:

There's no such thing as a certainty, Jim. How could you have been so stupid? And how could you do this? You were always so straight.

My father's voice now rose higher. The note of pleading was still there, but rage had entered now: the rage of a small boy defending himself against unreasonable persecution.

Will you try and *understand!* It wasn't as if I was stealing: I was just borrowing it over the weekend. I didn't see any risk. Les knew the owner.

Les! That damned scrawny creature. I knew that one day he'd lead you to this.

He knew what the horse could do, and so did the owner. There wasn't anything in the field that could touch it.

But it lost.

It lost by a nose. I believe the bloody jockey pulled it. If I'd backed it for a place I'd have been all right. But I backed it straight out. I wanted to go for broke, for once.

Well you certainly did that. A hundred pounds.

A hundred pounds. I just haven't got it. There's only ten in the savings account.

Another pause; and when my mother spoke again her voice had a resigned hopelessness.

That's such a lot of money. It's something like two months' wages, Jim. I'll ask my father if he can help, but I don't think he'll have that sort of money.

No. I wouldn't have you doing that anyway.

How soon will they know?

On the first day of next month. On a Friday, in just under three weeks. That's when I sit down and do the reconciliation with Paul Fitzpatrick. He'll see straight away that we're a hundred quid short, and he'll want me to explain it. That farmer's got my signed receipt, and Mrs Harris has got the copy in her receipt book. Paul won't show me any mercy. John's got a heart, but Paul's a hard little bastard.

Why, Jim? Why did you do it?

I wanted you to have those new carpets. Maybe take a holiday in Melbourne. I wanted us to have some real money, for once.

My father's voice now had lost its passionate defiance; it was low and weary and lifeless. There was another brief silence, and when my mother spoke again, her reproof was mingled with pity, as though she spoke to a child.

There must be something we can do. This could mean gaol, Jim.

They might not go that far. But it's the end of the job, and I'll be finished as an accountant. They'll be bound to report me to the ASA. So it's all over for me. I'm sorry, pet. I'm sorry.

His voice had become strained, and not itself; it seemed to carry a hint of tears. I didn't want to hear any more; I turned away and went into the dining-room. I turned on the radio on the sideboard, so that when my parents came in they'd think I'd been listening to it all the time.

Over the days that followed, they were silent and withdrawn. They didn't know what I'd heard, and it was clear that they wanted to hide the situation from me as long as possible. But I decided that I must try and rescue my father, and began to consider how I might carry this out.

The only truly contented children are probably those whose parents are entirely at ease with life: people who are constantly benign, and approving of what they've been given. That wasn't my situation. My childhood on the whole was similar to many others: a mixture of delight and despair, excitement and boredom. It would probably have been easier had it not been for my father, to whom I was something of a disappointment.

He's long dead, and has become in memory a dwindled, far-off form, his stocky figure planted with feet apart, one hand holding his chin in a posture that denotes thought, staring up from the tunnel of lost time as though seen through the reverse end of a telescope. This makes me more fond of him now than I was in life, so that I sometimes call out to him inwardly, in helpless sadness. (*Dad!*)

I was an only child, and my father expected great things of me – or rather, things that he thought were great. Foremost among these were good marks at school – leading eventually, he hoped, to my becoming a solicitor – and brilliant performances at football and cricket. I delivered none of these things. My marks at school were mediocre, I wasn't good at sport, and I wanted to be an artist, not a solicitor. I'd been born with a talent for drawing, and I'd already decided that I wanted to be an illustrator, like those early twentieth-century masters whose drawings decorated the classic English children's books to which I was devoted: artists like Ernest H. Shepard, Arthur Rackham, Edmund Dulac and W. Heath Robinson. This was a disappointment to my father, who saw no possibility of my earning a proper living by it. Neither did my mother, who would gaze at me reproachfully, shaking her head. Scottish ancestry had given her large, judgemental grey eyes, dark hair and a nature that veered between stoic cheerfulness and melancholy. Then she became a *mater dolorosa.*

My bedroom was at the back of the house. Intended as a sunroom, it was long and narrow, with sliding windows on two sides. Its door opened on to the back porch, which I must cross to enter the house through the kitchen. I liked my room, despite the fact that there was no lining in the ceiling, but simply the rafters supporting the iron roof. When it rained hard, the noise was very loud; but I found this dramatic, and enjoyed it. Here I did my drawing at a pine desk that had been bought for me by my father, who expected me to use it mainly for schoolwork. When he'd first noticed that I was talented at drawing, he'd bought me sheets of proper drawing paper, Indian ink, a special penholder, and a number of steel drawing nibs. I believe he came to regret this, however, when he found that I was obsessed with drawing to the exclusion of almost everything else, and that my homework suffered. The matter came to a head when I was eleven years old.

A Saturday evening in summer, not long before the meal at six o'clock we called tea, I was hard at work on an illustration of my own for *Treasure Island*, using a fine-nibbed pen. I had a cup of tea in front of me, brought from the kitchen where my mother had made a pot. It rested on the ledge along the top of the sloping desk. There was a sudden rattling, and my father opened the door that led onto the porch and looked in, holding the doorknob as he did so. He had an accusing expression, and I saw that he was in one of his bad moods.

Still at it?

Yes.

I finished the stroke I was making with the pen, and put it down. My father took a step into the room and stood with his hands on his hips, peering at my image of Long John Silver.

You draw well, I have to admit. But you ought to get outside and kick a football with your friends now and then, instead of crouching in here all the time.

I do get out. I just want to finish this.

My father sniffed once as though he had a cold – which he didn't – wrinkling up his nose. He continued to stand in silence for a few moments, his head on one side, and I saw that he was working out what to say next. He was of medium height, about five feet nine, and powerfully built, with wide shoulders, a broad chest and a broad head. He wore what he usually did at home: an open-necked shirt, an old grey cardigan hanging loose and unbuttoned, and grey slacks. His colouring was unusual: his eyes were brown, but his hair was blond. It had darkened a little (he was in his late thirties), but the yellow was still there. It was thick and straight and he wore it rather long; he had a habit of brushing his forelock off his forehead with the back of his right hand: a somewhat theatrical gesture in a man who was otherwise conventional. His features were regular, except for a rather short nose, and his shovel-shaped chin had a pleasing size and firmness. He was quite a good-looking man I suppose, and when he was in a good humour and cracking jokes he had an attractive, even whimsical personality. In his youth he'd been a keen sportsman, playing cricket and football and engaging in competitive rowing, which was what developed his chest: that chest which contained a fatal weakness.

He had chronic bronchitis. It had developed in his boyhood, and had greatly marred his life. It meant that he was given to constant chest infections, despite all his efforts at fitness, and although he'd tried to enlist in the Army as soon as the War broke out, he was refused because of his ailment. He was bitter and ashamed about this, and it added to a resentment which was already lodged deep in his nature.

He worked in the office of J. & P. Fitzpatrick's, the largest hardware store in the city, and I gathered from remarks that he made that his work sometimes bored and frustrated him. He seemed to hold Fitzpatrick's in contempt at such times, and the War must have looked like a marvellous escape: the greatest adventure life had ever offered him. At eleven years old, this meant little to me, particularly since my mother openly said that she was glad my father wasn't able to go. Why should she want him killed? Children have very little capacity for compassionate understanding, and when my father had bouts of wheezing and coughing, it also left me unmoved; it was just a disturbing noise to me.

Finally, he spoke again.

Where's it going to get you, this stuff? There are so many other things you could do in your spare time that'd be more worthwhile. You'll be twelve soon, and you've got to pass the exam this year to get into High School. I don't want you ending up in the bloody technical college. You should be studying.

I do study. But I want to be an artist. An illustrator.

An illustrator? You think you'll earn a living that way, when you grow up?

Why not? The artists who illustrate good books must earn a lot. The books are sold all over the world.

I waved my hand to indicate the world. As I did, I knocked my cup over, and tea flooded down the slope of the desk, ruining Long John Silver, mingling with the Indian ink, and rushing on in a brown and grey river. I stared in horror as it cascaded over my bare legs, poured onto the small blue and white rug on which my chair was set, and spattered the linoleum that covered the rest of the floor. Then I jumped up and met my father's gaze, incapable of speech.

Christ.

His mouth twisted sideways in a way that it did when he was utterly disgusted. He didn't move but stared at the floor and at me, and his voice remained ominously even.

Look at this bloody mess. You've ruined that rug – and it's one your mother's fond of.

I'm sorry, Dad. I didn't notice the cup.

You thought you'd be the *artist*, didn't you, having his cup of tea? You're so much in the bloody clouds you can't even see what's around you.

He sighed, and his voice became weary and resigned.

Go into the kitchen and get a cloth from your mother. Tell her what you've done to her rug, and then try and clean up this mess.

I saw now that he resented me; perhaps resented what I was. This was a shocking thing to realize about my father, and I turned away in silence and retreated from him.

The next day, in the late afternoon, he approached me again.

I was loitering on the railway bridge, leaning on the railings. It was calm and sunny, and long shadows lay across the lines. I heard a cough, and turned to find my father walking up to me, still wearing his weekend uniform of cardigan and slacks. He didn't speak, but instead moved next to me at the railings and leaned on the top one as I was doing, staring up the line and smoking a cigarette. I stared in the same direction and waited, looking towards Moonah and the hills.

I've been thinking, he said. I was probably a bit hard on you yesterday, son. I realize what happened was an accident. But it bothers me that you might fail your test to get into High School. And that's because I want you to do well. I want you to be a success in life. You understand that, don't you?

I said that I did.

I had a win at the races yesterday, he said. That'll pay for some new drawing things for you.

He looked at me with a faint grin, letting me know that things would now be all right between us.

His one indulgence was gambling on the horses. Every Saturday afternoon he went to the Elwick race track in Glenorchy with his friend Les Harrington: a tall thin balding man who always wore a green felt hat and a loose, sagging cardigan, a hand-rolled cigarette permanently in his mouth and a folded racing paper tucked under his arm. He looked like a jockey, although he was too tall for one. My mother seemed not to be impressed with Les; I once heard her say that he wasn't my father's type. But she tolerated my father's Saturdays at the races; it gave him a break, she said. I assumed that this tolerance was because he only betted small amounts; he never seemed to lose very much or win very much.

I want you to understand that there are no second chances in life, my father said. Not unless you're born rich. I learned that the hard way, in the Depression.

I had only a vague idea of what was meant by the Depression. But I wanted him to go on talking, and prompted him.

So you were poor, then.

You could say that.

He threw his cigarette over the rail on to the tracks below, where it lay smoking.

I never had a penny to spare, he said. But at least I had a job. A lot of people didn't. I was just a clerk, and I had to study at night to qualify as an accountant, and get promoted. Then I was a bit better off, and could afford to marry your mother.

He was speaking now as though I were grown up, and I felt flattered. We'd not had a conversation like this before.

But Grandpa Dixon's a lawyer, I said. So he wasn't poor, was he?

My father's mouth suddenly twisted, as though he'd tasted something sour, and his eyes went cold. It was an expression of great bitterness, which I'd seen before when Grandpa Dixon was mentioned.

No – your grandfather wasn't poor. Neither is my brother George, these days. That's because my father sent George to University to study Law, so that he could join the family firm. But the old man couldn't afford to send us both to University, because of the Depression. Or so he said. So I was put out to work at sixteen.

That wasn't fair.

No, Hugh. That wasn't fair.

He continued to stare up the line to where a gold light was deepening on the hills, and fell silent. Then he took a breath and turned to me with a smile that was like a wince.

Come on son, he said, and put a hand on my shoulder. Time to go in for tea.

I'm able to see now that my father was never at home in the world.

In his youth, a University education was only possible for those whose parents could afford to pay for it. And the chance came only once, at the end of secondary school; if it was lost then, it was lost for ever. Denied that chance, pushed at sixteen into a dead-end job in the office of a factory, my father had to depend on the same small salary as his workmates did, since my grandfather Dixon had no intention of supplementing what he earned. He was as poor as the other clerks at the factory; and yet he was seen as somehow privileged, without wanting to play such a role.

This was because he had the wrong accent and the wrong sort of manners for the level he'd come to inhabit. Born in 1906, he'd grown up in a prosperous Edwardian household that employed domestic servants. He'd been educated at a private school which worked hard to instil in its pupils the style and speech of the English ruling class – seen as essential to refinement throughout the Empire. A casualty of colonial history, my father had little hope of fitting in as a poor clerk. It wasn't for want of trying: he worked hard at sharing the jokes and manners of his workmates. But he never really succeeded; he'd been pushed out of the world where he belonged.

After a few years he'd left the factory, and had taken a clerical job at J. & P. Fitzpatrick's, where he'd stay. It was an old family firm, founded by an emancipated Irish convict in the nineteenth century and run now by his descendants, the two short plump and smiling Fitzpatrick brothers, John and Paul – pillars of the city's establishment, who never acknowledged their convict ancestry. They often assured the members of their staff that an employee of Fitzpatrick's was secure for life – and my parents, as children of the Depression, valued this assurance. Not long after being taken on there, my father began to study accountancy through a correspondence course, and ultimately qualified as an Associate of the Australian Society of Accountants. He was then put in charge of the office at Fitzpatrick's, overseeing the clerical staff. He'd achieved the sort of authority which insulated him against rejection or ridicule, and he was valued and trusted by the brothers Fitzpatrick. He earned a salary that wasn't large, but enough to support his family in reasonable comfort; and for a good deal of the time he was probably content.

As a small boy, I would be taken by my mother to call on him at the store. Fitzpatrick's stood in Elizabeth Street, the main street of the city, and was a stone-built, three-storey Georgian-style building of early nineteenth-century origin, conjoined with two others. The sign on the verandah awning over the footpath was in tall green lettering, and read: *J. & P. Fitzpatrick. Hardware.* My father's office was upstairs on the first floor, where customers came to a counter to pay bills, or discuss their business. Many were farmers from the country; as well as being a retail store, Fitzpatrick's manufactured such articles as water-tanks and roof trusses, and did a good deal of business with the bush. When my mother and I came up to the counter, I would see the book-keeper, grey-haired Mrs Harris, at work in a small cubicle; a little way off, my father sat in a big glass office, behind a desk stacked with files. Mrs Harris would go in there and let him know that we were here, and he'd emerge and walk briskly to the counter, youthful and immaculate in his three-piece suit, smiling with pleasure at seeing us.

I saw very little of my paternal grandparents when I was young. My parents hardly ever visited them, and nor did they come often to our house in Tower Road. The law firm of Dixon and Dixon was run by my grandfather Charles and his brother Walter. My father's brother George soon became a partner; and in contrasting himself with George, my father felt that he'd slipped below the level of his family. So he'd mostly ceased to socialize with his brother, and with the people he'd known in his youth. Then a final rift occurred that would never be healed, so that I never saw my Dixon grandparents again. The breakdown had come, apparently, when Charles Dixon suggested that my father join Dixon and Dixon as their chief accountant. The old man thought of this as a favour; but so deep was my father's resentment that he'd refused – and an already deep bitterness became deeper on both sides, ending in complete separation. By the time I was sixteen, both my father's parents were dead. They were thus only half-real to me, existing in fragmented childhood memories.

One or two friends from my father's youth remained in contact with him; they and their wives would come visiting, and my parents would visit them in turn, and sometimes play tennis with them. But my father's closest friend was Les Harrington, his companion at the race track.

Les was a motor mechanic, and not the sort of man with whom my father would normally have had much in common. Nor was Les the sort of man who would generally have been in sympathy with my father. But this was how it was – unaccountably, they were friends. I had only to see them greet each other to know this. They would grin, and a genuine warmth would light up both their faces. They were an odd pair, but they were clearly comfortable with each other. This association was mysterious to me, as a child; but later I formed a theory about it.

My father had two sides: two personalities. The dominant personality was the one that went every weekday to Fitzpatrick's, wearing his suit, collar and tie and the grey felt hat that nearly all men wore then like a uniform: an Akubra, set at a rakish angle – the only give-away, perhaps, to his other personality. This personality was the one that had wanted to escape to the War: the one that longed for adventure, and whose principal reading for relaxation was crime thrillers. In this incarnation, clad in a golf jacket and slacks and an open-necked shirt (but still wearing his hat), he enjoyed the risk involved in his modest bets, as well as the slightly disreputable nature of the race track, and of racing people. It was an escape from Fitzpatrick's; an escape from respectability.

Les Harrington was a racing man through and through: apart from his job, his life was horse-racing. My father had probably met him when he took his car in for repairs at the garage where Les worked. Les knew a wide circle of trainers, jockeys and owners – and this meant that, through him, my father penetrated the inner circles of the racing world. He and Les had beers with racing people in the bar under the grandstand, and sometimes visited them in the stables, gaining information as to whether a jockey was going to throw a race, or whether a horse was off-form. Talking to me about it – which he did when I was older – he would hint at such things with a smile that made him resemble a boy getting into mischief. Being with Les won him acceptance by the racing crowd – which could never otherwise have happened – and I guessed that Les enjoyed being guide and mentor to a man of Jim Dixon's type: a man whom he perhaps saw as cleverer and more educated than himself, but less worldly-wise, and certainly less knowledgeable about horses and the arcane world of racing.

Through the open door of my room on the back porch, I would often see Les arrive on a Saturday afternoon in his eternal loose cardigan, green hat pushed back on his high, balding forehead to free a strand of lank dark hair, his racing guide under his arm, a hand-rolled cigarette in the corner of his mouth. When my father appeared in answer to Les's knock on the back door, Les's narrow face would break into a sly grin.

G'day, Jim. Picked any likely ones?

There was a faintly mocking tone to this; and yet there was also a fondness, like that of a master speaking to a favourite apprentice. My father's eyes would warm with pleasure, and he would push back his thinning, straw-yellow hair with a gesture of anticipation.

Let's go, he would say.

Then they'd drive off in Les's big Studebaker to the Saturday adventure of the track: territory of release and exuberance; territory of ruin and disaster.

Descending into the 1940s, that archaic time before my eighteenth year and my father's disgrace, I find far, fine-spun webs of happiness. The flowering back garden of summer – irises, roses, marigolds, foxgloves – and the music of those days drifting from the radio through the open dining-room window. Paul Robeson singing 'I Still Suits Me'; Richard Tauber singing 'You Are My Heart's Delight'; Bing Crosby singing 'Please'. Pieces of star-shaped thistledown floating through the blue: children called them robbers, because they came through windows. My mother in the kitchen singing snatches of songs by Noel Coward and Stephen Foster, no doubt recalled from her youth. The mild, sunny air full of melody. Farther off, the voices of my friends along the street, calling me out to meet them in the road. Voices that the past makes ghostly, since the faces are half-forgotten.

It's 1944, and I'm eleven years old. Bob Wall waits for me on the corner of Main Road and Hopkins Street, at the entrance to Dickenson's Arcade. His white face is expressionless, his white-blond hair like dried grass in the sun. As I come up to him his glance shifts, as though he expects someone more important to be coming along behind. I smile, but he doesn't smile back. That's Bob's way.

We walk up Main Road together: the highway that's brought me here from the corner of Tower Road, taking me over the frontier of New Town and into the suburb of Moonah.

Moonah, southernmost suburb in the district of Glenorchy, is a zone of mythical possibilities. Skirted in the east by the spaces of the river, and on the west by the barrier of the hills, it's a poorer district than the one I live in, and is seen by my parents as less respectable; yet for me it's a territory of veiled promise. A wide, extending flatland of teeming bungalows, train lines, shops and small factories, with plumes of white smoke drifting in its distances, it's also the home of Bob Wall. I've previously caught the tram to school, but now that Bob waits to meet me, I come on foot. It's not very far to the school from here, and I suspect he has no money for tram fares.

He stares straight ahead as we walk, his dark blue eyes fearless and stern under level, low-set brows. He seldom talks much, so we walk mostly in silence. I carry a leather school bag on my back; Bob carries a battered canvas rucksack. I like to think that he waits for me each day out of friendship, but I know there's another reason: he wants to copy my homework, before lessons begin. Now he looks sideways at me.

Did you get it done?

The homework, you mean?

Yeah. The homework.

Yes, it's done.

Going to give me a look at it?

Okay. When we get to school.

He nods, and we walk on. I'm happy to help him in this way, because I yearn to penetrate his secret life. I don't even know what part of Moonah he lives in, and Bob won't say. Attempts to make him do so all fail: I'm met with monosyllables, or silence. When Bob doesn't like a question, he just doesn't answer. Sometimes

I wonder whether he lives in an ordinary house at all. I see him living out of doors, alone, like the gypsy Meg Merrilies in the poem we've learned at school, sleeping in some nest in the grass, or in a stable. His blue school shirt and grey shorts are shabby, and it's clear that he's quite poor.

Main Road in the summer is a magic highway. Straight and level, it runs north through Moonah towards the suburb once called O'Brien's Bridge and now named Glenorchy; after that come the borders of the country. In those distances to the north, as we walk along, the pale blue ranges seem to sing, like the telephone wires that loop overhead. The air is filled with little whirrings, and the far, wild cries of an unknown life. Everything out here is mildly and sweetly faded, in a way that I believe has something to do with the presence of a smiling, invisible race who are part of that hidden life: people who are different from those in the ordinary world. I find it hard to imagine the nature of the life they live, knowing only that it's connected with Moonah's sun-warmed fadedness; with the old grey boards of unpainted sheds and outbuildings, faded and baked and cracked by the suns of many summers; with the whitened grass that grows along paling fences, smelling like warm bread; with the little weatherboard shops out here, and the coloured, bleached-out signs that advertize tea and chocolate. Tram lines are part of it too, gleaming and shimmering in the sun like static streams of water. A green double-decker clangs by, its electric whine drowning the singing of the ranges. It recedes with infinite slowness down the long, straight line of highway, making occasional stops; it becomes a toiling green speck; it becomes a thing in a dream, vanishing into the haze that leads to the country.

The passing cars have charcoal-burners on the back: a device made necessary by the wartime shortage of petrol. But we no longer have to fear that the Japanese forces in New Guinea will invade Australia: American and Australian troops are driving them from their bases into the mountains, and will soon overwhelm them. Occasional horse-drawn vehicles go by:

delivery carts of butchers and bakers painted in carnival colours, the drivers giving double clicks of their tongues to urge the horses forward. The tool-laden cart of a Council road gang clatters beside the kerb, the group of lean men in ruined felt hats and ancient black waistcoats sitting with legs dangling, while one of them stands to drive, shaking the reins. Most of them are quite old; young men have nearly all gone to the War. The cart draws up at the iron horse-trough outside Cooley's Hotel, and the men roll cigarettes while the old draught horse drinks and drinks. Oat-smelling horse droppings that nobody minds lie piled on the hot grey asphalt. It's still a world in which horses have a part: one which will last a little longer, until after the War.

We reach the Moonah State School early, well before the bell, and sit on a bench under a peppercorn tree. Bob looks at me and waits. I unbuckle my bag, take out my homework book, and hand it over. Bob pulls a stained and crumpled exercise book from his haversack and sets about doing his copying, using a blunt, chewed pencil.

I decide to make another attempt to probe the enigma of his nature, and I ask him what would happen if he weren't able to copy my homework any more. He looks at me quickly, and his eyes narrow.

Why? Aren't you going to let me see it no more?

Of course. But I mightn't always be here.

You going somewhere, Hugh?

No. But *some* time or other you'll have to manage the work on your own. Won't you, Bob?

His tone grows sardonic, at this.

Some time or other: yeah. I'll worry about that when the time comes. Don't fuss, mate.

Why is it you don't try and do it yourself? You've got the brains.

He studies me for a moment and I grow tense, wondering if I've gone too far. Then he says:

Do it myself? At my place? You don't know what it's like at my place, when the old man's at home. He's there at the moment, and there's no fucken peace.

How do you mean, there's no peace?

I mean he's always liable to start belting me.

He looks at me directly from under his straight, low-set brows, as though warning me not to question him further. But I press on.

What about your mother? Doesn't she try and stop him?

He belts her too, when he's drunk.

I stare at him. I can think of nothing to say, and he looks away across the playground. Then he says:

My mother's okay to me. We get on well, when he pisses off from home. But the bastard always turns up again.

I want to tell him I'm sorry; but his hard, empty face warns me not to do so. He stands up.

Come on, he says. The bell's gone.

He's never said so much to me before, and I believe there'll come a time when he'll tell me even more. Then I'll enter his other life, and truly become his friend.

Trying to plumb these levels of the childish past – levels so deep in time that they seem to belong to a history not my own – I find it difficult to distinguish my real life from the life of dreams.

This is because I was visited then by two kinds of dream: those that came to me in sleep, and those that I encountered in waking life. There were certain people in the real world who seemed to have come from dream; I could not have said why. Particular landscapes and objects seemed also to belong there, even though they appeared in front of me in a perfectly real guise. One of these was the building I thought of as The Orphanage.

In my earliest years, I found this building frightening. It was located close to our home on the New Town side of the border, in a little street on the eastern side of the railway bridge, next to an empty field: a large, forbidding, two-storeyed Victorian structure of red brick, with three-sided turrets at each end, topped with small peaked roofs. My parents always referred to it as 'The Orphanage', and it was only after some years that I discovered that it wasn't an orphanage at all, but some kind of rooming house. Why they'd given it this name I never discovered; but I find it understandable. It had the grim, unforgiving air of an institution: an institution out of the nineteenth century, or a story by Dickens. One reason for my parents' error – or perhaps it was a joke – may have been that there were often groups of children playing in the street outside; and these children bore the stigmata of poverty which were common then, persisting from the Depression: bare feet, or clumsy boots that didn't fit, thin, hungry faces, and a mixture of clothes that might have been picked out at a jumble sale: dresses and trousers and shirts that were too big or too small; bulky sweaters and cardigans shaped by former owners. Sometimes a woman would come out and shout at these children, and drag one or two inside; or a swaying, drunken man would go through the front door.

When I went past there as an infant, my hand in my mother's, I would peer at The Orphanage's tall, narrow windows, all of which were masked and darkened by flyscreens of heavy wire mesh, as well as by holland blinds of a dingy yellow colour. These windows stirred in me a nervous curiosity: they were somehow both squalid and mysterious, and seemed to belong to a life that might reach out and claim me. By the time I was eleven I'd outgrown such fears; but my curiosity remained.

I sometimes went by there on my own, and the children loitering in front of the door would stare at me. One of them would look at me with particular interest: a thin, pale, brown-haired girl in a faded floral dress, with a sharp face and wide, unwinking eyes. Her expression was critical and amused, and I wondered what amused her. She looked about eleven or twelve, and I seemed to have seen her before, I couldn't think where. I imagined a name for her, and called her Rose.

One evening I wandered down the street past The Orphanage when it seemed to be deserted. There were no children to be seen outside; but then I caught sight of a figure out of the corner of my eye, in the empty field. A paling fence hid most of the field, but a broken gate stood half open, revealing an expanse of dry grass where the girl I called Rose was standing quite still and staring at me. When she caught my eye she smiled, as though there were some secret between us. Then she beckoned, a sort of gathering-in motion. I wanted to obey and go to her through the gate; but I couldn't imagine what doing this would lead to, and I hadn't the courage to find out. So I merely waved, and hurried on.

Was it months later that I saw her in the field again – or only weeks? The scene exists in the dimension of dream – and sometimes I wonder if this was what it was.

Walking by The Orphanage again, I'd paused by the broken gate that opened onto the field. Twilight, with the last light fading out, like the arrival of unconsciousness. Long red clouds, like the coals of a dying fire, suspended in the sky above the towers of The Orphanage. Grim and threatening, these clouds, seeming to signal something bad, happening far out in the world. Then, in the centre of the field, two figures suddenly appeared: the brown-haired girl and a man. He was lean and middle-aged, with a thin, sallow face and lank black hair, and wore a dark jacket and navy-blue trousers, like some kind of uniform. He had hold of Rose by the arm and was dragging her through the grass towards a tumbledown shed on the far side. She was wearing the same floral dress, and her legs and feet were bare. There was a wind getting up, and it blew the dress and her hair sideways.

I stared, not knowing whether to run or stay still. Neither Rose nor the man seemed to see me. She cried out once, a single thin sound like the call of a bird. The man smiled; and this was somehow more alarming than had he worn an angry expression. The girl frowned, her mouth an O, leaning back to resist him. But it was useless; he continued to drag her, and I saw that her hurrying feet obeyed despite her body's reluctance, like those of a child who puts up token resistance to punishment, knowing it must come.

Who was this man? Was he her father? Was he going to beat her? He dragged her into the shed, and I heard a final cry from inside, drawn out and pleading. Silence then, and darkness, and the grim clouds glowed and faded above The Orphanage.

I never saw the girl again: she didn't appear in the street after that.

Bob Wall was one of those people who came from dream.

I'd not actually encountered him in the dreams of the night; yet when I first saw him in the school playground, I recognized him instantly. Bob came from that other life, and it made me want to know him better. This meant that I was drawn towards someone with whom I seemed to have almost nothing in common: a boy whom I could hardly call a friend, and who showed none of the warmth of a friend. But his white, sternly closed face and his hard, untelling eyes were instantly recognizable: he had his origins in a dream I longed to enter.

Our true friendship only began when we discovered our shared enthusiasm for drawing: an enthusiasm which in both our cases amounted to obsession, even at that very early age.

In the weekly art lesson one day, we were both singled out by our class teacher as the best in the group, and our drawings were pinned up on the notice board. This must have been gratifying to Bob, since he was near the bottom of the class in most other things. We both liked to draw animals, and took our inspiration from photographs in magazines. I'd drawn a horse, and Bob had drawn a dramatically snarling leopard. There were murmurs of admiration for the leopard from around the room, and Miss Barrow called Bob up to the front to praise him, telling him how lifelike it was, and what a gift he had. She was a strict yet kindly woman, with greying fair hair drawn back in a bun and tired eyes. Bob stood stock-still, unsmiling, his mouth tight; but his face flushed bright red, in a way that I'd never seen it do before.

Later, during recess in the playground, we walked towards the seats under the peppercorn tree.

You sure can draw, I said.

So can you, he said. You're good.

He glanced at me and smiled briefly, and I knew that he'd accepted me as something more than a convenient acquaintance. After that, we began to show each other drawings which we brought from home. Both of us drew the fighter planes the War had made famous – Spitfires, Kittyhawks, Flying Fortresses, Messerschmitts – as well as battleships and tanks. Then I began to show him my illustrations for books. In response, he brought me examples of his own special interest: drawings copied from American comic strips, and attempts at comic strips of his own, heavily influenced by the masters of the form. His drawings were beautifully and meticulously done, though his only materials were cheap coloured pencils.

I still read comic strips now and then, as most boys did; but I'd begun to grow out of them, and to concentrate solely on books. Bob read few books; comics were his devouring interest. He wanted to be a comic strip artist, he told me.

This emerged during a lunch hour when we were sitting under the peppercorn tree. I'd shared my sandwiches with him, as I often did, since all he ever seemed to eat for lunch was a meat pie from the tuck shop, bought for sixpence supplied by his mother. I shuffled through his drawings, some of which I found quite strange. This was because a number were copied from strips that were unknown to me. They featured scantily-clad women, and were often graphically violent – and this gave them a shocking and even forbidding flavour. The more accurate term for these creations was 'adventure strips', since they were scarcely comic, and were aimed mainly at adults. Certain features in them –

clothing, cars, ships – didn't seem to belong in the current era, and I asked Bob where they came from.

He seldom had money to buy any comics, he told me, but he'd discovered a collection of coloured American comic books in a trunk under the house, possibly left there by a previous tenant. This was quite a find, since American comics had ceased to appear in Australia when the War in the Pacific cut off the passage of most goods from America by sea. The comics were also quite old: syndication dates in some of the frames revealed that they were survivals from ten years ago and more, in the 1930s.

Many of them were familiar – *The Phantom*, *Tarzan*, *Buck Rogers* – but others were not. One strip in particular which was quite unknown to me captured my attention. It was clearly Bob's favourite, since he'd copied more images from it than any other. This was *Terry and the Pirates*, by Milton Caniff, dealing with the adventures of Terry Lee and his muscular friend Pat Ryan on the China Coast of the 1930s, eluding Chinese pirates and warlords. When I expressed an interest in it, Bob brought the actual book from home and showed it to me. Looking through it, we sat side by side under the peppercorn tree in the lunch hour, heads bent close together. He didn't offer to lend the book; but I knew, as I watched the reverent way he handled it, that just showing it to me was a mark of his growing trust.

The coloured, yellowing newsprint pages gave off a musty scent that was obscurely tantalizing: the smell of the 1930s, when Bob and I were infants. There was something wicked yet deeply exciting about *Terry and the Pirates*, and the smell itself seemed part of this, as such things do at that age. The dialogue was unusually sophisticated for a comic strip, so that some of it was beyond our grasp. As though we viewed a difficult adult film, we pored over the speech balloons, trying to comprehend everything the characters were saying to each other, but knowing – as in certain films – that there was another level of experience here besides that of story: one that only adults could decipher, and which was somehow dark. Caniff's pictures, with their use of dense, dramatic shadow, seemed to contain cryptic messages never to be translated into words, but creating a longing for a life unlikely to be reached: a life both enticing and disquieting. There was nothing gross in the strip, and certainly no nudity, given the standards of the time; after all, it was a piece of mass entertainment from the pre-permissive age, operating within strict limits. But a veiled eroticism lurked in its pages, and subterranean glimpses of what used to be called depravity, since certain female characters emerge in recollection (though no inkling of this would have been possible for me at the time), as nymphomaniac or lesbian or both. *Terry* was for adults, and was uncompromisingly tough and realistic; and I saw why it fascinated Bob.

What I realize now is how perceptive he was in making Milton Caniff his mentor. When I came to study black-and-white illustration, and managed to obtain some ancient copies of *Terry and the Pirates*, I saw as others have done that Caniff had a kind of genius. He was the most original cartoonist of the pre-television era, and he would influence my work and Bob's as he did that of many other artists. He had revolutionized the comic strip medium with his use of chiaroscuro, deep shadow, dramatic silhouette and impressionistic rendering of detail, in drawings that resembled woodcut prints. He also used cinema techniques, such as long shots, close-ups and contrasting camera angles. He even influenced the cinema itself in the way that he used light sources to create mood, as black-and-white films would come to do in the B-grade crime dramas of my youth: the genre now known as *cinema noir*.

A comic strip that was actually comical, and which drew Bob and me together more than any other in his collection, was *The Captain and the Kids*. We sat bent over the book in the spangled shade of the peppercorn tree, chuckling and slapping our thighs, glancing at each other with glee. Bob seldom even smiled, and his laughter was very rare; now he laughed with open joy, and his face showed a warmth I'd not seen before.

We recalled episodes from *The Captain and the Kids* to amuse each other, in class and out of it. Bob would squint at me sideways, with a humorous expression.

Those two kids – Hans and Fritz. Eh?

This was enough to start us both laughing: a key to something only we understood. We talked more and more about the disruptive twin boys on their island in the South Seas, tormenting their plump Mamma and the fat, bearded Captain and his friend the tall-hatted Inspector: quaintly-dressed figures out of nineteenth-century Germany, via New York – a strip that I've since discovered was a favourite of Picasso's. We saw ourselves as the twins: Bob was blond Hans; I was dark-haired Fritz. The fact that the Germans were the enemy in the War made the game somehow funnier. We punched each other in the ribs, staggering about the playground, and Bob went pink in the face. We quoted lines from the dialogue:

'Dum frazzle your ding-busted hides!'
'Vot manners!'

There is a sort of innocent love that can spring up between small boys. It's like the affection of puppies, and manifests itself in the same way: through mock fighting, and rough and tumble. In the grassy playground at the school, where the boys were segregated in one zone and the girls in another, sporadic fights were always taking place between the boys – only a few of them serious, most of them ritual or play. In the shade of the gum trees that grew along the fence, Bob and I wrestled, still taking the parts of Hans and Fritz. (*'Take zat!' 'Dummkopf!'*) We were expressing our affection for each other; and as we rolled and grappled on the grass, I breathed in the odour of Bob's white hair, light and pleasant as hay.

We were together now on most weekends. Bob would never come to my home – though I invited him many times – so I would ride my bicycle out to Moonah and meet him in the usual place, in front of Dickenson's Arcade. He still avoided telling me where his own home was, and I suspected he was ashamed of it in some way. He didn't have a bicycle, and he clearly envied me my Malvern Star, which we took turns at riding as we moved about Moonah and Glenorchy – or else Bob straddled the luggage rack and I carried him as a passenger. We wandered for miles, catching tadpoles in jars in marshes beside the roads, tickling trout in the creeks that ran through Glenorchy down to the Derwent, trespassing into factory yards and vacant lots and climbing on old sheds. On hillsides beyond the town, we would run with our arms outstretched, making wordless shouts: cries of exaltation at the marvels of the world.

We also went into the bush beyond Glenorchy and smoked cigarettes that Bob stole from his father. On these occasions we lit small fires and pretended to be camping. Coughing, drawing on our cigarettes, we looked at each other across the flames with cunning outlaw grins.

Heh, heh. Craven A. Not bad fags, are they, Fritz?

Good. Very good, Hans. But won't he miss them?

Nah. He was so pissed when I took them, he won't know where they've bloody gone.

On one of these occasions, squatting in the grass beside the fire, Bob spoke to me about his father again. His expression was harder than usual, and I saw that something serious had happened. We were both wearing shorts, and he pointed to bruises on his legs.

The old man belted me again last night. Took a piece of kindling to me.

Jesus, Bob. Why did he do that?

He was punching my mother, and I told him to stop.

I looked at him in horror, while he drew on his cigarette. Finally I said: Why does she stay with him? Why don't you both leave?

My mother won't leave him. She keeps on hoping he'll stop drinking. She says he's all right when he's not drunk. Something in that. He's even nice to me, then. But he's drunk more and more. He doesn't even work much – just odd jobs. If my mother didn't work in the factory, we wouldn't eat.

He stared into the fire, his eyes as stern as a man's, and I knew I should be quiet, and not ask any more questions. After a time, he spoke again, still looking into the fire.

It's all right when he's not there. My mother's real nice to me. She lets me do my drawing on the kitchen table. But when he's home I have to stay in my room. There isn't a table to work on there. Now he's home, I keep hoping the bastard will go off drinking again.

He turned and looked at me, raising his eyebrows, his expression changing as though something had just dawned on him.

I'll tell you what, Hughie. I reckon I should run away. Take off into the bush. Want to come with me?

Sure. I'll come.

I was smiling, since I treated this as a game; but Bob's expression was serious, and now he put out his hand. When I took it, he gripped my hand hard.

We're comrades, aren't we, Fritz?

Right, Hans. Comrades.

This was an important word, and what Bob had said was serious. We two had declared ourselves inseparable, I thought. But I was wrong.

Some two weeks later, on a Monday morning in April, Bob was no longer standing by Dickenson's Arcade. I waited, under a grey autumn sky, until it grew too late to wait any longer; then I caught a tram out to the school.

At the beginning of the first lesson, Miss Barrow stood by her table in front of the blackboard, waiting for Grade Six to be still. We settled into our varnished wooden desks with their tip-up seats and sat up straight; but Miss Barrow didn't immediately start the lesson. Instead, she announced that she'd had a phone call from Bob Wall's mother. Bob had been missing from home since Saturday, and Mrs Wall wanted to know if any of us had seen him.

A cold wave went over me, and the fluttering voices around me seemed to come from a distance. The voices told Miss Barrow that nobody had seen Bob, repeating it many times until she held up her hand.

There's something else. On Friday afternoon after school, Donald Grant in Grade Five reported his bike missing from the bicycle shed. It was a blue Malvern Star. Its theft has been reported to the police. But over the weekend, one of our teachers saw Bob Wall riding a blue Malvern Star through Moonah. We can't be sure, but we wonder if he might have taken Donald's bike. So please keep your eyes open, and if you see him on the bike, you must report it to the school – or else ask your parents to report it to the police.

There was a silence, in which faces turned to each other with looks of solemn dismay, or else with those gleeful, scandalized grins that welcome the distraction of wickedness. But I sat stricken, looking away through the window at the glittering heads of the gums in the playground.

That night in bed, I found myself thinking of how Bob had talked to me once about the first comic strip he'd become devoted to: *Felix the Cat.* His mother had bought a *Felix* book for him, he said, when he was seven years old. She did it to console him after his father had given him a very bad beating; his father had gone out that night, and she'd sat on Bob's bed reading the comic to him before he went to sleep. Together they'd followed the series of black-and-white pictures in their frames, while his mother had recited the speeches in the balloons. She'd also talked to him about Felix. It seemed that the cat was a fading film star, who'd been very famous in her youth: one of the first animated cartoon characters. She'd often seen him in the silent, black-and-white cinema as a girl; the whole world had loved him then, she said.

Bob still had the *Felix* book she'd given him, and brought it to school to show it to me under the peppercorn tree. By peering at the minute dates in the frames of the various sequences, we discovered that these adventures, like those in *Terry and the Pirates*, dated from long ago: from the 1920s and '30s. Felix moved through an American world of skyscrapers, excitement and danger, alien yet familiar, like the terrain of dreams. And what Bob had admired most about Felix when he was small was that the little black cat always survived the dangers that threatened him; always triumphantly outwitted the enemies who pursued him. After one of his father's beatings, Bob would retreat to his bedroom with Felix and regain his hope and courage.

There were two kinds of backgrounds in the *Felix* strips: cityscapes, and peaceful outer suburbs near the country. The cityscapes, with their American streets and buildings, were infused with excitement. In contrast, the scenes in the outer suburbs were silent and calm. One of these in particular Bob contemplated often, he told me, even now that he'd outgrown the strip. He pointed it out to me. Felix was walking past an open, grassy hillside on which stood a single, gabled house: an American house of the 1920s that was not unlike some of the better houses in Moonah. When he was unhappy, Bob told me, he'd imagine that he could walk through the frame and go into that house. When he did, he'd meet the people who lived there, he said, and they'd be sure to be kind. I understood, and wanted to tell him so, but I hadn't the words, at that age. I'd seen that the house on the rise was his place of absolute peace: a refuge of perfect contentment, back in those 1920s where his father could never reach him.

Bob had noted the signature of Felix's creator in each final frame – *Pat Sullivan* – and he'd often tried to imagine what the artist was like. He was sure that Pat would be a nice fellow, he said: a clever, youthful American who would understand his ambition to be a comic strip artist himself. Today I know that Sullivan was no longer alive when Bob was studying his *Felix* book: the cartoonist had died in 1933. And he wasn't American, but an Irish-Australian from Sydney: a wild-natured, hard-drinking cartoonist who made his way to New York on a cattle boat in 1910, where he boxed for prize money until he got work in an animation studio and ultimately invented Felix – naming his cat after a New South Wales boxer called Peter Felix. He'd once spent nine months in gaol for raping a fourteen-year-old girl – after which he married a Ziegfeld Follies dancer who was devoted to him for the rest of their lives together, and who fell to her death from their New York apartment in 1932, leaving Pat to die of drink a year later.

Today, the impact of Bob Wall's crime would be very slight indeed. But then, in the 1940s, theft and burglary were so unusual that my parents seldom locked their back door when they went out, murder and rape were rare monstrosities, children could wander anywhere in safety, and violence on the streets was scarcely known. My native island, once a reformatory for the British Empire's criminals and a byword for depravity and misery, was now as free of crime as any society in history. London-style bobbies in their tall blue helmets paced the quiet streets in pairs, and serious crime happened in American gangster films, or in Agatha Christie novels. People were living in a bubble of public peace, even while violence of giant dimensions lay just beyond the horizon, where our troops remained locked in struggle with the Japanese in New Guinea. So the schoolyard theft of a bicycle, in that world of unquestioned order, was an event which excited shocked interest.

Bob Wall now became a criminal, to be viewed with virtuous hostility, or else with scandalized pity. But I secretly mourned him. Would I ever see my comrade again? It seemed unlikely, as the days passed by and Bob didn't reappear at school. He was gone, on the stolen Malvern Star, and by now he was probably miles out in the country: a wandering boy outlaw, hard blue eyes fixed on the road ahead, pedalling into the dream where he'd always belonged. He'd taken to the bush, as he'd said he'd do, and had not asked me to come with him.

June Leaman, who sat in front of me in class, was Miss Barrow's favourite when it came to reciting poetry. Miss Barrow often called on her to recite *Meg Merrilies,* which June knew perfectly by heart. None of us minded her being chosen as the best at recitation, because we all knew it was true – and also because none of us wanted to recite poetry if we could avoid it. She had probably been given private elocution lessons, and had what was called a 'good' accent: which meant as close to upper-class English as possible. Another reason that she wasn't envied as a favourite was that she was always friendly and cheerful, with a smile that seemed filled with delight. She was also pretty, with a somewhat Danish appearance: pale blonde curls and narrow, light blue eyes.

I was in love with her, and didn't know what to do about it. I sometimes tapped her on the shoulder and asked to borrow an eraser or a pencil during art class, even when I didn't need them; she always turned to me and obliged immediately, and for a few moments I would encounter her serene smile at close quarters. I sometimes managed to talk to her when Miss Barrow was out of the room; and on a few treasured occasions she actually turned and initiated the conversation.

This happened a week after Bob Wall's disappearance. An English lesson was beginning, and we were sitting in silence, looking through a story in our reading books, waiting for Miss Barrow to finish marking some papers at her table at the head of the room. June suddenly turned and looked at me, which meant that she wanted to talk. I leaned forward, while David Baxter next to me pretended to ignore us. June spoke in a whisper.

Did you hear about Bob Wall?

What?

The police caught him, and got that bike back.

I stared at her, my heart jumping. She wasn't smiling now; instead her expression was solemn.

What have they done with him?

He's been sent to the Hillcrest Boys' Home. That's what my father told me.

What sort of place is that? Where is it?

It's a home for boys who get into trouble. It's somewhere up the country.

When will they let him out?

Not until he's about sixteen, my father says. Most boys have to live there until they finish school.

She saw my expression, and added: I'm sorry. He was your friend, wasn't he?

This made me love her all the more, even in the midst of the despair I felt for Bob. I was about to speak again, when Miss Barrow looked up from her table.

June Leaman and Hugh Dixon, why are you talking?

Sorry Miss Barrow.

Sorry Miss Barrow.

There was a sniggering from some parts of the room, and Miss Barrow said:

Quiet, please. We'll have poetry, now. June, you can start us off by reciting *Meg Merrilies.*

June went briskly up to the front and stood facing the class with her hands behind her back and her head up-tilted. Her glad smile had returned, and she began as she always did, with a stress on the first word, which she pronounced clearly and beautifully, the O perfectly rounded:

> '*Old* Meg she was a gypsy,
> And lived upon the moors:
> Her bed it was the brown heath turf,
> And her house was out of doors ...'

But I sat stiffly in my seat, a dumb, appalled sorrow gathering inside me.

Bob Wall, the friend I'd loved, was gone. He'd carried with him always the promise of adventure: now that promise was gone too. I'd never see my comrade again, and would never comprehend his secret nature – the key to which had surely been his hoard of antique comic books: *Terry and the Pirates*, *Dick Tracy* and *The Captain and the Kids*. His pale, set face, seen only in memory, would remain unknowable forever – and I'd never be able to look at *The Captain and the Kids* again without tears.

2

When the disaster at the race track struck my father, it took me some days to discover the details. I knew it would be useless to try and speak to him about it, but by questioning my mother I was able to learn the whole situation. I think it relieved her to discuss it, even though she wept as she did so.

The fatal horse's name (I'll never forget it) was Noble Prince. My father had been assured by Les Harrington that it was due for a win, and just before the Saturday of the race he'd taken the one big gamble of his life. For some time, he'd been pursuing a certain farmer from the Midlands about a long overdue account for a hundred pounds, owed to Fitzpatrick's for water-tanks and tools. On the Thursday of that week, the farmer phoned him to say that his wool cheque had come in, and that he was coming in to Hobart the next day to pay his bill. He always paid in cash, and my father assumed that he'd do so this time. Usually Mrs Harris the book-keeper would have dealt with it; but she was away on leave until Monday, and my father told the farmer to come up to the office and ask for him personally. His plan was simple: he would give the farmer a receipt, place his bet on Saturday, and on Monday, winnings in hand, he would give the hundred pounds to Mrs Harris and tell her to bank it, together with the rest of the day's takings. She wasn't likely to query the fact that it had been received on Friday – but even if she did, he'd simply say that he'd been too busy to bank it, and had put it in his safe. When he sat down with Paul Fitzpatrick on December 1st to reconcile the ledgers and the bank statements for the month, the totals of the month's takings and the statements from the bank would match, and nobody would ever notice what had been done.

He was going against everything in his nature and training: he'd never done a dishonest thing in his life, I felt sure. But he'd been driven by the sort of sudden madness that can overcome a man in middle age who feels that life is fleeing from him.

Over those few days, I searched my mind for ways in which my father might be saved. The only idea that seemed feasible was an approach to his uncle: my great-uncle Walter Dixon. My father would never be persuaded to do it; I knew that. I would have to do it myself.

Just beyond Glenorchy, close to those tall, grey-blue ranges that formed an ultimate line of distance when I looked out from the railway bridge on Tower Road, lay a district called Montrose. It's now a nondescript little suburb where the town straggles to its end; in 1950 it was still a semi-rural area. Its border was Montrose Road, which went west off Main Road and wound into the first of the high, bush-covered hills. Not far from the end of this road was the property called Leyburn Farm: the original home of the Dixons, where great-uncle Walter still lived. My plan was to visit him there, and to describe my father's plight. I would then appeal for financial help.

Walter Dixon was a barrister of some repute in the city. At seventy, he continued to be a partner in the firm of Dixon and Dixon, which he and my late grandfather Charles had founded. Charles's son George was now the head of the firm, and Walter carried a lighter workload than he'd once done. But he was said to retain an alert mind and a dry wit, and had wide interests outside the Law: in literature, art and history. For this reason, he'd always been guardedly respected, in a town where anyone who was at all prominent was watched and discussed.

All this I'd learned from my father. In cutting himself off from my grandfather as he'd done, my father had cut himself off from Walter Dixon as well – though there was no bad blood between them, so far as I could gather. So my father's link with Leyburn Farm was also cut; and yet he would sometimes talk about the place with a sort of nostalgia, as though it belonged to some golden era. He had many memories of his uncle Walter, who seemed to both fascinate him and cause him to shake his head. Walter was 'a learned man', he'd told me; but although Walter was respected, he was not entirely liked. Some people sensed his contempt for the simple pleasures they enjoyed, and knew that his own pleasures were beyond their scope. His references both in court and in general conversation to such writers as Tacitus, Balzac and Anthony Trollope – from whose works he drew parallels with the follies and corruptions of human beings in general and of some of Hobart's public figures in particular – did not go down well, even with most of his fellow lawyers, whom he dismissed as philistines. He'd spent some years abroad, in England and on the Continent. In our small, remote, purely Anglo-Celtic island community, few of whose citizens ever travelled further than the Australian mainland, and where culture was regarded by most people with contempt or suspicion, this made Walter Dixon half a foreigner – despite the fact that his family had been pioneers here. Living abroad had made him peculiar, people said. He had a thespian style – both in court and out of it – which perhaps invited this judgement. Tall, courtly and intimidating, he was just a bit too elegant, my father said. His beautifully-cut suits were made for him in Melbourne, since no Hobart tailor would do for him, and his dressiness marked him out. He always had a flower in his buttonhole, carried an ebony cane, and wore spats – which were beginning to go out of fashion, in those years just after World War Two. He had a car – an ancient Buick, which sat in the stables behind the house – but he seldom took it into the city. Summer and winter, he drove it down Montrose Road into Glenorchy and then caught the tram, absorbed in a book all the way.

My notion of appealing to such a man was a desperate one; I knew that. But I felt that I'd do anything to save my parents from what loomed over them. I was both numb and fiercely determined. I didn't attempt to telephone Walter Dixon; I'd decided simply to turn up, on the off-chance that he'd be there. And so I set off, riding my old bicycle out through Glenorchy on a hot Sunday afternoon, in a clean white short-sleeved shirt and my best casual slacks, fastened at the ankles with bicycle clips. I was hoping for an interview with a relative I'd never met, so far as I knew – though I seemed dimly to recall a tall, pale man with a beaked nose who might have been Walter, encountered in very early childhood when my parents were still visiting my grandparents. As I pedalled, I tried to recall as well what I knew about Leyburn Farm and the family past. My father knew a good deal about it, and had often talked about his Dixon forebears with a painful mixture of pride, wistfulness and resentment.

Although the property was still called Leyburn Farm, much of its land had now been sold off. It had been owned originally by my great-great-grandfather, Henry Dixon, who had come to Tasmania – then the penal colony of Van Diemen's Land – in 1830, twenty-seven years after first white settlement. Henry was the second son of a prosperous farmer in Wensleydale, in North Yorkshire, close to the town of Leyburn. His father intended to leave the farm to Henry's elder brother, my father told me – and a familiar, bitter expression had crossed his face.

But that didn't mean Henry got nothing, he said. His father was a lot more generous than mine was to me.

When Henry was twenty-nine, with a young wife and an infant son to support, his father had encouraged him to emigrate to Van

Diemen's Land, and had given him enough money to buy land here. There were good reports of the place in newspaper articles and in letters being sent back to England by free settlers, and the elder Dixon had been told that the colonial government was doing everything to encourage well-funded free immigrants in order to develop the colony, and as a counterbalance to the large population of convicts and ex-convicts. He hadn't been misinformed. When Henry Dixon arrived, with a generous amount of capital, a good supply of farming implements, and an introduction to Lieutenant-Governor Arthur from his local Member of Parliament, he found his path made easy. Within a month he'd purchased a large brick and stuccoed house on one hundred and twenty acres of arable land at Montrose, some four miles from Hobart Town. The house had only been built the year before, and was elegantly designed by colonial standards, at a time when most houses in the colony were still rudimentary. The owner had apparently suffered some family tragedy, and wished to return to England as soon as possible; so Henry got the property at a reasonable price.

In honour of his place of origin, Henry named the property Leyburn Farm. He'd learned his skills well from his father, and was soon growing fine crops of wheat and barley, and running a small herd of cattle. As an approved settler, he was quickly assigned convict labourers and household servants by the government, at no other cost than supplying them with food and clothing. He shortly obtained a contract to supply the Commissariat Department in Hobart with meat and wheat, and his success was then assured. He also planted an orchard, producing apples and apricots, ideally suited to the cool marine climate of Van Diemen's Land. Four years after their arrival, he and his wife Margaret had a second son – the first native-born Dixon – whom they named Martin. He would be the father of my grandfather Charles, and of great-uncle Walter.

Charles Dixon had left the farm soon after he and Walter had established their legal practice together. Some sort of financial settlement had been made between the brothers, and Charles had bought his own house in Swanston Street, in New Town. So the property passed into Walter's hands, and he'd stayed in the old house all his life – though he gave all his time to the legal practice, not being interested in farming. He had sold off most of the land to his neighbours, keeping only the orchard, which he maintained as a sort of hobby, with the help of hired hands. He'd married quite young, but the marriage had broken up, and there were no children. He had never remarried, and apparently lived alone. When I had asked my father why the marriage had ended – a thing that was rare in Walter's day, and even in the period of my childhood – my father had looked at me with a sly expression, squinting sideways.

She left him, he said. I can understand why. Walter was a strange sort of cove. Learned, a brilliant barrister – but eccentric. Yes – I think you'd call him eccentric.

He would say no more than that, and I was remembering his words as I turned the corner into Montrose Road.

It was still and pleasantly warm: the sort of November warmth that promised a hot dry summer. I passed some small suburban houses near Main Road and then I was into the country, riding between orchards, lines of poplars and gums, and pastures where black Angus cattle grazed. Behind me was a glimpse of the Derwent, with twin-humped Mount Direction in the east; ahead were tall, blue-green hills of bush – near now, instead of in the distance. At a point where the road began to get steeper, I came to some farm gates on my right, standing open onto a gravelled drive. One of them had a faded wooden sign attached, whose ochre lettering read: *Leyburn Farm.*

I dismounted, wheeled my bike inside the gates, dropped it in a patch of grass and then began walking up the drive. There was no sign of life, and I couldn't yet see the house, which was hidden by a group of dark, spreading cedars, probably planted when the house was built. It was very still, and the air seemed to be filled with a soft, universal whirring, like that of insects. The sound was probably in my head; I was growing nervous. The garden, with its scattered bushes, was neglected: long yellow grass overwhelmed the flower beds, and the gravel of the drive had mostly been worn away. The drive ran in a curve, taking me past the cedars, and now the house came into view.

Not grandiose, it nevertheless had the elegance and authority of its period: a typical Georgian farmhouse of colonial days. Studying it, I felt a pang of regret. If it hadn't been for my father's feud I might have made childhood visits here, to this home of my great-great-grandparents; it might have been part of my own past. It was a long, single-storey, yellow-stuccoed building with two tall chimneys and an iron hipped roof painted green, which would once have been shingled. A verandah with iron trellis columns – also painted green – ran around the house on the two sides that I could see (and no doubt on a third), covered by an extra line of roof. In the front, four French windows with green shutters opened on to the verandah, set two on either side of the front door. I glimpsed a long brick stable at the back, still roofed with the wooden shingles of the nineteenth century. Above it the grey-green hills loomed, like shapes from that past.

The driveway had brought me between two tall stone urns. They framed the verandah and the four-panelled door, with its handsome fanlight. I stopped now, and clenched my sweating hands, trying to work up the nerve to make my approach. The verandah was paved with flagstones that were almost flush with the ground; flower beds ran along it filled with roses. These were in bloom, and didn't look neglected; nor were there weeds in the bed. So somebody was tending the garden, at least some of the time. The green shutters were closed over all the French windows, and I began to think that Walter Dixon was away. I also began to think of retreating, since my mission was probably hopeless. But I straightened myself, and stepped onto the time-hollowed flagstones. The scent of the roses seemed to grow stronger here, filling the waiting verandah. There was a brass bell-pull beside the door, and I jerked at it. A remote tinkling sounded from somewhere in the house, and I stood back and waited. The only other sound was a sporadic twittering of sparrows and honeyeaters, coming from a flowering red bottlebrush past the corner of the house: a sound which had an ineffectual urgency, as though the garden was held in a condition of stasis from which the birds struggled to escape. No-one seemed to be coming, and I began to turn away. But then I heard the sound of feet in the hall, and the door was swung open wide.

The old man who held it was somewhat as I'd imagined, but a good deal more vivid. He was imposing, being taller than me – over six feet – and lean and well-built, if a little stooped. He had a domed, pallid skull, entirely bald on top, but with white hair over his ears worn long, in two curving wings, like the hair of a nineteenth-century aesthete. This and the way he was dressed made him look quite unconventional to me. Men's hair was worn severely short in that year, and styles in male attire were rigidly limited – any departure from the conventional lounge suit and tie or drab-coloured sports coat and slacks being regarded with suspicion. Great-uncle Walter was dressed as though about to go to an English garden party, in an open-necked, pale blue shirt with a red cravat knotted at the throat, and a dark blue corduroy jacket. Male corduroy garments were considered then to be either scruffy or effeminate – usually being worn by men of an artistic or theatrical bent – but Walter Dixon's appearance could neither be called scruffy nor effeminate; instead, it had the stylishness of another era. His pale grey trousers had knife-edged creases, and his dark brown boots had a mirror finish. I assumed that he was going out somewhere, since he surely wouldn't be dressed like this on a Sunday at home.

We stared at each other in silence while I tried to summon up words, and he looked me up and down. His alert, deep-set blue eyes were very large, in someone of his age; they gave a single touch of youth to his appearance. He was the first to speak.

Well, young fellow? What do you want? Are you collecting for something?

No, I said. No. I came to visit you. I hope it's not a bad time. My name's Hugh Dixon.

Dixon, did you say?

His voice and white eyebrows rose. It was an aged voice, with the ghost of a tremor in it, but nevertheless strong and beautifully-produced, like that of an actor. To me, it sounded English; there was very little trace of an Australian accent. I remembered that Grandpa Dixon's voice had sounded similar, on the few occasions when I'd met him as a child.

Yes, I said. My father's Jim Dixon. Your nephew.

The old man stared at me for a few moments more, frowning slightly, as though searching his memory. His frown made me even more tense, and I wondered now if he'd ask me to leave. Instead, he let go of the door.

So you're James's boy. Yes – I can see that you are.

He gave me a small smile, not very encouraging, but better than nothing. Then he stood to one side and raised a large, pale hand, gesturing at the hallway behind him.

Don't just stand there. Come in.

I stepped inside, and he shut the heavy door behind us with a booming noise. I waited in the semi-darkness of the hallway, which had broad, polished floorboards and a dark red carpet runner down the centre. The hall ran for what appeared to be the full length of the house, and it smelled as the hallways of old houses often do: a combination of floor polish and something else, which I thought of as the lingering, mournful odour of a hundred years.

Walter Dixon came up beside me and took hold of my right elbow.

Come. Let me offer you afternoon tea, Hugh. Will that be acceptable, in honour of your visit?

Thank you, I said. But I don't want to take up your time, Mr Dixon. Perhaps you were going out.

Mr Dixon? That sounds awfully formal from a family member. No, I'm not going out – and I was about to have tea anyway.

Still holding my elbow, he guided me down the hall. At the same time, he peered sideways at me.

We'll decide what you can call me later. You *are* my great-nephew, after all. First, we'll discover what prompted this unexpected visit. Your father never visits me. I suppose you know that.

He led me through an open door halfway down the passage, and we came into a dining-room. It was a long room, running down the northern side of the house. Like the rooms at the front, it had two French windows looking onto the section of verandah here, and a pair of these glass doors stood ajar, together with their shutters, so that thick afternoon sunlight leaked in. It would have been funereal, otherwise. Its sombre green wallpaper was patterned with gold medallions, and a heavy cedar sideboard and equally massive dresser stood against one of the walls. A number of original pictures were hung about the room – among them (I'd later discover) a line and wash drawing of the Kimberley desert region by Russell Drysdale. A long mahogany dining table was placed in the centre, with a set of matching ladder-back chairs.

My great-uncle gestured towards the dining table.

Do sit down. I must leave you for a moment, to let Mrs Doran know you've joined me.

When he came back, we sat facing each other across the long table. Scones, jam and clotted cream, some small cakes and a large pot of tea were set out between us on a linen cloth, placed in the centre of the table. Our cups and saucers and side plates were of delicate bone china, with a pattern of roses. Large linen napkins lay beside them.

All this had been brought in by Mrs Doran, who appeared to be Walter Dixon's housekeeper. He introduced me to her as his great-nephew, and she murmured a greeting in a voice so low that I could only just hear it. After that, she said nothing, moving about the table, and soon vanished into the interior of the house again, moving very quietly. Everything about her was quiet, like her voice. She was a woman I guessed to be in her early thirties, with black hair, a contrasting fair complexion, and blue eyes that were unusually wide-set. She smiled with closed lips all the time she was with us; but she was one of those people who remain entirely expressionless even when they smile, and she scarcely ever looked at us. Instead, her gaze seemed permanently fixed on some remote distance, or perhaps on a memory that preoccupied her. Her figure was full and yet trim, and I thought her attractive – as far as any mature women could seem attractive to me, in that stage of my life. She appeared, like my great-uncle, to be dressed for an occasion, in a full-skirted dress with a floral pattern, over which she wore a white apron. I wondered if other visitors were expected; but nobody came, and Mrs Doran didn't appear again. I assumed that she'd gone to the kitchen, somewhere in a far part of the house. Through the open door to the hall, I could hear the distant sound of music on a radio, which I guessed was playing for her benefit.

While she was in the room, my great-uncle had made only neutral conversation with me, commenting on the warm weather and telling me that Mrs Doran made excellent scones and cakes and brought him the clotted cream from a local dairy farmer. Mrs Doran's prim little smile had remained unaltered, but her glance had flickered over to me for a few seconds, and had then returned to the inward distance she contemplated. Now that she'd gone, silence fell for a time, as we ate our scones and sipped our tea. Then Walter Dixon leaned forward, and his expression of pleasant civility vanished. His eyes were fixed on me with an expression of challenging enquiry, and I seemed to see him clearly for the first time. He put me in mind of a Roman portrait bust: a senator, perhaps, or one of the emperors. His large, thin white nose was like the beak of a predatory bird, and his lips, now that he'd ceased to smile, were thin, down-turned and forbidding.

Now then, young Hugh, he said. Would you like to tell me why you've come to visit an old man you've never met?

In the seconds in which I gathered my thoughts, trying to remember the speech I'd prepared, the distant radio from the kitchen became very distinct: the Glenn Miller band was playing 'Moonlight Serenade' for Mrs Doran. I sat up straight. My pulse was racing, but I managed to keep my voice even.

I've come to ask for your help.

He frowned. My help? What kind of help had you in mind?

It's not for myself. It's for my father.

His thick white eyebrows rose. For James? You mean he *sent* you to me?

No. He doesn't know I'm here.

Would you like to explain?

I explained. I told him all that I'd learned, and ended by saying how honest my father has always been, and that he should not go to gaol for this one mistake. As I spoke, the old man continued to watch me, no longer frowning but simply intent, as though trying to read something in my face that would tell him more than my words were doing. No doubt he studied people on trial in this manner, and the witnesses he cross-examined. He'd stopped eating, and didn't even sip his tea. When I'd finished, he said:

And how much money are we talking about?

A hundred pounds.

A hundred pounds. Serious – but hardly a vast amount.

It's a vast amount to my father.

No doubt. And he thought he could put it back, and no-one the wiser.

That's right.

Yes. So many poor bloody fools have thought the same thing.

He had picked up half a scone in his fingers and was holding it suspended. Now he looked down at it as though wondering where it had come from. Taking his knife, he topped it with jam and cream from two little bowls in front of him, put it in his mouth and sat chewing in silence. Then he dabbed his lips with his napkin, laid the napkin carefully beside his plate and cleared his throat.

And you say the money must be put back by the end of this month?

Yes.

I see. In a little over a week. So there's time.

My heart jumped. But I waited, and said nothing.

He pushed away his empty plate, looking through the open glass doors across the room, where the yellowish light leaked in, together with the sudden, frantic outcries of the birds. I could see the red flames of the bottlebrush out there; beyond was a glimpse of orchard, with apple trees out in leaf. Then the old man looked back at me.

And what are you supposing your father will do, if I give him this money? Regard it as a gift?

No. Certainly not. He'd pay it back. It might take him a while, but I know he'd do it.

I'd raised my voice; but my great-uncle's expression seemed to grow less severe.

You're very loyal to your father. No doubt what you're saying is true, and he's honest – even though he's been so bloody foolish. None of our family has ever been crooked. Very well: I'll tell you what I'll do. I'll give you a cheque before you leave, and you can tell your father to pay me back in his own time.

I began to thank him, but he raised his hand.

No need for that, young fellow. You're not out of the woods yet – your father could still bring disgrace on you, and could still be charged.

I stared at him, not comprehending.

He may refuse the money. He may refuse it because of that damn silly pride which made him stay away from his father all those years – which kept him from even visiting Charles on his deathbed, and kept him from visiting me. What had he against *me*? Nothing – except that I was his father's brother. I once invited him over here, but he made some excuse. He cut himself off from his whole family. So how will his pride allow him to take money from me now?

My face must have expressed desolation, because the old man slowly stood up, walked around the table, sat down on the chair next to me and squeezed my shoulder. He was smiling in a way that seemed almost kindly, as far as his severe features could express this.

Nil desperandum, Hugh. Your father must be made to see that if he doesn't take the money, he ruins not only himself but your mother and you – and he has no right to do that. I'll write him a note to that effect, and I'll make him understand that this is purely a loan, not an act of charity. That may work.

I'm very grateful, I said. And I'm sorry that my father wouldn't see you.

He turned his chair sideways to look at me, tilting his head back and narrowing his eyes as though reading fine print. For some moments he was silent, and I began to feel uncomfortable. Then he said:

I detect certain qualities in you, young fellow. You're certainly a Dixon – but a different sort of Dixon from your father. Poor James.

Why poor James?

I'll tell you why in a moment. Firstly though, let me ask you: do you know why he hated his own father so much?

Because he was put out to work at sixteen, and Uncle George was sent to University to study Law.

True. And has he told you any more than that?

No. He doesn't talk about it much.

I can understand that. There are wounds that men don't want to display, especially to their sons. But I'll tell you this much, so that you'll understand your father better. My brother always favoured George, from the time when George and James were boys. I never really understood why this was. George was the elder, of course, but that doesn't fully explain it. Sometimes men just don't *like* their sons, for no rational reason. In some cases, simply because they're unattractive, perhaps. But this can't have been the case with James. I remember him as a child – he was quite a pretty little boy, and his mother doted on him, and no doubt tried to make it up to him for his father's harshness. Charles used to crush James, and make him feel inadequate, while George was always praised.

But why wouldn't he let him study Law?

I asked Charles that once. All he would say was: 'He's not up to it. George is the bright one. And I haven't the money to back them both.' Well, it's true that money was short, then – but it wasn't true that James was stupid. He was quite intelligent, as I remember him.

So it really was unfair.

My great-uncle rubbed his chin, looking at me, and I saw that his mouth appeared cruel again.

Perhaps. But the way your father's life has gone can't only be put down to that. He had a defect of character, as I see it. He was dealt a bad hand – a lot of people are. But he didn't know the best way to handle it – which is not to brood on it, not to make it into a life-long grievance, but to put it behind you, forget it, and make your own luck. Life isn't always fair – and I hope you don't think it should be, or you'll fall into the same sort of hole as your father.

I sat silent. I knew that what he'd said was probably true, but I'd no intention of agreeing with him, and so I said nothing. He saw this, and smiled.

No need to comment. I don't expect you to. So tell me: what are *you* doing? Are you still at school? And how old are you?

I told him I was studying for matriculation, and was now eighteen.

Eighteen, is it? You look younger. No ugly whiskers yet.

He took in my embarrassment at this, and looked amused.

And you'll go to University?

That's what my father wants – if I can win a Government scholarship to pay the fees. He thinks I should be a lawyer.

The old man's eyebrows went up again. Ah. You'll achieve what he failed to do. And is that what you want?

No. I want to go to Art School.

Really? That's interesting. You mean you want to be a painter?

I want to be an illustrator.

An illustrator?

He looked puzzled, and I explained that I wanted to be a book illustrator, probably specializing in children's books, since few adult books now carried illustrations. He asked me what artists I admired, and I named some of my favourites.

All Edwardians. What a strange old-fashioned boy you must be! And do you really think you could succeed at it?

I told him coldly that I hoped so.

Come, come. I'm not laughing at you. You begin to interest me, young fellow. No Dixon has ever been an artist. I would have liked to be one myself – I once spent a year in Italy, studying the masters of the Renaissance, and producing some fairly mediocre paintings. I didn't have the talent to make art my career, and I had sense enough to realize it in time. Perhaps *you'll* have the talent.

He stood up.

I imagine you must be going now, Hugh – but perhaps you'd like to call again next Sunday? I'd like to get to know my nephew, and there are many things we might discuss. Come at about this time. And now I must go and write you that cheque.

I got to my feet, and he turned away. Then he turned back again, as though remembering something.

And would your father send you to Art School? Instead of University?

No. He won't agree.

I see. So history repeats itself.

He pinched his chin with his finger and thumb, looking at me abstractedly. He remained in this position, half turned away, seeming in two minds as to whether he'd move off or not. When he finally did so, he spoke over his shoulder.

Bring some of your drawings when you come. I'd like to see them.

My recollection of the exchange I had with my father that night comes back to me only in flashes. This isn't because it's dissolved into vagueness; rather the reverse. Its very intensity has jolted it out of perspective, like the memory of a road accident.

What I see most vividly, apart from my father's face, is the furniture of the dining-room, where the two of us have paused by the oval dining table, having cleared away the dishes together after the evening meal. My mother has gone to the sitting-room. Isolated as though in a vacuum, the Tasmanian blackwood table stands out vividly, together with the matching sideboard, where the green Bakelite radio that I've listened to since childhood sits next to the telephone at one end, and a brass bowl of fruit is positioned at the other. The room seems to be filled with a dull orange glow, gloomy and worrying, which memory can't account for, and which is not the normal effect of the electric light. Perhaps this too is a distortion of memory.

We don't sit down during the conversation that follows: we remain standing, facing each other like opponents. My father has taken off his tie and jacket and has unbuttoned his waistcoat. A sheaf of hair, streaked with grey now, hangs across his forehead, and I see how weary and old his face looks. The lines that run from his nose to the corners of his mouth seem to have got much deeper in the past week, as do the lines on his forehead.

I begin by telling him baldly that I've visited Walter Dixon – nothing more – and he looks at me in ominous surprise.

And you simply went there off your own bat? Without any warning, and without contacting him first?

Yes.

But *why*, for heaven's sake?

Because I thought that he might help us.

Help us? What are you talking about?

I thought he might get you out of trouble.

My father blinks at me, in the orange light. I haven't yet divulged my knowledge of what he's done; now, stammering slightly, I do so. The thought of his reaction to this has made me nervous ever since I formed my plan, and continues to do so. I'm taller than my father now, and don't fear him physically; but I'm nevertheless concerned that he might lose his temper and attack me in some way. Somehow a potential for violence always seems to be present in him.

At first, he says nothing. His fists are clenched, and his face is filled with a mixture of shame and anger. Finally he says:

So you went to my uncle and tattled about it. Well, thanks for that, Hugh. My life's ruined, and you've shared it with one of my nearest relatives. What did you think he'd do? Defend me in court? Christ almighty.

He attempts a scornful laugh, but it dies.

Walter Dixon's letter, which contains the cheque, is in the inside pocket of my green sports coat. I draw it out now and pass it to him, my arm at full stretch.

This is for you, I say.

Walter Dixon has addressed the envelope to Mr James Dixon. My father looks at it and frowns; then he tears it open. Before he takes out the note inside, he looks up at me.

Have you read this?

No.

He unfolds the note, and sees the cheque. He raises this in front of his face, holding it well away; his sight isn't as good as it was. Then he begins to read the letter, tilting his head back and screwing up his eyes in a peculiar way he has, like a jeweller assessing a gem. He reads it twice; then he puts it carefully on the dining table, together with the cheque. His face has no expression.

I told him you'd pay it all back, I say. So there's nothing wrong with taking it, Dad. Please take it.

He looks at me for a long time. You know what he's done? You know about this cheque?

Yes.

He shakes his head slowly, frowning as though adding up some figures. He appears bewildered, and looks down at the floor. Then he says:

I can't take this.

He said you'd say that.

He looks up at me. He appears dazed, and I suddenly find myself angry.

You *have* to take it, I say. You can't go to gaol, Dad. What would happen to Mum? For God's sake take it.

He says nothing, but I see that something has given way in him; he has a helpless, bewildered look, and I press my advantage.

There's nothing wrong with taking it, if you pay it back. He's your uncle. Why shouldn't he lend it to you?

He still has the same helpless look. He holds his chin, rubbing it slowly and staring at the floor. When he speaks, it's in a low, toneless voice.

You're right. I have to take it – if only for your mother's sake. And for yours.

He looks up. Slowly, reluctantly, he puts out his right hand, and for a moment I look at it blankly. Then I give him my hand, and he holds it in a tight grip. We remain fixed in this posture, and I begin to feel embarrassed. Finally he says:

I guess you've saved my life, Hugh.

No, Dad.

Yes you have, son.

He gives me a painful smile, and I smile back. At this, his grip grows even tighter; his expression becomes one of reluctant gladness, and a sort of sad warmth has entered his eyes.

Memory freezes us in this posture, smiling and holding each other's hands, while the dull orange light seems to brighten.

In preparation for my visit to Walter Dixon the following Sunday, I made a selection of my best drawings, and put them in a folio. Carrying this on my bicycle proved somewhat awkward, but I managed it, riding single-handed. I'd included illustrations for Hans Andersen's fairy tales, Charles Dickens's *Great Expectations*, and Rolf Boldrewood's bushranging novel, *Robbery Under Arms.*

My Hans Andersen illustrations were somewhat influenced by those of Edmund Dulac (though mine were in black and white, not colour), while my drawings for the other two titles no doubt betrayed how much I'd learned from Milton Caniff – and also from Rowland Hilder, whose illustrations for a pre-War copy of *Treasure Island* I'd pored over for years. Hilder's use of contrasting light and shadow was very similar to Caniff's; and although colour has been employed in his illustrations (as it was in the Sunday supplement episodes of *Terry and the Pirates*), they seemed to me essentially the work of a black-and-white artist, as Caniff's was. At this stage, that was how I saw myself: as a black-and-white artist.

Walter Dixon and I sat as before in the dining-room, and once again we were served afternoon tea by Mrs Doran: still silent, and still wearing her mysterious little smile. The scones and cakes were the same too, which pleased me; if I liked something, I was happy for it to be repeated indefinitely. My great-uncle was stylishly dressed again – this time more conventionally, in a grey-green Harris tweed sports coat, with a blue shirt and dark blue knitted tie – and I guessed that he must always dress as well as this at home, even if he wasn't going out, and even if he had no visitors.

I've had a letter from your father, Walter said. A very gracious letter. Perhaps he told you?

He only told me that he wrote to you.

Ah. He expressed his thanks for my cheque, and assured me he'd pay me in instalments. I'd invited him to call on me, in my letter, but he made excuses for the present. Something about needing time to get over his shame. He's a very proud man, isn't he?

I suppose he is. But he's very grateful to you.

No doubt. No doubt. But I don't think he wants any contact with a member of his family, no matter what the circumstances. Well, never mind. I prefer to have you to myself, at present.

I felt a little uncomfortable at this, and concentrated on cutting my scone in two. When I looked up again, I saw that the old man was watching me with a small, amused smile, his tea cup held just below his chin. Then he looked at my portfolio, which I'd put on the seat of the chair beside me.

I see you've brought me your drawings.

Yes. Some black-and-white illustrations.

Would you care to show me?

I said I would, and untied the ribbon. There was plenty of room on the long mahogany table, whose dozen ladder-back chairs seemed set for a large dinner party. Our afternoon tea, on its small linen cloth, was an island in the centre, and I opened the folio and began to set out my drawings on the area to my left. My great-uncle wiped his mouth with his napkin, stood up, and came around the table to peer at my work.

For some time he said nothing, but stood bent over the drawings in silence. He wore his severe expression, and his narrowed eyes seemed critical. When he reached the illustrations for *Robbery Under Arms* he drew a pair of spectacles from the top pocket of his shirt and put them on and stooped lower, peering at the drawings as though to discover a flaw in them. I'd written in pencil on each drawing to identify it, so I felt no need to explain, and kept my own silence. I could hear no radio from the kitchen today, and the stillness in the house was complete: a stillness that was fathomless and entirely without hope; the grave, heavy stillness of age and lost time, where everything had already happened, and where remedies and hopes were pointless.

Finally my great-uncle straightened up, put away his spectacles, and looked at me, unsmiling.

These are good. You have a talent, young man.

Thank you.

Don't thank me – thank God.

Still unsmiling, he walked around the table and sat down in his chair, gesturing for me to sit down again in mine.

And you want to be an illustrator, you say?

Yes.

In effect, a commercial artist.

With some vehemence, I told him that I didn't see the best illustrators in that way; they were true artists, in my view.

Well, well, perhaps so. And what about the great painters? Do you take an interest in them?

I told him that I liked the French Impressionists. I also named some of my favourite Australian painters: Roberts, Streeton, Dobell and Drysdale.

He nodded.

And what about the painters of the Renaissance? Have you given *them* any attention?

I don't know very much about them.

He raised both hands in a gesture of mock dismay.

We must do something about that. I have some books I can lend you. You should begin by reading Walter Pater's wonderful little essays on the Renaissance. Have you read Pater? What he's really writing about is beauty, and the rediscovery of beauty in that wonderful fifteenth century. It's there in the paintings of Leonardo; of Fra Angelico; of Fra Filippo Lippi; of the divine Botticelli.

He had half closed his eyes, his head tilted back. He seemed moved; the faint tremor in his voice was made a little more pronounced by this, and I began to feel that he'd made me his audience for a lecture he'd rehearsed in his mind many times. I'd never met anyone quite like him – in fact, I'd never had a serious conversation with so old a man.

The concept of beauty is at present somewhat out of fashion, he said. But take it from me, Hugh, nothing else matters. Remember your Keats: ' "Beauty is truth, truth, beauty," – that is all Ye know on earth, and all ye need to know.'

I ventured a question, at this point. Didn't different people see different things as beautiful?

He frowned at me, and I thought I saw a flash of anger in his eyes.

Beauty is in the eye of the beholder? Come, come, you know better than *that*, Hugh – or you should, if you have the qualities I detect in you. That line of thinking is a silly modern fallacy. There's a beauty that's *innate*, as Plato knew, and as Pater points out. People with refined souls respond to it immediately. Such spirits see it in particular pictures; particular books; particular music; particular landscapes. They see it in a Ming vase, or in the sculptures of Praxiteles – that's why such artefacts are immortal. Wordsworth saw it in the landscapes in the Lake District, and his joy in them gave us a new kind of vision in poetry. For those who have the temperament to respond, beauty is a mystery that both beckons and tantalizes us – and the finest critical minds have been able to recognize its features. I'm hoping you're one of those people who have the gift to respond. Then you may become a true artist.

I stared as though seeing him for the first time. Certain landscapes already moved me in the way that he'd indicated, as did some paintings. I felt that they contained a mystery that put them beyond the realm of ordinary reality; and to hear my great-uncle describe what I'd imagined to be an insight peculiar to myself filled me with surprise. He seemed to see this, and his expression became indulgent.

I'll lend you some of my books on the Renaissance artists, if you'll take great care of them. Then you'll understand more.

Thanks, Mr Dixon. It's very kind of you.

He raised his hands again, this time in protest.

Oh dear. This 'Mr Dixon' must stop. I don't think I want you to call me 'uncle', either. It had better be Walter, don't you think?

Without waiting for a reply, he said suddenly:

I like your illustration for *Robbery Under Arms*. Your Captain Starlight puts me in mind of Liam Dalton. You've heard of Dalton, of course? And Lucas Wilson?

Most people have.

You're not particularly interested in them?

Not really. I've never taken much interest in the old days.

He frowned as though I'd revealed some sad deficiency of character. Then his expression changed to one of gentle forgiveness.

That's a pity. Those old days should concern you. I hope to show you that, if you'll visit me in the future.

3

In the early part of that summer, as my High School days drew to their close, I was meant to be studying night and day for my matriculation exam. But I wasn't; I had too much to distract me. My visits to Walter Dixon, which continued every Sunday, were changing my thinking.

Walter had made me feel that my hopes for becoming an artist weren't foolish, as my father thought, but might actually be justified. He'd told me I had talent; he'd hinted at the possibility that art might be my life; and this had filled me with a consuming excitement.

He was genuine in these opinions, I felt sure. But the full nature of his interest in me, which he'd take some time to reveal, proved to be more complex.

Walter Dixon's infatuation with the past – a passion that had tied him permanently to Leyburn Farm – wasn't displayed to me immediately. I was only shown superficial signs of it on my third visit to the house.

On that Sunday, Walter took me on a tour of the place. It was a limited tour: I wasn't taken into any bedrooms, and nor did we go into the regions where Mrs Doran worked. Its highlight was the drawing-room.

Standing in the middle like a guide, Walter spoke of the fittings with a sort of remote pride, as though the house belonged to someone else. Privately, I found the room gloomy and oppressive. Now I realize I was looking at something rather remarkable: a perfectly preserved and elegant survival of the Victorian era, fixed in time. Nothing in the room appeared to date from later than the 1870s, and nothing appeared to have been moved or altered since that time. A round centre table, covered with a patterned cloth, was surrounded by a ring of balloon-backed mahogany chairs. Chintz-covered armchairs were arranged about the walls. A huge mirror, framed in carved mahogany, was set above the marble mantelpiece. The wallpaper was of a rich but faded floral pattern, matched by a similar faded pattern in the carpet. The room smelt of furniture oil and flowers, no doubt from the attentions of Mrs Doran – and I suspected that her hands had arranged the vase of fresh roses that stood on the centre table.

This is where I receive occasional visitors, Walter said. Not many these days, I'm afraid.

His voice had a wistful tone, and I wondered if he was lonely.

We passed on down the hall, and emerged through the back door on to the verandah overlooking the yard. Like most back verandahs in country houses, it didn't try to be elegant. A pair of gumboots which I guessed to be Walter's stood by the door. A large wooden box was crammed with firewood, and some brooms and garden tools leaned against a wall. Hanging on a peg was a stained, yellowish, broad-brimmed felt hat with a low crown, of a style I'd seen in pictures of settlers in the nineteenth century. Walter followed my gaze; he had a disconcerting habit of watching me.

That was my father's hat, he said.

It must have been hanging there, I realized, for an extraordinary length of time. I said something to this effect, and Walter looked at me coldly.

My father died in 1912. He'd been wearing the hat for at least twenty years before that. I see no reason to move it.

I felt it wise to make no further comment; but the hat caused me to reflect. It seemed that nothing had been allowed to change in this house since that old, serious century that was gone.

A middle-aged border collie ambled up to us, wagging his tail.

This is Jock, Walter said. He's growing old – like me.

As I patted the dog's smooth black-and-white fur, Walter pointed across the yard.

The old stable's not in good repair either, I'm afraid.

It was true: the shingled roof had small gaps in it, and the green doors were in need of a coat of paint – but I still found it an appealing building, with its orange hand-made bricks from the early days. Through some open double doors at the end, I could see Walter's big old Buick Century: a navy-blue relic from the 1930s.

Liam Dalton stabled his horses there, on the night he visited the place, Walter said.

I looked at him. He'd spoken casually, but something in his tone and the sharpness of his glance told me that I ought to be impressed, and I tried to sound it.

Really? Dalton raided here? With a gang?

Just one companion. A creature called Griffin.

He pointed to the tall, grey-green hills of bush that towered behind the stable roof; and now the tone of his voice changed again. It took on a melodic, almost elegiac note, seeming to recite a poem he'd long been familiar with.

When they left, they rode off into those hills. To somewhere up near Collinsvale, in a place that Lucas Wilson called Nowhere Valley. There was no such place as Collinsvale then, of course: it hadn't been settled. Just the wild mountains beyond Sorell Creek, where nobody wanted to go.

He'd been looking at the hills as he spoke. Now he turned back to me, and his tone changed again: it was matter-of-fact and challenging.

Do you think you'll matriculate, Hugh?

Probably not. I'll fail in French and Maths.

Why? You're intelligent enough to pass, surely.

I'm not interested.

I see. All you think about is Art School. Well, let's see what happens after the exams. Now I'll show you my library.

I'd never seen a private library. Most people were readers in that pre-television era, and most of the homes I'd been into had sets of bookshelves in their sitting-rooms, as my parents did in theirs – but none of them had what might be called libraries. The books my parents had on their shelves were pretty much duplicated in the homes of their friends. The classics were always there, stiff and perfect in their cloth and leather bindings: Shakespeare, Browning, Tennyson, Dickens, Scott – mostly unread, or else read once, a long time ago. The rest of the books were by the latest popular novelists and by those of the 'twenties and 'thirties when my parents and their friends were young: Somerset Maugham, John Buchan, Louis Bromfield, Philip Gibbs, Warwick Deeping, A.J. Cronin, Pearl Buck. Some of these books had given me pleasure, but I was ignorant at that stage of more formidable writers, and also of foreign authors, except for Dumas and Hugo. I often spent time in the city's lending library; but this collection too had its limitations, and few foreign authors were represented there either.

So the room that Walter took me into now was a new experience. It was a true 'gentleman's library' in the Victorian style, and had no doubt been maintained in good order for as long as the drawing room had. It was quite a large room, situated on the southern side of the house, with windows looking out across the garden towards the road. All four walls were lined with mahogany bookshelves, set on a series of cupboards of the same carved and polished wood. The ramparts of books rose to the high ceiling, and a wooden stepladder stood in a corner for access to the upper levels. A round cedar table stood in the centre of the room, with books and magazines stacked on it. Next to it, on a pedestal, was a bronze statue of a naked youth in a broad-brimmed hat, carrying a sword. As we passed it, Walter patted the youth's shoulder.

A copy of Donatello's *David*, he said. I bought it in Florence, in my young days. A very fine copy, don't you think?

I said that it was, speaking in perfect ignorance, and Walter led me off around the shelves, sometimes laying a hand lightly on my shoulder, as he'd done with the statue, and pointing out the categories in which the books were arranged. He seemed to be planning to allow me free use of the library, which filled me with anticipation. He continued to be a rather unnerving and unpredictable old man – a bit of an old aunty, I told myself – but I liked him and was somewhat in awe of him. It also began to seem that he was taking charge of me in some way – with what purpose, I couldn't imagine.

I stared about the shelves, surprised by the sheer numbers of books. The classic and established authors filled whole sections here: entire sets of Jane Austen, Scott, Dickens, Thackeray, Trollope and Hardy, and novels by authors of whom I then knew nothing: Balzac, Proust, Henry James, Joseph Conrad, Virginia Woolf and D.H. Lawrence. Some of the books, in brown calfskin bindings, looked very old; others were clearly more recent. Entire separate sections were devoted to poetry, biography, ancient and modern history, and travel. A collection that would take days to explore. As we moved on along the shelves, Walter began to question me about my reading, discovering which standard authors I'd read, and which ones I'd studied for matriculation. I talked about novels I'd liked, and his ever-active eyebrows rose.

You're quite well-read. But tell me, have you read the Russians? Chekhov? Tolstoy? Dostoevsky?'

I said I hadn't, and Walter turned away and moved off across the room, gesturing for me to follow. He pulled a book from one of the shelves and handed it to me. It was *Crime and Punishment*, by Dostoevsky.

You can borrow this, if you promise to look after it. When Dostoevsky gets you by the back hairs, young man, you'll wonder what's struck you.

Smiling, not giving me time to reply, he moved on, and we came to a whole section devoted to art: large, expensive histories of European painting, architecture and sculpture, and books dealing with individual painters, with colour reproductions of their work. Many of these looked far more lavish than any I'd seen in bookshops. Walter pulled his spectacles from a pocket of the dark green linen shirt he was wearing, whose colour combined tastefully with his olive-coloured corduroy trousers. I continued to be impressed by Walter's arty yet fastidious elegance, and began to hope to emulate it some day. He squinted carefully at the titles, made a selection, and held the stack in both hands; then he jerked his head towards the door.

Time for tea. We'll have a look at some of these books together. They might advance your education.

What followed in the dining-room, once we'd had afternoon tea, was an improvised talk by great-uncle Walter on the nature and spirit of Renaissance art. This was clearly one of his passions: Italy of the Renaissance was a country of the spirit through which he roamed constantly, it seemed – and I began to suspect that one of the reasons he invited me here was to make me an audience for his dissertations on the subject. Or perhaps to make me a convert to his religion: since art appeared to be his religion.

He spread out the books on the table and came and sat down next to me, pointing to the reproductions of particular paintings as he spoke. He was apparently unconscious of Mrs Doran, who came and went, clearing away the tea things. But I was far from unconscious of her; I found it difficult not to follow her with my eyes. I sometimes had the impression that I'd seen her before; but I couldn't recall when or where, and decided that I'd imagined it.

Today she wore no apron, and looked even more stylish than usual. A pale blue, pencil-style dress closely outlined her figure, accentuating her narrow waist and wide hips. Her small, close-lipped smile was in place as usual, and once she glanced at me quickly with an expression I couldn't read, but which seemed to be speculative. What did she think of my presence here? When she looked at Walter Dixon, it seemed to me that she did so with an expression that was somehow both respectful and indulgent. After she'd gone out, I plucked up courage and asked Walter casually whether Mrs Doran lived here.

He frowned and looked at me quickly, as though I'd intruded on his privacy.

Certainly not, he said.

But then he went on to explain Mrs Doran's position, as though to remove any false assumptions I might have. She lived nearby, he told me, here in Montrose. She acted as his part-time secretary, doing work that he brought home from the office, and so reducing his need to go into town. She had her own office, in a room down the hall. She also prepared his meals – except on Saturdays, when he usually went into town to his club. She came and went as it suited her, and did no other household work. For this he had a cleaner who came in once a week, who also took care of his ironing.

Mrs Doran is a good, intelligent woman, he said, and we get on very well. It's perhaps an unusual arrangement, but we're both happy with it. She's a war widow, with a small child to support, and doesn't want a full-time job. Her husband was killed by Japanese fire in New Guinea.

He closed his eyes for a moment, and paused as though in respect. Then he resumed his lecture on the paintings. A short time later I heard the phone ring in the hall, and the murmur of Mrs Doran's voice answering it. She came into the room again, and spoke softly to Walter. It was the first time I'd heard her speak at any length, and I found her voice musical and agreeable.

It's a client, Mr Dixon. He wants to speak with you.

Walter looked up at her fiercely. On a Sunday? Good God. It's *known* I won't speak to clients on a Sunday.

His tone was dauntingly stern; I sensed his capacity for sudden anger, and expected Mrs Doran to become nervous. But her face remained entirely calm, and her voice low.

I told him that, Mr Dixon. But he said it was important.

Tut. Tell him it can wait until Monday, Mrs Doran. Make it clear I'm engaged. *You* know how to handle these things. And perhaps we'll have another pot of tea, if you've time.

She nodded once, and went out again.

Walter leaned back and looked at me, raising his forefinger as he no doubt did in court.

Most of these paintings I'm showing you come from the fifteenth century. Let me quote to you what Walter Pater says of the period in his essay: 'That solemn fifteenth century which can hardly be studied too much.' That's when the miracle began, young Hugh: in the fifteenth century in Italy. That's when all we inherit in art and culture first came to the boil: when classical antiquity was rediscovered, and new directions were taken that led beyond it. That's when men of genius took fire in Florence. Look at this.

His long fingers seemed to tremble as he grasped one of the big art books, turned its pages and laid it flat. I found myself looking at a fine colour reproduction of Botticelli's *Primavera*: a picture I'd not seen before.

When I first stood in front of the original of this in the Uffizi in Florence, Walter said, I got dizzy with joy. It's all here, you see: the legends of antiquity combining with the poetry of the Middle Ages, and a new sort of beauty being born. You and I will never experience the excitement of the *mind* that men like Botticelli knew: an excitement at entering the marvellous world of the ancient Greeks, for the first time.

He spoke as though to himself as well as to me; and I was following his words with difficulty. His finger moved over the images.

No-one fully understands this picture. But here are the three graces, and blind Cupid, and a mysterious woman who may be Venus. And here's the nymph Chloris being transformed into the goddess of Spring by the touch of Zephyr, the West Wind. In a poem by Ovid the nymph says: 'I was Chloris, who am now called Flora.' Botticelli would have read his Ovid, and known her by that name.

I studied the gesturing, glowing figures in front of their dark green tapestry of woodland; and I found an excitement growing in me that answered the old man's. I was sceptical of it at first, as youth is always sceptical of enthusiasm in old people, but it wasn't to be checked. The graphic imagery and the contrast of light and dark that I'd admired in my favourite illustrators were raised here to a magical level; and to this was added a private discovery that transfixed me as Walter pointed to Flora, in her flower-teeming gown. The face that looked towards me, with calm inscrutability, was the face of little June Leaman, vanished with childhood and now transformed into a woman from myth.

I became aware that Walter was asking me to comment on the painting. I've forgotten what sort of awkward reply I made, but it seemed to satisfy him, and he smiled at me almost benevolently.

Since you seem to like Botticelli, you may care for this, he said.

He turned the page to a reproduction of *The Birth of Venus*. The goddess – whom Walter referred to by her Greek name of Aphrodite – stood on her scallop shell, carried on the sea towards the shore in serene and perfect nudity, while roses fell from the air around her, and distant promontories glowed in the dawn. While Walter expounded, I struggled to pay attention to his words. I'd reached the age when any portrayal of female nakedness was both arresting and intensely disturbing, since I'd never seen a living naked woman. Pornography for the masses had yet to be unleashed, at that time; children had yet to make the acquaintance of sexual depravity on their video screens, and even depictions of female nakedness were rare. They were mostly found in paintings and reproductions like this one, and such images had an effect more powerful than the present generation might imagine. I found that I was developing an erection, and I shifted in my seat, crossed my legs to trap my telltale member, and strove to keep my expression noncommittal.

Walter continued to smile, peering at me as though to read my thoughts.

She's a good deal more beautiful than your pinup girls, I should think?

At this moment Mrs Doran glided in with our teapot and cups on a tray. Looking up at her, I had the feeling again of having seen her somewhere before, a long time ago. As she set the tray down, she glanced at the picture and then at me, and her smile seemed to have a knowing quality. I was mortified to find myself flushing, but Walter seemed quite oblivious; he went on speaking, as though Mrs Doran weren't there.

Here's Zephyr again, together with Aura, the gentle breeze, blowing Aphrodite on her shell towards the shore. And here's one of the Horae, the female divinities of the seasons, holding up a cloak to cover Aphrodite's nakedness. If you can forget about that nakedness, young fellow, I want you to look at the marvellous movement and rhythm in these figures. And although this painting may seem an image of pure pleasure, look again: there's a certain melancholy here – as Pater points out. Do you see? The light on the sea's cold, and the face of Aphrodite has an odd expression, don't you think? A mixture of calm and sadness: an expression that tells you that love will always bring sorrow – something you'll eventually learn, young Hugh.

These words gave me little concern, but I glanced at him now with a flash of sympathy, imagining that Walter had suffered in love in some ancient phase of his life – perhaps in his broken marriage. Now that I'm old myself, I find it quaint to recall how very ancient he looked to me then, in spite of his elegant dress: an alien being, quite outside the springtime of life that I inhabited.

I studied the face of Aphrodite. It was the face of a woman from dream, who gazed into an eternal distance with profound serenity; with a knowledge beyond conjecture. I would see this face often, as Walter showered me with the images in his sumptuous art books; it seemed constantly to haunt the works of these Florentine and Venetian painters, and it mingled with scents from the garden beyond the French windows, and the buttery taste of Mrs Doran's scones. Another face which I found arresting was that of Crivelli's Mary Magdalene. In her sumptuous fifteenth-century gown, with her sculptured scrolls of fair hair, this aristocratic beauty hardly seemed like the repentant loose woman of the Bible; but this was not what interested me. Her closed, still face and her long, grey-blue eyes seemed to contemplate some uncanny, secret knowledge: and in this she resembled Mrs Doran.

I only half took in all the paintings that Walter introduced me to that afternoon; my mind whirled with crucifixions, with chaste images of the Virgin and Child, with the worldly-wise faces of Florentine and Venetian nobles, with female figures out of myth and legend, conjured into sensuous life by Titian, Giorgione and Tintoretto. Finally, Walter stood up to dismiss me, as he always did. I got quickly to my feet and turned to him.

Thank you, I said.

No need to thank me, young man.

But you're giving me so much time, Walter – I wonder why you're doing it.

The words had come out without my thinking about them, and I saw with concern that Walter was frowning at me in what looked like anger.

You silly young fool – don't you *know* why? Because I believe in your talent.

I stared at him, embarrassed and flattered, unable to summon up a reply. He saw my discomfiture, and his expression and voice softened.

You're becoming important to me, young Hugh. Your uncle George has two boys – so I have two other great-nephews besides you. But they're dull, philistine creatures, and don't interest me in the least. And of course, I have no children of my own. You're the only Dixon with a spirit I can see might possibly be similar to mine. That's why I've decided to pay to send you to Art School.

I stared at him, and Walter began to laugh.

No need to say anything. We'll talk about it again after your exams. Now get along home. Go on. I've reading to do. You know the way out, don't you?

It was the first time that he hadn't escorted me to the front door. Digesting what he'd said, I was only half aware of walking out into the dimness of the hallway. I then became conscious that somebody had come up behind me, and turned to find Mrs Doran.

I'll see you out.

It was the first time she'd addressed me directly, and my heart jumped. I thanked her, but could think of nothing to say as she moved ahead of me towards the door. I expected her to open it; instead she halted and turned to me in the gloom. We were now standing quite close to each other, and her pale face looked paler than ever, framed by her black hair. She had to tilt her head a little to look up at me, and her wide-set eyes had a confiding shine in them, as though at a shared joke.

You don't remember me, Hugh.

No. Should I?

I was a teacher at your primary school in Moonah. You were just a little boy then. I didn't take your class.

That's why I didn't remember you, I said. I would have, otherwise. But I knew I'd seen you somewhere.

My heart was still thumping, and I was embarrassed to find that my voice was dry. I could smell her perfume, and it almost seemed that her body's warmth was tangible across the space between us. No adult woman had ever stood so close to me, or had such a marked effect on me; it was something quite different from the excitement created by the High School girls I'd taken out, grappling with them in the back rows of cinemas, or in shadows by front fences at night.

There's no reason why you should have remembered me, she said. It's so long ago. But I used to notice you in the playground. You were a nice-looking little boy, and rather quiet. And now you're a handsome young man.

She saw my embarrassment at this and smiled, her eyes lit with an amusement I couldn't read. Was she mocking me? She turned, and opened the door; but still she paused.

Your uncle's very fond of you, she said. He really looks forward to your visits. I suppose you realize that.

I cleared my throat of its dryness.

I look forward to coming here. I learn so much from him.

Good. We'll see you next week then, she said.

I moved out on to the flagstones of the verandah. She had said 'we', I thought: perhaps this meant that she looked forward to seeing me too. The importance I attached to this was absurd, and I knew it. But I was suddenly in the grip of a secret elation: one which was mindless, and wouldn't be checked.

I failed in my exams, as I'd expected to do. I gained Honours in English and History, but my poor results in French and Maths meant that I hadn't matriculated, and I braced myself for my parents' disappointment.

My mother adopted a face of tragic despair when I gave them the news, and told me I'd ruined my chances in life. But my father was strangely quiet, and at first made no comment. Instead, he asked me to come for a walk with him.

We walked up the road towards the railway bridge. My father stopped there and leaned on the rail, and we stood side by side as we'd done when I was a child, staring up the tracks towards the hills. It was now January. The westerly gales and rain that came in the spring had dropped, and warm, still days had set in. We both squinted against the morning sun, and my father fumbled in his shirt pocket and pulled out a packet of cigarettes. He'd promised my mother to give up smoking, but I often found him having a furtive cigarette in the garden.

You're still hooked.

He grinned ruefully, lighting up. Don't *you* start nagging, Hugh. And don't take up smoking yourself – it's bloody hard to quit.

He blew out a long stream of smoke, and said nothing for over a minute. I hadn't yet told him about Walter Dixon's offer, but I intended to do so now. I wasn't as tense as I might have been. Since Walter's loan, my father had changed. He'd become almost humble, and was more friendly towards me than he'd ever been. He seemed to feel that he had to do permanent penance; he'd given up going to the races, and had made a resolution never to place another bet. His friendship with Les Harrington continued, but now they went to the football together, when Les was prepared to skip going to the track. He cleared his throat now, and looked at me with a neutral expression.

So what do you think you'll do, son? Now that you've failed?

I told him that I still wanted to go to Art School, and my father nodded.

I thought you'd say that. But I can't afford the fees on top of keeping you, and paying you an allowance – you know that.

You won't have to, I said; and now I explained a proposal that Walter had made to me on my latest visit. He would pay the fees, he'd told me, if my father would agree to continue giving me room and board and pocket money.

For some moments, my father stared at me in silence, his lips pursed, his cigarette held poised in front of his chest. His expression wasn't hostile; it was simply thoughtful. Then he said:

I'll have to go and visit Uncle Walter.

Does that mean you agree?

Don't get carried away. I'll need to know exactly what Walter's proposing about these fees. Whether it's in the nature of a loan.

It's not a loan. He wants to do it. He says he believes in my talent.

Maybe so. But you can't take this as charity. You'll need to promise that once you start earning your living, you'll repay him. If he'll agree to that, I'm happy to support you here at home, and to give you a small allowance.

I thanked him, and he said:

You were always going to do this, weren't you?

I said nothing, and he nodded. When he spoke again, his voice was low, with a tone in it I'd not heard before: a sort of nostalgia.

Maybe you've got more sense than I had. I'll tell you something. When I was young, working in the office at the factory, there was another clerk there I made friends with. Dan Brennan, his name was. He was a wild little bloke, but a lot of fun. We used to go to dances, and go out with girls together. We decided to save up and have a trip to Melbourne in our holidays. It took us a while but we did it, and went over on the steamer. After we'd been there a few days, Dan told me he wasn't going back. He said he wanted to see the world, and he was going down to Port Melbourne to see if he could get a job as a deckhand on an overseas cargo ship. And he asked me to go with him.

He paused, and glanced at me quickly.

I thought he was crazy, and I didn't agree. I wanted to go: I wanted to see the world, the same as he did. But I thought I wouldn't be fit enough, with this bloody bronchitis of mine – and maybe I just didn't have the nerve. Dan did have the nerve, and he got himself hired on a Port Line boat, and off he went overseas.

Maybe you should have gone too, Dad.

He didn't seem to hear me. He was looking away up the tracks, his eyes narrowed, as though he watched Dan's ship receding there. He stayed silent for another minute or so, stroking his chin. Then he said:

Dan used to say to me: 'Come on Jim, you can be crazy like me, if you try.' I never saw or heard from him again, little Dan Brennan.

He turned back to look at me again.

It's better to do what you really want to do when you're young, no matter what happens. I can see that now.

Walter had invited me to lunch the following Sunday, instead of afternoon tea. I felt I was being honoured; it seemed to mark a new phase in his interest in me.

Full summer had come. The French windows of the dining-room stood open; a panel of thick sunlight lay across the floor, the air in here was hot and motionless, and the chirping of the sparrows and honeyeaters outside came faintly through the shimmering heat from a dimension that was static and eternal, removed from the ordinary world. Mrs Doran served us with herb omelettes, salad, biscuits and cheese and brewed coffee. The coffee was novel to me, and somewhat exotic: all through the War it had been almost unobtainable, replaced by a substitute made from chicory. Coffee was still expensive, and most people still drank the chicory.

As Mrs Doran cleared away, I managed to catch her eye. She smiled at me with a polite and pleasant expression; nothing more. Then she was gone, and didn't appear again.

Walter lit a thin cigar. I hadn't seen him smoke before; this too seemed to mark an occasion, though he didn't offer one to me.

James came and visited me at the firm, he said.

My father had said nothing about this. I waited, and Walter looked at me with a confiding expression, squinting through the smoke, the cigar jutting upwards from his lips.

You didn't know? I see. A pity he didn't come out here to the house. When he telephoned me, I invited him to do so, but he preferred to see me in my chambers in town. He probably felt it was more businesslike.

He smiled with an air of tolerance.

I think we may say that everything is satisfactory. Your father is happy with the arrangement I've offered – on the basis that you pay back the fees when you're working.

He put the cigar down in a large ceramic ashtray, looked at it thoughtfully, and sighed.

Proud. James is very proud. And tense. He's a tense man, isn't he? You needn't answer that.

I didn't, and Walter sat back in his chair.

It was strange to see my nephew after so long. He appeared somewhat careworn – but he has the Dixon looks. He reminds me of my father Martin: the fair hair, the long jaw.

He picked up the cigar again and drew on it.

But you're a less typical Dixon. From what I recall, having met her many years ago, you've inherited your mother's looks: dark brown hair and soulful grey eyes, I seem to recall. But you also inherited the Dixon jaw. A sign of determination, I hope. More coffee?

He chuckled, pouring from the tall silver pot. He seemed to enjoy making me uncomfortable with personal remarks like these.

As for those fees, he said, don't worry about them.

But I must. I will pay you back, Walter, I promise.

As you like. It's not important.

He waved his hand with the air of impatience he always assumed when he wished to dismiss something. Then he sat back, sipping his coffee.

Fathers are a problem, he said. What happened in *my* father's early life deprived him of his peace of mind, and made him pine for a life he could never regain. He was also troubled by guilt. You know about that, I suppose?

I said I didn't, and he looked at me, shaking his head.

Good Lord. How little James has told you about us. This is his own grandfather we're speaking about. Your great-grandfather.

He paused, seeming to consider how to continue; or whether perhaps to continue at all. But then he went on.

As a very young man in the mid-1850s, my father spent time with Lucas Wilson and Liam Dalton, out in Nowhere Valley. He even published an article about it in one of the Hobart Town newspapers of the day: *The Hobart Town Courier.* That did him very little good, I'm afraid. Soon after the article was published, stories were put about by the gossips in the town – stories that were even published in a newspaper in competition with the *Courier.* My father claimed that he'd gone with Dalton purely to get Lucas Wilson's story for the *Courier.* But what the gossips said was that he stayed out with Wilson's band by choice, long after he could have come back. It was even claimed that he took part in their raids – which made him a criminal. The family always denied it, of course; but the rumours never went away.

At this, I assumed an expression of polite surprise. Walter, watching me closely, seemed satisfied with this: he sat back, folding his large white hands on the table and went on.

When I was in my twenties and he was in his seventies, my father began to tell me all that had happened out there. There was no-one else left to talk to. My mother was dead, and my elder brother Charles had long ago married and left home. So I was the only sympathetic listener he had. The fact is that the newspaper article contained only a fraction of what he'd experienced. He'd never spoken about it to anyone else – except presumably my mother. And I've never made public anything he told me.

He looked at me now with an air of suspicion, cocking his head.

But does this have any interest for you, Hugh? I suspect you'd rather be out and about with your friends than listening to me.

Of course I'm interested, I said.

I was lying, and thought he'd detect it; but he nodded, and seemed reassured. So this is one of the reasons he wants me to visit him, I thought. To talk about this, as well as art and ideas. But instead of interest, my actual feeling now was one of unease. For Walter, this yellowing segment of family history was clearly significant; but the prospect of hearing about it in detail had little attraction for me. Although I'd become attuned to the Victorian formality of his way of speaking, I was afraid he'd lose my attention if he dwelt too long on the past. Even when it connected to our family, the past was a topic that was mostly boring and oppressive to me at that age, and the preoccupations of old people had little meaning for me. To hide this, I searched for a way to indicate engagement.

So Liam Dalton was actually here. In this house.

Walter gestured at the dining table.

He sat at this table, on one of these chairs. He joined the family at dinner, and took a glass of wine with them – not by invitation of course. He had a pistol beside his glass.

Everyone had heard of Liam Dalton, who was always courteous to women, and who had once escaped from Port Arthur, and I asked Walter what his father had thought of Dalton.

He seems to have grown fond of him, Walter said. Dalton turned himself in not long after my father came back, and was given a remarkably light sentence: only seven years. He became respectable, and ended his days running a little orchard near Berriedale. My father had testified to Dalton's good qualities in court – and apparently lent him the capital to start his orchard. That gave the gossips ammunition to claim that my father was somehow criminally involved with him, and therefore biased. But Dalton wasn't vicious: he was just a big reckless Irishman who'd been driven to theft by the Famine. And it was Lucas Wilson who most fascinated my father, as I've told you. Wilson, as you surely must know, was not your ordinary bushranger, and certainly no ordinary thug.

His eyes released me now, moving away to stare through the open glass doors at the orchard, where the sun lit the deep green tops of the apple trees.

My father's brother William was thrown from a horse and killed at twenty-six, he said. That was the year after my father spent time with the Wilson band. This left my father as sole heir to Leyburn, and old Henry expected him to run it after he died. So my father shouldered the burden for life. In many ways, he was fond of the place – but farming wasn't really what he'd wanted to do. Martin was quite a cultivated man, given the circumstances of the time.

His father had done well at school, Walter told me, and had gone on to study at Christ's College: the colony's first university. He'd wanted to be a scholar – a teacher, perhaps. But Henry Dixon had sent him to the College purely to get a bit of polish – not to take up scholarship as a vocation. That idea alarmed old Henry so much that he took Martin out of the College before he could graduate, and set him to work helping to manage the property.

Martin always resented that, Walter said, but he had a strong sense of duty. Leyburn Farm was Henry Dixon's great achievement: as his heir, how could Martin walk away from his inheritance? He seems to have felt he had little choice in the matter; he stayed here for life, and did his best. I won't say his life didn't have its good side – though in his late years he became a little too fond of the whisky bottle. The farm would have been neglected if he hadn't had a good manager. When your grandfather Charles and I grew up, we had no intention of running the place: we'd both chosen the Law as our profession. That's why we sold most of the land when our father died – but not the house. Charles would have sold it, but I didn't agree. No. I could never leave this house.

He broke off and continued to look out through the doors, as though seeing images in the heat that danced above the trees.

When he spoke again, his voice had become soft and slow, taking on the same melodic cadences I'd heard in it on the back verandah, when he'd looked at the hills where Dalton had gone.

Sometimes I think my father's real life ended at twenty, out in the bush with Wilson and Dalton. He kept re-living that time, in his old age; his head was filled with it. He'd killed a man out there – but nobody ever knew that, and I won't go into it now. One thing I feel certain of: when Liam Dalton raided this place and took my father out to the wilderness, he bound him to Wilson for ever. He was obsessed by Lucas Wilson ever afterwards.

He was still staring out into the heat, his old voice trembling a little more than usual. My attention had begun to drift again, and I tried to adopt an interested expression when he finally turned back to me.

But I'm probably boring you, he said.

I protested that he wasn't.

I trust not. Still, it must be time for you to go, young Hugh. Shall I see you next Sunday?

I'm looking at two early photographs, inherited from Walter Dixon. Both were taken in the mid-1850s. One is a portrait of my great-grandfather, Martin Dixon. The other is a portrait taken by Martin himself: the outlaw Lucas Wilson.

The back of the studio portrait of Martin Dixon carries the legend: *H.H. Baily, Photographer, Hobart Town.* It's typical of the period. Martin is posed behind a round, polished table in front of a floor-length curtain, formally attired in a dress coat, stiff white shirt and narrow bow tie secured with a pin, his hand resting on a book: no doubt to indicate his identity as a budding scholar. He seems to be about twenty or so. His long, youthful face contains opposite elements: mature determination is combined with a hint of that childish vulnerability which sometimes lingers after adolescence. A lock of fair hair falls diagonally across his forehead, spoiling the formality of the pose; one can imagine him pushing it back. His hair and the set of his long jaw give him a distinct resemblance to my father, but his eyes are obviously blue, since the antique picture makes the irises very pale, as early photographs tend to do. He looks at the viewer from under his brows, which are set low above the eyes. He's tall and thin, and stands in a slightly slouching manner: a scholarly stoop.

The portrait of Lucas Wilson shows Martin to have been a gifted amateur, since he was working in the very early days of photography. The man who stares out through the reddish-brown screen of the past is somewhere in his thirties. He wears a bush-worker's blouse over a striped shirt, and a neckerchief is knotted at his throat. The picture has been taken out of doors, against the wall of a weatherboard house, and his left hand is outstretched to hold the barrel of a shotgun that's propped on the ground. His thick hair, which appears to be a darkish brown, is swept straight back. He's clean-shaven, apart from his side-whiskers, with a long upper lip and high cheekbones, and his eyes have a strange look. Like Martin Dixon's, they must actually have been blue, since they too are drained of colour by the technology of the time – but in his case the effect is more drastic. The irises are white, baleful discs, the pupils minute, fixed on the viewer in a way that's intimidating – an effect that's emphasized by the severe line of the upper lids.

Walter left this portrait to me in his will, together with the one of his father. It's the only known photograph of Lucas Wilson, and has never been published – though it would certainly arouse considerable interest among historians. This is because Walter never revealed its existence – perhaps because he had some irrational notion that it gave him a secret ownership of Wilson. As for me, I've never been in a hurry to release it either: something holds me back. Perhaps, like Walter, I prefer to keep Lucas Wilson hidden for the time being. Eventually, I'll leave it to the Archives.

How often did Walter study this image? Often, I imagine. Often.

That summer after I'd finished school was one of the happiest of my life. I'd submitted some of my drawings to the Art School in town and had been accepted, and enrolled in the Fine Arts course. Walter had given me a cheque, and the first term's fees had been paid. At the end of January, when the school reopened, I'd begin my classes. For now, I was entirely free. I went swimming with friends, walked in the bush, or worked on my drawings. And every Sunday, I visited Walter – usually for lunch. He would often let me browse alone in the library, but always, late in the afternoon, he'd join me there or in the dining-room, and we'd talk.

I was happy to make these regular visits, since I felt deeply grateful to him, and I was more and more impressed with his erudition. He knew as much about literature as he did about art, and he lent me many books – poetry, and novelists who were new to me – and these were mostly what we talked about. Just once, I told him I couldn't come the following weekend, as I had another engagement, and I was disconcerted by the expression on his face: disappointment was mingled with veiled disapproval. He made no protest, but it was clear to me that I'd broken an unwritten rule: I was always to be available on Sundays. Since I had plenty of time on my hands, this presented no difficulty: but it reminded me that I was beholden to him – and also that I was important to him in a way that wasn't entirely clear. I was his captive listener.

Mrs Doran didn't see me to the door again, since Walter always did; so I had no further opportunity to talk with her. Perhaps because I had no current girlfriend, I thought about her a good deal. I found her both enigmatic and attractive. I told myself that this growing infatuation was absurd, since she was somewhere in her mid-thirties – almost middle-aged. But it made no difference. When she smiled at me in the dining-room, my heart would jump, and my mouth would go dry.

My visits on those Sundays have a tendency to dissolve into one another, in memory. They've now become a single, infinitely extended afternoon: an afternoon in which Walter and I sit always in that long dining-room, at the long mahogany table that had come out from Yorkshire in 1830, while his sonorous voice, like the voice of an old actor, goes on and on, rising and falling, measured and inflexible, sometimes engaging, sometimes tedious, punctuated at times by the outcries of the sparrows and honeyeaters that float in through the open French windows: cries that I tell myself resemble those of prisoners, seeking to escape from their condition. Art and family history are Walter's two passions. He speaks mainly of painting and literature; but he often returns to the story of his father and the Wilson gang, and to that old, serious century that's gone.

It becomes my impression that a little of his father's obsession has rubbed off on Walter, and I begin to see him as a hostage in the house of his birth – and perhaps a hostage to the past. At times I imagine that Wilson and Dalton ride through Walter's dreams, haunting his odd single life in this house which he seldom leaves except for his visits to his office in the city and occasional trips to Melbourne: a house which sits stranded and immured in the nineteenth century. Sometimes, I think, he must stand on the back verandah where his father's hat still hangs (this would happen at twilight), watching the bush-dense hills that loom behind the stables and imagining the sound of hooves: riders from that old, lost century of his childhood and his father's youth, coming down to the flatland across a hundred years, from out of the mountain wilderness that lies not very far to the west: that region once empty of settlement, its forests unexplored; a country beyond human laws and consolations, snowbound in winter and with no other name than the one that was given it by Wilson: Nowhere Valley.

BOOK TWO

*

Martin Dixon

1

The two men lay on their bellies on a little hill, in the shadow of a drooping casuarina. This was in the summer of 1854. Their faces and hands were webbed with cuts and scratches, and their coarse fustian clothing was torn and shredded, hanging in strips. The jackets resembled those of clowns: pied garments in yellow and black, the sleeves differing. On the back of each jacket, the letter F was stamped. Felon.

The night air was mild and still. The only sounds here were the lonely piping of plover, and the far barking of a dog. Supporting themselves on their elbows in the tussock grass, the men surveyed the wide expanse of Pitt Water: an inlet from Frederick Henry Bay which was almost landlocked, and which was now the colour of pewter, under a full moon. They'd come to a country of water, and of low, round hills.

After a time, one of them spoke in a whisper.

Where are we, Dalton?

He had an educated accent, at odds with his wretched appearance. He was in his late twenties: slightly built, with a sharp, long-nosed face, very pale. His head had not long ago been shaved, and his hair was in dark bristles. His unshaven jaw looked black against his pallor.

Sorell, Dalton said. It's called Sorell. I've been in these parts before.

You mean you've raided here. With Wilson.

Sure, and I might have done, Dalton said.

His tone invited no further questions. His voice was deep, and his accent Irish: the soft brogue of Galway. He was a big man in his early thirties, around six feet tall and strongly built. He too had short-cut hair: coppery bristles. He pointed beyond the inlet, to an area of open grassland in the distance. Two small orange lights were glimmering feebly out there, some miles apart.

Farms, he said. See? I'm thinkin we'll pay one of them a visit at sunrise. We'll be needin weapons, and food.

No doubt of that. I'm fucking starving. But how do you propose to take their guns?

We've surprise on our side. And these are poor people, out here. Probably no servants to help them, and the village a good way off. Are you with me or not, Griffin?

Griffin turned quickly to look at Dalton, grinning in the dark.

You know I'm with you. I won't leave your side. You won't get rid of me, comrade.

Dalton and Griffin had escaped from the penal settlement at Port Arthur eight days ago. Their achievement in doing so was unusual, since the Tasman Peninsula, where the settlement was situated, was itself a natural gaol.

It extended into the sea in the extreme south-east of Van Diemen's Land, and was joined to the Forestier Peninsula in the north by a narrow strip of land called Eaglehawk Neck. Forestier Peninsula was linked in turn to the mainland by another narrow neck. Both necks were patrolled day and night by sentries, and Eaglehawk Neck was guarded as well by a line of dogs, chained six feet apart. Should a convict attempt escape, however, there was no way to go but this one: the way that led north, across the two necks, to the areas of settlement on the mainland. Any other way led to disorientation and death by starvation, since both peninsulas were mountainous and clothed in dense wilderness, largely unexplored, whose undergrowth was so thick that progress was painful and at times impossible.

A few escapees in their ignorance had gone south instead of north. These had come to a barrier more appalling than the bush: the Southern Ocean, beyond which lay Antarctica. Starving, they then wandered in despair on a coast of merciless beauty, whose rocks had been shaped aeons ago by an immense volcanic upheaval. The seas of the Roaring Forties exploded against tall, dark, infinitely receding capes composed of giant pillars of dolerite – structures suggesting the walls of a prison more pitiless than Port Arthur – while from out of the sea rose fantastic dolerite columns like those of sunken temples, reaching a height of a thousand feet, and beckoning the escapees with mirages of a titanic civilization. But here, on this final and empty edge of the world, lashed and frozen by Antarctic gales, the lost little London pickpockets and burglars finally starved, and left their bones on the rocks.

The authorities had been confident that there was no way out of Port Arthur by land. But then Liam Dalton made his first attempt at flight.

He did so by skirting Eaglehawk Neck and its guards, and swimming the bay. The bay was a small one, but it was said to contain sharks: a rumour with little foundation, encouraged by the authorities. Dalton chose to risk this, and emerged unscathed on the Forestier Peninsula; but he was caught in the bush there when he collapsed from exhaustion, having eaten no food for four days. The feat had made him celebrated in the settlement, and drew particular attention from Roy Griffin.

Dalton and Griffin worked in a quarry on a hill at the edge of the settlement. They belonged to a gang of four convicts who pushed truckloads of sandstone along a tramway: doing the work of horses, they propelled their wagon to a pier down on the harbour. Late on a hot December afternoon they stood waiting in the quarry while another gang reloaded the truck. Talking was permitted at such times, and they had begun to know each other.

You're going to try it again, Griffin said suddenly. Aren't you?

He spoke very low, glancing furtively at the two other members of their gang nearby, in their black-and-canary uniforms. These men were lounging against the truck, and paying him and Dalton no attention. Other convicts, well out of earshot, were working with picks at the quarry face or cutting the stone into blocks, while the overseer, himself a convict, was standing some distance off, watching the stone-cutters. Above the quarry, the olive-green bush began: the endless forests of eucalypts that were the final walls of their prison.

Dalton looked blankly at Griffin. The smaller man's eyes were an odd bottle-green, bright and disturbingly penetrating. Nothing could be read behind them.

I'm right, aren't I? Griffin said.

And why would I be gabbin about that to you, even if it's true? You might grass on me, Griffin.

Never. You surely can't mean that. You can trust me, Dalton: I swear it. I admire you, I truly do. And I believe that next time you'll succeed.

There won't be a next time, I'm tellin you.

Griffin moved closer, his face inches from Dalton's.

Yes there will. I know it.

It's bloody nonsense you're talkin. How would you know it?

I know such things. I have that power. And I know that only you can do it.

Griffin's voice had sunk to an ardent whisper, while his gaze never left Dalton's.

Trust me, he said. I swear you can trust me, Dalton. And I'm asking you: please take me with you when you go.

Dalton shook his head, and made no reply. But Griffin smiled at him, seemingly not discouraged. He had an engaging smile: one which asked that others like him, and believe in whatever he said.

Please think about it, he said. Two heads are better than one – and you'll be glad of a comrade.

When Dalton still said nothing, Griffin's expression became beseeching.

I *beg* you, Dalton. I've got to get out of this fucking place. I've been flogged once, and I can't bear any more of it. I'm not a man who should be here.

Dalton raised his brows and then looked away, studying the picturesque blue bay below them, whose surface sparkled cheerfully in the sun. The Isle of the Dead, with its convict cemetery, lay at the bay's centre, and the Government schooner *Eliza* was anchored by the pier. His gaze travelled on over the settlement: a town in the wilderness, ruled by the military. Its main purpose was the punishment and reform of convicts who'd committed fresh crimes in the colony, as he and Griffin had done; and yet it resembled a pretty English village. English oaks lined the roads, and its cottage gardens were filled with displays of English flowers. Its stone buildings, erected with convict labour, were substantial and well-designed: a military barracks, a hospital, offices, stores, residences for the officials and overseers, a bakery, a lunatic asylum, and a big, freestone Gothic church with a steeple. Only shops and taverns were absent. At the settlement's centre, just above the port, was the massive Penitentiary, past which the tramway from the quarry ran, to end at the jetty. In the south, on a rise above the Commandant's cottage, stood a giant semaphore, with three pairs of double arms. This machine was one of many devices whose aim was to foil any attempts at escape. There were thirteen such semaphore stations on the two peninsulas, and messages passed between them within four minutes, relaying the name and number of any escapee. An intermediate semaphore at Clarence Plains provided swift communication with Hobart Town, sixty miles away, so that details concerning bolters reached every military station in the south of the island within a quarter of an hour. Beyond the semaphore, like sombre thoughts, the olive-green forests began. Looking across there, Dalton narrowed his eyes. Then he turned back to Griffin.

Sure, and I'm sorry for you, he said. But that's just it, Griffin: you're a gentleman, and not cut out for this kind of thing. It's hard goin in the bush, and my guess is that you'd not be able to bear it.

You're wrong. I'm stronger than I look. And I can use a gun. I'm a dead shot. Please, Dalton. I implore you. I'll find a way to repay you, I swear it.

I'll think about it, Dalton said. I won't say I agree, but I promise you one thing.

What's that?

If your tongue wags, I'll find a way to kill you.

Five days later, on the second of January, Dalton and Griffin stood by the truck again, while the quarry gang filled it with a fresh load of sandstone blocks. It was two in the afternoon, soon after dinner, cloudless and very hot. There was little shade in the quarry, except under the slope of the hill from which the stone was cut, and the sun shimmered and danced on the stacks of sandstone in a way that made the yellow-and-black-clad figures move with dreamlike slowness. The convict overseer, in a plain grey prison uniform, sat with his eyes half-closed on a stack of blocks by the quarry entrance, and all sounds here had a quality of trance: the muted reports of the picks wielded by the prisoners at the face of the quarry, a murmur of voices, and the gurgling calls of magpies from out of the wall of bush that ran along the top of the bank.

When Dalton and Griffin strolled slowly away from the truck, they did so in an idle, purposeless manner, heads down, as though sleepwalking. They didn't speak, but Griffin watched Dalton's face. After a few moments, the big man looked sideways at him and winked.

Instantly, Griffin ran to the bank of the quarry and began to scramble up it, agile and comically urgent, stumbling a little on the stones but moving very fast. Dalton was close behind him, hurling himself upwards with remarkable speed for so large a man. At the top of the bank, barely pausing, he reached behind a fallen log, drew out a small canvas sack, and ran on. Then, while shouts rose from the quarry, he and Griffin plunged into the dark green fathoms of the wilderness, fighting their way through the dense, prickly undergrowth that grew between the ranks of tall blue gums, ignoring the twigs and thorns that were lacerating their faces and hands. As they smashed and burrowed their way forward, new and more distant sounds came up to them: the blowing of whistles, a rifle shot, and the raised, commanding voices of soldiers. But they were quite invisible from below in these mazes of vegetation, and the sounds soon faded behind them as the guards lost time in preventing a general break.

Dalton didn't pause. It was not until some twenty minutes later that he came to a halt, panting to recover his breath, his chest heaving. Griffin, speechless, stood gulping in air and watching him, bent forward with his hands on his knees. Dalton wiped away sweat from his face, the sack dangling from his other hand. After some moments he took a few steps to one side and looked back through a gap in the trees. He beckoned to Griffin, and pointed. Some of the settlement's buildings could still be seen on a ridge in the south: the military hospital, the barracks and the officers' quarters. Above these, the semaphore stood out against the sky, moving its arms like a giant damaged insect. Dalton laughed.

Look at that now. It's wettin their britches the bastards are, sendin out the news about us. Well, they'll not get me this time.

He slapped the canvas sack.

I've stowed some grub in this swag. One of the cooks was a friend to me. We'll not starve, the way I did before.

You're a marvel. So what next? Shall we start heading north?

Dalton squinted upwards through the canopy of gums and silver wattle, searching for the position of the sun.

No. We'll go south: to Mount Arthur.

Griffin stared at him. But the Neck's in the north, he said.

Aye. And it's there they'll expect us to go, and it's that way they'll be movin. We go south, and lie low at the foot of Mount Arthur. There we'll stay snug for two or three days, until the noise dies down.

Griffin laughed, and shook his head.

Clever, he said. You're a very clever man, Dalton.

The scrub at the foot of Mount Arthur, south of the settlement, was pathless and almost impenetrable. With Dalton in the lead they fought their way through it and finally reached a small creek. Here, deep in the bush, they settled down to wait, sustained by two loaves of bread from Dalton's sack, and water from the creek. The sack also contained a supply of flour, which Dalton was saving for later in the journey.

This was the warmest time of the year and it rained only once, during the second day. They slept at night under a clear sky with burning white stars: stars which seemed brighter and closer to the earth than those in the hemisphere from which they'd come. They took turns at keeping watch, but there were no sounds of pursuit: they heard nothing but the snoring noises of quarrelling possums and the low calling of a mopoke. Dalton warned Griffin to watch out for snakes, which he said were deadly in this island; but none were seen.

On the evening of the third day, Dalton led the way north through the bush. By midnight they were skirting the prison settlement on its western side. Some four miles further on they crept across the convict tramway that ran from here to Norfolk

Bay, and then across the rough, narrow road that took the same route. It was only five miles along this road to Norfolk Bay, and another three to Eaglehawk Neck. But Dalton refused to take to the road, since police patrols moved on it constantly. Instead, they re-entered the bush near Signal Hill, north of Port Arthur.

They were now faced with a wilderness more dense than before: one that had never been explored. Tonight, Dalton said, they'd hide in the scrub on the far side of Signal Hill, and in the morning they'd move north-east.

At this Griffin grew uneasy.

How can you know your way, in this fucking wilderness?

Dalton explained. He'd once worked with a party of prisoners carrying provisions to some soldiers on Mount Arthur, and had been to the summit. From there, the entire peninsula could be scanned, all the way to Eaglehawk Neck. He'd memorized the whole line of country, and some of the old lags had pointed out its landmarks to him. He'd got through before, and he'd do it again.

There was only a faint quarter moon. Going up Signal Hill, they moved through near-total darkness, and the undergrowth here was so dense that they must crawl on their hands and knees for a good deal of the time. This continued for some hours. Griffin became tormented by thirst, hunger and lack of sleep, and began to complain.

I've had enough of this, Dalton. I've got to have some rest.

You'll get no rest until I say so. And stow that bloody whining or I'll leave you here to rot.

At this, Griffin's face became contorted with private rage, but he followed Dalton in silence. Coming down the other side of the hill, he stumbled and crawled behind his guide through a black, eucalyptus-smelling underworld of ferns and damp mosses, where the knife-like thorns and twigs slashed at his face and clothing as though with venomous intent, and sharp stones cut his knees. He constantly feared that snakes were attacking him, and muttered obscenities at this whole gloomy and alien country where no wild berries or plants grew that might be eaten, and whose black and barren womb seemed to have swallowed him. Finally, with a faint dawn light entering the sky above the gums, they found themselves on the floor of a gully where another small creek was bubbling, and Dalton called a halt.

Griffin collapsed on his belly, greedily drinking the ice-cold water. As soon as he'd done, he rolled over on his back in the grass and fell instantly asleep, his sharp white nose pointing at the sky. Dalton did the same.

They slept heavily, and woke late in the morning, roused by the sharp remarks of nameless native birds. The sun glinted on the leaves of the gums above their heads, raising their spirits. The gully was well hidden from the world outside, and Dalton decided that they were far enough away from the settlement to make damper for breakfast. He lit a small fire in a hollow tree with one of some hoarded lucifer matches, and let it burn to ashes. Then he took out all the flour in his sack, mixed it with water on top of the sack, kneaded it to dough, and cooked it on the coals.

Griffin chewed his hot damper gratefully, and became ingratiating again. This is good, he said. You're a clever fellow, Dalton, I must say.

Enjoy it. It's almost the last thing you'll be eatin on this bloody peninsula. I'll save this last bit of damper – but after that we'll not eat again until we lay our hands on more provisions. And now it's time to be movin.

Again they moved through dense bush, keeping to the valleys. This went on for some hours; then they climbed another towering hill. The blue gums and wattle grew farther apart here, and the two men stood in a clearing at the top. Dalton pointed.

There's Norfolk Bay, he said. Not more than two miles off. And you can see the track around the bay that leads to Eaglehawk Neck. We must keep that in sight on our left.

Below them, after the confinement of the gullies, lay a landscape of freedom, extending to infinity under a huge sky. Out in the north-west, Norfolk Bay gleamed in the afternoon sun, half-enclosed by a hook-like arm of the peninsula. Beyond it in the north lay the mauve-grey hills of Forestier Peninsula, linked to this one by the thin, just-visible thread of Eaglehawk Neck. On the east of both peninsulas lay a blue and jade sea, with white cumulus clouds towering above the horizon. Beaches and dark, wild capes receded south in endless succession, growing minute with distance, dwindling into nothing at the empty end of the world.

Griffin drew in his breath. By Jesus, he said. We've almost done it.

We've still the hardest part in front of us, Dalton said. We'll cross the Neck tonight, all bein well.

He put a hand on Griffin's shoulder.

I've been a little hard on you. But I had to be, Griffin, or you'd not have got through. You've done well so far, for a gentleman of delicate constitution.

Griffin looked at him quickly, and Dalton smiled. But Griffin's answering grin was empty and ambiguous.

At eight o'clock that evening, with the island's long summer twilight not yet over, they lay on a hill above the road that skirted Eaglehawk Bay. Below them on their right, perhaps half a mile away, was the narrow, sandy isthmus of Eaglehawk Neck.

It was covered with white cockle shells, laid down to shine in the dark, and a row of lamps stretched across it from end to end, already lit in the dusk. Red-coated sentries were clearly visible, standing at intervals. So were a succession of dog kennels, with mastiffs chained in front of them. Armed, blue-clad constables were patrolling on the road. A semaphore stood on a hillock behind the guardhouse, its arms working. Beyond it was a row of sandhills, glowing gold in the setting sun, and on the other side of these stretched the final, dark blue bar of the sea. They could hear the hollow booming of the surf.

Look at those redcoat cunts, Griffin said. And the fucking constables are here as well. Nobody could get across there.

He bit nervously into a hunk of cold damper, and chewed.

Sure, and you knew that already, Dalton said. We'll not be concerned with the Neck.

He pointed across the road below them to the calm, leaf-green expanse of Eaglehawk Bay: an indentation of the larger Norfolk Bay. It became quite narrow here, close to the Neck, and on its far side was yet another ridge of bush.

That's where we'll be crossin, Dalton said. When it's dark, we'll swim the bay just here. It's no more than a quarter of a mile.

Christ, Griffin said, and his voice was small.

What is it that troubles you?

It looks wider.

It's not. I hope you'll not be losin your nerve, Griffin? You can swim – have you not told me so?

Yes, I can swim. It's the sharks I'm thinking about. You say it's just a story, put about by the traps to scare us. Is that really so?

Maybe. But even if it's not, that's the chance we take. Better the sharks than Port Arthur, by Christ. And never a shark showed his head when I crossed before. But let you not be thinkin of the risks now, Griffin. It's too late for that.

And what about those bastards of police? Look at them. They're up and down this road all the time.

That will be the hard part. We must wait until dark, and creep across when we get the chance. We'll see their lamps comin, if there's any of the buggers close by.

Griffin became quiet, and they lay in the grass in silence, watching the shadows lengthen on the road.

At eleven o'clock they came down the hill and crouched behind some bushes at the road verge. A constable passed within yards of them, boots crunching on the gravel, carrying his lantern. As soon as his footsteps had died away and his light had vanished around a bend, they took off their heavy prison boots, crept across the road and went down among the trees to the shore.

In minutes, they stood white and naked in the dark, making their trousers, shirts and jackets into bundles and tying their boots together by the laces. Then they stood hesitating on the stones, in the feeble light of the moon. It was very quiet, but every sound seemed loud: the lapping of the water on the rocks, distant military voices at the Neck, and the sudden deep barking of a dog. Griffin looked at Dalton with an expression that might have contained some sort of appeal. He was shivering. Dalton ignored him, and hung his boots around his neck. He waded in with as little sound as possible, tied his clothing on his head and slid into the water. He began to swim breaststroke, his head held high above the surface.

Griffin followed, and Dalton turned once to look for him. The smaller man was swimming strongly, his narrow white face just visible in the dark, tilted upwards as though in supplication. Dalton then concentrated on reaching the opposite shore. When he got there, crawling onto the rocks, he found that Griffin was only a few yards behind him. The two of them hobbled panting across a tract of sharp stones, anxious to be out of sight.

Once in the bush, they found themselves climbing a steep, rocky hill. Its thorny scrub was more tormenting than anything they'd yet come through, and their night now became miserable. It had turned cold, and a south wind was blowing. Their prison suits had been splashed with water, and the coarse, heavy fustian clung to them like clay. They reached the top of the hill and collapsed, too tired and weak from lack of food to go further. They bedded down as best they could in the grass and bracken and lay shivering throughout the night, too cold to sleep except in snatches.

When the sun came up, they surveyed the scene below them.

It was an overcast, cool day; they could not get warm, and were now very hungry indeed. On the other side of the Bay they could make out the line of sentries on the Neck, and police patrols beating the bush in the hills above the road, searching for them. The dark blue figures were quite close to where they'd been last night.

Christ, Griffin said. Those bastards'll find us soon.

Dalton turned away without a word and led the way down the other side of the hill, walking stiffly but very fast. Muttering, Griffin followed. Within minutes, they were moving above the road that ran from here to the East Bay Neck, some fourteen miles off, where their crossing to the mainland must be made.

There's a guard-hut that I know about down there, Dalton said. Some lags under a convict overseer are posted there: good-conduct men. They're mendin the roads. They'll be away in the daytime, at work. There'll be plenty of grub in there. We'll have to crack it.

What if someone's there?

Sure, we may have to use persuasion.

They reached the slab hut late in the morning. There was smoke coming from the chimney. Dalton came through the door with a heavy stick in his hand, Griffin following behind him.

The hut was empty except for the cook: an aged, grey-haired convict stirring soup in a pot at the fireplace. He threw up his hands immediately, and begged not to be harmed. He knew who Dalton was, he said, and was glad to help him; there was plenty of time to pack some food before the road gang was due back for dinner.

Served by the cook, they each drank a bowl of hot soup, shivering with gratitude. Then they set about filling a sack with beef, bread, tea, sugar and salt, as well as knives, plates, mugs, a billycan, and a box containing some lucifer matches. They tied the old man up to prevent his giving the alarm – or to make it appear that he'd been prevented from doing so, since he swore that he wouldn't betray them. Then they made off into the bush.

Griffin had imagined that they would now head north again, keeping close to the line of the road. But instead, Dalton went deeper into the bush, moving east. He halted at evening in a gully far out in the wilderness, in an area which he said had never been penetrated by the authorities. By raiding the hut, he told Griffin, they had signalled their presence on the Forestier Peninsula. The semaphores would by now be sending out the news, and the searchers would have moved on to this side. They must lie low here for three days; but this time they'd be warm and well fed.

That night they camped in a grassy clearing surrounded by tall gums, close to a creek. Dalton had once again made a fire in a hollow tree, in order to produce as little smoke as possible, and they sat cross-legged facing it, staring into the low flames, enjoying the warmth. They were replete from a meal of beef and bread, their clothing dried, mugs of hot tea in their fists. The billycan sat perched on the coals of the fire. It was a still night, and the air was filled with the scent of eucalyptus from the burning twigs. Throughout their journey, they'd held very few conversations; their exchanges when they'd rested had been minimal, since discomfort and exhaustion had made them disinclined to talk. Now, however, in their state of wellbeing, they began to converse.

So tell me, comrade, what are your plans? Griffin said. Will you go bushranging again?

It's all I'm good for now. They've made me an outlaw, and an outlaw I'll stay, unless I take ship out of this bloody island. Besides, I'm good at it.

That you are, from what I hear. You and Lucas Wilson are famous.

Sure, and it's Lucas that's famous. I'm just his lieutenant.

And yet they didn't hang you, when you were caught.

They didn't hang me because I've not killed a man, and have never insulted a woman. I've been in gunfights with the traps, sure, and winged a few – but I've not yet taken a life. I've not had to. So they gave me twelve years. I said to myself: I'll never serve that, if I can help it – and I've not done twelve months.

He laughed, drank off his tea, and looked into the fire for a time. Then he looked sideways at Griffin.

And what of yourself? How did a cove like you come to be transported? Let me guess: the gentleman's crime, was it? Forgery?

Something like that. My father's an attorney in Taunton, Somerset. I was studying Law, and intended to be his partner, but I fell in with a fast set of fellows. I had gambling debts I couldn't pay – and I forged a promissory note to get me out of my difficulties. Instead, I was sentenced to execution – commuted to transportation for life. So you might say I've been lucky.

He grinned without amusement, while Dalton looked at him with a puzzled expression.

But an educated man like yourself generally lands a nice soft situation here. They've a need for educated men. How did you come to be put in Port Arthur, now?

You're right. When I arrived, they made me a clerk in the Convict Department, in Hobart Town. But I got into some trouble.

What kind of trouble?

Griffin looked away into the trees, and his mouth twisted.

Trouble that shouldn't have happened. A fucking constable told lies about me.

Dalton waited, but Griffin said no more. The fire's dying flames were reflected on his face, making the blackness of the stubble on his chin look blacker.

Well now, Dalton said, whatever it was, it's behind you now. So what will you do, once we get through? You'll not be wantin to show your face in Hobart Town again, I'm thinkin.

I thought I'd come with you to Captain Wilson.

Dalton narrowed his eyes, still looking sideways at Griffin, who had adopted a winning smile.

I'm afraid I can't let you do that, Dalton said.

Griffin stared at him, his smile fading.

No? But why not?

You'll know that Wilson has never been tracked down, Dalton said. Not him, and not any of our gang – except me.

Of course I know that. And yet he controls whole sections of the country – isn't that so?

Dalton leaned forward, and stirred the coals of the fire with a stick.

Aye. And the reason he's never been taken is that our headquarters is secret, and none of us will ever betray it. I got taken because I was fool enough to go into the town of New Norfolk, pursuin a silly little girl there. Her brother it was who betrayed me to the peelers, God's curse on him. I broke one of our rules in doin that – but I went alone, and put none of our people in danger. We take no-one into our band who might do so. We admit no strangers – and I'll not wish to offend you, Griffin, but it's a stranger you are.

I see. After all we've come through, I'm a stranger.

You're a stranger. I know little about you – and you a gentleman, unused to life with a gun in your hand. So let you not think about joinin Captain Wilson.

Griffin imitated Dalton by picking up a stick and stirring the fire with it. He frowned, staring into the coals in silence, and his face had taken on a disturbing expression. It was perhaps simply one of disappointment; but the low firelight was causing his features to resemble a malign mask, and Dalton studied him with greater attention than before. After some moments Griffin blinked, and seemed to make an effort to collect himself. He turned to look sideways at Dalton, and his expression had changed to one of humble entreaty, his green eyes wide with it.

But Wilson's a gentleman too, isn't he?

Aye. But he's also a soldier.

Griffin drew in a breath and sighed. He shook his head and looked down again.

Maybe when we get through this – that's if we do – you'll have come to know me better. Then you might change your mind.

Maybe, but I don't think so. It's Wilson who makes the rules we live by. I just obey them.

Like a soldier.

Aye. Like a soldier. And now let's get some sleep.

At sunset over three days later, they reached Mount Forestier. They stood on a thickly wooded slope looking down on East Bay Neck, the isthmus linking the peninsula to the mainland. It was about half a mile long; a military guardhouse stood there, and sentry boxes were dotted along it from one shore to the other; but there was no line of dogs. On its western side was Norfolk Bay, and on the east, Blackman Bay. Beyond lay the distant ocean. The blue-green water was glassy and still, and the low-lying promontories were cradled in a deceitful spell of peace. Dalton pointed.

We'll need to go past the Neck, he said. The bay gets narrow there, see? We'll swim it tonight.

They came down out of the bush close to midnight, and crept along the deserted shore. It was overcast and dark. No sign of habitation; but behind them were distant lights, strung across the Neck. They reached a point where the width of the bay was less than half the distance they'd swum at Eaglehawk Neck. They had stripped and swum across it in ten minutes, and entered a patch of scrub on the mainland of Van Diemen's Land. Their escape was complete, and they now began a night-time trek around the western shore of Frederick Henry Bay, entering a country that Dalton knew, headed for Sorell.

On Saturday, January 14th, four days after their arrival at Sorell, Dalton and Griffin appeared at sunset in the Bridgewater district, on the eastern side of the Derwent River, some twelve miles from Hobart Town.

They were now on horseback, and were entirely transformed. Their prison suits were gone. Both were clean-shaven, and each was well-clothed, though their styles were very different. Liam Dalton might have been taken either for a modest squatter or a stockman. He rode a bay gelding, with a shotgun in a leather scabbard strapped to his saddle. His low-crowned, wide-brimmed hat was woven from the leaves of the New South Wales cabbage-tree palm, with a green silk band tied around the crown. He wore a red serge blouse over a striped shirt, secured at the waist by a leather belt, and a black neckerchief. Two leather shot flasks and a brass gunpowder flask were attached to his belt, and his moleskin trousers were tucked into a pair of Hessian top boots. Griffin, mounted on a black mare, was attired as a gentleman – but a somewhat odd gentleman, difficult to classify. He might have been in some kind of commerce. His handsome grey felt hat had a round crown and a wide brim, and his white buckskin trousers were set off by patent leather top boots. Despite the mildness of the evening, he was enveloped in a long, coat-like, dark grey mantle, fitted with a circular cape and fastened at the throat. The effect, together with his sharp, pallid face, was funereal.

Since they'd lain on the little hillside at Sorell, they'd carried out two raids.

The first had been on one of the small dwellings whose lights they'd seen from the hillside. They had arrived there at six o'clock in the morning, and the place had proved not to be a farm, but merely a shepherd's hut. There was a wood-heap outside with an axe lying beside it, and Dalton had armed himself with this before entering by the unlocked door, with Griffin behind him. There was no-one inside but the shepherd's wife. Her husband was out with the sheep, she told them. At first she'd been terrified, but Dalton had spoken to her soothingly, explaining that they had no wish to harm her, nor to steal their possessions. All that he wanted was a gun, he said. She gave him the double-barrelled shotgun supplied to her husband by the grazier he worked for, together with two shot flasks, a flask of gunpowder and some wad paper. She and her husband were both ticket-of-leave convicts, she said, so she wished them well, and hoped they'd get away. She gave them cups of tea, and filled a sack with bread and cold meat and cheese to take with them.

Out in flat open pastureland, with a bright morning sky above them, the two moved west towards a line of low, dome-like hills, some clothed with bush, some mostly cleared of trees. Beyond these, Dalton said, was the village of Richmond. They were now too far from Port Arthur to be pursued by the military or police forces stationed on the peninsulas; what they had to fear now was the police in Sorell or Richmond being alerted to their presence.

We should have taken some clothing from that hut, Griffin said. We need to get out of these fucking Port Arthur uniforms, before we're sighted. We have no cover here.

He was glancing nervously at a number of small houses in the flatland to the north.

I'll not rob poor people like those, Dalton said. There's a gentleman's property that I know of near Richmond. Good pickings – and now that I have this gun we can surprise them. Then we'll be as well-dressed as you please.

That night they slept in the bush out in the hills, having eaten the provisions given them by the shepherd's wife. During the next day they rested there, since they could not risk moving far by daylight in their prison clothing. In the valley below them, sheep-dotted pastures and fields of wheat extended for miles, with Richmond at their centre: a village that might have been in England, with red-brick cottages, stone Georgian houses, English elms and oaks and a church with a castellated tower. At sunset they set off again, going downhill under cover of the trees, keeping close to the road that led to Richmond. It was easy bush to move through, with sparse, spindly gums and none of the dense undergrowth of the two peninsulas.

An hour later, having skirted Richmond in the twilight at a distance of some miles, they crossed some empty grasslands and reached the property Dalton was looking for. It bordered the Jerusalem Road, north of the village, and its two-storey Georgian-style stone house was set well back from the road, surrounded by acres of grazing land and fields of wheat and barley. Waiting for full darkness to fall, Dalton and Griffin hid in a clump of trees and studied the situation. There was a long brick outbuilding not far from the house with lit windows, and with smoke coming from two chimneys; it evidently housed the servants. They watched two farmhands go into it at seven o'clock, their work over for the day. At eight o'clock, Dalton announced that it was time to make their move.

They moved across the fields to the main house, where a light burned in one of the windows. The back door was unlocked, and they made their way up the hall to the sitting-room, where the owner and his wife were seated in armchairs in front of a fire. Dalton trained his shotgun on them and demanded that the grazier lead him to where his guns were.

In a small room off the rear passageway, the grazier handed Dalton a double-barrelled shotgun: the house had no doubt been visited by bushrangers before, since the gun was kept loaded in readiness. There was a cap-and-ball pistol there as well – a Navy Colt – and Dalton took possession of it. Back in the sitting-room, he handed Griffin the shotgun and ordered him to search the rest of the house to make sure it was empty, and then to go out and get the farmhands and any other servants he found, and bring them into the house.

Griffin came back herding two farm workers and a young housemaid in a mob cap, who looked flushed and agitated. She kept glancing at Griffin with a terrified expression, and drew back when he moved close to her, crossing her hands on her breast. But Griffin was grinning with an air of great good humour: the situation seemed to excite him, and his eyes shone. Dalton ordered all of the servants to sit on the floor and told them that nobody would be hurt if they kept quiet. He then explained to the farmer what he wanted: clothing, money, a small supply of food, some soap and a razor, and two of his best horses. The grazier began to curse him; he was a big, red-faced man in his fifties, plainly of an irritable disposition.

You damned Irish rogue, he said.

Dalton raised his rifle and held the man's gaze until he fell silent.

You'll do what I say, Dalton said. You'll also get me all the money that's in the house, or I'll blow out your brains. Am I clear, now?

When they left, Dalton had in his saddlebags a pouch containing a hundred guineas, and some food. A scabbard held his shotgun, and Griffin had the Navy Colt in a holster. Their prison suits were gone and they had put on their new outfits, selected from a wardrobe in the grazier's bedroom and from the bedrooms of his two grown sons, who were away on a visit to Hobart Town. The grazier's size in boots had fitted Dalton well; but they were too big for Griffin. A pair belonging to one of the sons had suited him better.

Now they rode side by side across the long timber bridge that spanned the Derwent River, crossing from the Bridgewater side to a point on the western shore called the Black Snake. They had ridden across country from Richmond, having slept last night in a deserted barn. The country they had passed through had been largely unsettled, and they had encountered no-one except a few friendly convict shepherds. It was a country of gentle hills and open, straw-pale grasslands, easy to cross on horseback, but sometimes strange: there had been sinkholes there, and caves going into the earth. They had skirted the Meehan Range, following bridle tracks where they could, and had arrived here at Bridgewater in the early evening, sooner than Dalton had expected. They had ridden through the village to get to the bridge without attracting undue attention, and Dalton paid the toll using one of his new store of guineas.

The bridge was connected to a stone causeway on the western side. Since the Derwent was wide here, the whole structure extended for nearly three quarters of a mile, and it took some time to cross it. They were exposed as though on a stage, and Griffin shifted uneasily in his saddle as farming couples in gigs and farm workers driving spring carts piled with vegetables glanced curiously at them, going by. But Dalton gave them all a genial smile, tipping his hat to the farmers' wives in the gigs. When they reached the Black Snake, he reined in his horse at the edge of Main Road, and Griffin did the same. They sat in silence, gazing at the river, which was dotted with black swans. Beside the road stood a low, roughly-built stone building: an abandoned convict watch-house. A little further on, a steep-gabled weatherboard building was visible on a rise. A number of gigs were drawn up outside; horses were tethered to its verandah rail, and a throng of men and women loitered there, talking and laughing.

There's the old Black Snake Inn, Dalton said, and pointed. Sure, I've had many a drink in there, and some good times with the wenches hereabouts.

A glass of wine or porter would go very well now, Griffin said, and licked his lips. I've not had a drink for so long. Shall we, Dalton?

I think not, Dalton said. There'll be notices out offerin a nice reward for us now, and we're not far from Hobart Town. It's time to take stock of things, and to go our separate ways. Have you any plans, Roy? You might go up to Launceston: that's a nice little city, and far enough away. I'm happy to give you half the money we got from our friend the grazier.

Griffin stared at him from under his hat brim. His large green eyes had grown tragic and astounded, like those of a woman betrayed, and his mouth was pursed as though he fought back tears.

I've *no* plans, he said. I thought you might have come to trust me, Liam. I hoped against hope that you'd take me to Wilson. Didn't I back you up well, at the house in Richmond?

Aye, you did well enough. But I've told you, man: I can't do what you ask. There's no knowin whether the Captain would take you in or not – and if he should decide not, you'd go away knowin where our headquarters are. And that we can't allow, do you see?

At this, Griffin became melodramatic. He thumped his fist on his heart through the grazier's expensive mantle, the worryingly feminine eyes continuing to appeal to Dalton with mesmerizing insistence. Then kill me, he said. I agree that you can kill me, if I'm not seen to suit. Only take me to Lucas Wilson. I admire him; I respect him. Everything I've heard about him tells me that he's a man I'd follow anywhere. I've burned all my bridges; I've nowhere else to go – why should I betray him? Just *take* me to him, Dalton. Explain to him that you and I are comrades.

Dalton put his head on one side, frowning at Griffin in silence. Then he raised both hands in a gesture of surrender.

Sure, you're very persuasive, he said. All right, then – but hear what I say, now. You'd better hope that I don't regret this. There's something queer about you Griffin – something I don't like. But I'll let Lucas Wilson work you out.

Griffin seemed not to hear these last words; or else chose not to. His instant smile was full of joy; he leaned sideways to hold out his hand, while his mare pawed the ground.

Thank you, Dalton – thank you. I won't forget it. Comrades, then?

Dalton took the offered hand and shook it briefly; but he made no response.

You *won't* regret this, Griffin said, I promise you. I'll be an asset to the band in ways that you can't imagine.

His exuberance now was like that of a man intoxicated. His eyes shone, his face worked, and he almost seemed to wink, as though his words hinted at something he expected Dalton to guess at. But Dalton still made no answer. Instead, he straightened himself in his saddle and gestured at the highway.

We'd best start movin, he said.

Which way? North up the road?

South. And not on the highway. We'll leave it as soon as possible. We'll go by the hills.

South? Towards Hobart Town?

Aye. But not to the city. We'll be bound for a little small place called Montrose, near Glenorchy. And there's less risk of some nosy bastard takin an interest in us if we go through the hills. There are not many people out there to trouble us. Just a few little farms, easy to avoid. And plenty of bridle tracks goin through the bush.

Does that take us to Wilson?

It's on the way. But there's a property I want to visit first, at Montrose. I've had good information about it. It's a fine wealthy farm, and I'll not be goin back empty-handed to the Captain.

Griffin stared at him, his look of glee returning. Good, he said. Excellent. Lead on, comrade.

Dalton showed no amusement at this theatrical turn of phrase. He shook his horse's reins and went off at a trot down the road, without looking back.

2

In the summer when they came, Martin Dixon was twenty years old.

It was a Saturday evening at the end of the second week in January, a little before ten o'clock, and the family was finishing a late dinner. They were all in their usual places around the long mahogany table with its ladder-back chairs: Henry Dixon at the head, his wife Margaret on his right, and his eldest son William on his left. Martin sat next to William. Opposite him was Lucy, the youngest of the family, who was seventeen. It had been a hot day, and the French windows nearest to Henry Dixon stood open, letting in the cool evening air. Full dark had come, after the long summer twilight, and the bronze Argand oil-lamp that hung by long chains above the table had been lit. Candles had also been lit in the candelabrum on the sideboard, on the inner side of the room. A flame would occasionally tremble, in the flow of air.

They had finished their soup and roast mutton and were sipping glasses of claret, and the housemaid had just brought in an apple pie and had set it on the sideboard. She was standing there distributing slices of the pie into dishes when the visitors arrived. They came not from the verandah outside as might have been expected, but from inside the house. They entered the dining-room through the door from the hall: a door which was near the top end of the room, and so behind Henry Dixon's back. But Martin, who sat facing that side of the room, saw immediately what was happening, and what kind of visitors these were.

Liam Dalton entered first, in his cabbage-tree hat and belted blouse, a Colt revolver in his hand. Roy Griffin followed behind him: a dubious-looking gentleman in a grey felt hat and long grey mantle, levelling a double-barrelled shotgun at the family. William saw them a few seconds after Martin did, and exclaimed loudly. Henry and Margaret Dixon swung around in their seats, and Henry stared at the intruders with an expression of puzzled outrage. Then he, William and Martin pushed back their chairs and rose to their feet.

Please don't go any further, gentlemen, Dalton said.

He had moved along the wall to the sideboard and stood next to the housemaid, his revolver pointed at Henry Dixon. Griffin remained by the door, his shotgun covering them all. Henry and his sons stood fixed in their places, and Dalton removed his hat and made a bow. He was the type of Irishman who manifested both Celtic and Viking ancestry, Martin saw: tall and big-boned, his short-cut hair a reddish colour. He was clean-shaven, and his narrow, intimidating grey eyes had a humorous gleam.

Good evenin to you, he said. My name is Liam Dalton. You may have heard of me.

Martin studied Dalton intently; then he looked at his father. In spite of being short and stocky, Henry Dixon always had a commanding air, and he was managing to maintain it now. His long chin was set and truculent, and he addressed Dalton in the tone he used with erring convict servants.

Yes, I've heard of you, Dalton. You're a wanted criminal, and there's a good-sized reward out for your capture – you and your friend here. What have you done with my servants?

Your men are tied up in their quarters. And your cook is tied up in the kitchen. They're all safe enough. And if you know who I am you'll know that I'll do you no harm if you do none to us. And that your womenfolk are safe from insult. So do sit down again, gentlemen.

He looked at Mrs Dixon, who appeared to be frozen with fear, her right hand clenched in front of her mouth.

Ma'am, don't be frightened, Dalton said. You've no need to be, you have my word on it. Nor has your daughter here.

His deep voice and soft Irish accent were almost reassuring, and Lucy, half-turned in her chair, was looking at him in awed fascination. She was wearing a pink taffeta dress, her blonde hair shone in the lamplight, and her fresh colouring gave her a childish attractiveness. Clearly Dalton thought so, from the way in which he smiled at her; and Griffin, holding his shotgun, scarcely took his eyes from her. His expression, unlike Dalton's, was somehow repellent. It was not lewd, not insulting, and yet it made Martin uneasy.

William spoke next. He was a large, fair, heavily-built young man, with his father's prominent chin.

And what about your friend? He says nothing. Are we safe with him?

Griffin grinned at him, and spoke for the first time. You're quite safe with me, I assure you, he said. And may I say what a pleasure it is to be among gentlefolk.

As he spoke, his gaze moved from one to the other of the family, all of whom were formally dressed for dinner: Henry Dixon in a dress coat and cravat from an earlier era, his sad-faced wife in a gown of rich green silk, and his sons in lounging jackets, narrow bow ties and shirts with turned-over collars. Griffin's eyes lingered on these details with a look of wistful pleasure, as though encountering a world long lost to him.

As to that, you're not here by invitation, Henry Dixon said to him. And if you were ever a gentleman yourself, you've plainly ceased to be one. Come to the point. You're here to rob us. What is it you want to steal?

His flat Yorkshire voice expressed open contempt, and Griffin looked back at him in silence for a moment. His expression caused Martin to experience another stab of uneasiness: it hinted at an eagerness to do harm. But Griffin made no answer; instead he glanced across at Dalton, and it was Dalton who answered.

Well now, Mr Dixon, this is somethin that needs some discussion. I'll not be askin a great deal from you, but what I do want is rather special.

As he spoke, he moved to the table and sat down next to Lucy and laid his pistol in front of him, replacing his hat on his head.

With your permission, I might join you all in a glass of claret. I'm sure my friend would like one as well, but unfortunately he won't be able to join us at table, since some of you may get ideas.

Griffin looked at Dalton with a reproachful expression, but stayed mute, his shotgun still raised. Henry Dixon took a deep breath through his nostrils, glaring down the table at Dalton. Then he signalled to the housemaid.

Get a glass, Betty, and pour some claret for this – *gentleman.*

Betty filled a glass from the decanter on the sideboard and brought it to Dalton. He drank nearly half, set it down, and exhaled with satisfaction.

Sure and that does me a power of good, he said.

He grinned, looked sideways at Lucy and winked, and then looked at Henry Dixon again.

The first thing to be said is that none of you ladies and gentlemen will be tied up when we leave – so you'll be able to free your servants. But should anyone have ideas about goin to the police at O'Brien's Bridge perhaps, I'd advise against it. One of us will be watchin the farm for half an hour after we leave, and anyone who comes out in that time will be shot. Understood?

Henry Dixon nodded. He watched Dalton, his lips compressed.

Good, Dalton said. Now let me explain what I want, Mr Dixon. I know a little about you. I understand for instance that you have a fine collection of guns, includin the very latest thing in pistols. I mean the Adams revolver.

Henry Dixon's small eyes widened. What in God's name gives you that idea?

I have my sources of information. I know that you purchased it in Hobart Town, and where. The finest revolver yet made: England's answer to the Colt. Double action. Automatically cocks itself, so you don't lose your aim. Hand-made, of beautiful quality. Am I right, now? I see by your face that I am. Well now, this is the weapon I want – and whatever else takes my fancy in your gunroom.

Henry Dixon clenched both fists on the table in front of him.

What a pity you got out of Port Arthur, Dalton. But you'll hang in the end, be sure of it.

At this, fear for his father made Martin's stomach hollow. But Dalton merely smiled. His expression was amused; even light-hearted.

That may be. But it's a hard, sour man you are, Mr Dixon, and mine will be a merrier life than yours while I live it. And now let us have no more words. Let one of your sons here take me to your gunroom – for I'm sure you have a gunroom. I'll make my selection, while you remain here with this good companion of mine. Then, if your cook will be good enough to let us have some victuals, we'll be on our way, and trouble you no more. But let you not give my comrade any cause for alarm. He's a man who's quick to rouse, and I'd not want to see him do you a mischief.

Martin stood up. As soon as he did so he found Dalton's pistol trained on him; but he ignored it and spoke to his father.

I'll go with him, sir.

Henry Dixon looked at Martin and frowned. When he answered, he was looking at Dalton as he spoke.

Very well, Martin. It seems this villain gives us no choice. But mind how you go.

They stood in the gunroom together. Martin had led Dalton here through his father's study, unlocking the gunroom door with a key from the desk.

It was a small, bare room with one barred window, high up. Henry Dixon took trouble to make it secure, since not all his guns were kept for practical purposes: he was also a collector, who cherished his hoard of antique weapons. There was a smell of oil in here, and of the linseed used for cleaning the stocks of the guns. The only furniture was a workbench, scattered with equipment for stripping down and maintaining weapons: cleaning rods, screwdrivers and other tools. There was a safe in a corner for storing gunpowder. Along one wall was a set of tall glass cases resembling bookcases, lined with green felt, in which rifles stood in racks – artefacts that gave Henry Dixon more pleasure than any books. Pistols were stored in shelves under the cases.

Dalton stood in the middle of the room, his revolver pushed into his belt, hat tilted back, his hands on his hips. He apparently saw no need to be wary of Martin; instead, all his attention was given to the guns. His eyes glinted, and he smiled with frank pleasure. He had a small white scar on his left cheek, running to the corner of his mouth. He looked even bigger, in here: the gunroom seemed too small to contain him. He swayed, and Martin became aware of the odour of his sweat, mingling with the smells of oil and linseed. He'd evidently not bathed for some time.

Jesus, Mary and Joseph, Dalton said. Quite a collection, to be sure. I was told your father had some fine weapons. I can see that it's the truth, now.

He looked at Martin.

Well now, he said. Do you think you could find that Adams pistol for me?

Martin drew it from a shelf and passed it to him, and Dalton balanced it delicately in his hand and sighted along the barrel. Then he put it carefully on the bench.

Aye, that's the one, he said. A lovely piece.

May I ask how you knew about it?

How? No harm in tellin you, I suppose. Captain Wilson and I have a friend in Hobart Town who deals with certain gunsmiths – and that friend knows all there is to know about their business. He knows when the latest weapons come to them from England, and on what ships, and which wealthy farmers buy them. Men like your father, do you see. And he told me about this revolver just over a year ago.

Really? I'd no idea that bushrangers were so well informed.

Dalton squinted at him.

Aye. But you seem like a sharp one, so I'd better tell you no more of our business. And now, Mr Dixon, I'll just take a look at some of these other beauties, with your help.

While Martin opened the glass cases, Dalton moved beside him, exclaiming softly at what he discovered. He fingered the rifles, and bent to draw out the pistols from their shelves. Finally he selected two modern weapons which he placed beside the Adams pistol: a big Colt Dragoon revolver, and a Colt revolving rifle.

Sure, and Captain Wilson will be pleased with this baby, he said. He gestured at the rifle. This is the very latest – the finest to be had. I doubt there are more than half a dozen in the colony. You've used it yourself?

I've hunted kangaroo with it. Six-shot cylinder, and it takes a long cartridge. I'd better give you a supply of those.

Dalton glanced at him in surprise.

You're very helpful.

It's no trouble. I've heard a lot about you, Mr Dalton, and not all of it's bad. Now may I ask you a favour? I'd be really obliged if you'd not take any of the antique guns. My father sets great store by them – and some of them have been handed down through our family in England from the last century. It would break his heart to lose them.

Aye, I'm sure it would. Well, I'm in no position to sell them – and our need is for guns we can use. So no, I'll not take them. Even so, I'd be interested to see some more of these old weapons, before I take my leave – just for pleasure.

I'll be very happy to show them to you.

Martin opened more cases, and showed Dalton a Ferguson breech-loading rifle used in the American War of Independence, and an eighteenth-century flintlock fowling piece with delicate silver filigree work inlaid in the stock. He produced pistols of the same period furnished in silver with touches of gold, a pair of duelling pistols by Nock of London, and a top-quality flintlock pistol from 1820, made by the famous William Parker.

All of these Dalton handled with great care, murmuring in admiration. He stood holding the Parker pistol for some time, turning it over in his hands and sighting along the barrel.

Jesus, he said softly. Will you look at this now? A weapon like this is a work of art. And I'll tell you somethin, Mr Dixon. When I was a boy in Ireland, we knew about weapons like these, but we also knew we'd never put our hands on them. These were gentlemen's guns, and only the gentry could own them.

He handed the pistol back.

You seem to have a knowledge of the guns, he said. Are you a good shot?

Pretty fair.

Captain Wilson could use a likely young fella like you. You'd better come along with me.

His smile asked Martin to recognize that what he'd said was a joke. Instead, Martin looked back at him seriously.

That's just what I was going to suggest.

Dalton put the pistol down on the bench, searching Martin's face. Then his smile returned.

You're jokin with me.

I'm not. But I'm not wanting to turn bushranger either.

So what is it you're sayin, now?

What I'm saying is that I'd like to spend time with you, and get to know Lucas Wilson. I'd like to hear the true story of his life, and write it for one of the newspapers here.

You write for the newspapers, is it?

Not as a rule; I'm kept too busy on the farm. But I once published a story in *The Hobart Town Courier*, and I'm sure they'd take another.

Dalton smiled.

You're a bold one, and no mistake. A lot of people would like to meet Captain Wilson, but he allows nobody to do so. Why would he agree to meetin a young gentleman like yourself?

Because I believe I can write about him well. I'd show him the other story I've published, to prove I have the ability. Captain Wilson is a very unusual man; his story ought to be told, and I'm the one to do it.

He broke off, holding Dalton's gaze as though to compel his agreement, and Dalton laughed. Then he became solemn.

You're right in one thing, he said. The Captain's story should be told; he wants it told, and the record set right. He's often said so. Some day he may write it himself, so that the world will know of his ideas.

But I can help him, do you see? I can write it *for* him. I'll write down whatever he wants, and I'm sure the paper will publish it. And Captain Wilson would have my word that I'd never talk to the police, or tell them his whereabouts.

For nearly half a minute, Dalton studied him in silence. Then he looked down at the floor.

*In*terestin, he said. I must say that's *in*terestin.

Then he looked up again. I'll tell you somethin, Mr Dixon. If I could do this for you, I would, since you seem a clever young man. I've always believed that the Captain's story should be known, and the lies that are spread about him shown up. But I can't do it. You would know then where we are – and only a fool would depend on your word not to talk.

Then blindfold me.

What?

Take me there blindfold – and if Wilson won't see me, take me out of there, as far away as you like, still blindfolded, and turn me loose.

And what would your father think of this?

I don't care what he thinks. My father and I don't agree. I'm sick of my life here.

I see. So that's how it is.

Dalton studied the floor again. Then he looked up with an air of decision.

You've got a horse?

Yes.

I can give you ten minutes to get your story from that newspaper to show to the Captain, and to dress yourself for the bush and saddle up. While you do that, I'll pay a visit to your cook and get a few provisions. And if you're not in that hall outside in ten minutes, we'll be gone, I promise you. I can't risk more time here.

Martin was already turning towards the door, his expression one of triumph, and Dalton began to gather up the guns.

Ten minutes, he said. And don't forget that supply of cartridges.

Now there began for Martin a journey conducted in darkness.

He was mounted on Chief, his grey Welsh pony, and a thick woollen scarf (his own) was tied tightly about his eyes. He had not gone back into the dining-room to take leave of his family; instead he'd left a note for his father in the gunroom. He had changed into clothing he hoped was suitable for the expedition: a soft felt hat, a pea jacket, corduroy trousers and top boots.

His saddlebags contained a small change of clothing, writing materials, and the clipping of his piece from the *Courier* to show to Lucas Wilson. As well as this, a leather case and two tripods were tied to his saddle. He hoped to take a portrait photograph of Wilson, and the case contained a camera, a set of glass plates and a portable darkroom. As he'd mounted up, Dalton had glanced dubiously at this paraphernalia, but had said nothing.

They came out the front gate of the farm on to Montrose Road with Dalton riding next to him and Griffin riding behind. Dalton's threat to keep watch on the farm had clearly been a bluff.

Turn right, Dalton's voice said, and Martin felt a large, rough hand briefly touch his own where it held the reins.

Since they were turning right he knew that they were headed west towards the hills, and not east towards Main Road, with its string of little settlements. In this direction, less than a mile away, Montrose Road came to an end; and there all human habitation ended as well. There was only one other property on the way, after Leyburn Farm: a small mixed farm with a simple weatherboard cottage near the road, belonging to a struggling farmer called Logan. After that the bush-covered ranges began, where they would no doubt lose themselves.

He had been up this road so often from boyhood that he could sense when they were passing Logan's farm. A dog barked, and Griffin swore under his breath. They rode by in silence, and five minutes later Dalton's hand touched Martin's again.

Turn left, Dalton muttered. And take it easy. We're goin into the bush. We'll be on a bridle track now.

In his darkness, Martin tugged on the reins and turned his pony, and the sharp sound of its hooves on the stony road was replaced by soft thudding on the earth. He could smell the pungent scent of the eucalypts, and once some leaves brushed his face. It was a still, cool night, and all sounds were distinct: wild, fleeting cries of plover, and a cow lowing somewhere below –

probably at Logan's farm. They were going uphill here, and Chief was moving reluctantly. Martin had to urge him on, pressing him with his knees and clicking his tongue. He was not inclined to apply the spurs. Once the pony baulked at something, and he murmured to reassure him.

Easy now, Dalton's voice said next to him. You've got a strong young pony there, good for climbing hills. Just let him take it how he wants it.

Behind them, Martin heard Griffin's horse whinny, and Griffin curse again.

Stow that! Dalton called. Don't be puttin the spurs in. We want no bloody noise until we're well away.

Martin tried to calculate where they were headed. Turning left probably meant that they were moving south-west. It seemed quite likely that they'd move in a westerly direction, since that way lay the wilderness, while going any other way meant encountering settlement. On his right he could hear the rattling of water over stones. He knew this to be the Islet Rivulet, a creek he'd often played in as a child, and which ran near his father's property. It came down from Goat Hills in the west, and passed through Montrose to join the Derwent. They might be making for the region of the Rivulet's source: the wild, uninhabited country around Goat Hills, where the mountains began, and where few people ever went. But he couldn't be sure, and the longer he remained in a state of blindness the less certain he became.

Their ascent on the bridle track continued for what seemed hours, during which nobody spoke, although Dalton's hand sometimes touched his to caution or guide him. Sometimes the rushing of the creek would fade out, but then it would come back. Leaves were brushing Martin's face more often now, and he noticed that the air had grown cold: the sharp, clear cold of high country. He guessed that the track had become rudimentary, and was very little used. Certainly it had grown much steeper; he now had to brace himself in the saddle, and Chief often stumbled over rocks. He decided to question Dalton.

It must be very difficult for you, finding your way by night in rough country like this.

Dalton's voice came back to him with unnatural clarity.

There's a moon. I can see well enough.

But finding your way must still be hard.

I know this country. It's not hard for me. But we'll have to dismount soon, and lead the horses.

They rode on, always uphill; the track got steeper, and the branches and leaves thrashed Martin's face more and more often. He'd lost any clear idea of the time, but guessed that it must now be the early hours of the morning. Finally Dalton called a halt, and told them to dismount. Martin stood holding his pony's reins, waiting in his darkness. The air had grown colder still, and he buttoned his pea jacket. He could hear the rushing of the creek again, quite loud.

Now then, Mr Dixon, I'm goin to let you remove that blindfold, Dalton said. There's no way you can lead your horse, otherwise.

Martin reached behind and undid the scarf. It fell away to show him a forest of tall gums, almost too dense to walk through, on the edge of a small gully. The creek was running fast through the gully, only a few yards off. There was a full moon above the trees, its white disc making him blink, and the white stream of the Milky Way ran directly overhead. A variety of eucalypts grew here, as well as smaller trees common in the bush: blackwood, dogwood and wattle. The massive stringybarks, with their shaggy trunks, rose to heights of over two hundred feet, and the blue gums were almost as tall, their smooth white branches gleaming in the moonlight. Both trees were in flower, the small, dim stars like reflections of those that blazed overhead. The sloping ground was rocky, with clumps of long white grass growing between the boulders. Smells of damp earth came up from the gully, though the weather was fine, and runnels of water ran across the upward-sloping track. This and the sharpness of the stars made Martin sure that they were near the mountains. But he could gain no idea of their location, since no distances could be seen through the gums. As for the track, it had shrunk to a mere suggestion of a track, and he could see why they would now have to lead their horses through the trees. And something in his spirit drew back at the sight of this forest, which seemed to press in on them.

Although he'd grown up near the edges of the wilderness, he'd seldom ventured very far into it. Few people did, for any length of time. These hills were where the west began, and the colonists had left the west uninhabited, since it defied settlement. The further west you went, the more inhospitable the island became, its stony mountains and valleys clothed in impenetrable bush on which unceasing rain fell – rain that was carried by the gales of the Roaring Forties, the westerly winds that blew around the globe from Cape Horn. Van Diemen's Land was one of the most mountainous islands on earth, and you were never very far from hills. Only the Midlands were level and open; and they were an ancient lake floor. Like most people he knew, Martin preferred those mild, park-like lowlands, with their big sheep properties and little villages and towns strung along the Main Road. He liked the fertile valley of the Derwent in which he'd grown up, with its pleasant farms and hopfields. He liked the small city of Hobart Town, where he'd gained his modest education: southernmost city of the Empire, and a storehouse of that transported culture whose artefacts – books, magazines, musical instruments, scientific equipment – were carried by ship from his parents' lost home in England, together with the fine wines and condiments and fashionable luxuries the colonists prized. England was his home too, though he'd never seen it – he'd been made to understand that from childhood – and the civilization that England embodied was certainly preferable to wilderness. This thought had come to him with some force, looking at the wall of trees. The tall hills and mountains had always been a picturesque backdrop in his life; a mirage on the horizon, nothing more. Beautiful at a distance, they were sombre and overwhelming near at hand, and to wander very far into them had always seemed uninviting and pointless. Now, however, a point existed, and he would have to come to terms with it. He set his mouth and shoulders and put aside a feeling which had not been fear but something like it: something profound yet without definition, like the wilderness itself.

He turned to find Dalton studying him.

Well now, Mr Dixon: have you any idea where you might be?

None.

Aye, as I thought.

Dalton turned away and unfastened a billycan that dangled from his horse. He handed it to Griffin.

Go and get some water from that creek.

Griffin looked at him for a moment; then he took the billy and obeyed, climbing down the bank.

While he was away, Dalton and Martin gathered sticks, and Dalton lit a fire. Then he carried over the sack of provisions he'd acquired at the farm, and the three sat on a flat stretch of grass between some boulders, close to the flames. They ate bread, sausage and cheese, accompanied by mugs of tea.

When they'd drunk the tea, Dalton said:

Hold out your mugs. I've somethin here that'll put some heart into you – courtesy of your father, Mr Dixon.

He held up a bottle of French brandy, and Griffin laughed.

Cognac! You're a wonder, Dalton. A proper drink at last.

His eyes shining in the flames, he held out his mug at arm's length, and Dalton poured. Griffin waited until Dalton had poured for himself and Martin, and then held up his mug.

Success! Success to the Wilson band!

Dalton nodded, but without any answering enthusiasm. Aye, he said. Success.

They all drank, and Griffin exhaled loudly. By Jesus, that's good after so long.

He tipped the mug up again, drank it off, and set it down in front of Dalton.

Another, if I may.

Dalton set the bottle down in the grass between them. Help yourself, he said. I'm goin to take a piss.

He walked away from the fire and disappeared behind a nearby stringybark. Pouring his drink, Griffin grinned at Martin.

Your father has good taste in brandy. This is nectar, after all I've endured.

I'm glad you're enjoying it, Martin said.

Griffin drank deeply, looked down into the tin mug, and then looked up again.

You live well, at Leyburn Farm, don't you? A genteel life. I lived that way myself, once. Looking at your family around that table, I may tell you I was close to tears. It reminded me of all I've lost.

His eyes were fixed on Martin now with a tragic expression, and Martin wished that Dalton would come back, since Griffin made him uncomfortable.

Yours is a fine-looking family, Griffin said. He poured himself a third brandy, and then held the bottle out to Martin, who shook his head.

You've an especially fine-looking sister. A beautiful girl. Have any young fellows come courting?

Not yet. She's too young.

Not too young to lie with, though. Perhaps you've fucked her yourself?

Martin felt something explode in his brain. He stood up, staring down at Griffin, who smiled up at him. His full lips, wet from the brandy, were parted in a loose smile.

What did you say?

Come now. You wouldn't be the first man to fuck a pretty sister. You can tell *me*, my dear. There's no-one to hear, in these woods, and I wouldn't blame you in the least. I have a feeling that we might become friends, you and I – friends who can confide in each other. And my feelings are generally right.

His voice had become caressing, and his eyes stayed on Martin's face with a look that was a parody of tenderness. Staring back at him, struggling with his outrage, Martin found that Griffin's bottle-green eyes had grown larger, filling his field of vision. In that moment, he found himself powerless to speak, or even to look elsewhere. This alarmed him; and when he finally managed to answer, he found himself stammering.

I should beat the life out of you. How dare you talk like that to me?

Griffin ran his tongue across his lips, and his smile remained in place. You must be tired, he said. What have I said that could possibly offend you, my dear?

But even as he spoke, his confiding, mocking gaze, like that of a flirtatious woman, said that they both knew better. Searching for words, his heart hammering, Martin glimpsed the tall figure of Dalton walking back from the line of trees. He took a deep breath.

If you say anything like that to me again, I swear I'll thrash you.

Griffin raised his heavy dark eyebrows, still smiling. You threaten me with violence? A genteel young fellow like you? Unwise, Mr Dixon – but I forgive you. When you know me better, you'll be glad to be my friend, and to tell me all your secrets.

Dalton stepped abruptly into the firelight. Pack up, he said. We'll give the horses a drink in the creek, and then it's time to be movin.

When they came to the top of the final hill, some three hours later, it was five-thirty by Martin's pocket watch, and dawn had arrived. The paper-pale trunks of a group of peppermint gums, formal as the columns of a temple, were lit by the rays from the east. The sky had lightened to a pale blue, its few clouds tinted with pink and copper, and birds had begun to call in the branches overhead. It was as though a giant lid had been lifted, freeing them into the light.

Nearly there, Dalton said. Soon it'll all be downhill.

They emerged from the trees, leading their tired horses, to find themselves on an open, level, yellow-grassed expanse that was studded with lichen-covered boulders, and dotted with the tiny white flowers of ground clematis. They could see for miles, to all points of the compass. The effect, after their long imprisonment in the darkness and the bush, was exhilarating, and Martin forgot his tiredness and his aching back and legs. He even managed to put from his mind his conversation with Griffin, whom he now avoided looking at.

They halted their horses in front of a group of tall, spotted grey boulders on the utmost edge of the hill, looking north. A landscape of great beauty extended below them, more vast in its extent than any Martin had seen. Scanning its full circumference, he found it at first to be empty of any human signs: virgin as it would have been before the colony was settled. In the west, beyond hill after deep green hill of bush, two flat-topped mountains rose against the sky, blue and violet in the sunrise: extinct volcanoes, like so many peaks in the island. He tried to recognize them and failed; and yet they seemed vaguely familiar. They might be part of the Wellington Range, but he couldn't be certain. He could only be sure of one thing: he was looking at the frontier of the island's western wilderness – that wilderness he knew to be largely unexplored. Next he looked east, and was startled to see a distant silver bend of the Derwent. Here was something familiar: he was not so far from home after all. This was confirmed when he looked behind him to the south, and discovered on the horizon a shoulder of Mount Wellington, the peak that rose behind Hobart Town.

Finally he looked north, examining the valley that lay at their feet; and now he found that settlement existed here after all. Small with distance, a number of cultivated fields and an enigmatic scatter of buildings could be seen down there, glowing in the strengthening sun like a village in a fable. Behind, like protective walls, rose the tall hills of bush; and beyond these again the long blue ranges rolled wave after wave into infinity: to a country of which he knew nothing.

Dalton mounted his horse and pointed. We go down there, he said.

Griffin also mounted. He leaned forward over his horse's neck, studying the distance. He spoke in a voice that was close to a whisper, as though subdued by the valley's beauty.

It looks like Paradise.

Paradise or Hell. It's men who decide what it is.

So what's this place called?

Nowhere Valley.

Really? That's its name?

That's its name. The name that Lucas Wilson has given it.

Dalton pointed to the buildings.

And there's our community. The community that's governed by the Captain.

Martin woke slowly. For some moments, he was uncertain where he was. Nor did he know whether it was day or evening, since the room he lay in was dim. Then he recalled that he was in Liam Dalton's house, in Liam Dalton's bedroom, and that today he'd meet Lucas Wilson.

The quick anticipation of youth drove away his drowsiness and fatigue, but a sense of unreality persisted. His clothes were piled on a trunk beside the bed; his pocket watch lay next to them, and he picked it up and squinted at it. Nearly noon. He discovered that the room was dim because shutters were closed over its only window, but a thin blade of sunlight was coming between them. Sounds came through them as well: the drawling of domestic fowls, like the sly, protesting voices of old women, and a regular hammering, and male voices, and what sounded like the far-off voices of children. But the presence of children here seemed unlikely; he decided that he was hearing bird-calls.

He recalled undressing and falling into this bed after the long ride down from the hilltop, and sleeping instantly. Dalton had brought him in here, and had slept in a bed on the other side of the room. But Dalton was gone now; his bed was empty, its possum-skin rug thrown back.

Martin sat up and looked around. The room was fairly basic, like one in a bush hut, but far less primitive than those in most bush huts, with their unlined ceilings and earth floors. Certainly not the kind of room he'd expected to see in a bushrangers' hideout. The ceiling and walls were lined with eucalyptus boards, and the floor was of the same timber. The boards weren't dressed or painted, but they were well-fitted and pleasing to look at. The bed he'd slept in was a camp stretcher, with a straw mattress covered by a blanket, a pillow with a cotton slip, and a handsome possum-skin rug for covering, like the one on the other bed. Dalton's bed was clearly the work of a capable bush carpenter: a wide, solid four-poster made from dressed eucalyptus wood. The room's other furniture was no doubt the work of the same craftsman: a square timber armchair, also made from well-planed eucalyptus, and a basin-stand of the same material, on which stood a china jug and basin.

He threw back the rug, crossed to the window in his underdrawers and vest, and opened the shutters. The window was glassless, and the sun and air of noonday flooded in. Dazzled, he shaded his eyes.

The air was cool and crisp: the air of the high country. In these first few seconds, it was the distance that came into focus: the two flat-topped mountains he'd seen from the hilltop at dawn, deep blue now, and seeming quite close. The mountains! His heart began to race, as he took in their strangeness. Nameless and commanding, they belonged in another dimension, their blue so dark that it seemed almost black; and they told him once again that he'd arrived in a country that was alien: one far removed from the territory of home; one beyond safety and the law. But this gave him little concern; instead, he was filled with elation.

He shifted his gaze to what lay close at hand, and found himself looking at a farmyard. This surprised him. He'd expected some sort of stronghold here: a cluster of crude huts behind a stockade, perhaps. Even a kind of fortress, where Wilson and his men would repel any intruders. Instead, here was a peaceful farm: and one, as far as he could tell, that was quite extensive. Immediately in front of him was a wide, open area which had patches of grass and wild flowers but was mostly bare earth, where the fowls he'd heard were pecking about for food. A European ash grew at its centre, and a slab-built barn stood on its far side, with a plough standing by the door. A bull terrier was chained there; it barked twice when it sighted Martin, and then lost interest. Out in the centre of the yard, a thin, fair-haired woman in a long cotton gown was passing with a wooden bucket, headed in the direction of the barn. The bucket was clearly heavy, and she was bent a little to one side. Feeling Martin's gaze on her, she glanced across at him, and her eyes widened in what might have been alarm. She neither smiled nor greeted him, but hurried on and passed out of sight behind the barn. The hammering he could hear was coming from somewhere over there, but no other human beings were visible.

He turned away. His saddlebags were lying on the armchair where he'd thrown them when he came in at seven o'clock, and he was relieved to see that the case containing his camera and portable darkroom was also here. He opened one of the saddlebags and pulled out fresh underclothes, a shirt and a pair of heavy lace-up boots for wear in rough country. Soon, having washed at the basin-stand with water from the jug, he was ready to leave the room.

As though he'd been watched, the door was flung open. Liam Dalton, in striped shirt and moleskins, his feet bare, stood stooped beneath the lintel, looking at him from under his eyebrows, head lowered. Martin noticed again how sharp and unnerving Dalton's grey eyes were; but the glint of humour was still there.

So it's awake you are. Come and get a bite to eat, Mr Dixon, or there'll be nothin left.

He gestured for Martin to follow him, and led him across a central passageway into what appeared to be a dining-room. It was filled with odours of smoke and frying bacon, and a log fire was burning in a deep stone fireplace: one tall enough for a man to walk into. Griffin, who was sitting at a table here, looked up at Martin and smiled, and Martin had a sinking sensation in his belly. He did not smile back, but nodded briefly. Griffin was now dressed for rural life, in a serge shirt and fustian trousers; but he still wore his patent leather top boots. A young girl was squatting by the hearth with her back turned, attending to a long-handled frying pan filled with bacon and eggs that was set on iron bars above the coals. She looked once at Martin over her shoulder like a cat, and then turned back to the fire.

Sit down, Dalton told him, and we'll all be havin bacon and eggs and damper. Not the fancy food you're used to, I'm thinkin.

It smells good, Martin said.

He found that he was ravenously hungry. He sat down opposite Griffin at the bare wooden table, where knives and forks and willow-pattern plates and cups were set out. There was a large teapot in the centre; Griffin lifted it, poured him some tea, and gestured at a jug of milk and a bowl of sugar. He remained silent but continued to smile, and he shot Martin a quick, confiding glance, as though they shared a secret. Martin looked away, fighting down a surge of revulsion. He had decided to behave as though the conversation of last night had not taken place.

Dalton had moved to the fireplace and stood next to the girl, close to where a camp oven hung. The black iron pot was suspended above the flames by a hook attached to an iron bar, and the bar was hinged to the side of the fireplace. Dalton swung it out now so that the pot hung above the hearth. Using a cloth, he removed the lid and drew out some round loaves of damper, dumping them onto the table one by one. He picked up a kitchen knife and cut two slices and dealt them out to the others on the point of the knife.

Eat, he said. You'll be hungry after that ride last night.

By Jesus, Griffin said. Hunger isn't an adequate term.

Head on one side, he tore with his teeth at the warm unleavened bread. There was something more than appetite in the way he did this, Martin thought: an unpleasant animal greed.

Dalton sat down with them, and the girl began to move around the table with the frying pan, serving bacon and eggs on to their plates with a spatula.

This is May, Dalton said. She does my cookin for me, and does it well. Isn't that so, darlin?

The girl made no response except to smile timidly at Dalton. Her large, dark blue eyes moved quickly over the other two men and then fled away, and Martin saw now that she was no more than twelve or thirteen years old: thin and frail-looking, with a pale, narrow face, prominent cheekbones and a shock of straight brown hair that made her head look too heavy for her neck. She wore a loose grey cotton smock whose hem was uneven, making him suspect that the garment had been made by somebody with little skill at dressmaking. Her feet, like Dalton's, were bare.

They ate in silence. Then, when Dalton had pushed aside his plate and was pouring a second cup of tea, Griffin looked at him.

So tell me, Dalton, shall we meet Captain Wilson now?

Dalton set his cup down and sat back, wiping his mouth with the back of his shirt-sleeve.

No you won't. You'll not be meetin him until this evenin.

Oh. Why is that?

Because the Captain says so. I've already been and spoken to him. He'll be out huntin wallaby today. I'll take you to him before supper.

Griffin raised his eyebrows, but said nothing.

In the meantime, Dalton said, I'll show you both about the place. And we'll find some jobs for you to do.

Jobs? Griffin said. You mean you'll put us to work as farmhands?

Sure, and that's exactly what I mean. This is a farm, and let you not forget it. We all do our bit. Anyone who didn't would soon find himself with nothin to eat. How else do you think we manage, up here?

Griffin stared at him for some moments. Then he licked his lips and smiled.

By raiding, he said. Surely.

By raidin, is it? Let me explain somethin. We raid only for those things we can't grow or make for ourselves – or for money. That's the rule the Captain's laid down. And every year there are less and less things that we're needin from down below – which is what the Captain's aimin at. He'll explain it all himself, when you meet him. The day will come soon, he says, when we won't need the world, and the world won't trouble us. Then there'll be no more raidin.

Griffin continued to stare at him, his hands resting palms-down on the table in front of him. A small frown was creasing his brow now, and his expression had changed to one of profound surprise. When he spoke, his voice was soft.

No more raiding? But raiding was what I came here for.

Then you came to the wrong place, and I'd tell you to turn around and ride out again, except for one thing – and you know what that is.

You can't let me go.

No. Havin got here, you can't be allowed out again. So you'd best be thinkin about keepin our rules and makin yourself useful.

He looked at Griffin's top boots.

Ye'll need to get rid of those fancy ridin boots, for a start, and put on some workin boots – like Mr Dixon here. We've a store with a good supply. You can pick some out for yourself.

Griffin said nothing, his hands still on the table in front of him, his lips compressed, staring. Dalton smiled amiably.

The Captain will explain what we're about, a lot better than I can. He might even change your way of thinkin, Griffin. He surely changed mine.

There was silence, while May moved softly about the table, taking away the dishes. Griffin's eyes shifted to follow her; then they turned back to Dalton. He returned Dalton's smile with tight, closed lips.

Maybe he will, he said. Maybe he will. I look forward to hearing his ideas.

Green and tawny among its mountains, wide yet sheltered, the valley called to mind the illustrations Martin had seen in books on Austria and Switzerland. And yet it was different: a hollow in the last primal uplands of the world.

On its eastern side stood a belt of peppermint gums and silver wattle, bright green and blue in the afternoon sun, and he sensed that the land fell away behind them, no doubt to level out finally in the safe and orderly world he'd left below. Between these trees, blue-grey ranges could be glimpsed on the horizon, frail as mirage and seeming to dream. In the west, much nearer, were the deep blue mountains he'd seen from Liam Dalton's bedroom. Dalton had told him that in winter they'd be covered in snow, and that the valley would be snowed in then for days at a time. But now the mild air was filled with the scents of flowering gums and wattle, and of summer-bleached grass.

Dalton called this place 'the farm', and sometimes 'the community'. As he led them across a stretch of level ground, Martin saw that a community was what it was, rather than a farm. In fact it resembled a village, being a whole collection of buildings, with well-worn tracks leading through the grass from one to another.

Dalton's house was the kind of slab dwelling common in the bush, built from split eucalyptus logs set vertically, the cracks between them sealed with mud. But it was larger and better-finished than most, with a well-crafted roof of wooden shingles, wooden guttering, and a downpipe to take rainwater into a barrel by the door. Behind it on the northern side, and close to the barn Martin had seen from the window, was a long, slab-built set of stables where their horses had been installed last night and provided with oats and water. Beyond the stables was a field dotted with stooks of harvested oats, and to the right was another slab-built house that looked less well-finished than Dalton's, its roof being made of sheets of bark. This, Dalton told them, was the bachelors' quarters.

They were walking south. Dalton had now put on boots and a wide-brimmed felt hat, battered and stained. Their first stop, it seemed, would be at what he called the commissariat store. This was a term the Government used for its supply depot in Hobart Town, and the function of the store here was apparently the same. Clothing, boots, guns, ammunition and many other necessities and luxuries were stored there that couldn't be manufactured in Nowhere Valley: loot from raids into the flatland. The commissariat would supply Griffin with work-boots, Dalton said.

Griffin received this in silence, darting curious glances around him. Martin did the same, already forming in his mind the notes he would make for his newspaper article. No other people were to be seen here, and he asked Dalton where they were.

Workin, Dalton said. And some are out shootin game.

As he spoke, they came to the most impressive building in the settlement. It was a long farmhouse, similar in style and finish to those in the settled areas below, being built of properly dressed horizontal weatherboards, painted dark red. It had glass windows, a shingled, steeply-pitched roof, and a side wing. There were two stone chimneys, and a deep verandah ran along the front. One feature made it different from the conventional farmhouse: a square tower, at the end opposite the wing. This too was built of weatherboards, with windows at the top and a four-sided pyramidal roof, also shingled.

This is the Lodge, Dalton said.

He halted, and the other two looked at him.

Captain Wilson's quarters, he said. He pointed at the wing. That part is where we have our meetins. That's why it's called the Lodge.

You have meetings? Griffin said.

Aye. Regular. We discuss things.

What kinds of things?

You'll find out in due course.

Griffin lingered, still contemplating the house. He smiled, and his expression was quizzical.

It's very handsome, he said. Not easy to build, up here. You'd have had to haul some of the materials up from below. The glass, for instance.

Aye – we're able to do that. We have pack horses.

Captain Wilson is very privileged.

Dalton looked at him. And why should he not be? We owe everythin to him.

I'm sure you do.

Griffin nodded with an air of eager enthusiasm, but Dalton frowned. As they turned away, Martin asked him what the tower was for.

Lucas does his book work there, Dalton said, and he likes to observe the stars through his telescope.

A little further on, moving south, they passed another farmhouse resembling those in the flatland. Built of weatherboard like the Lodge, it also had glazed windows and a front verandah, but it was smaller than the Lodge, and clearly older. The brown paint of the weatherboards was worn away in places, and the shingles of the roof looked aged and in need of replacing. There was a front garden with a brushwood fence around it where roses and foxgloves were in bloom. Outside the fence were a child's seesaw and an abandoned ball. Behind the house a grassy bank led down to a fast-running creek, where a line of English willows grew. The creek appeared to form the boundary of the settlement: on the other side, the tall trees of the wilderness rose like a wall.

Dalton pointed. That's Sorell Creek, he said. That's where we get our extra water. And this is Bill Bosworth's place. Bill was the one that settled this valley. He hadn't much money, bein a ticket-of-leave man, and he bought the land cheap from the Government, years ago. He let us settle here – and no other bugger has ever come up to disturb us. Why would they? The soil's poor, the winters are hard, there are no roads, and it's a long way to shops and taverns and all the good things of this world. And that's the way we like it.

He smiled, but Griffin was frowning.

And what about the police? They never come here?

No. In all the time we've been here, never a police patrol have we seen. Nor has Bill Bosworth, either. The bastards are too idle to ride into this country – and why would they want to do so? There's nothin up here but the wild mountains, and the wild bush for miles.

Nobody comes here?

Sure, once a pair of surveyor fellas turned up, so Bill tells us. But that was years ago, and nobody since. And if they do come, what do they see? A farm, that's all. That's the beauty of it. Bill Bosworth's a law-abidin man – not one of us.

A farm? It looks more like a whole bloody village.

Sure, and there's no law against Bill puttin up extra buildins, is there?

And he's let you and Lucas Wilson settle on his property and put him and his family at risk? Why would he do that?

You're askin a lot of bloody questions. What's your trouble, Griffin?

Griffin had been kicking in the dirt with his heel, studying the ground. Now he looked up again at Dalton.

No trouble. But there are big rewards out for you and me. And descriptions. Suppose the troopers *did* turn up? What then?

Dalton drew in an impatient breath, his mouth gone thin.

We have dogs chained about the place. They'd give us plenty of warnin. But if the traps did surprise us, they'd not ride out again. Does that satisfy you, now?

It does, Griffin said quickly. It most certainly does, comrade.

But Dalton continued to stare at him, and Martin grew tense. The Irishman had been amiable and easy-going until now, even when he was in the process of holding up Leyburn Farm, but it seemed he had a different side. He was clearly prone to sudden anger, and probably capable of killing if he thought it necessary.

Griffin said no more, and Dalton turned on his heel and jerked his head.

Come on, he said. I'll take you to the store. We're wastin time, and there's work to do – whether you've a taste for it or not.

The store was a little way on past Bosworth's house, and was also just above the creek. Like the stable, it was long, low, and built of horizontal slabs. Its only doorway was in the centre, with small windows on either side that were glazed and barred, so that it looked somewhat like a gaol. As they approached, the strains of a flute could be heard, coming through the open door. Dalton led the way in.

Just inside the door sat a monk. He wore the brown woollen habit associated with Franciscan friars, secured around the waist by a big leather belt. The effect was only marred by the fact that instead of sandals he wore heavy boots. He was a big man, and also very fat. He was completely bald except for a fringe of brown hair over his ears, and clean-shaven, with a pink, smooth face and pate and a vast pink jowl, putting Martin in mind of a giant infant. He was holding a flute in front of his chest and looking up at them with large, bright blue eyes which he shaded against the light through the door with his other hand. Behind him, a multitude of chattels lay crowded on trestle tables and on shelves around all four walls: tools, crockery, sacks of tea and sugar and flour, bottles of ale and spirits, clothing, and rack after rack of guns. At the far end, a closed interior door indicated a second room.

Hello Alan, Dalton said.

The fat man's eyes became wider and brighter, and he smiled with an expression of delight. He laid the flute down on the table next to him, heaved himself up from the armchair he sat in and hurried forward, his arms outstretched, his robe flapping.

Liam! The Captain told me ye were here – and told me of your marvellous exploit. Welcome back, man! It's a joy to see ye.

Sure now, Dalton said. And you too, Alan.

They embraced, while the fat man chuckled.

Ye look well, Liam, despite your trial. I thought ye were lost to us for ever, man. But I might have known they couldnae hold ye. To get away clean from Port Arthur – what a feat! It's never been done, and never will be again, I'd take bets on it. I'll be composing a song about it, to see that ye go down in history.

I'm sure I will do, Alan, if you put me in one of your songs. Gentlemen, this is Alan McLeod. This store is also his home, and he guards it well. He's no holy man, I'm afraid, even if he's dressed like one.

I find it comfortable, McLeod told them. I carried this garment away from a religious institution near Hobart Town – along with some other sacred objects I found there. Candlesticks. Silver plate. Little things I thought the Church mightn't begrudge a poor sinner.

He giggled suddenly with his mouth open, like a boy recalling some mischief: a high, falsetto eruption that caused his belly to shake and his face to grow pinker. Dalton shook his head; then he introduced Griffin and Martin Dixon.

Mr Dixon isn't wanted by the police, he told McLeod. He writes for the newspapers. He wants to tell the Captain's story.

As McLeod shook Martin's hand, his smile faded, and he turned to Dalton with a puzzled frown.

Is this wise, Liam? Writes for the newspapers, do ye say? What a wonderful story *that* will be – to be able to tell his readers where Lucas Wilson and his band are hidden! Man, have ye no thought about that?

Alan, Alan, Dalton said. Of course I have, and so has the Captain. Martin assures us that he'll tell no-one where we are – and at present he has precious little notion. We're satisfied with that.

I've given Mr Dalton my word of honour, Martin told McLeod. And I'll give it to Captain Wilson, when I see him.

The fat man stared at him.

Aye, he said. I'm sure ye will, Mr Dixon. And I suppose we must believe ye're a man of your word. But ye do understand, now, that it's a heavy responsibility ye've taken on? It might be said that ye hold our lives in your hands.

His smile had returned; but this time it held no warmth.

When they left the store, Dalton led them back along the land above the creek, passing Bosworth's farm and taking them to the eastern end of the settlement.

Here, on a stretch of ground that bordered the edges of the bush, a wagon laden with gum logs was standing, a draught horse between the shafts. As they came near, Martin saw that the wagon had been halted next to a saw-pit. One of the gum logs was laid across the pit, and a bearded man stood crouched at the edge, working on the log with a crosscut saw, pushing and pulling in harmony with an invisible partner in the pit.

Here's where we cut up the timber for our buildins, Dalton said. That's Bill Bosworth there – him that owns the farm. We're needin slabs for a new blacksmith's shop at present. He looked at Griffin. You two fellas can lend Bill a hand until this evenin.

Griffin tightened his lips but said nothing.

When Bill Bosworth caught sight of them he halted his motion on the saw, straightened up, and said something to his partner below. Then he wiped sweat from his forehead with the back of his hand and smiled at the three as they approached. He was powerfully built, and growing thick around the middle; his beard and his rusty brown hair were greying, and Martin guessed him to be in his late forties. He had a plain, good-humoured, stoical face: the face of a man who had dumbly resigned himself to a life he'd never chosen. Martin had often seen such faces among his father's convict servants.

Hello, Liam, he said. Are these the coves you told me about this mornin?

Aye – these are the ones, Bill.

Dalton introduced Martin and Griffin; then he pointed to the saw-pit.

And who have you got in the hole?

As though on cue, a pair of small hands appeared on the edge of the pit, followed by the face of a man whose lank brown hair was covered in sawdust. He had apparently climbed a ladder to reach this level, and stood peering at the group with an expression that mingled theatrical woe with a jaunty self-mockery. It's me, mates, he said. And what I'd like to know is this: why is it always me in the hole?

Liam Dalton laughed, while Bosworth put out his hand to take his companion's arm, hauling him over the edge as though he were a child. And indeed, he wasn't much bigger than a child, Martin saw – a twelve-year-old boy, perhaps, since he wasn't much over five feet tall. He stood licking his lips and brushing sawdust from his hair and striped shirt, grinning as though he contemplated some dubious joke. His East End accent and pinched yet whimsical little face put Martin in mind of a visiting comedian from London whom he'd seen at the theatre in Hobart: the sort of man who would always appeal for laughter.

The hole's where you do best, little Joe, Bosworth said. You've been in worse places, ain't you?

I have, in the days when I was naughty, Joe said. But I ain't naughty now, and I deserve better things, don't I? Maybe one of *these* two coves can take my place.

He grinned at Martin and Griffin, his eyes surveying them with open curiosity.

I reckon not, Bosworth said, and looked at Dalton. I'd like 'em to unload them logs from the wagon. Joe Jarvis can carry on with me.

Then that's what they'll do, Dalton said. He raised his hand in farewell, and walked away.

A few minutes later Martin and Griffin were lifting the heavy gum logs from the cart, taking an end each. Staggering, they laid them in a pile near the pit, where Bosworth and Jarvis went on sawing them into eight-foot palings. Griffin worked silently, but once Martin heard him cursing under his breath. Then, after they'd lowered the latest log onto the pile, Griffin straightened up and paused, looking across at Martin.

And how does *this* occupation suit you?

I've had better, Martin said.

His tone was cold, and he said no more. He'd resolved to discourage any conversation with Griffin.

But Griffin persisted.

I'm sure you have. As for me, I expected something else from our bold bushrangers than to turn me into a labourer. And on a bloody Sunday, as well.

Martin said nothing. Instead, he walked over to the cart and waited to pick up the next log, staring at Griffin in silence. At this, Griffin smiled.

Still sulking, are we? There's really no need, you know. You and I can be friends.

I don't think so, Martin said. The less we have to do with each other the better.

Griffin shook his head, and clicked his tongue. You've misunderstood me, Mr Dixon. I really could be your friend. And I will – you'll see. You might be surprised how much I could teach you.

Unable to help himself, Martin let out a contemptuous breath.

Teach? Do you see yourself as a schoolmaster?

Griffin laughed. Oh no, my dear. Not a schoolmaster. Something much more important than that.

He reached for the end of one of the logs, standing at the other end of the cart.

Shall we carry on with our slave labour?

At close to seven o'clock they were led by Dalton to the Lodge. He had first taken them back to his own house, where they'd washed, changed their sweaty clothing, and eaten a supper of soup and potatoes.

I'd rather hoped the Captain might ask us to dine with him, Griffin said.

You'll likely wait a long time for that, Dalton said.

They came up to the dark red house, with its odd tower. The valley lay bathed in late sun, but as soon as they stepped into the shadow of the verandah, Martin felt a chill. Despite the season, it was going to be cold in these hills at night, he thought; but he knew that the chill was mainly caused by the nervousness that gripped him. His heart was beating unevenly, and his palms were sweating. He was trying to imagine what Wilson would be like, and could not.

The solid-looking, six-panelled front door was painted white, with a brass knocker. Dalton walked up to it and rapped three times. It was opened almost immediately by a woman who appeared to be in her early thirties, with light brown hair drawn back in a bun. She was wearing a brown print, ankle-length house dress with long sleeves and a high-necked bodice, and held herself very straight. Her expression seemed to Martin to be one of frozen sadness; but perhaps it was simply an absence of expression. This and the chaste, unadorned dress combined to create an impression of severity; yet Martin thought her handsome as well as austere.

Dalton removed his hat and bowed, smiling with a warmth which Martin thought the woman must surely respond to. But she remained impassive, her brows slightly raised.

Good evenin, Frances, Dalton said. I believe the Captain is expectin us.

I believe he is, the woman said. You'd better come in.

She stood aside, and Martin and Roy Griffin followed Dalton through the door. Frances surveyed them with a single quick glance; then she turned and led the way down a hall that ran through the centre of the house. Close to the end, they came to a door on the left. Frances opened it and stood back, looking at Dalton. He went in, and the other two followed him. Martin heard the door close behind them, and turned to find that Frances had gone. As he did so, he heard Dalton say:

Good evenin to you, Captain. Here are these two fellas that are waitin to meet you.

They had entered what appeared to be a combined sitting-room and library: one that might have been found in a reasonably prosperous grazing property down below. And yet it was subtly different, since its furniture was unlike any sold in the stores of Hobart Town, or imported from the home country. No lamps had been lit, and the casement windows, two of which were open, were letting in late sun which lay across the furnishings with the density of dream, giving to the room the glow of illusion, like an apartment on a stage. On its far side, some twenty feet away, a fire blazed in a big, walk-in fireplace with boarded walls. Beside it, in an unusually large armchair of polished wood, Lucas Wilson sat looking across at them; and he and the sun-hushed room made a picture that might have been arranged to impress his visitors.

He'd been reading a book, which he now set aside on a small round table. He stood up, but didn't advance to meet them. He was a lean, fine-featured man in his mid-thirties, with a long face, a long upper lip, and high, knob-like cheekbones. Like Liam Dalton, he was well above the average height: somewhere over six feet. His chestnut hair, swept straight back and springing up high around his forehead, was so luxuriant that it resembled a mane. He was clean-shaven except for his side-whiskers, and his skin was tanned, with a high colour in the cheeks from recent exposure to wind and sun. He waited like a high official, hands at his sides, while the group advanced across the floor. When they came to a halt, he smiled.

Good evening to you, gentlemen.

He had a cultivated accent, with the faint hint of a Scottish brogue. He put out his hand to Martin.

You must be young Mr Dixon.

His hand was warm and dry and somehow reassuring. At close quarters, he seemed to Martin to resemble an actor rather than a bushranger – partly because of his looks, but also because of his dress: a grey, single-breasted lounge jacket in the latest fashion; a fine linen shirt; a green silk scarf knotted at the throat. He now turned to Griffin.

And you are Roy Griffin. The man who escaped Port Arthur with Liam. You'll be remembered for that exploit, won't you?

It seemed to Martin that there was a faintly mocking quality in this question; but if Griffin detected it, he gave no sign. As though taking his cue from Wilson, he was standing very erect, hands at his sides, and his expression was one of good-humoured modesty.

I doubt that, Captain. The escape was entirely Liam Dalton's achievement. I was merely his fortunate accomplice.

Wilson put his head on one side and examined Griffin carefully. His eyes were of a blue that was both light and intensely vivid: so arresting that it was difficult to look away from them. The upper lids, slanting slightly downwards, had a hard line which gave him a daunting appearance, even though his expression at present appeared to be genial. After some moments he held out his hand to Griffin, as he'd done to Martin.

You sound like an educated man. Is that the case?

I was studying to become a solicitor when I fell foul of the law.

And you don't wish to go back to legal practice, after serving your sentence? It could be done in this colony, you know. They're not very fussy about such things.

No. I preferred to come to you.

I see. And in doing so, you make yourself an outlaw, with little hope of a pardon. Little hope of returning to a civilized life. Is that really what you want?

Exactly. To join your band – that's my highest hope.

You see how it is, Liam, Dalton said to Wilson. He wouldn't take no for an answer.

Studying Griffin in silence, Wilson nodded slowly and narrowed his eyes. This, like any small change in his expression, had a dramatic effect, causing Griffin to straighten himself still further. The Captain was certainly like an actor, Martin thought: one who was perhaps too conscious of his good looks. Wilson now turned away from Griffin and raised his open hands, surveying them all.

But what am I thinking of? I mustn't keep you standing here, gentlemen – pull up some chairs to the fire. The summer's never certain up here, and there's a chill in the air this evening.

Liam Dalton dragged three upright chairs away from the wall beside the fireplace so that they formed a semi-circle around Wilson's big armchair. All the chairs, Martin saw now, were the work of a bush artisan, like the furniture in Dalton's house, but these were of a much higher standard. They were not made from eucalyptus, but from the local myrtle: a handsome, pinkish wood of far better quality, which had been beeswaxed and polished so that it shone. Each of the upright chairs had a cushion on the seat, and there were a number of cushions in Wilson's armchair, whose unusual size and high back made it resemble a throne. And perhaps this was calculated. When Wilson sat down in it with his hands resting on the arms, whose ends had been carved into scrolls, he had a kingly air – an effect that was emphasized by the fact that the chair was somewhat higher than those on which Martin and the others sat. For some moments the Captain surveyed them in silence, still faintly smiling. Then his gaze rested on Martin again.

So you've come here to write a newspaper story about me. Is that it, Mr Dixon?

Yes. If you'll allow it, Captain.

Wilson rubbed his chin, seeming to muse, and said nothing for some moments. Then he said: That remains to be seen. You and I must have a serious discussion. I may see you tomorrow evening.

He looked at Griffin again, who was sitting very straight in his chair, like a schoolboy preparing to be examined. He had put on the fine leather top boots that Dalton had made him remove for work, and his eyes shone with an eager light.

Let me tell you something, Mr Griffin, Wilson said. When my lieutenant brought you back with him, he broke our most important rule: that nobody is ever to discover where we are.

His voice had now become measured and deliberate. It was a fine, resonant voice, and Martin suspected that he knew it. Liam Dalton, whose long legs were extended in front of him, had been gazing into the fire. He looked quickly at Wilson; but his face was expressionless.

I understand he did it because you gave him no peace, Wilson said. You cajoled and begged and pleaded, and he finally gave in.

He paused – an actor's pause – letting these words hang in the air. Griffin's eyes seemed to flicker; but he gave no other sign of unease. He sat absolutely still. Before going on, Wilson slowly raised his open hand, holding it in Dalton's direction.

Liam Dalton is my right hand, he said. I trust him absolutely. He also has a good heart – an Irish heart, that sometimes puts generous sentiment before cold calculation – and it seems he felt sorry for you. I can't judge him harshly for that. And I give you credit for the fact that you supported him in his escape. But you must realize one thing, Mr Griffin: you'll never leave here, now – unless we decide to get rid of you.

The crackling of the fire and the hiss of sap in the gum logs became much more distinct, as Griffin sat staring at the Captain. But then he nodded.

I do realize that. I've told Dalton so.

So Mr Dalton tells me. But you've got to be clear about something else. If you should change your mind, and if you should slip away alone and get down below – we'll find you.

Wilson sat forward, his hands lightly gripping the arms of the chair, and his expression had changed. His light blue eyes were eerily empty, as though he'd entered a trance.

Depend on it, Mr Griffin: you won't find anywhere to hide from us, in this little colony – we've too many friends and informants. We'll find you, and we'll kill you. Do you fully understand that?

All warmth seemed to Martin to drain from the room. Wilson's threat was more chilling than anything that might have been uttered by some brutish lout; and it also caused him to suspect that his own arrangement with Liam Dalton might be put aside, and the same penalty for coming here imposed on himself. Yet Griffin showed no sign of alarm. Instead he was smiling at Wilson, as though what he'd heard was pleasing to him.

Of course that's understood, he said. I wouldn't have it any other way, Captain. You might even say that it's part of the reason I've come here.

Wilson frowned. Oh? How so?

I've heard talk, Griffin said, when I was working for the

Government in Hobart Town. Talk of what sort of man you are, and what you're trying to do. And I admire it.

I see. And what might you have heard?

I realize such talk might not be accurate, Griffin said. Rumours and guesses, merely. But the people out in the bush – the poor farming people, the convict shepherds and such – they admire you, and they talk about you, and it gets back to town. You're a legend, sir, you don't need me to tell you that. You control many areas of the countryside, though the Government pretends not. And the people there love you for what you've done for them – you and Liam Dalton. I've heard that you give them money and food and clothing in hard times. I've heard that you've helped convicts escape the probation gangs, and got them away into the bush, and even out of the colony. I heard a story that you bailed up a cruel master at Broadmarsh – a man who was always ill-treating the convict pass-holders who worked for him. You flogged him with his own horsewhip, in his own yard, in front of his servants. What fun that must have been.

He licked his lips and grinned.

Wilson did not smile back. Fun is not how I'd describe it, he said. But let's keep to the point, Mr Griffin. What is it you think I'm trying to do?

To stick your thumb up at the world. To be free of its rules. To make your own rules.

Wilson sat back and raised his chestnut brows, studying Griffin carefully.

You put it rather crudely – but what you say has some truth in it. What we're trying to do here is *to start again.*

He had spoken in a tone of some vehemence. A light of cold enthusiasm had entered his face, and Griffin leaned forward abruptly in his chair, projecting an answering enthusiasm.

Yes. Of course. You're creating a Utopia up here. Am I right, Captain?

At this, Wilson's brows rose even higher.

You have some acquaintance with Sir Thomas More's book?

I've browsed through it. His ideas appealed to me greatly.

I'm glad to hear it. And if you have any Greek, Mr Griffin, you'll know why Thomas More named his imaginary island as he did.

Griffin shook his head. I have some Latin. But no Greek.

Wilson raised his right forefinger like a schoolmaster.

'Utopia' is a pun based on two Greek words: *eutopia*, meaning 'good place', and *outopia*, meaning 'no place'. In other words, 'nowhere land'. That's why I've named this settlement 'Nowhere Valley'. This is our Utopia, as you've guessed. And what we're trying to build here is a society that's more just and free than the corrupt and unjust one that's rejected us. Do you see?

It's what I've often dreamed of, Griffin said. It's what I hoped for when I followed Dalton up here.

Then perhaps you may fit in. But that remains to be seen.

Wilson stood up suddenly from his throne-like chair.

Gentlemen, let me offer you a drop of Spanish sherry. It's a fine one – from the cellar of a grazier in the Ouse district.

He walked over to a sideboard on the far side of the room, next to a set of bookshelves that rose to the ceiling. He poured from a decanter into four small glasses and carried them back on a round silver tray, holding it out to each man in turn. As he settled back into his armchair again, and they began to sample their drinks, Martin became aware that the light out the windows was fading a little, and dusk was beginning in the room. The strongest light here now, since no lamp had been lit, came from the fire, and its flames were reflected on their faces. The glow turned Wilson's skin to a deeper tan, making his knob-like cheekbones resemble polished wood. He was now looking at Martin.

And what about you, Mr Dixon? Have you read Sir Thomas More's work?

I'm afraid not. I only recall that Henry the Eighth had him beheaded.

Yes. Because Thomas More was a man of high principle, who could not be broken. I admire that sort of man greatly. You ought to read *Utopia*, Mr Dixon, it will help you to understand what we're doing here, if you come to write your article. I may lend you my copy. In More's island nation, all men are educated alike, the land is owned communally, all must work, everyone contributes to society, and society's order is respected by all. Does that appeal to you?

Certainly, Martin said. But I wonder if it could ever be achieved in the real world?

Liam Dalton shook his head, and spoke for the first time. The real world's too bloody wicked, he said.

Wilson laughed. Right as usual, my Liam. You've never been one to be deluded by dreams.

He turned to the others. But this is the point – do you see? Up here, removed from that world below, we can put Thomas More's dream into practice. We all contribute to creating the wealth of this valley, and we all take what we need. When we can eventually manufacture everything we want, we'll have no more need of the world below at all.

But at present, you must raid, Martin said.

Wilson looked at him without expression. Aye. At present we must raid.

More seemed to allow the pursuit of pleasure in his Utopia, Griffin put in. Was there any belief that was prohibited?

They didn't tolerate atheism, Wilson said. They said that the soul was immortal, and created by a God who meant it to be happy. And they believed that we'd be rewarded and punished after death according to our behaviour in this world. I'm inclined to agree with them – although I don't insist on it here. What do *you* think, Mr Griffin?

Griffin paused, seeming to deliberate. Then he ran his tongue across his lips and his expression became conspiratorial, as though he had a secret to impart.

I'm sure of one thing, Captain Wilson. There's certainly a life outside this one. An invisible world lies all around us, and we're watched by invisible beings.

Wilson looked at him quickly, his sherry glass suspended halfway to his lips.

Indeed? Is that your notion? You and I must talk further about this. I'd be curious to hear more.

I'd be delighted, Griffin said.

He smiled at Wilson in a way that was clearly intended to be winning. It seemed to succeed, since Wilson looked back at him with an expression that had become almost encouraging.

Griffin had presented a new and surprising aspect of himself; but it failed to impress Martin favourably. Although what he'd said might have been seen as interesting, or at worst, harmlessly eccentric, Martin found it instead to be disquieting, since the man himself was disquieting.

He noticed that Dalton seemed to share his response. The Irishman was staring at Griffin with an expression that was deeply dubious.

3

Follow me, Wilson said.

He went through a narrow doorway leading off the hall, and began to climb a staircase so steep that it resembled a ship's companionway. Martin followed him, and they emerged into the large square room that occupied the top of the tower. Wilson was carrying an oil lamp, which he set down on a table in the centre of the room. There were casement windows on all four sides of the tower, all without curtains. Their glass reflected the glow of the lamp, creating reflections that obscured what was outside. But then Wilson walked across and pushed two of them open.

Blue-black and cloudless, the night sky filled the frame, its expanse uninterrupted by treetops, since the land sloped away on this side of the Lodge. The swarming stars were more numerous than any Martin had seen from his home below: a dizzying infinity of pulsing white lights, brilliant in the clear, thin air. Wilson turned to him and smiled with satisfaction, as though at a display he'd arranged for Martin's benefit.

There's the road to Heaven for you, he said. It's nearer to us, up here.

It's magnificent. Is that why you built this tower?

Partly, Wilson said. He gestured at a telescope that stood in a corner of the room. I like to observe the stars, he said. A hobby of mine. The southern hemisphere is still strange to me, and I try to make charts. This month is the best of all, for looking at the constellations.

He beckoned Martin over to the window, and pointed.

We're looking north. There's the belt of Orion high up – instead of in the south, where you'd see it if we were back in old England. See how bright the Dog Star is from here? And there's Aldebaran – the eye of Taurus.

He was silent for a moment, his face tilted upwards as though praying. Then he turned to Martin again, seeming to come back to himself.

But the southern sky isn't as strange to you as it is to me, is it? You were born here, I believe. Sit down, Mr Dixon, and we'll talk.

Please – call me Martin.

Martin, then, since you're such a young fellow. Most people here address me as Captain. You might as well do the same.

Of course, Captain.

They sat facing each other in two straight-backed chairs of the local pink myrtle, placed beside the table. These and two other chairs and the table were the only furnishings here, except for the telescope, a set of bookshelves, and a Persian carpet on the floor. The walls and ceiling were of beeswaxed eucalyptus boards, and a small iron stove stood in one corner, giving out a low heat, its pipe going up through the ceiling. Wilson liked to have extra warmth, it seemed, even in the summer, but this eyrie of his was otherwise austere: clearly made for solitude and simplicity. Tonight, as though in harmony with this setting, he was much more simply dressed than before, in a blue serge shirt, black cotton neckerchief and corduroy trousers: clothing a bush worker might have worn, except for ankle boots of fine brown leather.

Well now, I've read your newspaper story, he said.

He reached for a pile of papers that sat on the table beside him and shuffled through them, drawing out the cutting from *The Hobart Town Courier* that Martin had brought up to the Valley in his saddlebag. It had been passed on to Wilson by Liam Dalton, who had told Martin this evening that the Captain was ready to talk to him. Wilson held up the cutting like an exhibit.

You write well. You deal with a trial here, I see: this fellow in Hobart Town wrongly charged with embezzlement. You seem to have a good knowledge of the Law.

A little. My father has a friend who's a lawyer, and he gave me advice.

I see.

Wilson put down the cutting and was silent for a moment, staring at Martin with his uncannily light eyes. They were changelessly cold, Martin saw, even when Wilson was smiling. This made it difficult to relax in his presence, and Martin found himself sitting very stiffly in his chair, anticipating some kind of challenge. It came immediately.

You want to write my story, Wilson said. And to publish it in a newspaper.

That's right. I'll be very grateful if you'll consider it.

But why should you want to do such a thing? And why should I allow it?

I believe it would be a story worth telling. The articles in the newspapers condemn you, but the men who write them know very little about you – except that you're said to be an educated man and a former soldier who turned to bushranging. In the more vulgar papers, they call you the Captain of the Ranges. It's said you raid the big property-owners, but give help to small farmers and bush workers in hard times. That makes an interesting story – but what would make it even more interesting to readers would be to learn why you went bushranging, and what really brought a gentleman like you as a prisoner to this colony.

He stopped and waited, nervously brushing back his forelock from his forehead. What he'd said must convince Wilson to accept his proposal, and Martin feared that he had only a very slight chance of doing so.

Wilson had been listening intently, his head on one side. But he merely nodded, watching Martin steadily with his disturbing gaze, as though waiting for something more.

It's said you were transported for assaulting a superior officer, Martin said. But there must have been a reason for that.

Yes, there was a reason. I was grossly insulted. And that's what brought me to where I am now.

I suspected something like that. I guessed that you were no common felon – and now that I've heard your ideas on Utopia, I know it to be so. That makes your story more interesting still.

Wilson took a long breath through his nose, continuing to stare hard at Martin.

I've killed a man, he said, since I became an outlaw. A police constable. What do you say to that? Does it make you squeamish?

I read about it, of course, in the papers. I suppose it was in self-defence.

It was. It was him or me. But if they ever catch me, they'll hang me – and there's a large price on my head, as I'm sure you know. You might think of claiming it, Martin, if you get back below.

Martin noted the use of 'if'. It made him even more tense; but he managed to maintain a calm expression.

I'd never do that, Captain. I'm here to learn your ideas, and to tell your story: nothing more.

Now Wilson seemed to look through him, into a remote distance. His eyes had widened, he raised his right hand in a theatrical manner, and when he spoke again he surprised Martin by beginning to recite poetry. His voice signalled this: it had become strong and resonant again, its rhythms more than ever recalling the style of a stage actor.

'The world is too much with us; late and soon, Getting and spending, we lay waste our powers. Little we see in Nature that is ours …'

He broke off, and Martin added: 'We have given our hearts away, a sordid boon!'

Wilson's eyebrows rose. Then he smiled widely, showing his teeth, and for the first time exhibiting something like warmth.

You know that sonnet, then? You know William Wordsworth?

I love his poetry, Martin said. I began to read him at school, and I still read him.

I see. I see. Well now, young fellow, that puts a different complexion on things. A man who loves Wordsworth must love nature, and has a lot to recommend him. But I quoted this poem for a reason. What I've done in establishing Nowhere Valley is to escape that world which is too much with us. Do you see?

I think so. You've left it all below.

Exactly. Here in this beautiful place, we're in a territory that's never been spoiled: one that's just as it was at the beginning of time. Think what a wonderful gift that is! The birds, the flowers, the trees: all new and strange, waiting to be discovered, like those stars out there – like a country in a dream!

Wilson's expression now was one of abstract yet fervent enthusiasm. He had fallen into a mode which Martin suspected was habitual with him, the cadences of his speech similar to those he'd employed when reciting from Wordsworth's sonnet. And Martin found himself being drawn into the spell that Wilson wished to create. He resisted this, at first. He reminded himself that Wilson was a criminal, and told himself that the Captain had something of the poseur about him. He attempted to view him dubiously, with youthful irreverence; but he found this impossible to maintain. The power of Wilson's personality was too strong; it overwhelmed Martin's puny scepticism. The Captain was revealing an ability to make himself captivating – and in spite of himself, Martin began to feel honoured that these passionate and poetic confidences were being offered him, up here in this tower where Wilson communed with the stars. He wanted to know the Captain better; to hear whatever it was that he might choose to reveal.

This is a place, Wilson said, whose air will never be fouled by the smoke of towns and factories. A place where we till the soil as our ancestors did, free of those vile machines that are robbing the world of its beauty. A place that's free of the bloody vultures who run the mills and coalmines. Free of those damned authorities who herd men into prisons, if they dare to rebel.

His eyes were now shining with indignation. One fist was clenched on the arm of his chair, while he ran the fingers of his other hand through his great mane of chestnut hair. It was an indignation that Martin found alarming, even though it was not directed at him. But then, in seconds, the Captain relaxed and changed entirely, looking at him with a mild expression.

So we've left all that behind to start again. And the soul of these mountains is one that's untainted by the wickedness and misery below. Have you noticed that, young fellow? Is yours the kind of spirit that responds to it?

He waited, and a reply seemed necessary.

I believe so, Martin said.

Yes: I believe you may have such a spirit. If you do, you'll have sensed there are no memories in this air of treachery and war and oppression, as there are in the ancient air of Europe. No blood has ever been shed here, unless by those poor aborigines our corrupted civilization has driven out. We're truly able to start anew here. It's a place where what Wordsworth called the shades of the prison house can never close around us.

He sat back, and reached for a long churchwarden pipe that sat on the table beside him, together with a leather pouch of tobacco. As he filled the pipe, he continued to hold Martin's gaze.

I go out walking here, he said, as William Wordsworth did in his dales, and I find myself in forests of native myrtle where no-one of our kind has ever been before. That's what nourishes my spirit.

I think I understand, Martin said. But what if the world comes up here to you?

Wilson's face tightened. It won't. We own this bit of land – and nobody wants it anyway. Poor, rocky soil. Steep valleys that are no good for sheep pastures. A hard winter. No – they don't want it. But if they ever came too close, we'd go deeper into the wilderness.

He struck a lucifer across the sole of his boot and lit his pipe, his cheeks hollowing as he drew in the smoke, its blue clouds rising into the room; and Martin decided now to steer the conversation back to its main theme.

What drove you to this wilderness in the first place, Captain? From what I've read, you committed no fresh crime after you arrived in the colony. You could have led a law-abiding life, and been given a ticket-of-leave.

Wilson looked up from under his brows, still puffing on the pipe. Then he released another cloud of smoke and took the pipe from his mouth. He smiled again, but this time with little warmth.

You're a determined young chap, he said. You still want my story. Very well, we'll make a start. I hope you have a notebook?

Martin nodded and reached into the pocket of his pea jacket, drawing out his notebook and pencil.

I grew up in the village of Charing, Wilson said, at the foot of the North Downs, in Kent. My mother was a widow – a Scottish gentlewoman from Berwickshire. She'd been married to a poor clergyman who died young, leaving her almost penniless. Her father hadn't been able to do much to help her – he was also poor. He'd lost his property and most of his money through risky investments. This happened when I was only an infant. So I have no memories of Scotland – nor of the man she told me was my father.

Martin looked up from his notes and stared, but Wilson raised his hand.

I'll come to that. My mother was an educated woman, who had taught at a school for young ladies before she married. Now that she found herself destitute, she answered an advertizement for a governess, to tutor the children of a wealthy squire in Kent. His estate was close to Charing. His name was Sir John Mountford. She came south and was taken into his household, where she stayed for two years. Then she gave up the position, moved into a cottage in Charing, and set up a little school there for the village children. I attended it myself, when I was small.

He paused; his pipe had gone out. He knocked some ash out into a dish on the table, tamped the tobacco into the bowl with his thumb and then lit up again, speaking from the corner of his mouth.

My mother was a good and kind woman. I was very fond of her, and still am. But she lied to me – and only confessed the lie when I'd almost come to manhood. Her late husband wasn't my father: Sir John Mountford was.

Martin said nothing, his pencil poised over his notes. The look on Wilson's face told him not to comment, and he tried to make his own face blank.

My mother had been young and childless when she came to England, Wilson said. The squire was married, and his wife was alive and well – but this didn't prevent him from taking advantage of my mother. He promised to leave his wife and divorce her, but this never happened. When my mother became pregnant, Sir John made it clear that he could not give up his marriage. Instead, he provided for her financially, buying her the cottage in the village, paying for the establishment of the school, and providing her with a small additional income so that I would be taken care of. When I was ten years old, the squire paid for me to be enrolled as a boarder at a college for boys in Canterbury. He paid my fees and other expenses until I completed my schooling. Then, when my final year at school had ended, and I was seventeen, he told my mother that I must look for employment, and make my own way in the world.

He paused, staring in front of him as though he'd lost the thread of his narrative. Martin paused in his note-taking.

But that wasn't what *I* wanted, Wilson said finally. I was a good scholar, and I loved learning. I'd won the Latin prize in my final year at school, the headmaster thought I should continue my studies, and what I wanted now was to go to University – to Oxford or Cambridge. My mother wrote to Sir John asking that he support me in this, but he told her that I was setting my sights too high. I'd never met him, you understand – and he refused ever to see my mother now, communicating only by letter, or through one of his servants. But now I decided to go to him, without her knowledge, and beg him to help me. So I went to the manor, and told the servants who I was, and asked to see the squire. The message came back that he wouldn't receive me.

He was silent for a time, releasing a stream of smoke from the side of his mouth, the long stem of the pipe gripped between his teeth, his eyes narrowed. When he spoke again, his voice was flat.

So I ran off to London, and I never went back. I worked as a clerk in an office for a time, soon got sick of that, and ran wild for a few years in ways I needn't dwell on. I worked as a sailor on a coastal trading vessel for a while, and then I went about the countryside in Essex with a friend of mine, hawking various goods. I also worked for a bookseller, and found time to read a lot of his books. Then, in 1843, when I was twenty-two, I joined the army as a common soldier. Had Mountford acknowledged and supported me, I might have gone to the Royal Military Academy and become a commissioned officer – but that wasn't to be. I never held the rank of captain – though my followers like to call me that.

He had gone into the army as a result of an encounter in a tavern in Knightsbridge, he said. This was at a time when his fortunes were low. A number of tall cavalrymen in the blue uniform of the Royal Horse Guards came into the taproom; their barracks was nearby. Wilson fell into conversation with one of them, paying for his drinks. He had decided, on the spur of the moment, that he wanted to join their regiment, and asked what the requirements were. He was told that a man must be fit, and over six feet tall. Wilson informed him that he was six feet two, and asked what his chances were. At first the soldier thought that he was joking, since he'd taken Wilson for a gentleman – but when Wilson convinced him that he was serious, the soldier said he'd recruit him immediately, if Wilson would take the King's shilling.

The next day Wilson was taken to the commanding officer at the barracks, who was apparently impressed with him. A medical examination followed, he was found to be healthy, and he was soon installed as a soldier in the Blues: part of the Household Cavalry. Over the following year he was trained in horsemanship and the use of the broadsword and lance, and attracted favourable attention. He was promoted to the rank of non-commissioned officer, and was now a lance-corporal. He had a natural way with horses, and he enjoyed the service, despite the frequent tedium of army life. The Horse Guards saw no military action, but his rank meant that he was employed on special duties at the royal residences at London and Windsor, taking part in the many ceremonies and spectacles that were attended by Queen Victoria.

But then, after six years of service, when he was twenty-eight, a single incident changed his life, and turned him into a felon.

It happened when we were stationed at Windsor, Wilson said. The races at Ascot Heath were being held, and a number of us were granted liberty to go to them. We had a fine time there – and a good deal to drink. By the time we got back to barracks, we were all pretty elevated: in fact, quite drunk. An argument began between myself and the corporal-major of our troop, a fellow called Johnson. It was over a matter so trivial as to be not worth recalling – but he and I had never liked each other, and it grew quite heated. He taunted me – told me I gave myself the airs of a gentleman when I wasn't one, and ended by threatening to put me under confinement. I was angry, and the liquor caused me to lose control. I told him to try it, and I'd make him sorry. Upon which, he called me a bastard.

Martin put down his pencil, and looked up. Wilson had laid his pipe aside, and his hands rested on his knees. His face was taut, and his eyes searched Martin's face as though he expected a comment. Martin decided it was best to remain silent; but he wasn't allowed to remain so.

He called me a bastard, Wilson repeated. Perhaps you'll understand my feelings about that?

His expression hinted at controlled rage, and Martin feared to give the wrong answer. He cleared his throat, and licked his lips.

Of course I do, he said. He insulted you.

Wilson nodded. Then you may understand what I did next, he said. I laid Johnson out with one blow to the jaw, and it took him some time to get up. When he did, I told him that if he ever used that term to me again, I would do him in. That was a very rash thing to say to a superior officer – but I was drunk and angry. It didn't take long for me to discover what a mistake I'd made. I was reported to the captain of my troop and ordered to be confined. I was seized and dragged to the guard room, and thrown into a cell they called the black hole. I was kept there for some days to meditate on my situation. At that stage, I thought my punishment wouldn't be too severe, since Johnson and I had both been drunk. I soon found that I was wrong.

He was now told by the colonel in command of the regiment that to threaten the life of an officer was a very grave offence, and that he must soon prepare for a general tribunal. After some weeks, he was taken to the Regent's Park Barracks in London, handcuffed and under escort, and was advised to plead guilty to the charges against him. This he refused to do, claiming that he had spoken in liquor, and had not had any serious intention of killing Johnson. He then spent a month in confinement, waiting for the outcome. It arrived with considerable pomp and ceremony. A general parade was ordered, to which he was taken under guard. The entire regiment of the Blues was drawn up in line, and the colonel read the minutes of the court martial. Having done so, he gave the finding of the court. The prisoner was guilty, and was sentenced to seven years' transportation beyond the seas.

Now I understood what I'd brought on myself, Wilson said. This may sound foolish, but it hadn't been real to me until then. I'd not believed that a drunken row, in which a stupid bloody oaf had grossly insulted me, could lead to this. Well, I was wrong; the British army takes a threat to a superior very seriously. I was removed to the Millbank Penitentiary, put into the uniform of a convict, and confined in a cell. After two weeks, I was transported to Woolwich, where the hulks lie: those wrecks that house convicts awaiting transportation. And very soon after that I was taken to the convict transport that would bring me here to Van Diemen's Land.

How terrible, Martin said.

He had spoken spontaneously, and Wilson granted him a thin smile.

Yes, I suppose so, he said. But you find you can bear most things if you have an aim in view. I had such an aim now, and got through the voyage pretty well by keeping it in mind.

And what was your aim?

To make a break, as soon as possible after we reached the colony. To escape the society that had done me this injustice. More: to have my revenge on it. And this proved to be not too difficult to set in motion – since the authorities out here made the mistake of being lenient with me.

He leaned back in his chair, faintly smiling, puffing on his pipe and looking out at the stars. He seemed to have relaxed now, all sign of anger gone.

When the transport docked in Hobart Town, he said, the officials came on board with their registers to take the particulars of their new load of felons. They grew quite sympathetic when they learned about my background and degree of education. One of them even said that my sentence seemed unduly harsh for what I'd done, especially since my military record was otherwise good. As an educated man, my abilities could make me useful to the colony's administration – and if I behaved well, I'd no doubt get a ticket-of-leave in a fairly short time.

He gave a brief laugh. I suppose I was expected to feel grateful, he said. I pretended to be, since what they were proposing for me meant that I could put my plan into operation sooner than I'd hoped.

He was employed as a clerk in the Colonial Secretary's office, and they paid him a meagre wage. He was housed at night in the dismal Prisoners' Barracks in Campbell Street; but like a number of other privileged convict clerks he had far better quarters than the other felons. He was even allowed to buy his own clothing, instead of wearing the grey convict uniform. So in a limited way, he was able to lead the life of a free citizen, provided he stayed within the bounds of the city, and returned to the Barracks at the required time in the evenings.

He bided his time for some months, learning what he could about his new environment and the way the colony was run, and he soon saw that there were ample opportunities here for a man who was prepared to be ruthless. After two months, on an evening in early summer, he made his move. Instead of returning to the Barracks, he simply walked out of Hobart Town.

It was quite easy, Wilson said. Had I been wearing the convict uniform, I would have attracted attention; I was very fortunate in being able to wear my own clothing. I had very few possessions – I couldn't afford them – but I had on a pea jacket to keep me warm, and carried a small handbag with a change of linen in it, and a few other necessaries. To the casual observer, I was simply a private citizen out for a stroll. I walked out through New Town, on through the village at O'Brien's Bridge, and so into the country. By then it was coming on dusk. I had no set plan; but I knew that what I had to get my hands on was a horse and a gun. This wasn't going to be easy, but I kept my eyes open for opportunities. Between O'Brien's Bridge and the Black Snake, one presented itself.

He was now in an area of small farms, and noticed a shepherd's hut out on a hillside. He'd been told that every shepherd had some sort of firearm, and he moved quietly up to the hut, where a lamp was burning. He burst in suddenly, to find the shepherd grilling chops over a fire. He was a small, timid man, and proved easy to overpower, Wilson said. He tied him to a chair with some rope he found on a chest. He then left with a double-barrelled shotgun he found behind the door, and a supply of gunpowder and shot.

He broke off and took a deep breath, stretching his arms above his head and smiling.

I next came upon a prosperous-looking property out beyond the Black Snake, he said. There I held up two convict farmhands in their quarters, some distance from the main house. I explained to them that I wanted a good horse and gear, and asked them to lead me to one without raising an alarm. If they did, I wouldn't disturb them further – if not, I'd shoot them on the spot. They understood me perfectly, and seemed happy to oblige. They even gave me some bread and cheese to take with me. I've often found convict servants cooperative – they have little love of their masters. And so my career as a bushranger began. I worked alone, at first – and then I met Liam Dalton. We made a fine team, and I think you might say we've been successful. We have secret control of a good deal of the country below, from Bridgewater to the Midlands.

He rose abruptly, and walked to the open window. Framed by stars, he stood with his back to Martin. When he turned back again, his face wore an expression that was perhaps one of exultation, but which also had in it the muted anger he'd exhibited before.

Tell me: have you ever seen Shakespeare's *King Lear* performed?

No, Martin said. But I've read it.

Then you may remember Edmund's speech. Edmund, who is illegitimate.

Wilson's voice rose to its full actor's resonance, and he threw up one hand.

'Edmund the base Shall top the legitimate. I grow. I prosper. Now, gods, stand up for bastards!'

He began to laugh loudly, throwing back his head. Martin joined in, but without much gusto; what he saw in Wilson's face unnerved him.

Enough for now, Wilson said, and his voice had become low again. That's all you need to begin with. You've got it all down?

Martin said he had and stood up, pushing his notebook into his pocket.

Good, Wilson said. I want it all known, so that people can judge me for themselves. Let me see what you've written, when it's done. Then I'll decide whether it's worth talking to you further. I hope for your sake that I *can* decide that – if not, you'll present me with a problem.

He smiled, but his smile now was without any warmth, and his eyes were empty.

Martin went down the stairs of the tower with his heart beating unevenly.

Years later, he would lie awake at night, summoning up Nowhere Valley and the events there that had reshaped his spirit, changing him in a way that was irreversible. Then the immense gullies would yawn at his feet again: deep, steep entrances to the Underworld, giving out their scents of eucalyptus and leaf mould, their floors so far down that they lay in permanent shadow. The giant gums that had their roots there climbed from darkness into light, where sudden bursts of sun would strike their upper terraces, changing their olive-greens to a brief, astounding gold. And always in the background, like guardians of Wilson's Utopia, the two nameless flat-topped mountains stood sharp against the sky, concealing a country forever unseen.

In this first week in the Valley, whatever lay waiting to be discovered also remained unseen. His life was tantalizingly quiet, following his interview with Wilson: he continued to work as a farmhand. On their next two days in the settlement, he and Roy Griffin went on labouring with Bill Bosworth and Joe Jarvis – this time going into the oat field, where they stacked the wagon with stooks and took them into the farmyard, unloading them in front of the barn. The settlement had no mill, so the oats must be threshed and winnowed by hand, ready to be put through a grinder; and this was their next task. Griffin, who had yet to be interviewed by Wilson again, had become increasingly given to resentful remarks in an undertone, inviting Martin to join him in his discontent; but Martin refused to be drawn.

On the fifth day following their arrival, Dalton finally informed Griffin that he was to go and meet Wilson on his own, presenting himself at the Lodge after breakfast. Meanwhile, Martin was to work at hoeing weeds in the communal vegetable garden.

This lay close to Bill Bosworth's house, and Bill was there to meet him when he arrived. He instructed Martin on how he was to hoe between the rows of swedes and potatoes, and then left him to work alone; but a few hours later he came back to inspect Martin's progress.

He proved willing to answer questions when Martin asked him how self-supporting the settlement actually was. The soil was poor, Bill said, but horse and cow manure were slowly improving it. The work was hard; they must carry water up from the creek in buckets to water this garden. Everyone took some part in the farming. They'd found it best to concentrate on swedes, cabbages, carrots, peas and potatoes. When it came to harvest time, everyone picked up a scythe, including the Captain. Oats provided them with porridge, as well as feed for their horses. The kangaroos they hunted were their main source of meat, but they also slaughtered some of their pigs and chickens from time to time, and brought in occasional supplies of meat from down below. They made candles and soap from tallow, but items such as tea, coffee, flour, sugar, tobacco and whale oil for the lamps had to be bought in one of the villages. Money wasn't a problem, he said, and smiled briefly; Liam and the Captain saw to that.

Bill was proud of his skills in carpentry and blacksmithing and general building work. Very few others here were skilled artisans, he said, except for Alan McLeod, who was good at blacksmithing. Together, they'd built a smokehouse to cure pork and bacon, and a stone oven to bake bread in. Bill did most of the baking for the settlement, and seemed proud of his bread; he was also proud of a hop beer he brewed. Martin asked him about his family, and Bill told him he had an eight-year-old son and a daughter of twelve. This was May, the girl who cooked meals for Liam Dalton, and cleaned his house. In return, Dalton helped him in a number of ways that Bill didn't specify.

That's the way we do things here, he said. Mutual favours – you see, Mr Dixon? I've a much better life since the Captain and Liam Dalton joined us here, *I* can tell you – it was bloody hard before. The missus had to help me with the heavy work outside, in them days. Now she doesn't, thanks to the Captain. He's a great man, and what he's doing here is a wonderful thing.

He smiled, fingering his greying brown beard. He seemed a decent, likeable man, ex-convict though he was; but the fact that his farm was a haven for a community of bandits, and that its economy was boosted and underpinned by their raids on the law-abiding world below seemed in no way to trouble him.

That evening, as he'd done the evening before, Martin worked on writing up his notes on the table in the dining-room after supper, a candle burning beside him, while Dalton and Griffin sat beside the fire. Griffin had changed, since his interview with Wilson; he wore a small, complacent smile. When he attempted conversation with Dalton, Liam discouraged it, answering only in monosyllables; so the dining-room was mostly silent, and there was little to distract Martin from his work. Griffin seemed unconcerned about these rebuffs; whatever had taken place between himself and Wilson must have gratified him, and he lay back in his chair with an air of secret satisfaction, toasting his stockinged feet in front of the flames.

After an hour, Martin had finally completed the account Wilson had given him of his life, and he asked Dalton to tell the Captain that he was ready to show him what he'd done, and would like to talk to him further.

I'll do that, Dalton said. But don't be in a hurry, now. No doubt the Captain will send for you again when he's read it.

Martin nodded, but he now nursed an impatience similar to Griffin's. His life here was becoming a monotonous routine of farm labour, and nothing else; and he began to wonder how soon he would be able to complete his story, and be free to go home.

Martin still slept in Dalton's bedroom, while Griffin continued to sleep in the dining-room. There was a lean-to at the back of the house which housed the kitchen and bathroom, with a crude latrine attached whose can they took turns at emptying into an ash pit. They washed in a tin bath with hot water poured from a kettle. May usually cooked their dinner and supper in the kitchen; but she always made breakfast over the fire in the dining-room.

Dalton generally rose at dawn, and was gone on unknown errands before Martin was properly awake. He would then come in for his breakfast at around seven-thirty. He was not yet back when Martin came into the dining-room this morning. But Roy Griffin was, and what he was doing caused Martin to halt abruptly. He sat by the fire with May perched on his knee, one hand holding her waist, the other stroking her hair. She wore the same grey smock as always, and a pair of black ankle boots that looked too big for her. She didn't seem comfortable; her pallid face flushed when she saw Martin, and she shifted slightly, as though trying to escape. But she didn't speak, and Griffin apparently held her too firmly to allow her to get down.

Good morning, comrade.

He looked at Martin across the kitchen with a guileless expression. He had stopped stroking the girl's hair, but continued to hold her securely.

May and I are having a talk, he said. Do you know, she's never been to school? Her mother taught her to read a little, but there's much more to be learned than that, isn't there, my dear? I might give you some lessons – what do you think?

May said nothing; she was now looking down into the fire.

Perhaps you should let her go, Martin said. She has work to do.

Come, come. She and I are just getting to know each other – aren't we, darling?

Griffin bent his head to smile into her face; but the girl wriggled, and now spoke for the first time. Her voice was very soft, and had a pleading sound.

Let me down.

Aye. Let her down, Griffin.

Liam Dalton had come into the room to stand behind Martin; he had spoken loudly close to Martin's ear, causing him to start. Griffin stared, no longer smiling, and seemed to search for words. His grip on the girl's waist loosened, and she suddenly wriggled free and stood looking at Dalton, her eyes wide and unblinking.

Go out to the kitchen, May, Dalton said. Bring us an extra loaf of bread. I'm famished.

This time he'd spoken very softly. The girl obeyed, hurrying out the door that led to the lean-to, her head bent. As she did so, Dalton moved quickly across the room to Griffin. He took him by the front of his shirt with one hand, lifted him from his chair and suspended him against the wall at arm's length.

Listen to me now, and listen carefully. May is only a child. So let you not get any nasty ideas about her.

For heaven's sake, Dalton – you do me an injustice. Her education has been neglected. I could be a tutor to her.

With his free hand, Dalton slapped Griffin hard across the face.

You're not hearin me, Griffin. Don't lay hands on her again. If you do, I'll have to make you sorry for it.

Griffin's eyes had widened in shock, and his mouth hung open. He clawed vainly at Dalton's arm. When he spoke again, it was in a low hiss.

You'll regret this, Dalton. You've completely misunderstood me.

Still holding him at arm's length, Dalton slapped him again, harder this time. It left a livid mark on Griffin's cheek.

Regret it, will I? Let me promise you somethin, Griffin. It's you who'll have regrets, should you touch that child again. Now get out of this house.

He relinquished his hold on Griffin's shirt, and Griffin stepped back, crouching and holding his cheek. His large green eyes were swimming with tears, but they were glaring at Dalton defiantly, and his face was contorted with a hatred that made him look deranged. He turned without speaking again, and went out through the door, sending a last glance at Dalton as he did so.

Dalton turned to Martin.

And now we'll be havin our breakfast.

Martin worked in the vegetable garden again that morning. When he came back to the house for his dinner at noon, he was somewhat apprehensive, anticipating tension between Dalton and Griffin. But he found Dalton and May alone in the dining-room, with no sign of Griffin.

May was standing by the camp oven that hung above the fire. She had made a stew the day before, and was now serving it again: potatoes, onions and pieces of kangaroo meat. Dalton was already eating, and when Martin sat down at the table, May ladled a portion onto his plate. He thanked her, and she gave him a timid smile. She seldom smiled, and never spoke unless spoken to.

Griffin's late, Martin said.

He won't be comin.

Dalton cut himself a slice of Bill Bosworth's bread, mopped up the last of his gravy and sat chewing. May was moving out the door to the lean-to, and he watched her go. When she'd gone, he looked at Martin.

He won't be eatin here, and he won't be sleepin here. I told him to move into the bachelors' house, with Joe Jarvis. No-one else lives there at present, so there's plenty of room. You can sleep on the couch here, from now on. It's warm, and you should be comfortable.

He stood up, his set expression discouraging any questions.

When you've eaten, go down to the stables. I'll meet you there in five minutes. You and I are goin kangaroo huntin. You said you were a fair shot. Let's see if you are, now.

When Martin reached the stables, he found Dalton waiting for him with a pair of guns under his arm: a single-barrelled shotgun, and the Colt revolving rifle taken from Henry Dixon's gunroom. His bay horse stood beside him, and two big kangaroo dogs sat at his feet, gazing up expectantly, their long bodies tense. Scottish deerhound crossed with greyhound, they were highly trained, valuable animals, used here since the early days, but becoming less common now that guns were more accurate.

Dalton handed him the shotgun.

This is yours. Holland and Holland: it ought to serve you well.

Yes. I've used one before.

There's gunpowder and shot flasks and a sling for the gun lyin on the feed bin in the stable by your pony. I'll be tryin out this beauty of your father's. It should have a good range: we'll see how it goes with wallabies. Get saddled up now, and we'll be off.

Dalton led them south-east out of the settlement and into the bush, following a track that went steeply uphill. The day was warm, with the sun coming and going behind high cloud. The kangaroo dogs trotted behind Dalton's horse, glancing up at him with frequent looks of enquiry, but never barking. They'd been trained not to do so, and the only sound they made was an occasional whimper of impatience. Within half an hour Dalton led Martin out of the trees and on to an area of open grassland, similar to the one from which they'd first surveyed the Valley, gently sloping and studded with rocks and small bushes. On its western side was a forest of eucalypts. Dalton pointed in that direction and whistled.

Go on, he called. Find them, Belle. Find them, Rufus.

Still noiseless, the grey, long-haired hounds leaped away and surged through the grass towards the trees, their noses close to the ground.

Dalton turned to Martin. You've hunted with these dogs?

No – we don't use them at home. I've usually hunted at sunset, when the roos come out to feed.

Aye. They'll be asleep in the grass, now – but the dogs'll stir them out, see, and drive them to where we'll get a shot. So get ready, now.

Are we after big kangaroos?

The foresters? No, they're not so plentiful these days – nearly cleaned out. We get the little wallabies. They make the best eatin, and the only thing that hunts them in the bush is the dog-tiger. It's a pretty slow animal, and they can easy get away. But these dogs are so fast the roos don't stand a chance. They'll soon find them – so get loaded and ready.

Martin began muzzle-loading his gun with the powder and shot from the flasks that hung from his belt. As he cocked the hammer, he heard Dalton give another low whistle.

Good dogs, he said, and Martin saw that the hounds were racing through the grass with three dark brown wallabies leaping ahead of them, headed for a clump of gums on the other side of the clearing. The wallabies looked quite small, in contrast to the dogs – not much bigger than hares – and Martin felt a momentary pity for them; he had never hunted for pleasure, but only to protect his father's crops. Both dogs kept a little to one side of the wallabies, herding them like sheep, and Dalton raised his gun.

Plenty of time, he said. The dogs will head them in a circle.

He fired and missed. Then he fired again, and the wallaby in the lead dropped.

Now let's see what you can do, he told Martin.

Martin was already training his gun on the second wallaby, which had gone a considerable distance and had almost reached the trees. He fired, and it dropped immediately.

Good. No need for you to reload, Dalton said. The last one's mine.

He aimed with the Colt again, brought down the third wallaby and laughed.

What a gun! No reloadin, and I've still got four bullets left in the cylinder. There's no doubt about those Yankees, they know how to make a firearm.

He whistled to the dogs, and they raced across to him, panting. He reached into a kangaroo-skin knapsack that hung from his saddle and drew out some pieces of meat, which he threw to them. Then he turned to Martin, and the expression on his face was more friendly than usual.

Sure, and you're quite a good shot, he said. You weren't just braggin to me. And now I'll be havin a smoke before we start back. Those roos will be enough for us to carry – we don't want more. We'll pick them up in a minute.

He dismounted, and tied his horse to a spindly eucalyptus sapling. Martin did the same with Chief, and they sat down together in the dry yellow grass beside some lichen-covered boulders, with the dogs lying nearby. All around them grew odd little bushes of a kind Martin had never seen before, to remind him that he was in alien country: bushes with clusters of long spiky leaves like bright green stars. The afternoon sun was warm now, and they tilted their hats against its glare. Dalton drew a packet of small cigars from his pocket, put one in his mouth and then held the packet out to Martin, who took one and thanked him. Dalton nodded. He lit Martin's cigar with a lucifer, and then his own. He lay back to rest on his elbow, releasing a long stream of smoke. The bright air was static, and the smoke hung almost still before finally drifting off. Dalton said nothing for a time, and the soft twittering of birds filled the silence like sounds half-heard on the edge of sleep. Out to the north, in the direction from which they'd come, the low blue waves of the ranges could be seen, rolling to that horizon which lay beyond the zone of anything real.

Unwilling to initiate conversation, Martin waited for Dalton to speak. He was still on his guard with him, but no longer as wary of him as he had been. He now judged him to be hard but not vicious, and he had to remind himself that Dalton was a criminal. He smiled, considering what his father would think of such a judgement.

What is it that amuses you?

Martin started. He became aware that Dalton had been looking at him from under the brim of his hat, his cigar jutting from his teeth.

I was just thinking about my family, and what they'd say to my being here.

You're missin them?

Not really. But I'm wondering how soon I can finish my talks with Captain Wilson and get back home.

Dalton's narrow grey eyes narrowed further. He took the cigar from his mouth and studied the tip.

That will be up to Lucas. But you have to consider that he may not let you go at all. I'm not sayin he won't – but he may not. It will all depend.

A wave of cold went through Martin. The sunlight seemed to fade, and he felt a tightening in his scrotum.

Depend on what? I thought it was agreed that I'd go back once my story was written. I thought since I came here blindfold that you'd know I have no idea of where you are, up here.

Sure, we had no agreement as such. That was your idea. As to your bein blindfold, you'll soon work out where you are by lookin around you. You'll have seen Mount Wellington in the south, and the Derwent in the east – and it's only five miles downhill from here to Berriedale, on the Main Road. So we can only let you go if we're sure we can trust you – and it's the Captain who'll decide that. He'd have to reckon that he can depend on you never to give us away to the authorities. And that's a very big gamble, I'm thinkin.

And what about you, Mr Dalton? Do you not trust my word?

Liam. You can call me Liam – and I hope I can call you Martin. Sure, I'm gettin to trust you: I believe you're bein straight with us. Lucas Wilson is impressed with you too: says you're quite a learned chap. But he's dubious about lettin you go, and I can understand his thinkin. You may have good intentions, but who knows what might happen when your story is printed in the papers and the traps begin to ask you questions down there?

Martin sat silent, looking away to the ranges, the cold that was gathering around him seeming to deepen.

Don't be too afraid, now, Dalton said. He was smiling at Martin in a way he'd not done before, his face open and friendly. After all, is it so bad here? Sure, you might grow to like it.

What are you saying? That you might not kill me after all?

Drawing on his cigar, Dalton looked amused.

Kill you, is it? Who ever spoke of that? No, the Captain might decide that you have to stay here – that's what I'm sayin.

And turn bushranger?

Well now, that would be up to you. But I'd not advise it, or you could finish on the end of a rope. No, you'd live in the community – make yourself useful. Wilson needs people who know how to farm, and educated fellas like yourself. We need more women here, so there's bound to be more children, later on. They'll need educatin – you could set up a school. Just leave the bushrangin to Lucas and me and Alan McLeod.

Tell me, Liam: why does the Captain do it? He could have had his freedom here, if he'd wanted. Why would a gentleman like him choose a life of crime?

Bushrangin, you mean?

Now Martin thought that he might meet with a rebuff. But the jocular light was still in Dalton's eyes.

Sure, you ought to have worked that out by now. You've had a good talk with the Captain, and heard his story. He's a gentleman who hates the gentry: that's what it is. He hates them for what they've done to him. That's why he'll only raid them big property-owners: the favourites of the Government, like your father – beggin your pardon. What we need from them is their money, as well as their watches, rings and jewellery – which Bill Bosworth takes to Hobart Town to sell to a fence we can trust.

He began to chuckle.

We've often had some fun on those raids, Lucas and me. On one occasion we took over a gentleman's property at Hamilton: Baxter, his name was. He had a wife and a grown son and three grown daughters, and we surprised them all at supper. He was a nasty, ill-tempered, constipated-lookin cove, with a red face. He took a high tone with us, tellin us we'd be hanged. So Lucas slapped his face to quieten him down. Then he told me to go and get the workin hands we'd tied up in the men's hut, and bring them into the dining-room. He invited them to sit down at the table, and he made Baxter and his family wait on us all, bringin us food and wine. The hands loved it, but old Baxter was ravin angry. 'How *dare* you?' he says. 'How *dare* you?' I found that amusin.

He looked sideways at Martin, keeping a straight face; but he was plainly holding back laughter.

Martin began to laugh spontaneously, and then Dalton joined in. Looking at each other, laughing without restraint, a feeling of warmth flowed between them; and Martin began to think that they might form a kind of friendship.

Dalton's laughter ended in a wheezing cough. He ground his cigar out in the grass, thumped his chest and grew serious again.

But you leave that kind of thing to us. You could make your own contribution, here in the Valley. You must know a lot about farmin, as well as book-learnin.

But farming's not what I want to do.

Is it not? And you with that beautiful property to inherit. How does your father feel about that?

He's not happy about it. He and I don't see eye to eye.

That's sad, now. Some day you may regret not gettin on with him. I'll never see my old father again, and it fills me with sorrow. Sometimes he comes to me in dreams.

Can you never get back to Ireland?

That's a bloody foolish question. Let any felon like me try and board a ship, and he's seized instantly. And even if I did so, what would I go back to in Ireland?

Silent for a moment, he looked towards the trees. When he spoke again, his voice had become low and subdued.

I come from Connemara in Galway, far in the West. Most people only speak Irish there, but when I was a boy I learned English and a good deal else in a hedge school. In the winter of 1846 – the year I was convicted – the Famine came. I've seen whole families like skeletons then, wanderin the roads. And when people had no more to eat and nowhere to turn, they stayed in their cabins and died there. The fever came as well, and no-one would go near those who caught it – when they died, they were burned in their cabins.

He fell silent again, and his silence warned Martin to say nothing.

My old father was like most people in that part of the country. He rented a cabin and five acres of land from the big landlord of our parish, General Parker. My two brothers and I helped him farm. Our mother had died long before, and that was probably a mercy. When the potatoes went, we grew oats and barley, but it wasn't enough. General Parker was a good landlord – not like some of the graspin cruel bastards who turned their tenants out and destroyed their houses. When we couldn't pay rent any more Parker didn't put us out, and he even gave us some work on his property – but little enough he had to offer. My brothers went on the public works in Galway, and my sister was employed as a house servant by Parker. I stayed on with my father, still tryin to scratch a livin from our land, and not really managin to do so. But then, when we were half-starved, I got into trouble.

One of the dogs was lying next to him; he reached out and scratched it behind the ear.

I had some friends who were worse off than we were. Their families were near starvin to death – and those boys had taken to sheep-stealin. They kept askin me to join them, and finally I did. My father was poorly, and I was thinkin what a good meal of mutton would do for him. So off I went with the boys at night, and we stole some sheep. They were General Parker's sheep, and I felt badly about that. We were caught, of course. Tried in Galway city, and given seven years' transportation.

He paused, patting the dog's head.

And your father? What became of him?

I'll never know. I'll never find out. He can neither read nor write, and neither can my brothers or my sister. I wrote a letter to them once, care of General Parker, but nothin came back. Maybe

Parker tore my letter up – I wouldn't blame him. He was good to us, and I shouldn't have stolen his sheep.

He stood up suddenly, adjusting his hat.

Time to get back. I've talked too much, I'm thinkin.

Martin stood up, and they faced each other.

No, Martin said. I'm very glad you told me this, Liam. I'll never see you now as a criminal.

Dalton's face remained expressionless, but he suddenly put out his hand and patted Martin on the shoulder.

You have a good heart, young Martin.

He turned away and began walking across the clearing, calling back to Martin as he went.

Come on, squire. Let's pick up these roos.

There was a touch of sardonic humour in his use of 'squire', but Martin read into it no sly mockery or disrespect; instead it seemed to confirm the growing good will between them.

As they rode back, their horses side by side, they passed through patches of sun in a silence that Martin found companionable. Dalton was humming a tune to himself, and Martin recognized a mournful plantation song by the Irish-American Stephen Foster: 'Massa's in the Cold, Cold Ground'. At one stage Dalton softly sang a verse: he had a pleasant voice.

Just before they reached the settlement, Dalton spoke to him again.

You say I'm not a criminal. I am now, of course, and no doubt bound for Purgatory. But not for Hell, I hope. I pray to the Blessed Virgin often enough. Maybe she'll intercede for me.

He had spoken matter-of-factly, as though about some practical legal matter, but Martin felt faintly uncomfortable with this display of Papist devotion.

I didn't intend to go bushrangin, Dalton said. The first two years I was here I was on a probation gang, doin hard labour on the roads. I behaved myself well, and was given a probation pass – which meant I could work for wages on a farm. But the property-owner I worked for was a bullyin bastard, and I allow no man to bully me. At last I gave him the back of my tongue, and got charged with insolence. I was sent back to work on a gang again, out in the bush.

He ducked under an overhanging branch, and glanced at Martin with a return of his humorous expression.

Then I got into more trouble. If you have a bad supervisor on a gang, he can make your life a misery – and that's what ours did. He'd been a convict himself, and he was a nasty bugger, God's curse on him. He took a set against me, and I bore it for a time – but I have a short temper. So one day I went for him, and I threw him in a creek. Fortunately I had no irons on, and I got away into the bush and wasn't caught, and then I went bushrangin. It was soon after that I met Lucas Wilson, and we teamed up. Without him, I'd just be a poor wanderin rogue, in constant jeopardy. He's shown me a whole new life. And if he succeeds in what he's aimin for here, who knows, we may give up crime altogether.

We've a number of men working on our farm who are ticket-of-leave, Martin said. They seem quite decent fellows, now that they've served their time. It's often made me wonder whether some men are born to be criminals, as most people think.

There are different kinds, Dalton said. Some have had desperate hard times, in the old country, and had little choice but to steal. When they get out here, all they want is a quiet life, and they'll give no more trouble, so. But there's another sort. Now and then you get a man who's born evil. There aren't many of those, but I've met one or two. Sure, they'd make your flesh crawl. They have a black demon in them – you can see it in their faces. And now I've gone and brought a creature like that up here.

Martin stared at him.

Aye. You know who I mean.

Roy Griffin?

Griffin. Lucas Wilson is mighty impressed with him just now – and a lot of lyin wicked nonsense Griffin is fillin his head with.

What is it he talks about?

Spirits. He talks about spirits. Lucas is interested in that kind of thing, and Griffin knows how to lure and bewitch him with it.

He leaned from his saddle and spat.

And I'll tell you somethin else about the man. Two mornins ago, I took a little ride to a property near Berriedale, just down the track. I'd gone there to talk to one of the convict hands: a fella that Lucas and I have dealins with. Turns out that this cove was in the Prisoners' Barracks in Hobart Town at the same time as Griffin. Roy, bein educated, was in a nice soft situation then: he worked as a clerk in the Convict Department, and could move about the town a bit in the daytime. But he tried to rape a young housemaid in a lane behind a taproom – this in broad daylight. She screamed, and he was collared by a constable. That's why he was sent to Port Arthur. I've told Lucas about it – but Griffin's convinced him that the constable was lyin, and the girl was willin. I don't think so. That's why I'll not have Griffin in my house, or anywhere near young May.

He glanced quickly at Martin through the sun and shadow, and pulled his hat low over his eyes.

Now I've warned you about the bastard. So take heed.

4

I've read your piece, Wilson said. You're a talented young man. I've written in a few corrections, but otherwise I approve. You've told my story pretty well, so far.

Leaning back in his throne-like chair, he smiled at Martin with a new sort of warmth. It was five o'clock: the Captain's hour for receiving. Sun came through the casement windows as before, lighting the spines of the books and glowing on various pieces set about the room that Martin guessed had once decorated some fashionable drawing rooms down below: a pair of candlesticks in engraved glass shades; a tall Royal Worcester vase containing wildflowers; a bell glass set over an arrangement of ferns and mosses; a mahogany writing-slope.

Frances has read it, Wilson said, and she thinks the same. Don't you, my dear?

Yes. It's good, Frances said.

Her voice was soft, and rather deep. She'd just set down a tea tray on the small round table in front of Wilson's chair, and had poured out coffees for the three of them. Now she sat on a chair opposite Martin, sipping from her bone china cup and glancing at him over the rim. Until now, he'd thought her to be a single woman who was taking the role of servant; but Liam Dalton had told him last night that she was Wilson's mistress. Martin had been curious to know something of her origins; but Dalton had told him very little. All he would say was that her full name was Frances Lambert, and that she was a free settler – not an ex-convict – who had come out to Van Diemen's Land with a husband who'd ill-treated her, and whom she'd deserted.

Martin found her large blue eyes beautiful; but there was a hint of some blank desolation in them that made them difficult to meet: the sadness he'd noticed the first time he'd seen her. She wore a long-sleeved, full-skirted cotton dress with a pale violet print, similar in style to the one she'd worn the first time he came here. It was modest, with a high neck; but because it had a tight bodice and narrowed at the waist, it outlined her full figure. She was certainly a handsome woman, he thought, though her wide mouth was of a kind that some people might find too sensual – even coarse. How old was she? Thirty? Thirty-five? A matron, certainly.

So it's agreed, Wilson said. You've begun the article well, and must soon go to the next stage. Frances and I have high hopes for the way it will turn out.

As he spoke, he looked at the woman with a confiding and indulgent expression, making Martin feel like a youth who was the topic of conversation between two adults. This gave him a stab of annoyance, and he decided to move the discussion on to another level – even if it meant raising questions that Wilson might not wish to answer.

I'm glad you approve, Captain, he said. So far, it's an account of the experiences in your life that led you to where you are at present. But now I want to deal with the more difficult part: your ideas.

Wilson pursed his finely-shaped lips, and frowned.

My ideas? What ideas are you thinking of? My theories about our Utopia? I believe I've already spoken about those to you.

Why, yes. But I need to discuss other things as well. Your larger theories. You're setting up a new society here, and you've said that it's one in which everyone will share equally. And that's caused me to wonder about a number of things. It's made me ask myself questions. Is everyone truly equal here? And are they to live in a state of nature, with nature as their religion – as Jean-Jacques Rousseau said men should do?

Now Wilson's expression changed again. His eyes narrowed further, and he ceased to smile. It was as though Martin had proved to be not quite the person he'd thought, but someone else: someone with whom it would be necessary to be cautious.

I told you he was well-read, he said to the woman, and then turned back to Martin, putting down his cup and saucer and rubbing his chin.

So: Rousseau, is it? There's a fellow to conjure with. I've been mightily impressed with his theories, Martin, but I see him as a dreamer, in the end. I doubt that he had to deal with the practical realities I've come up against.

And what are they?

Wilson didn't answer at first. Instead he gazed out the window to where the light was being invaded by an ancient gold. When he spoke again, his voice had taken on those bardic rhythms that had the power to overwhelm Martin's scepticism.

Some day, when we achieve absolute harmony here, and have all that we need – when we've only to reach out our hands to take what we want, since our orchards will be laden, and our pastures will be full of fat cattle, and no man need envy another – then, young Martin, there'll be no leaders and no followers, and I can lay down my burden.

He leaned forward abruptly, his expression suddenly grim, his pale eyes shining. His voice deepened, and filled the room.

But until that time comes, *I must lead* – and my authority must not be questioned. If it were, we'd have chaos here, and worse. Do you see?

I think so.

I hope you do. Now as to Rousseau's idea of a religion of nature, replacing those trappings of power the Christian churches have erected – that's another matter. The fellow spoke truly there – just as he spoke truly about the evils of our civilization. Its machines have produced a race that's no longer natural. Its people devour each other, like animals in a trap. And why?

He paused, looking from Martin to Frances. She sat very still, her sad eyes fixed on Wilson, her expression one of solemn devotion, as though she listened to a priest in the pulpit.

Because men no longer live in their natural situation, Wilson said. They no longer live as servants of nature, aware of the movement of the stars, and the growth of plants, and the feelings and needs of animals. Here in this valley we've discovered all that again. A new bud on a fruit tree is a miracle to us. The birth of a calf is a miracle. The water running in that creek outside is a miracle and a blessing. Our forefathers knew all that, and thanked their Creator. I know it, and do the same.

He surveyed the room, where the yellow light that came from outside was growing thicker, so that objects in corners became dim. Like Frances, Martin now kept very still, compelled by the Captain's beautiful voice – which would have compelled him no matter what Wilson chose to speak about. Suddenly, Wilson looked towards the nearest open window, which framed a native bush of a type unknown to Martin, with spiny branches and clusters of starry white flowers. A honeyeater was perched on one of the twigs, taking nectar from the flowers: a small, olive-green bird with a brilliant yellow throat. It raised its head as they watched, and uttered a small sharp cry.

Look! Wilson said. He pointed, his face filled with delight, his tone confiding; almost caressing. Look at that little honeyeater. See what he does? See? After each sip from the flower he throws back his head and gives a little call. He's thanking his Creator.

As though in obedience, the bird repeated its performance, sipping from a flower, tilting back its head and releasing its small, sharp sound.

Frances smiled, for the first time.

You're right, Lucas. That's just what he does! You notice everything.

All three of them now watched the honeyeater, and in that moment, Martin warmed to Lucas Wilson without reserve. That he was somewhat vain, and conscious of his looks and magnetism, no longer mattered. Martin knew now why Liam Dalton gave the Captain his absolute loyalty. Wilson was a great spirit, he thought, capable of ruthlessness but also of the utmost gentleness, and filled with a special vision of the world and its riches. And Martin decided that he was in no hurry after all to go back down below; he wanted only to be with Wilson, and to learn all he could of his ideas and his nature. By staying here with the Captain, he would learn how to ride the highest air-currents of the world; he would thrill to excitements granted only to a few; he would be freed forever from life's tedious back lanes; he would never again be bored, or without true purpose. This was his life's turning-point.

Wilson was looking at him again, gazing in an almost musing manner, his lips still touched with a half smile. He had lit his long pipe, and held it poised in his hand. And what he said now sent a small shock through Martin: it was as though the Captain had read his thoughts.

I hope that answers your question, young man – or begins to answer it. But there's much more that you and I can discuss. I've needed to explore ideas with a fellow of your education, and there are none up here I can do it with. So you mustn't be in a hurry to go – you've been sent here with a purpose.

I know it, Martin said.

He was conscious of a thickness in his voice; and he saw, out of the corner of his eye, that Frances was looking at him curiously.

But he didn't turn his gaze away from Wilson, who smiled more broadly now and nodded, putting the stem of his pipe back in his mouth.

Good, he said. Good. You're one of us, Martin, if you want to be. And now let's get back to the point.

He raised a long forefinger.

My religion is nature – you'll have understood that now. God is in nature, and I need no temple to worship him in. When I go out into our myrtle forest, then I have my temple. But this doesn't mean that I don't seek further to understand the religious mysteries.

He waved the pipe at his books.

I read. I read.

You read too much, the woman said. All those books. They'll turn your brain, Lucas.

He turned to her fondly, and spoke without condescension.

So you say, my dear. But you have a wisdom not given to men like me. You need no books.

He turned back to Martin with a wry expression.

A woman like Frances is naturally close to the spirits of nature – but a fellow like me must look hard to get a glimpse of them. I must look for wisdom in books, as well as in nature. I read my Bible, but I also read about those ancients who had other beliefs besides the Christian. Plotinus, now. Have you read him?

Martin had to confess that he hadn't; and now Wilson spoke of a supreme being called the One, and of the World Soul, which created the souls of all living beings. The rhythms of his voice gave his talk a mesmeric quality, and it would later mingle in Martin's memory with the semi-rustic charms of the sitting-room: with the dying glow on the pink bush furniture and the books; with the mingled odours of smoke from the fire and from Wilson's pipe; with the faint scents of the wildflowers on the table.

We can reach those higher realms of the World Soul if we have the refinement to do so, Wilson said. Then we can unite with the One. But if we fail, we're bound to the lowest levels of the material world, where the sources of evil are.

This sounds like the beliefs of the Gnostics, Martin said. They were heretics, weren't they?

The Church saw them as that. You can see why, but their ideas are interesting. The world not created by God, but by a demon. God removed altogether from this world, having nothing to do with it. A notion that's rather frightening, I admit. Roy Griffin's interested in Gnosticism.

Yes, he would be, wouldn't he?

Frances had spoken suddenly, and they both turned to her. In the gathering dimness, her face looked paler than before. She stood up now and began to walk away, speaking over her shoulder.

Demons would suit him, I believe.

Come now, Frances, Wilson said. This is just superstition. Griffin knows a lot about the spirit world.

Too much, perhaps.

She had reached a table in the centre of the room, and had picked up some lucifers. She struck one of them and lit an oil lamp that stood there. Its soft glow, coming through the glass chimney, illuminated her face as she looked across at Wilson, and flared in her sad eyes.

You'll be wanting supper soon, she said. I'll start getting it ready. Will Martin be eating with us?

Not tonight, perhaps, Wilson said. Next time. He'll be very welcome. He and I have much to talk about.

He looked at Martin sideways, and Martin was filled with a pleased anticipation: with a proud elation like nothing else in his life.

That night, lying under the possum-skin rug on the couch in Liam Dalton's dining-room, memories of home revolved in his head.

The scent of clean sheets, instead of this smoke-smelling quilt of animal skins. Good food at the well-set family dinner table. His room, with its books and newspapers. Scents through the window from the farm in the morning, and the murmuring voices of the servants. His sister's laughter from a neighbouring room, and the cook's loud voice from the kitchen. The friends he visited in Hobart Town: part-time journalists at the cluttered office of the *Courier*, eager to share the gossip of the town; fellow-students from his College days, with whom he talked books, and visited the theatre, and debated and laughed. Left behind such a short time ago, the solid substance of the only life he'd known had become unreal: flimsy as a dream.

He regretted the anxiety he must be causing his family; but with under a week gone by, he didn't yet miss them. His brother William and he had little in common. He was fond of Lucy, but there was little they could talk about either; neither she nor William had any great love of books or ideas. As for his father, it was good not to look at his obdurate face for a time, thin lips moving to utter reproofs and to forbid him the life he wanted.

Everything in Nowhere Valley was just beginning, he felt sure, and unimaginable dimensions lay in front of him. His one misgiving was that he might become involved in breaking the law – and he suspected that even this might be acceptable, against all his principles and better instincts. The talk this evening had created an intoxication in his brain, and he could imagine Lucas Wilson leading him anywhere.

The next day was Saturday. In the evening, Martin went for a walk after tea. He'd done this before, and had enjoyed the solitude. This time, however, an encounter took place.

Nowhere Valley fell into shadow early. The summer twilight continued longest on the hills that enclosed it, and he decided to make his way up the nearest of these, in the east. He'd been there on a previous evening. From the top of it, a remote silver bend of the Derwent could be seen, like a memory of the world below.

The hill was only sparsely grown with gums. Wilson had begun to have it cleared, in his ceaseless efforts to open up the countryside for grazing, and its stretches of tussock grass and wildflowers were pleasant for walking. Martin's long shadow moved in front of him, while behind him in the west the sun sank towards the rim of the flat-topped mountains. It was utterly quiet, except for the evening twittering of birds and the distant lowing of cows in the settlement, as they came in to be milked. When he sensed that he was being followed, he didn't at first turn around; he decided that he'd imagined it, and that this was merely a manifestation of that sense of being watched that was with him much of the time here. But the feeling persisted, and he finally looked over his shoulder.

Roy Griffin was toiling up the hill behind him. His shadow, fantastically elongated, reached across the dry yellow grass almost to Martin's feet, as though it were an independent entity determined to catch him up; and Martin had an unpleasant sensation of alarm, causing his heart to race: a sensation all the more unpleasant for being without justification, since Griffin presumably offered him no harm. But he hadn't forgiven Griffin for the insult to his sister; he'd avoided being thrown together with him ever since they'd arrived here, and it annoyed him considerably to encounter the man now, in a place so deserted that he could hardly find an excuse to avoid conversation. He guessed that Griffin was following him expressly for that reason, and there was therefore nothing else to do but to stop and wait for him.

Griffin came up to him, smiling. It was an ingratiating smile, but one which suggested unguessable intentions. He looked much as he usually did, except for a grey wideawake hat which he'd no doubt acquired at the commissariat store, and which made him resemble a travelling tinker.

Good evening, Mr Dixon. You're out for a constitutional?

Obviously.

Griffin compressed his lips in a parody of concern.

Oh dear. You're still angry with me.

I'm not angry with you. I simply want little to do with you. That ought to be evident.

Griffin rubbed his chin, but seemed in no way affronted. Nothing, it seemed, could have that effect on him, and he grinned as though at a good joke.

Oh yes, my dear fellow. You make it very evident.

Then why do you follow me?

To ask you to change your mind about me – and to offer you an apology. I shouldn't have spoken to you as I did, when we came here through the bush. We both know what I refer to. I can only ask you to understand something, Mr Dixon. I'd been a prisoner, and I'd made my escape with Liam Dalton by going through an ordeal that was almost beyond my strength. I was exhausted and half-starved – and when I drank brandy, it was after a period of long abstinence. It went to my head, and I spoke in a way that I'd not have done sober. I must ask you to forgive me. Will you do that?

Martin hesitated. Something in Griffin's face made him doubt the man's sincerity: a kind of smugness, as though he forgave himself. But then Martin considered that he might be misjudging him in this; so when Griffin held out his hand he took it, and reluctantly agreed to forget the incident. Griffin's look of satisfaction at this ought to have been reassuring; yet even this somehow struck a false note, making Martin feel he'd been tricked into a reconciliation against his will.

Griffin waved his hand towards the top of the hill.

Shall we go on? The view from the top must be fine.

They toiled on up the slope. For a few minutes Griffin was silent; then he spoke again, glancing at Martin quickly from under his shapeless hat.

You and I have good reason to be friends, you know. Captain Wilson thinks that we should be.

Oh? Has he said so?

Not in so many words. But he's spoken about you to me, and has said that you and I should have much in common. He wants us to visit him together, to discuss ideas. He's starved for the sort of intellectual company you and I can give him. He calls you a highly educated young man who'll be a valuable addition to his community. He's very much impressed with you.

Martin made no response to this, but stared straight ahead, conscious of Griffin's ingratiating sideways stare. Deeply put out, he tried to maintain a neutral expression, while digesting the fact that Griffin's presence at any future meetings would take all pleasure from his discussions with Wilson.

The Captain told me a little about your latest talk with him, Griffin said.

And what did he tell you?

They were nearing the brow of the hill now, and Griffin increased his pace without at first replying. Close to the top, he halted by a group of tall, lichen-covered stones, swung around, and looked back at Martin.

That you've read such philosophers as Plato and Rousseau. He's very much impressed with that. And I believe he found you were even acquainted with the Gnostics. The Gnostics interest me too, my dear. Before I began to gamble and carouse, I studied them: I didn't entirely waste my time as a scholar.

His grin now had a sly quality, as though they were to discuss a mutual interest in something dubious.

The Captain and I merely touched on such things, Martin said. I have no great knowledge of Gnosticism.

You're very modest, Mr Dixon. However, it's possible I can tell you things about that system you may not have heard of. They certainly interested the Captain. They might be of interest to you too.

Martin recalled now what Liam Dalton had said concerning the 'lying wicked nonsense' Griffin spoke about to Wilson, and his unease increased. Yet in spite of himself, he began to be curious.

Perhaps so, he said.

Griffin nodded, seeming to consider his next words. His eyes held Martin's as they'd done by the fire in the bush; and as before, Martin found them filling his field of vision. Time paused, it seemed. The two of them were bathed in gentle sun up here, but the shadows of the rocks and trees were spreading far across the grass, while much of the valley below lay in shade.

As you may know, Griffin said softly, the Gnostics said that we're trapped in a prison, here in this world. Our task is to escape it. We can do this through the help of the wise serpent – the one who was the enemy of the false God of the Old Testament. He offers us secret knowledge – as he did to our first parents. Then we can reach our true home: the source of the Divine Light.

Heresy, surely, Martin said.

Not heresy: magic! The ancient Gnostics knew that we live in a magical universe, filled with magical beings. Some are good, some are evil, and want to devour us. What we have to do is to find the ones who are helpers. They'll lead us to knowledge, and the light.

And you believe these things?

Of course.

Griffin waved his hand toward a line of eucalypts on the far side of the hill.

There are magical beings all around us now. This place is full of them: they're over there in those trees. If you paid attention, you'd see it.

Martin laughed, attempting a note of incredulity, and said that he doubted it. But Griffin didn't smile in response; instead he stared back at Martin without expression, his face becoming mask-like. A faint breeze had sprung up, stirring the tops of the gums he'd pointed to, and Martin began to feel chilly: more chilly than was natural on such a mild evening.

We'll talk about this again, said Griffin, when we meet with the Captain. You'll need to open your mind, as he does.

I must be getting back, Martin said. He'd spoken abruptly, but he suddenly wanted to get away from Griffin as quickly as possible.

Must you, indeed?

Griffin's expression told Martin that he'd read his discomfiture, and was amused by it.

Well, good evening to you, he said. I'll stay up here for a while. It's a good place to think, and look out over the world.

Martin muttered some sort of goodbye, raised his hand, and began to walk down the hill. He turned once, halfway down, and looked back. Griffin was sitting on one of the stones, and seemed to be watching him. From this far off, though, it was hard to be sure. The distance and the late, glowing light distorted his face, making it resemble a gargoyle's, under the wide-brimmed hat.

That night, he had bad dreams. Most of them were confused, but what all of them had in common was that he found himself walking through strange and repellent landscapes: places that he badly wanted to escape. Griffin was walking there too, and he was no longer smiling. Instead he looked at Martin with a spiteful expression; and all the while he was talking, talking, talking.

What was he saying? Martin didn't know; nor did he know why the scenes they moved through had such threat in them. Dark, empty landscapes with few trees, in which it was neither night nor day, they seemed innocuous on the surface: without visible threat. And yet they created an inward despair and dread whose nature was difficult to define. He only knew that the dread was of some kind of tedium – and that the tedium was the key to the nature of the dread.

Waking in Dalton's dark dining-room, he had the conviction that these had been no ordinary dreams – and that Roy Griffin had somehow invaded them. Such a thought was absurd and outrageous, and he tried to dimiss it. And yet it would not be dismissed. In the dark before dawn, under his possum-skin rug, he was possessed by the notion that the Griffin of real life had actually done this with intent, having planned it after their meeting on the hillside.

He sat up, lighting the candle that stood on a trunk beside his couch, and tried to shut Griffin out of his thoughts. But very soon the man was back, floating in his mind like one of those banal melodies that sometimes revolved in the brain, however much one tried to blank them out.

Two days after his encounter with Griffin, Martin attended his first meeting in the Lodge, at eight in the evening.

Halfway down the big room was a huge stone fireplace in which a generous fire burned. An oil lamp hung on chains from the sawn-timber ceiling. On two rows of benches sat the members of the community: the whole population of Wilson's Utopia. Martin was seated on the front bench on the right, together with Liam Dalton and Alan McLeod. Frances Lambert was sitting in the front row opposite, together with Bill Bosworth and his family: his wife Emma, the girl called May, and Benjamin, a boy of about seven. Emma Bosworth was the woman Martin had seen in the farmyard on his first morning here: lean and worn-looking, with lank fair hair. He realized now that she and Frances were the only adult females in the settlement. On the bench behind this group sat Joe Jarvis and Roy Griffin.

At the head of the room, a table and a chair were placed on a low wooden dais. Here Lucas Wilson sat alone, sombrely attired for evening in a dark blue lounge jacket with brass buttons. He was silent and grave, studying his flock, apparently waiting to begin the meeting. Both elbows were propped on the table, his hands locked under his chin. Two candles on the table lit his face with a lemon glow: an effect that was somewhat theatrical. People shifted and coughed, speaking in low murmurs. There was no laughter, and Martin wondered if this was because they were all a little afraid of the Captain. He wasn't sure what he'd expected from this meeting in an outlaw hideaway: a night of gossip and carousing, perhaps? Instead he might have been attending a civic gathering in some law-abiding town, and he took it in with bemused surprise; with a sense of unreality.

There was a slight stir at the back, and heavy feet advanced up the aisle between the rows: two men had come in late, and seated themselves now in the second row opposite, next to Roy Griffin and Joe Jarvis. Liam had told Martin about these men, but this was the first time he'd seen them. They were escaped convicts whom Liam and the Captain had recently come upon in the bush near Goat Hills, and who'd begged to be given shelter. Their names were Henry Hand and Isaac Smallshaw, and Martin didn't like the look of them. Was this prejudice? No, he decided; their looks would have repelled him no matter whether they were convict or free.

Hand was a big, powerful man in his late twenties, with a heavy, clumsy-looking body, a pasty face, and close-cropped hemp-coloured hair. His large, bulging eyes had dark rings under them, and his expression was sullen. Smallshaw was stocky and dark: about thirty or so, also with prison-cropped hair. He hadn't shaved for some time, and his chin was black with stubble. His expression was resentful and suspicious, and he darted looks everywhere, as though in search of something that would confirm his suspicion. Roy Griffin, who'd arrayed himself for the meeting in a fine white shirt and cravat, leaned sideways now and said something to Smallshaw. The dark man glanced at him quickly, but appeared to make no reply.

The Captain stood up now, both hands on the table, and voices died away quickly.

Welcome, friends, he said. Before we come to business, I thought we might ask Alan McLeod to give us some music.

There was a murmur of assent, and the fat man made his way up to the platform, carrying his flute. He wasn't wearing his monk's habit tonight; instead, he was prosaically clad in a voluminous blue blouse secured by a big leather belt. He looked about the room with his open-mouthed smile, his eyes wide and innocent.

I'll give ye a little air from my native country, he said. It's about a place where we go when we die, called the Land of the Ever-young. It lies west of the Hebrides, beyond the sunset.

His playing was highly professional, and the air he played was one Martin found wistful and charming, and unlike anything else he'd heard. Could this man really be a rogue, who produced sounds of such beauty? Yet he was: Liam had said that McLeod had been an expert forger back in Glasgow, and had been convicted again of forgery out here – escaping after that to join Wilson's band. When his performance was done, Wilson led the clapping. Alan then agreed to sing, inviting Joe Jarvis to accompany him. Little Joe produced a concertina from under the bench and hurried up to the platform: a jaunty gnome, looking smaller than ever beside McLeod's massive figure. The song that they performed was unknown to Martin, and he was startled to hear that it began with his own name. Alan had a fine tenor voice, high and true, and little Joe joined in the last line of each verse with a plaintive, reedy voice which was also true, grinning at the audience as he did so, and nodding waggishly at Martin when the young man's name was pronounced.

Oh, Martin said to his man, fie, man, fie,
Martin said to his man, who's the fool now?
Oh, Martin said to his man, fill thou the cup and I
the can,
Thou hast well drunken, man, who's the fool now?

I saw the man in the moon, fie, man, fie,
I saw the man in the moon, who's the fool now?
I saw the man in the moon clouting at St Peter's shoon,
Thou hast well drunken, man, who's the fool now?

The repetition of 'who's the fool now' seemed to amuse Wilson's community like a private joke: they joined in with Joe on the last line, and laughed every time this occurred. Alan and Joe left the platform to loud applause; and Martin sat smiling with delight. This strange little ballad of the people had sent a wave of exhilaration through him; it had heightened his sense of the uniqueness of his situation, so that while the music had lasted, he'd been able to tell himself that by coming to this hidden valley, he'd entered a place like the faery hill of fable: a region that nobody down in the flatland could ever know.

What followed caused his romantic intoxication to fade.

Wilson, seated at the table again with a notebook in front of him, now opened the meeting for discussion. The purpose of this, it turned out, was for the people to discuss issues and problems: in particular, to draw attention to shortages of items necessary to the working of the farm, and of any other necessities that couldn't be manufactured in the Valley. Bill Bosworth, who apparently did most of the blacksmithing and carpentry here, requested certain extra tools for his forge and his carpenters' shop. Emma Bosworth needed material to make new clothing for her son Benjamin, who was growing fast. Alan McLeod said that they were running out of tea, sugar and whale oil for the lamps. So it went on, while Wilson made lists in his notebook with a pencil. Finally he looked up, throwing down the pencil and sitting back.

All noted, he said. Bill, you'll be able to buy quite a few of those items down in Berriedale – I have just enough money in the chest. You might even go in to Hobart Town. I want you to bring me newspapers from there, and some books that I'll note down for you. Some other things – and a fresh supply of money – will have to be left to Liam and me. We'll need to pay a visit to some properties below.

He looked across at Dalton and smiled faintly.

I believe that's all, he said. Unless anyone has something to add?

I have, Captain.

The voice was loud and hoarse. Henry Hand had stood up, looking larger than ever on his feet, wearing the sullen expression that seemed to be permanent with him.

You say you and Liam Dalton will be going down below. You'll be raiding some properties, won't you?

Wilson merely stared at him, and waited.

Because if that's right, Hand said, we'd like to come with you – me and Isaac here.

I'm afraid that won't be possible, Wilson said.

Why not?

Isaac Smallshaw had spoken now, still seated, his voice a low growl. Wilson looked at him, his face blank.

Because Dalton and I carry out these operations alone. We prefer it that way. Taking more people only makes for confusion.

But look here, said Hand, and his tone had become threatening. We thought this was a bushranging gang. We joined you to see some bushranging. We ain't cut out to be farmers – that's not the life my mate and I want to lead.

Wilson studied him for a moment without replying, and his light eyes had taken on the empty look Martin had seen in them before. When he answered, his voice was unusually low and even.

Let me remind you that you begged us to bring you here, Mr Hand – you and your friend here. You were fearful of being taken, and you wanted refuge. We said we'd give it to you, and we told you the terms you must agree to if you joined us. What's changed? Is there something you didn't understand?

We didn't understand that we'd be nothing but bleeding farmhands. We're willing to do some work – but we expected to come raiding with you, as well. We expected to get down below and have some good times.

Hand was still standing – the only person in the room to be on his feet – and he turned to survey the group, as though in search of support. But all faces were blank, like Wilson's. Hand frowned, his mouth working, his chest rising and falling. He appeared to be striving to control his temper. When Wilson answered, it was as though he was instructing a difficult child.

Let me explain, Hand. We don't see raiding as good times. It's merely a necessity. As to contact with society below – that's what we try to avoid.

Now Smallshaw got to his feet, his expression as rebellious as Hand's.

That's all very well, Captain Wilson. But what gives you the right to rule over us like this?

Again Wilson was silent for a moment, contemplating the two of them while they glared back at him. Then, without haste, he drew a revolver from somewhere inside his jacket, and cocked it. The click of the hammer in the silent room was distinct. He placed the weapon on the table in front of him, and Martin saw that it was the Adams from his father's gunroom.

This does. Do you want to argue with it?

As he spoke, Martin became aware that Liam Dalton had got up quietly from the bench beside him and had moved to stand with his back to the opposite wall. He too was holding a revolver, suspended in front of his shoulder to point at the ceiling. Like Wilson, Dalton was expressionless, his eyes fixed on the two convicts, and Martin had the impression that he and Wilson had performed this tableau often in the past.

Hand looked at Dalton, and then back at Wilson. So did Smallshaw.

We ain't able to argue with them bloody guns, Hand said. That's clear.

He sat down, and Smallshaw did the same.

Good. And now let me ask you a question, Wilson said. Are you prepared to be proper members of this community, and to pull your weight, or not? If not, you're free to leave.

You told us no-one could leave, Hand muttered. Otherwise, you'd croak them.

I'll let you both leave, if you wish, and take your chances.

What does that mean? said Smallshaw.

We'd give you half an hour's start. We'll even give you guns. It's the kind of challenge that Mr Dalton and I enjoy.

There was silence. Hand was now looking sulkily at his boots, while Smallshaw stared at Wilson with an incredulous expression. Wilson seemed to smile back, but his smile had a wooden and chilling rigidity; he scarcely seemed the same man with whom Martin had held cultivated discourse.

Well? Wilson said. I need an answer.

We don't have no bloody choice, Hand muttered. That's plain. We'll stay.

Wilson nodded.

I'd like you to understand that Dalton and I aren't threatening you, he said. You asked what our authority was – that is, how we protect ourselves against betrayal and rebellion – and I've shown you. We've started a new community up here, free of the world below and its laws – and the law of the gun is the only one we have. When we achieve complete harmony, the gun will no longer be needed.

He looked away from the two convicts, his gaze moving about the room, and his voice took on a fervent, almost passionate note.

Believe me, I long for that day. In the meantime, since you chose of your own free will to join us, and since that can't be undone, I want you to be happy here, I assure you. I'll talk with you both later, and see what kind of work you'd prefer, and I'll do my best to accommodate you. As to going below – when we know we can trust you, that might be arranged, provided there's no violence. I can't speak fairer than that. Now: will you cast in your lot with us, with no hard feelings?

His smile now was warm, and he leaned towards them and opened both hands, like a preacher giving a blessing.

Hand was silent for a moment; then he nodded, and muttered yes. Smallshaw did the same, and Wilson stood up, surveying the room with a genial expression.

I believe our main business is over. If you'd all like to go to the table at the back, there are glasses of Bill's beer for everyone, and some pies.

Voices rose in conversation, and people began to move to the back of the room, with backward glances at the two convicts. Martin stood up, conscious that he was damp with perspiration under his shirt. Walking towards him, Liam Dalton looked at him with a straight face, and winked.

Wilson and Dalton set out on their expedition to the world below the following day. Soon after the noon meal, Martin walked down to the stables to see them off.

Wilson was already waiting, mounted on a black stallion that Martin had admired before now, but had not seen ridden. It stepped about restlessly, but Wilson easily controlled it. Dalton led out the bay gelding he'd brought up here from Richmond, swung himself into the saddle and sat looking down at Martin.

We'll be back tomorrow, he said. Anything you need, see Bill Bosworth.

He and Alan McLeod are in charge, Wilson told him. They're both well armed. If there's any trouble, go and see them.

Both tall men, appearing even larger on horseback, were looking at Martin now with their eyes narrowed against the sun. Both had rifles in their saddle scabbards, and were dressed almost identically, in broad-brimmed felt hats, dark blue pilot coats and top boots. There was another similarity between them, Martin saw, more profound than the matching of their outfits. It was the appearance that soldiers had: the seasoned and impassive look of men whose job was to deal with violence as a matter of routine. Lucas Wilson, his tanned, knob-like cheekbones reflecting the direct sun like polished wood, his eyes almost blank in its rays, was no longer the genteel, elegantly-clad philosopher of the Lodge. Another self had emerged, which seemed most likely to be his true one.

Dalton jerked his head, looking beyond Martin's shoulder.

You might help Alan by keeping an eye on those three coves, while we're away.

Turning, Martin saw that Liam was indicating the doorway of the bachelors' house, just beyond the stables. The two convicts had emerged there, together with Roy Griffin. They'd no doubt been having their dinner; now they'd come to watch Wilson and Dalton leave, and all three wore an identical expression: one of sullen, deep resentment. Wilson looked across at them briefly, but said nothing; he seemed already to be somewhere else, and he swung his horse around and set off at a trot.

Goodbye now, Dalton said. He raised a hand to Martin, and then followed after Wilson.

Watching the two ride away, Martin saw them now as Griffin and Hand and Smallshaw must be seeing them: as raiders. All other aspects of their natures and personalities had faded into insignificance, and they'd become deeply enviable to the trio in the doorway, who hungered to join them, who were filled with anger at being denied it. They had taken on the magnetism of warriors: raiders from outside the zone of civilized order; heirs of a tradition going back to prehistory: men whose vocation was to descend on the placid, hard-working people of the lowlands and plunder the products of their labours. And just for a moment, understanding the hunger of the watchers, Martin was disconcerted to find that he shared it. Briefly, he too yearned to go with Wilson and Dalton; he too wanted to be a raider.

Looking across to the hut he found that Griffin's gaze had turned to him; and Griffin nodded, seeming to signal an awareness of their common longing.

Martin made no response; he turned away abruptly and began walking back to the house.

5

February, and summer at its height.

Up here, in spite of the season, it would suddenly cloud over, and rain showers would weave across the Valley. These were brief, and often accompanied by slanting rays of sun. The landscape was never the same. Gold would light up one hill, while another, at an opposite point in the land, was veiled in rain. Nothing was static. The weather changed by the hour, and sometimes a look of false winter would arrive. Hard surfaces, cool stillness, and a dramatic clarity in things. Blue-grey light, and a sense of crisis behind appearances. The promise of a larger life elsewhere: in some unfound region, perhaps.

Wilson invited him to come walking at this time, and their walks became quite frequent. They would go up on to the hilltops in the early afternoon, and survey the world and talk. Mostly it was Wilson who did the talking, and Martin would listen; but Martin's interjections and questions seemed important to the Captain, and would set him off in new directions.

These hills inspire me, Wilson said. Look at them, Martin: their forms are an endless mystery.

He pointed across the land that lay everywhere below them. The afternoon was sunny, with a faint breeze, and they were walking across one of the hills in the east, through an open area of grass and boulders. They seemed to walk close to the sky, and Martin was buoyed up by an illusion of limitless freedom. Below them on the western side of the hill stretched a green open pasture where the dairy herd grazed, enclosed by a post-and-rail fence. Beyond this, on the far side of the valley, the dense hills of bush rose above the roofs of the settlement, and beyond these again stretched those long blue ranges, hazed with sun, which seemed to belong in another dimension. It was to these that Wilson had pointed.

I study them for hours, he said, and I ask myself what is it they hide. Not just unexplored country, surely. No – something more. The entrance to a sphere beyond our knowledge. The dimension of the divine, perhaps.

He turned to look at Martin as they walked, his chestnut mane fluttering in the wind, and Martin hesitated, unsure whether this suggestion was serious, or one of those poetic flights which Wilson sometimes indulged in. Before he could attempt an answer Wilson had turned away and had fixed his gaze on the ranges again, seeming to muse as he spoke.

You asked me yesterday whether I truly believed in God. Sometimes I'm not sure – but I know I believe in the mystery of the hills.

I suppose you mean the mystery of appearances, Martin said. What the philosophers argue about. Whether the world we perceive is created by our senses, or is really something quite different.

Wilson thrust out his prominent lower lip with an expression of contempt.

Philosophers! he said. I know the kinds of fellows you're talking about. Berkeley. Hume. Kant. Am I right?

Yes. I had to study them at College.

I've had a look at them. Heavy reading – and they all say the same thing.

He pointed to a nearby eucalypt.

That tree is green only because I see it as green. What it really looks like, outside our senses, we can have no idea. We're trapped inside our heads, they say. Well I say no! All those fellows are talking about is the mind. But it's not my mind that perceives the mystery in those hills – it's my spirit. And the spirit isn't trapped in the head, or limited by the senses. The spirit can go anywhere. That's what Wordsworth knew – and poets know far more than your philosophers. You remember Wordsworth's great ode? He speaks of a time in his boyhood when the meadows and groves of Grasmere were filled with a heavenly light – 'the glory and the freshness of a dream'. Then, when he grew older, the light faded – as it does for nearly everyone once childhood's gone. Well I tell you, Martin, it hasn't faded for me. Here, in this island at the end of the earth, it's returned. I've only to look at the hills.

He had come to a halt, head thrown back, hair flung about in the breeze, hands on his hips, smiling at Martin triumphantly. How he loves to strike an attitude, the young man thought; but despite this secret irreverence, he was moved. Wilson's voice had become deeper; he'd employed those theatrical cadences he always did when he spoke of poetry – an effect that came close to being comically extravagant, but which Martin still found impressive – and he'd given expression to things that Martin had formulated dimly in his own mind, but had never imagined hearing articulated by anyone else. This excited him, and caused his admiration for Wilson to grow stronger: to approach a sort of veneration.

They walked on, and Martin introduced the topic of Utopia. He needed guidance, he said, on how Wilson wished him to write about Nowhere Valley in his article. He needed to know more about Wilson's ideas.

I've been thinking about that, Wilson said. It's a very large topic – too large for a newspaper article. What I think we should do is work on a book together. I believe that you're the fellow to do it with me. You have the intellect and imagination. What do you say, Martin?

For some moments, Martin said nothing, and Wilson watched him obliquely, slowing his pace.

I'm honoured that you want me to do it, Martin said. But that could take a long time – years, even. I wasn't expecting to stay up here so long.

No. But dealing with the unexpected is the mark of an outstanding man. I'm sure you'll come up to the challenge. We can really get down to it in the winter, when the cold and the snow keep us indoors much of the time. I need you here, Martin. I have no-one else with your understanding and education. I need a partner with those gifts. I hope you won't refuse me.

They had come to a halt again, and were facing each other. The breeze had become stronger: their words were whipped away as soon as spoken, and they had both raised their voices a little. Staring at the Captain, whose luminous, narrowed eyes were fixed on his face, Martin thought: It's not a partner he wants; it's a disciple. He was trying to keep his equilibrium, and his thoughts were in confusion. He had wanted to stay longer in Nowhere Valley, compelled as he was by Wilson's powerful and seductive personality, but he'd not thought about it realistically in terms of time. The idea of committing himself to years here was daunting; and what added to his unease was the suspicion that Wilson's appeal to him to stay was a mere gesture, and that even he would prove to be no exception to the Captain's iron rule: that nobody who came to the Valley was ever allowed to leave. He also reminded himself that there were two Lucas Wilsons: the cultivated and seemingly gentle individual who stood on this hilltop with him, and the remorseless lawbreaker in whom a cold, wild rage was always close to the surface.

Let me think about it, Captain, Martin said.

Lucas. It's time you called me Lucas, since we're going to be literary partners.

Lucas, then. I'm happy to be able to call you that.

It was true: an absurd thrill of gratification flowed through him, as though he'd been granted a rare honour.

I do value our talks, he said. I'm also very happy to stay here for some time – but I hadn't planned on years.

Plans can change, when life beckons you in a new direction. I know you'll give it serious thought, Martin. Meanwhile, we're partners in this undertaking, aren't we?

He held out his hand, smiling, and Martin shook it and nodded his agreement. Then Wilson looked at the sun.

Time to be getting back, he said, and they set off down the hill. After a time, Wilson said:

We'll discuss Utopia in detail when next we meet. But if you have a particular question you'd like me to think about, ask it now.

Martin had already formulated a question which he believed to be more important than any other; but for a moment, he hesitated. He feared that it might cause the second Wilson to emerge – the man whose anger was sudden and unpredictable. Martin was frankly frightened of that Wilson; but he summoned up his courage.

I understand perfectly that you hope in the end to create a community where all are equal, and where all share in the wealth they create. When that's achieved, there'll be no more need for obedience to an armed leader. But what I wonder about is this. It seems to me that it will work with people of equal understanding – people who share your ideals. But what about those without that capacity – men who are brutish?

Wilson turned his head and looked at him hard.

You're thinking of those two convicts.

I suppose I am.

Yes. Of course. And you've put your finger on the greatest problem that I have, young fellow: I won't deny it.

Wilson walked on without speaking for some moments, jerking downhill. Then he spoke in a low voice, almost to himself.

Such people are children – and I've made another world for them here. I've given them peace and security and freedom. Yet for some of them, it's still not enough.

He shook his head, and his lower lip crept out, rather in the manner of an aggrieved small boy. In that moment, Martin saw that there was a childish side to the man: one which might prevent him from ever engaging with the problem realistically. Yet it didn't cause him to lose his respect for Wilson, since Martin was not far removed from the actuality of childhood. Instead, it woke a surge of sympathy in him, and he decided not to trouble Wilson further.

We can discuss it next time, he said.

Yes, Wilson said. Next time.

Martin had not forgotten Roy Griffin's claim that a meeting was supposed to take place in which the two of them would exchange ideas with Wilson. But as time went by and Wilson made no suggestion of it, Martin suspected that the proposed meeting had been an invention of Griffin's: a lie intended to unsettle him.

His life here was agreeable now, with its quiet and unvarying rural rhythms, and he began to feel that he'd been in the Valley for a good deal longer than in fact he had. Time here would have seemed almost static, had it not been for his pocket watch. His tasks on the farm had grown lighter – probably on Wilson's orders – and he often went hunting wallaby with Wilson and Dalton together.

It was following one of these hunting trips that he persuaded Wilson to pose for his camera. The three had stabled their horses and had delivered the wallabies to Bill Bosworth, who would skin them and carve them up for meat and store the hides. Now, as they walked on towards Dalton's house, carrying their guns, Martin asked both Wilson and Dalton to pose. Both refused.

I'd prefer not, Wilson said. I don't want my likeness getting into the wrong hands.

That's right, Dalton said. Who knows where such a picture might end up?

Martin gave them his solemn word that he would show the pictures to no-one. He would keep them, and leave them to his heirs – and some future generation might value them, if Nowhere Valley was successful.

This calculated flattery clearly appealed to Wilson, and he agreed to pose. But nothing would change Dalton's mind. He shook his head with a stubborn expression, and walked off into his house. Perhaps, Martin thought, there was an irrational part of Liam that saw the camera as a dubious form of magic or trickery, to be avoided by sensible men. There were still quite a few who saw the new invention in that way.

At first Wilson wanted to change into more formal clothing; but Martin persuaded him to stay just as he was, in his serge blouse and neckerchief and moleskins. He wanted him to be seen, Martin said, as the sort of man he was in everyday life, sharing the work of the settlement. This appeal also worked, and Wilson waited patiently while Martin went inside the house and brought out his cumbersome equipment: his camera, glass plates, tripods and wooden portable darkroom, with its collection of chemicals and bulky tent. With Wilson watching him quizzically, Martin was now quite nervous. He was using the new wet plate process, which had only been in use for three years: a complex procedure which had to be completed in ten minutes, from the dipping of the plate in chemicals and its exposure in the camera, to the developing process, which had to take place while the plate was still wet. He set up his camera and miniature darkroom on their tripods and went to work. He took only one picture of Wilson standing by the house. The negative on the plate seemed to be satisfactory, and he examined it with secret excitement, under his tent. There on the glass in ghostly reverse was this man of contradictions who had come to dominate his life: captured forever.

The next morning, out in the sunlight behind the house, he set up a small printing-frame on a table. He aligned the negative over a sheet of high-quality, light-sensitized paper he'd prepared in a processing bath, and watched as the sun printed the picture. It came out perfectly, coloured a rich reddish-brown which did justice to Wilson's chestnut hair. Martin was well satisfied, and produced an extra print for Lucas. That evening, he presented it to him.

Wilson studied it for some moments in silence, without expression.

I look like a bandit, he said.

Martin stared at him. It wasn't possible to tell whether he was joking or not.

In the evenings, Martin usually went to the Lodge to discuss the proposed book, and sometimes he was invited to stay and dine. He and Wilson and Frances would eat by candlelight off fine china; and Frances was an excellent cook.

All this time he saw little of Griffin; when he did, it was usually from a distance. Once, coming back to the house for supper at dusk, when Dalton was away in the bush, he saw Griffin talking to May, standing by the rainwater barrel. Neither was aware of his approach. Griffin was smiling, but the girl looked reluctant: head bent, half turned away. Griffin moved closer to her, seeming to try and hold her with his gaze. But she turned, and began to walk off. He reached out and grabbed her arm, and began to drag her towards him. She frowned, leaning back to resist him: a child trying to escape punishment. Martin was about to call out when she shook herself free, and vanished through the door of the house. For a moment Griffin stood staring after her; then he walked slowly away.

I ain't cut out for this kind of work, said little Joe.

Striving to keep up with Martin, he was staggering uphill from the creek towards the vegetable garden, his childlike body bent sideways by the weight of a bucket of water. The afternoon sun was hot, and they were both tiring. They'd been going back and forth with their buckets for an hour or more, watering the rows of vegetables that would soon be ready for picking. When they'd emptied their buckets along the last row of carrots, Joe looked at Martin with an air of invitation.

What do you say to a rest, Martin? I believe we've earned it.

They sat in the shade of the group of English willows that Bill Bosworth had planted here: a delicate, light green island among the endless olive tones of the bush. For some minutes they were silent, their ears filled with the bubbling and rattling of the creek. Unlike Martin, Joe wore no hat; his small, pointed face was dewed with perspiration, and he pulled off his neckerchief and mopped his brow with it.

It's a prime crop of vegetables, he said. We've plenty of those, ain't we, and plenty of wallaby meat. But don't I miss a roast haunch of mutton in a nice cosy chophouse in London. I should say I do.

You're homesick, Joe?

The small man adopted an expression of whimsical self-pity, more than ever resembling a sad comedian.

Of course I'm bloody homesick. I wish I could be transported back home tomorrow – but it ain't going to happen.

What were you sent out for, Joe?

Joe turned his wistful eyes on the fast-flowing creek.

I had a nice little business in Dudley Street, near the Seven Dials. A shop that sold old clothes, and curiosities. I did a fair trade, but I never got rich. Then various rogues started to bring me things to sell for them. Quite valuable things, and I got tempted. I got nabbed for receiving, and they gave me fourteen years.

That's a long sentence.

They're hard on fences, the beaks are. If I'd been a bloody pickpocket lifting pocket handkerchers and watches, I might have only got seven. I'd have faced doing my time, then, and got my ticket-of-leave. But I couldn't face fourteen. No. That's why I escaped to the bush with two other coveys, and found my way to Liam Dalton. He and I had known each other on one of the road gangs, and he took me in – even though I ain't a fighting man.

Well, you're safe here, Joe. You believe in what the Captain's doing, don't you?

Joe looked at him without at first replying. As far as his face could become grave, it was grave now, and Martin saw that the small man was not just a joker: he had a kind of shrewdness about him.

Do I believe in it? You mean, do I believe that Nowhere Valley can last? Well now, that's the big question – ain't it, Martin?

I agree. What's your opinion, Joe?

Joe leaned closer, speaking only just loudly enough to be heard above the bubbling of the creek. His tone now was the urgent and intimate one common to dedicated gossips and conspirators.

I'll answer you, Martin: but first I want to know that you'll repeat what I say to no-one.

Of course I won't, Joe.

Well then. I admire Captain Wilson, and I admire Liam Dalton – they're fine men. And I think the Valley will last for a while longer. But I'm scared it may fail in the end.

Why is that?

Joe looked over his shoulder, as though fearing eavesdroppers.

A number of things. Firstly, it ain't really free here, is it? Everything depends on obedience to the Captain. And two people control the money and the goods: the Captain and Bill Bosworth. It's doled out as they see fit, while the Captain and Bill and Alan McLeod keep the accounts. People won't accept that for ever, will they? It ain't in their nature. They'll rebel. And there's another reason they'll rebel. People want some fun in their lives, and they don't get it here. They're supposed to keep their heads down and work, while the Captain and Liam Dalton and Alan McLeod go down below and get some excitement. You saw what happened at the meeting with Hand and Smallshaw. I don't like sharing the bachelors' house with those villains – nor with that queer cove Griffin. He makes my flesh crawl, that one – and he keeps stirring the other two up.

He leaned closer, his face only inches from Martin's.

One of our problems in the Valley is the lack of women. Liam Dalton has a sweetheart in Broadmarsh he rides down to see on the quiet – but no-one else can do that. That's one of the things I hear Roy Griffin talking about to Hand and Smallshaw – and I've seen how they watch Frances Lambert and Mrs Bosworth and even her young daughter May. It ain't nice. I don't like it. I believe it will lead to trouble.

If there's trouble, the Captain will take care of it.

The Captain? Believe me, I respect him, and I know he has grand notions about this place. But the more I think about it, the more I see that there's another reason why the Valley can't last.

He took a long breath and looked down at the creek. Then he looked back at Martin.

They call Captain Wilson and Liam Dalton the last of the bushrangers – and that's very likely true. The Government and the gentry want the colony to be respectable now, and that's the way it's going. They stopped bringing convicts here last year – it ain't to be a penal colony any more, and there's respectability everywhere. It's getting like England: soon there won't be a district left that ain't patrolled. And sooner or later they'll take an interest in this valley, and begin to ask questions. And what then?

You know what the Captain's aim is, Martin said. He'll give up bushranging, when the settlement supports itself. Then this will be a community that's independent of the world.

Joe smiled. You think so? You're very young if you don't mind me saying so, Martin, and you've got innocent notions. That's good – and I'd like you to be right. But I wonder if you know what keeps this place going: what gives the Captain his power? It ain't just the raids – that ain't enough. There's a whole lot of farming people down below who do business with us. The Captain and Liam Dalton deliver them kangaroo skins, and get flour, meat, gunpowder and such things in exchange. And the Captain and Dalton have been known to move very large flocks of sheep off some of the big properties, and re-brand them. Then they deliver them to other big property-owners who are friends of the Captain's and who pay well – not wanting to know where the sheep have come from. Turning a blind eye – see?

He grinned, seeing the surprise in Martin's face.

Oh yes. And the Captain's got friends and spies all through the countryside down there, and ain't never been betrayed. But how long can it last? Already the trade's falling off, and his friends are shrinking in number. Why? Respectability. Respectability's taking over.

Let it, Martin said. The Captain will move the settlement farther out into the bush, if that happens. To country that's never been settled.

Joe cocked his head, adopting an expression of comic incredulity.

Will he? And that means those ranges out in the west – don't it? Do you know what's there, Martin? Nothing. Nothing but forest, where it rains the whole bleeding time. No good for farming. No good for anything.

Martin frowned at him. He half suspected that what Joe was saying was true; but he would not give up the dream that Wilson had woven for him.

There'll be good country somewhere, he said. A place not yet explored. The Captain will find it.

Joe looked at him for a moment, brows raised; then he shrugged, and his serious expression vanished, to be replaced by the half-jaunty, half-wistful grin that was his usual mask.

We'd better hope so, he said. I could be wrong – and I want you to be right. But sometimes I think we're all fools.

He winked. He'd become the jester again.

*

A week later, Martin sat alone in Liam Dalton's dining-room, finishing his evening meal of wallaby stew and potatoes. May had cooked it tonight in the camp oven over the fire; having served it, she'd gone home. Yesterday, Dalton had ridden below with Wilson, and Alan McLeod had gone with them.

Martin pushed his plate aside and was pouring himself a final cup of tea when Dalton came in. In the light of the oil lamp that burned on the table, his face looked drawn and weary. He was unshaven, and grey showed in the stubble on his chin. He threw his hat on a chest by the wall, and nodded once to Martin.

Martin.

Hello Liam.

Is that stew I can smell? Get me a dish of it, will you, squire? I'm beat.

Martin picked up a plate from the dresser, went across to the fire and began to ladle out stew from the black iron pot, while Dalton slumped in a chair. He brought with him what Martin thought of as the smells of outlawry: gunpowder and the sweat of horses. Martin sat down opposite him and sipped his tea. Dalton ate hungrily, head bowed, saying nothing. When he'd done, he threw down his fork and sat back, staring towards the dying fire.

I'll tell you how it is, Martin. This game of ours is gettin to be not worth the candle.

His voice was harsh, and Martin waited, saying nothing.

We ran into trouble, Dalton said. We decided to visit a property at the Back River, near New Norfolk. Owned by a Mr Bradshaw. On the way, we ran across a shepherd who's a friend to us. He told us there was a body of police stationed near the Back River who were protectin the neighbourhood, and who had a great notion to capture me and the Captain, should we appear. Alan and I were all for retreatin – but not Lucas. So we hid our horses in the bush and went forward on foot.

He got up, fetched a bottle of brandy and two glasses from a cupboard, and poured a good quantity for each of them.

You left the horses?

We always do. There are too many people about these days, in places like that. We'd draw attention.

He drank. At first it went well, he said. We tied up the servants in their hut and bailed up Mr Bradshaw and his family in the house and gathered a good swag of money and jewels. But then Alan looked through a window and saw people movin about near the men's hut. They were traps. So we moved out on to the verandah and challenged them. They opened fire, and we fired back. Alan hit one of them in the leg, and another that Lucas hit went down: not dead, but not inclined to get up. After that we got away into the bush, and found our horses. No-one rode after us – but we were lucky.

He drained his glass, and set it down with a rap.

We were lucky, he said again. But the game can't go on. It's not like the old days. There are too many people and too many bloody traps, and they're everywhere. I've told Lucas: we'll soon have to quit goin down altogether.

That's what little Joe says.

Dalton smiled; but there was little humour in it.

Aye. Little Joe's got a clever head on his shoulders.

In the last week of February, Wilson informed Martin that he was to move into the Lodge. He'd be provided with a room of his own and a desk to write at, making it easier for him to work on their projected book. It would also enable them to discuss ideas whenever they wished, and he could make use of Wilson's library.

In spite of his misgivings about the future, Martin felt greatly honoured by this. The Captain, like some prince of the Renaissance giving patronage to an artist, was creating a unique and privileged position for him, drawing him ever closer into his life. Martin continued to eat most of his evening meals with

Dalton, but two or three times a week he would dine at the Lodge with Wilson and Frances Lambert.

A new phase in his life here had begun.

He sat at his desk, in the late afternoon. It was a simple, flat-topped desk, made by Bill Bosworth from the local eucalyptus. His room was also plain, furnished only with a single bed, a bedside table, a wooden armchair and a chest of drawers. But it pleased him, and he savoured its privacy.

Sitting at the desk, Martin could see from his window the two nameless flat-topped mountains. He noticed with surprise that they were capped with snow today: a premature warning of winter. The afternoon was bright, and the streaks of snow were brilliant. The days weren't yet cold, but their warmth was ebbing: next month, autumn would put out its feelers. Time was slipping away, and Martin didn't welcome the thought of the Valley's hard winter. Time was slipping away, and there were very few landmarks up here to mark its passing. Time was slipping away, and it seemed to have no features here: it was almost as though Time had no existence, in these wild, unvisited valleys.

He sat very still, and thought about Time. If he stayed here, it would be almost as though Time didn't exist. The events and the calendars and the goals that punctuated it in the world below were all absent. So were fresh newspapers from London, arriving in Hobart Town by ship with their regular reports from the arena of great events: that opposite hemisphere where everything mattered, and which his parents and most other colonists called home. These were the things that made Time real. Up here, all that would make him aware of Time's passage would be the turn of the seasons, and the wheeling of those brilliant constellations which Wilson tracked through his telescope. Meanwhile, his life would ebb away unheeded.

At the thought of this a kind of muted panic seized him. He looked at his pocket watch, which lay on the desk in front of him. For some minutes he stared at its dial as though hypnotized, listening to its ticking. He couldn't recall seeing anyone consult a watch up here – not even Wilson, though no doubt he had one. He recalled Lucas saying that they were liberated in the Valley from mechanical time: that they lived and worked in harmony with nature's rhythms. No doubt they did, getting up at dawn and going to bed when darkness fell, like the people of the Middle Ages. But wasn't this really a sort of bondage a bondage from which the medieval world had been freed by the mechanical clock, enabling people to work at times that weren't dictated by nature? And did Wilson himself work to nature's rhythms? He did not, Martin thought: he sat in his tower at all hours of the night, reading and studying the stars – and it was rumoured that he sometimes slept late.

He sighed, and put aside these rebellious thoughts. He picked up the copy of Thomas More's *Utopia* that Wilson had lent him, having asked him to read it carefully before they began to plan their book. He began to read.

> *And if any king were so smally regarded, and so lightly esteemed, yea, so behated of his subjects, that other ways he could not keep them in awe, but only by open wrongs, by polling and shaving, and by bringing them to beggary, surely it were better for him to forsake his kingdom, than to hold it by this means; whereby though the name of a king be kept, yet the majesty is lost; for it is against the dignity of a king to have rule over beggars, but rather over rich and wealthy men.*

*

The Captain had established certain routines for the evenings when Martin dined with him.

After dinner, he and Martin would sometimes go up into the tower and discuss the book on Wilson's projected Utopia, while

Martin took notes. Wilson approved of much of the outline of Utopian society in Thomas More's work – but not all of it, Martin found.

More's Utopia was a whole country, and the scale was thus different from their small community, Wilson pointed out. It wouldn't be feasible in Nowhere Valley to have an elaborate structure of government, with elected officials. Instead, when the population grew larger, the Valley would be organized in a way that would resemble the early Benedictine monasteries, running to changeless rules to which all were agreed. As to the nature of the society itself, he hoped it would be managed on very similar lines to the one in More's pages.

It would consist of a cluster of households, whose members would meet regularly, as they did now. He hoped eventually to have a common dining hall, as the monks did, where elevating literature would be read aloud while people ate. The occupation that every person would have to follow would be farming – but in addition to that, each person, male or female, would be taught a trade or skill. In order to cease raiding, they would have to manufacture such things as their own clothing – by spinning and weaving, and also by making suits and moccasins out of kangaroo skins, as many of the early settlers and bushrangers had done. There would be a six-hour working day (as in More's Utopia), with the people going to bed at eight o'clock, and sleeping eight hours. Other hours would be spent in recreation, or cultivated pursuits. They would build a proper mill for threshing the oats, and a school and a hospital would have to be founded, to achieve independence from the world. To do these things, they would have to attract skilled people: individuals such as Martin.

At this point, Martin began to ask questions. If there was to be no government, who would be in charge? Who would deal with trouble, if it came? Who would ensure that people kept to the rules? Would Wilson and Dalton continue to do so indefinitely – through force?

A faraway look came into Wilson's eyes at this, and he took some time to answer. Finally he said:

You surely don't imagine that human beings are equal?

Not in capabilities, no. But they should have equal rights and freedoms.

Think, Martin, think. The big societies out there make a pretence of giving people those freedoms – but a pretence is largely what it is. What are the police and the Army for? To protect us from criminals and enemies, certainly – but also to ensure that governments aren't overthrown. And this is because men aren't equal. If the armed guardians were taken away, even for a day, what would happen? The stupid and the vicious would wreck and overwhelm society. Even More's Utopia elected a prince, who ruled for life. The more secure and happy a civilized society is, the more it depends on strong rule, with efficient warriors to defend it. The Romans knew it. The British know it. As for the Benedictines, their life was based on obedience. You'll have heard of the Benedictine Rule? It forbids what St Benedict called *muttering* – meaning grumbling. He knew that grumbling leads to rebellion. So think how necessary it is to have a steady hand on the gun in *this* little community! You saw what happened at our last meeting. I spoke then of a day when harmony would make the gun unnecessary: and I'd truly like to believe in it. I offer it like a dream to those around me – and it's a dream worth offering. But between us, Martin, I have to allow for the fact that a dream is what it may remain. And that means, when Liam and I grow old, capable leaders will probably have to succeed us. I hope not, but I think it likely.

It sounds like Plato's Republic, with its philosopher guardians.

Does it? Perhaps. But once *my* Rule is accepted, people will live in absolute peace and harmony, without fear of poverty or the demands of slave-driving masters. And once we stop raiding, there'll be no need to keep this place secret – so those who wish to leave it will be free to do so. What's wrong with that, young fellow?

*

On other evenings, they would move to the sitting-room and sit by the fire drinking sherry: Wilson on his throne and Frances and Martin in chairs on either side. There they would have a poetry reading, with books taken down from the shelves of Wilson's library. It had begun one evening when Lucas had asked Martin to read aloud, giving him a volume of Shakespeare's sonnets. He had listened with raised brows and a blank face, making Martin nervous; but at the end, had lightly clapped his hands.

Good. Good. You read well, Martin – I knew you would. It's a pleasure to hear poetry read with such understanding. Now: may I read you some Shelley?

He read *To a Skylark*, and read it beautifully, his deep voice resounding like a musical instrument. The exultation he expressed was so exactly suited to the ascent of the skylark that Martin told himself that this was surely how Shelley himself would have read it. He said so when it was over, and Wilson smiled with a quick, rare warmth.

I'm in sympathy with Shelley because his spirit and mine are alike. He would have understood me, rebel that he was.

After this they read to each other every evening, selecting their favourite poets from the shelves; and these were supremely happy occasions for Martin, like no others he'd experienced. All his reservations about staying in the Valley would dissolve, and the hold that Wilson exerted over his imagination would deepen still further. While they read, Frances would sit and listen intently, keeping very still, her face showing no emotion. But sometimes she would nod, and say that she'd liked a poem. She never elaborated on this, and once she said:

I don't really understand poetry.

Ah, but you do, my dear, Wilson said. You understand it in your soul. He turned to Martin. Frances has a poetic spirit. She understands poetry instinctively.

Sometimes, when Lucas was reading, Martin would look up to find Frances's large, melancholy eyes fixed on his face. She didn't look away when this happened; she held his gaze steadily, as though trying to convey something to him. This sent a thrilling wave through him, since he continued to find her both attractive and disturbing; at the same time he was concerned that Wilson might notice and take offence, though the purpose of her gaze was no doubt quite innocent or perhaps simply abstracted. But Wilson saw nothing when he was reading, since his eyes were either on the book or fixed above their heads.

All this time there had been no further mention of Roy Griffin, though Martin knew that he called on Wilson, and had long conversations with him. It seemed that Wilson preferred not to see the two of them together, and this suited Martin very well. But one evening in the first week of March, when their poetry session had drawn to an end and Martin had stood up to say good night, Wilson said to him:

It really is time that you learned something of Roy Griffin's ideas. Have you spoken about them with him?

Only a little. He talked about Gnosticism, and magical beings.

Martin chose his words with care, not wishing to show his dislike of Griffin, since Lucas apparently remained impressed with him. He was conscious at the same time that Frances's gaze was fixed on him. It was raining outside, the drops streaming down the closed windows; the first chill of autumn was in the air, and they had all drawn close to the fire.

Did he now? Wilson said. He's very interesting on that subject. He has some strange notions. I'd like to have your opinion of them – so I suggested that Roy talk to you. He's asked that you meet outside the Lodge at six-thirty tomorrow evening, after supper. Will that suit you?

Martin stiffened. He agreed that it would suit him only because it was clear that Wilson's wishes were not to be refused.

*

Martin came out of the Lodge at exactly six-thirty. It was still light, but the shadows were lengthening. The distant strains of little Joe's concertina could be heard coming from the bachelors' house, where early lamplight showed in the windows: he was playing 'Sweet Polly Oliver', and the tune sounded full of yearning. At first Martin didn't see Griffin; then Griffin stepped from the shadow of a single wattle tree that grew nearby.

He wore the same shapeless grey hat as he'd done at their last meeting; yet he seemed in some way different. It had nothing to do with his dress: the change was in his demeanour. He no longer looked sly or mocking; his expression was almost humble, seeming to ask for understanding. When he spoke, his voice was unusually soft.

I'm glad you agreed to meet me, Mr Dixon. I've been afraid you were still avoiding me, and that seemed a pity.

The Captain seems to think that we should discuss your ideas. So here I am.

Here you are indeed, thanks to the Captain. He says that you and I have the best minds in the settlement, and that we should be brought together. I must say I agree. Shall we walk on the hill again?

Side by side, walking in silence, they climbed the slopes of tussock grass. Martin had no wish to open the conversation, and it seemed that Griffin was not yet ready to do so. The March air was cool and sharp, and a vast grey cumulonimbus cloud, tinted with copper by the setting sun, was sitting above the mountains in the west behind them, threatening rain. When they'd almost reached the top of the hill, Griffin stopped by the same group of tall, lichen-covered stones where they'd halted before. He turned to gaze at Martin with his continuing air of humility, and Martin's resolve to treat him with cold reserve was weakened.

Lucas tells me that you've been discussing Gnosticism with him, he said.

Yes. Lucas is interested in achieving the consciousness of the World Soul that Plotinus talks about. A fine ambition, but I've explained to him that to do that, he needs to escape from the material world altogether.

Martin raised his brows. He began to suspect that Griffin's ideas were eccentric in the extreme.

As I told you before, that was what the Gnostics understood, Griffin said. There were some sects who managed to achieve it – people who possessed the divine spark. For them, the material world wasn't the creation of the true Godhead, but of an inferior god: the Demiurge. And since this was so, they had no obligation to any earthly laws or government. They could do as they pleased.

Is that what you believe, Mr Griffin?

Of course. I'm that kind of Gnostic.

But that would mean that anything's permitted. You can break any law. Commit any sin.

Of course. Fucking, killing – it's all one. That's why I've come to the Valley, my dear.

He smiled; his expression now was a gloating one, and Martin tried to hide his repugnance. It was the same repugnance that Griffin had woken in him before – but he wanted now to discover how such theories could have compelled the interest of a man like Lucas Wilson.

You said that some Gnostics escaped the material world. Surely that's impossible.

You must open your mind, Martin. I do hope I may call you Martin? And please call me Roy. You called this heresy before – but there are powers you know nothing about that make it possible. Some Gnostics invoked angelic helpers, being Christians. There are powers even more potent – powers that existed in the ancient world, long before Christ and the Gnostics. When I was a student, I met people who introduced me to ways of summoning them up. But before I say any more, let's go right to the top of the hill, shall we? It's a rather special place.

The hilltop didn't look special to Martin, except for its dramatic view of the country below. It was treeless and open, under a sky of immense grey clouds: a place of flat boulders, small bushes and more tall stones, mauve-grey in colour and coated with white lichen. Griffin led the way to a pair that resembled obelisks, with an opening between them like a doorway. Here he stopped, and leaned against one of them. Martin halted beside him, and turned to survey the landscape.

The light was fading, and all colours were sombre and stark. The rain-cloud over the snow-capped western mountains had grown even larger and darker, and the approaching sunset had made its copperish tinge deeper: a colour that Martin now found grim. The breeze up here had a touch of ice in it, and he buttoned up his pea jacket and moved close against the shelter of the stone. Griffin wore only a shirt and blouse, but seemed not to feel the cold. He now began to speak again.

I brought you up here because it's a place of power.

What does that mean?

You'll find out shortly. First, my dear, let me explain what I mean by powers that can help us escape the material world.

His gaze was fixed on Martin again with that insistence the young man found worrying. Pure green eyes are rare, and it was no doubt for this reason that Griffin's eyes compelled the attention in the way that they did. As he spoke, they seemed to grow larger, as they'd done on past occasions, and Martin found it impossible to look away.

There are many roads to achieving escape, Griffin said. The people I mentioned to you showed me some of those roads. They showed me that there's a circle between this world and the next – the domain of the gods, and of supernatural beings. That circle can be reached. There are ways of opening the door.

And what are they?

Not so fast. There are many. One of them is to call on the Goddess.

And which goddess is that?

She has many names. Ishtar, Artemis, Aphrodite – it doesn't matter. She brings you to the circle between the worlds.

Martin managed now to unlock his gaze from Griffin's and to look towards the east. There, the far-off Derwent could be seen below: a reminder of home, and normality. Twilight was falling now, and the breeze grew even colder. The little bushes with their spiky green leaves tossed backwards and forwards as though they had their own power of motion. He decided that the time had come to be forthright.

And is this the pagan nonsense that Lucas Wilson finds convincing? I can scarcely believe it.

He thought that Griffin would grow angry at this. But when Griffin replied, his tone was quiet and reasonable.

Lucas has understood that magical beings are all around us: beings who can help us. I've taken him out into the bush and he's experienced their presence: they're very strong in these mountains. They're especially strong on this hill. That's why I've brought you here.

He paused. Then he spoke in an intense, hissing undertone quite unlike his usual voice. It was as though someone else had spoken from inside him.

Open your mind, Martin! Open your heart!

Martin started, and looked at him directly again. Griffin's eyes were wider than ever, and once again it was very difficult to look away from them. He moved closer to Martin, and his voice changed again. Now it was confiding and soothing.

They're here. Quite close. Don't you feel them?

No.

Be quiet, and listen.

Martin could hear nothing but the sighing of the breeze.

This is a very strange time of day, said Griffin. The magic time. But there's no need to be afraid. Just wait.

A sudden, violent gust of wind hit them, and then died away with unnatural suddenness.

That was a sign, said Griffin.

The hilltop, with its dry grass and boulders and little bushes, now lay in a strange, attentive silence.

They're here, Griffin said. He smiled with an air of triumph, and pointed across the hilltop towards the east.

Beyond the next group of tall stones, it seemed to Martin that a shadow had moved across the grass, its motion oddly brisk, like that of a living creature. But then it had gone. The fading of the light was draining the colours from the land, and there were many shadows here now. He decided that what he'd just seen was one of them, and said so to Griffin.

But now Griffin was pointing again.

And that? Is that a shadow?

A small figure was standing by one of the stones. It looked like a child, and the colours of its clothing were brown and grey; but the dusk made its face difficult to make out.

It's a wallaby, Martin said. But a wave of intense cold went over him.

You know that it isn't. Look again.

Martin began to walk towards it. As he advanced through the grass, it seemed to him that the figure was fading like smoke, and when he got up to where it had been, there was nothing there. He turned to Griffin.

What was it?

You know what it was. It came here for *you*, my dear.

As Griffin spoke, drops of rain began to fall, and he squinted into the sky.

It's time to go down, or get a soaking. But you'll come back up here, I'm sure. Your helpers will be waiting for you. You must tell Lucas about it. He'll understand. He's seen them too.

He laughed, and began to trudge off down the hill. The rain had grown heavier, and Martin turned up his coat collar and followed. He was trembling, and felt curiously light, as though he'd just avoided a dangerous accident.

*

Maid Margret stood in her bower door,
Kaiming down her yellow hair;
She spied some nuts growin in the wood
And wished that she was there.

She had nae pulled a nut, a nut,
A nut but barely one,
Till up started the Hind Etin,
Says, Lady, let they alone!

But he has tane her by the yellow locks,
And tied her to a tree,
And said, For slighting my commands,
An ill death shall ye dree.

All through his sleep that night, *Hind Etin* was repeated in fragments. Lucas Wilson had recited this poem to him a number of times, reading from an aged collection of Scottish ballads acquired for him in Hobart Town. Martin found its theme rather ugly, but he hadn't said so since Wilson was fond of these traditional songs of his ancestors, the tunes of which were lost.

What made the ballad more ugly now was that the voice reciting it was not Wilson's, but Roy Griffin's. This made it somehow threatening, and he wanted it to stop. When it finally did, it was succeeded by Alan McLeod and little Joe Jarvis singing 'Who's the Fool Now'. But instead of being enjoyable, as it had been before, this time the song was mocking him personally.

Thou hast well drunken, man. Who's the fool now?

He could hear Griffin laughing: a sniggering noise that grew louder. *Fucking*, he said. *Killing.*

At this, as is sometimes the case in dreams, Martin grew terrified without there being anything specific to account for his terror, and woke with a sudden shout. He fumbled for a lucifer on his bedside table and lit the candle there and propped himself up in a leaping and shifting semi-darkness as the candle flame swayed and flickered; there was a draught in the room. He was thankful that Wilson and Frances Lambert slept in a bedroom a good way removed from his, and wouldn't have heard his cry.

He lay back again, listening to the autumn wind moaning about the Lodge, its voice sounding almost human. *Ghosts and spirits of the air*, he said. It was a long time before he could bring himself to put the candle out again.

Griffin, it seemed, was constantly in their minds at present: his and Lucas Wilson's and Frances Lambert's. Certainly he dominated their conversation.

They sat in front of the fire in the sitting-room after dinner. During dinner, Lucas had been somewhat silent and moody; now he asked what Martin had thought of Griffin's ideas.

Martin sipped his sherry, giving himself some moments to formulate an answer. He was aware of Frances watching him intently.

He'd been interested, he said, to hear about the different Gnostic sects and their notions: Griffin was very knowledgeable about them. But the Gnostics were dualists, and he could hardly subscribe to a dualistic position himself. After all, he was a Christian, and a member of the Church of England, and believed in one God. Two Gods in the Universe really wouldn't do. Also, he didn't believe that it was possible for any human being to escape the body, as Griffin claimed some of the Gnostics had done.

He'd employed the kind of light yet measured tone he would have used in a Philosophy tutorial as a student, and he noticed as he spoke that Wilson's brows were drawing together in frustration. Now the Captain held up his hand.

You don't believe it? You should think again. Griffin maintains it's possible. He says he's done it himself. He says his spirit has left his body and travelled great distances.

Before Martin could reply, Frances spoke. She did so directly to Wilson, and her tone was half-protesting and half-pleading.

Oh, please, Lucas! Surely you don't believe that nonsense.

The two stared at each other in silence, while Martin sat still with embarrassment. It was plain that they were returning to a theme they'd often wrangled over, and he almost felt he shouldn't be here. Finally Wilson answered, glancing at Martin at the same time. His tone was reasonable and courteous, as it always was with Frances.

I don't believe it's nonsense, my dear; you know that. An unseen realm exists beyond this one, of which we know very little. Many wise men and mystics have known that to be true. And Griffin is able to get in touch with it – he's convinced me of it.

Wise men and mystics, you say. You mean holy men and saints. *They've* had visions of God – it's all in the Bible. But I don't believe that Griffin is a holy man, and I don't believe he has visions of God.

Her tone continued to be protesting – almost passionate – and Wilson glanced at Martin again.

What, then? What sort of visions does he have?

Demons, she said. I believe he talks to demons. There.

Wilson sighed. Then he turned to Martin.

Frances is a woman of considerable wisdom. She senses things that I don't, and I'd be foolish not to heed her. She sees something bad in Griffin – so does Liam Dalton, and I must say that I suspect it too. You may have noticed that I've never asked him to dine here – and I'm not likely to do so. Very well. So far, Frances and I agree. But demons? I can't believe that. I think that Griffin is simply one of those people who are able to contact the spirit world. It's a rare gift, and it interests me greatly.

He sat forward in his chair, his hands on his knees, and looked at Martin with a severe expression.

So now we come to the point. I've been out in the bush with Griffin, and he's shown me things. I'm not a gullible fool, Martin. He called up spirits there, and I actually saw them.

You imagined it, Frances said.

Wilson ignored her, continuing to look at Martin, and his voice took on its tone of authority.

I want you to speak honestly with me, young man. I don't want to hear about your philosophical debate with Griffin – that's not the reason I asked you to see him. I did so because I wanted your personal judgement of his ideas about the supernatural. I'm sure he'll have spoken of them – am I right?

Martin began to feel trapped. He'd not intended to discuss his experience on the hill with Griffin. He'd decided to assume that the things he'd seen were imaginary, and he was trying to dismiss them from his mind. But it began to be clear that he could no longer be evasive.

He spoke to me again about spirit helpers, he said.

He paused, and Wilson leaned closer.

Yes. And then?

I seemed to see them.

Ah. You're sure?

No – I'm not sure. I might have imagined them.

You didn't imagine them. I tried to tell myself the same thing, at first – but now I know it's not so.

Wilson threw himself back in his armchair and smiled triumphantly, looking at Frances again.

You see, my dear? Martin saw them too. There are spirits in this high country of ours, and Griffin is able to summon them up.

Spirits? We're told not to have anything to do with such things. The Bible warns us against it – even I know that, and I was never much of a churchgoer. Why do you *want* this, Lucas? Isn't the world as it is enough for you?

Wilson thumped his fist down on the arm of his chair, breathing hard.

No! No it isn't! I need something more than this dull reality! The Bible isn't enough – I want the other world to be *revealed* to me. I want what I feel when I ride fast and hard, with musket balls whistling around me. Then I'm truly alive – don't you see?

His words excited Martin, and part of his spirit responded to them: hadn't he had similar thoughts himself? And yet he had the sudden sense that the Captain was weaving some ultimate destruction for himself.

Wilson stood up now, reached out for Frances's hand, drew her to her feet and put his arm about her shoulders.

Come on, my dear, don't fret. Griffin won't enter this house – I've made that decision because you dislike him so much, and because Liam Dalton mistrusts him as much as you do. Liam tells me that he was charged with filthy behaviour to a woman in Hobart Town – but we must be fair. Griffin says the police lied about it; and that wouldn't be unusual in this colony. In the meantime, what I'm trying to do is simply to draw on his peculiar abilities.

He turned to Martin.

Thank you, Martin, you've helped me as I knew you would. And now let's away to our beds.

Down below, March was the gentlest month of the island's year: an interval of dreaming stillness, when all winds and gales had died away, and day followed day of mild sun, and Time was slowed by the spellbound calm of autumn. It proved to be the same up here in the mountains, where Time was neither fast nor slow, but instead seemed not to move.

On the last Friday of the month, Wilson and Dalton and McLeod rode off to the country below again. That evening, Martin dined with Frances Lambert.

This was the first time they'd been alone in the house together, and both of them were constrained, sitting in the large kitchen-dining-room. During the meal they made only the most banal remarks to each other. He still found Frances attractive, though he told himself that the difference in their ages made such a feeling absurd, as well as being disloyal to Wilson. He tried to dismiss it; but when her lucent, melancholy eyes rested on his face she stirred pangs of desire in him, making him feel guilty and foolish. Martin's only experience of love had been with the eighteen-year-old daughter of a farmer in Montrose who was one of his father's friends; he had visited her at home with her parents' approval, had sat with her in their parlour, and had gone on walks with her in the countryside. But the affair had progressed no further than holding hands and a few chaste kisses and had somehow faded, and he was still at a stage in his life where passion was a closed door. His inexperience made concealing the effect a beautiful woman had on him difficult to do, and he tried not to look at Frances too long or too often.

As soon as he'd helped her clear away the dishes he told her he had work to do, and retreated to his room. He sat at his desk for over an hour, writing up notes he'd made when he and Wilson had discussed their joint book on Utopia. A single candle, burning on the desk, was the only illumination he had, so that most of the room was in shadow. He'd begun to think of going to bed when there was a soft knock on the door. He called come in, and Frances stepped into the room's dimness: a nebulous form beyond the circle of candlelight.

He got hastily to his feet, looking at her in surprise. She moved into the light and halted in front of him, still wearing the green ankle-length house dress she'd had on at supper, a white lace fichu draped about her shoulders. She was clutching it at her neck with one hand, in a way that appeared to be nervous.

Excuse me for interrupting you.

You're not interrupting. Please – sit down.

He waved at the armchair, but she shook her head.

No. I won't sit. What I want to say won't take long. I wouldn't have come here if it weren't important. I thought of speaking to you at supper, but I couldn't bring myself to do it. I'm sorry to trouble you this late.

She had let go of the fichu now, and was clasping her hands together in front of her. Her eyes seemed larger than ever, and more than ever sad. When she spoke again, it was in a rush of words.

You must know how much Lucas thinks of you. You're like a son to him. I've come here to ask you to speak to him – to try and make him see something. He might listen to you.

What is it you want me to say?

She looked down at the floor. When she looked up again she failed to answer his question.

Don't you miss your home, Martin? Your parents? Your friends?

Sometimes. But I'm not ready to go back. And Lucas doesn't want me to go back at all.

I know that. But you shouldn't be here – a clever young man like you, with your life in front of you. And to stay here for ever? That would be madness: you'd be wasting your life.

Lucas wants to build a new society here, and he wants me to be part of it. Don't *you* believe in it, Frances?

She frowned, and bit her lip. When she spoke again, her voice was low and flat.

No.

No?

She shook her head. No, I don't believe in it. I wanted to, but I can't any more. It's never going to work. There'll never be enough people, or the sort of people that would hold it together. Lucas is dreaming.

He stared at her.

But you're Lucas's partner in life. I thought you believed in him.

She frowned. When she answered, he heard something like despair in her voice.

Believe in him? He's an extraordinary man, and I've adored him from the moment I met him. But he lives in his head. He's a dreamer, and unless he can be made to listen, he'll be killed because of his dreams. That's why I've come to you, Martin. I want you to convince Lucas to get away from here – and to take me with him.

He looked at her now in simple amazement. She was breathing quickly, her eyes shining in the candlelight, and he saw now that she was in a state that was no longer balanced: a state that mingled excitement with desperation.

He'd never do it. You must know that, Frances. And even if he did, they'd hang him if he went back down below.

No. I've thought about this. He and I would have to find a ship that would take us out of this wretched colony. A ship that would get us to America, where the authorities couldn't reach us. Others have done it.

He'll never agree.

Then *you* take me, Martin. Tomorrow – while he and Liam are still away. We can take two horses and go down to Berriedale, on the Main Road. From there we can soon get to Hobart Town. I'm afraid to go alone – but I'd be no trouble to you after that. I have friends in Hobart I can go to.

She met his astounded gaze, her lips open and moist.

But how could you do that to Lucas? Don't you still love him?

Yes, I love him. And that's why it might be better to run away – because if he asked me to stay, I couldn't bear to refuse him. He loves me, in his way, but I never feel I know him, or know what he'll do next. And I won't watch him shot by the police, or taken away to be hanged. I know that will happen in the end, if we stay here. If he can't be made to see that, I must go – and hope that he'll follow me.

But you must have believed in him when you came here. And you must have known what he was when you met him.

For a moment she made no answer. Then she said:

You think I'm a bad woman.

No.

I wasn't when I came to this colony. Yet I deserted my husband and left my two children to join a gang of criminals.

You don't have to tell me this.

I'd like you to understand. I met my husband back in England. My father owns a flour mill in Sussex; Mr Lambert was a grain dealer then, and he used to sell grain to my father. He brought me out here when we married, and set up an importing business in Hobart Town. He thought he'd make his fortune – but he failed. Then he bought a store in Green Ponds, in the Midlands. That was a sad descent after his venture in Hobart – but because Green Ponds is a coaching stage, he thought he'd do well. He didn't; we barely made a living. He took to drink, and began to beat me.

Martin found it difficult to look at her. I'm sorry, he said.

I wanted to leave him, but he wouldn't let me take the children, and the law says they're his. And I had no money. I wrote to my father for money, but he said I should stay with my husband: he's very strict like that. I was trapped. Then Lucas came, and he took me out of the trap.

She was no longer looking at him, but staring into the candlelight. He knew that she would tell him everything now; or perhaps tell it to a confessor in her mind.

Wilson and Dalton had come into Green Ponds late one night, she said, having held up a property near Bagdad. The store was closed, but they knocked at the door of the house, wanting provisions. Her husband, who was drunk, let them in. She was sitting in a chair in the parlour, bleeding from the nose. Lambert had punched her, and she was trying to stop the bleeding with a wet towel. Wilson quickly understood the situation. He beat her husband unconscious, and tied him up in a back room. Then, while Dalton was packing what they wanted to take from the store, Wilson cleaned away the blood from her face and gave her a drink of brandy.

He talked to me for a long time, she said. He was very gentle, and I could see that he was attracted to me. He asked me to come with him to Nowhere Valley, where I'd be looked after. So I did.

She frowned, and looked at Martin again.

I know: it was mad. Lucas was an outlaw – but he was so refined, and a very beautiful man: not like any man I'd ever known. You know how he can make you feel that anything's possible? That's how he made me feel that night. I fell in love with him; and I was desperate to escape my husband. And I suddenly *wanted* to be mad. Lucas told me about the Valley and his plans, and I believed it because I wanted to believe it. For a long time we were happy – but I'd left behind my five-year-old son and ten-year-old daughter, and I missed them all the time, and still do. Lucas keeps saying that we'll capture them and bring them here – but that isn't easy to do. To have left them was wicked – and now I'm paying for it.

Suddenly she began to weep, bending forward, the handkerchief pressed to her eyes. Martin put his arm about her shoulders, pity making his throat swell.

Please, he said. Don't. I'll talk to Lucas, I promise.

She looked up at him with an imploring expression, her lips parted as though to speak; but no words came. He held her closer, his hands on her back, and now her body was pressed against his: this body he'd often longed to hold. But it was quite different from the body of a girl, he found. Through her dress, he felt the dense female flesh of maturity, and he knew once again that his desires had been absurd, that a gulf lay between them, and that the only true emotion he might feel for her was compassion.

When they broke away she examined his face in silence, her eyes red from weeping.

You won't do it? You won't come away tomorrow?

I can't. But I'll talk to Lucas when he gets back tomorrow night.

She nodded, her expression desolate. Then she turned and hurried from the room, her dress rustling, not looking back.

When Martin came into the dining-room at seven-thirty, Frances wasn't yet up, as she usually was. He took some firewood from a box by the door and laid it under the iron colonial oven in the chimney cavity and lit it. The kettle that stood on top of the oven had already been filled with water, and he sat down at the table and waited for it to boil for tea.

Outside were bird-calls and the crowing of a rooster. Otherwise everything was silent. Usually at this time he would hear the distant voices of Bill Bosworth and his family, who were early risers; but there was no sound of human activity. The stillness began to seem unnatural, and he stared through the window at a grey, overcast sky, and grew faintly uneasy. He got up and went out the back door and walked around to the front of the Lodge.

There was no sign of life in front of Bosworth's place, nor near the distant bachelors' house. Stillness and silence. No smoke came from either of their chimneys, and this was unusual, since at this time breakfast would usually be cooking. The settlement looked deserted, and Martin stood on the brink of the windless autumn day and stared about him, frowning. He had a sudden irrational feeling that everything had changed.

He walked across to the bachelors' house. He and Joe had agreed to share the milking of the cows today, and he decided to make this an excuse for calling on him. When he knocked on the door nobody answered. He waited, then opened the door and went in.

He'd never been inside the house before. He found himself in a dark kitchen which smelled of smoke and old cooking fat and the general putridness of a place shared by men with no interest in housecleaning. In the middle of the floor, next to the kitchen table, Joe Jarvis sat tied to a chair.

A neckerchief was tied about his mouth as a gag, and a folded sheet of paper was pinned to his shirt. There was a purple swelling on his forehead the size of an egg. His eyes bulged, staring at Martin, and urgent falsetto noises came from beneath the gag. Martin untied it. As soon as it came away, Joe sucked in air and began to speak.

Thank you mate, thank you. Now get these ropes off, for Christ's sake. I've been here most of the bloody night. God rot them, the bastards. God rot that wicked swine Griffin. Me legs are killing me, they're that stiff. I thought the bloody night would never end.

Martin undid the last of the knots, and straightened up.

What happened, Joe?

Joe stood up and began to limp about, flinching at the pain in his legs. He picked up a jug of water that stood on the table and tipped it up and drank most of its contents.

You know what today is? All Fools' Day. April first. And we're the bloody fools.

Joe. What happened?

It's that fucking Roy Griffin. He's run off, and persuaded those other two to go with him. They took horses: I heard the hooves. He wanted me to go too, but I wouldn't. They nagged at me, wanting me to change my mind. When I wouldn't agree, Griffin told Smallshaw to take care of me, so I wouldn't raise no alarm. Those two obey everything he says. Smallshaw knocked me out with a piece of wood, and I woke up tied to that bloody chair.

He raised his fingers to the lump on his forehead, and winced. Then he said:

So they never came near you?

Martin shook his head.

No. I wouldn't have thought so, Joe said. All they wanted to do was get away. They knew that Wilson keeps guns in the Lodge, and they probably thought you'd give them trouble – I heard Griffin tell them you was a dead shot. What about Bill Bosworth and his family?

I don't know. We must go and see.

Griffin pinned this note to me, Joe said. He said it was for Captain Wilson.

He unfastened the single sheet of notepaper pinned to his shirt, and handed it to Martin. Martin took it without reading it, pushed it into his pocket and hurried out of the house to make for Bill Bosworth's place. Joe limped after him, having emptied his bladder at considerable length in the grass.

Terror had come, it seemed; but Martin only understood its extent when he and Joe stood in Bill Bosworth's kitchen. Bill and his wife Emma and their young son Benjamin sat gagged and roped to chairs just as Joe had been. There was no sign of May. When Bill's gag was removed he began immediately to shout, his eyes bulging, glaring at Martin and Joe in turn.

They've taken her! They've taken May!

His face was red; the veins stood out on his temples, and there was spittle in his grizzled beard. He twisted and turned while Martin worked at untying him.

D'you *hear* me, for Christ's sake? Roy Griffin's taken her!

Are you quite sure? Martin said.

Jesus Christ, of course we're sure. Our daughter's taken.

She's gone. And we know why he's done it.

Emma Bosworth had spoken in a low, toneless voice, while little Joe was untying her. Her worn face looked more tired than usual, and drained of blood. Her lank fair hair was uncombed, and hung about her shoulders. Her faded blue house dress was torn open at the neck, so that a bruise showed on the top of her breast.

D'you see what they did to her? Bosworth said. She tried to stop them takin May, and Griffin laid hands on her and tore her dress. I'll kill that bastard, I swear I will.

We know why that man took her, Emma repeated. May told us how he annoys her. She's only twelve. Twelve. Oh God, why wasn't Captain Wilson here?

She began hopelessly to weep, standing up and chafing her wrists as Joe freed them from the ropes.

Bill Bosworth also stood up, flinging away his ropes. He put his arm around his wife's shoulders and straightened her torn dress, and his voice became low.

Don't you worry, my Emma. We'll find them.

He looked at Martin and Joe. We'll go now. Come on.

Joe had been untying the pale-faced little boy, who appeared to be struck dumb, and who stared about him as though in disbelief.

Hold hard now, Bill, Joe said. Where will we go, the three of us? We ain't even to know which direction they went in. And what we need to know first is: are they armed? Did they break into the commissariat?

That wouldn't be easy, Bill said. But I never liked it that Alan wasn't there at night to guard the weapons. He should never have gone below, with those villains among us. See what's happened now, by Christ.

He hurried towards the door, his mouth working, his voice breaking as though on the edge of tears. Martin and Joe followed.

Dalton had often remarked to Martin that the commissariat would be very hard to break into. When Alan McLeod was away, its one exterior door was secured with a giant padlock, to which only Wilson, Dalton and Bosworth had extra keys, while all its windows were barred. But Griffin and his comrades hadn't attempted to deal with the padlock: instead, they'd climbed onto the roof, torn away some shingles and entered that way. When Bosworth led Martin and Joe inside, they found that a number of shotguns and pistols were missing, together with a supply of ammunition, and flasks for shot and gunpowder.

So they're well armed. And I know they've taken horses, Joe said.

In silence, the three walked across to the stables.

Wilson's black stallion was gone, together with the bay gelding and the black mare that Dalton and Griffin had brought from Richmond. There were five horses left, and Martin was relieved to see that Chief was among them. Close by the stables, chained to their kennels, lay the bodies of the two hunting dogs, Belle and Rufus, both shot through the head.

Come on, then. Let's get some guns and saddle up, Bosworth said.

Bill, Joe said. Bill. I understand your feelings, but you're not thinking straight. This is a job for the Captain and Liam Dalton. These are very nasty buggers. I'm no use at all with a gun, you're not a fighting man and neither is young Martin here.

Fuck all that, Bosworth said. My May's been taken, and we're losing time. Are you two with me or not? He was trembling visibly, and breathing hard through his nose.

I'm with you, Martin said. But he felt himself grow cold as he said it.

Joe held up his hand. Despite his small stature and whimsical face, he'd taken on a sort of authority. Perhaps it was the calmness of his voice, and his reasonable tone.

Look, Bill, they could be anywhere out there by now. It's going to take time to find them, and it's going to need good information to track them down – the sort only the Captain can get. We have to wait. The Captain said he'd be back today. Wait.

Bosworth looked at him, and then at the floor. He sat down on a feed bin, and his shoulders slumped.

At two in the afternoon the settlement lay quiet again, and Martin found himself alone. Wilson, Dalton and McLeod hadn't yet returned: they didn't usually do so until the evening. Bill Bosworth had confined himself to his house with his wife and young son; Joe Jarvis had gone to his room to sleep, exhausted by his ordeal on the chair, and Frances Lambert was also sleeping. It was as though a narcoleptic spell held the Valley.

Martin had spoken to Frances that morning, and had told her what had happened. She'd listened to him with careful attention, but had shown little emotion; she was pale and listless as though from an illness. When he'd done, she sat biting on a thumbnail, eyes narrowed and fixed on the floor, saying nothing. Then she looked up.

It's come sooner than I thought. You see? I was right.

Yes, you were.

It's the end, Martin. The end here.

Lucas won't think so.

Oh no, Lucas won't think so. And he'll go after them, won't he? He and Liam.

He'll have to. There's that child.

Oh yes. The child. She's ruined already, of course. And what about you?

I'll go too.

Please think again, Martin. You'll get killed.

I don't think so. I'll go.

Frances closed her eyes and shook her head. You're young. The young have no sense. But you'll speak to Lucas as you said, when it's over?

Of course I will.

She reached out and touched his cheek. Thank you, Martin. It will do no good, but thank you. I'm frightened. It might be Lucas who'll die, not you. Young men are lucky. He's been lucky for too long.

Her eyes suddenly filled with tears, as they'd done last night. She turned away quickly, and disappeared to the bedroom she shared with Lucas.

Now, in the early afternoon, he wandered about the silent, deserted stage of Lucas Wilson's dreams. It had rained recently: the grass was still damp, and the shingles on the roof of the Lodge and Liam Dalton's house glistened with water. Smells of damp earth and damp animals hung in the air. By four o'clock, the cows would need to be milked again, and he and little Joe would have to go and do it. There was still an extensive grey cloud cover, but weak sun was leaking through. April, and the long drift towards winter.

He walked out of the settlement and on up the hillside where he'd often gone with Wilson. He was thinking of what Frances had said, and began to consider the possibility that a rifle ball might find him if he went out with Wilson and Dalton. He knew that they'd try to dissuade him, but he also knew that he'd go. He paused, looking towards the west, and a deep uncertainty gathered in him.

It was now a time of mists. Lines of fog lay stretched across the hilltops like abandoned linen, and the olive-green miles of bush had turned almost black. On the horizon, the feet of the two flat-topped mountains were hidden by a bluish-white screen, above which their ancient cones rose sharp against the sky, their colour changed to a sombre indigo. And suddenly he understood where he was, and how things were. This wilderness, which covered most of the island, was the true and final nature of the place: indifferent, dispiriting and frightening. The two little cities and the string of townships that the colonists had so recently erected were mere timid gestures at civilization on the edge of an aboriginal abyss, and the beauty that Lucas had so often spoken about was mere fancy – something he'd grafted onto this landscape through a spirit he'd brought from the hemisphere of his birth. But it had no validity, that vision. There was really neither beauty nor ugliness in the wilderness, and neither was there significance, comfort or hope. There was only obscure, struggling life, and inevitable death and decay.

Suddenly he was homesick for the warm, domestic lowlands, where the other hemisphere's illusions were cherished, and made to seem real.

To Captain Lucas Wilson, Esquire

Dear Captain Wilson,

You will no doubt be displeased by our departure, and by the manner of it. However, you have only yourselves to blame – you and your henchman Dalton.

I came to this valley because your reputation had caused me to admire you exceedingly: I mean your reputation as a daring and reckless bandit, and a rebel against society. I'm an adventurous man, not lacking in daring myself, and I wanted to give you my support by becoming a member of your band. I had thought that I would join you in your raids on this colony's prosperous landowners; but you quickly made it clear that this was not to be, and that I was to see myself as a farmhand. Worse: I would not be able to escape such a life, and would be killed if I attempted to do so. Hand and Smallshaw, also daring men, were faced with the same fate. Very well, then: this is our answer to you.

We have absconded with the intention of forming a Utopian community of our own. We will quickly gain recruits among those prisoners and ex-prisoners to be found about the countryside who seek a more exciting life, and who will enjoy taking revenge on their former masters. I shall be the leader of this merry band, which will call itself Lucifer's Brothers.

Why am I so confident of success? I will tell you. What you have never quite understood, my dear Wilson, is that I have direct contact with those otherworldly powers in whom you showed such interest. They are powers that give an initiate such as myself the ability to control the minds of others; to bring ill-fortune to my enemies; even to visit illness and death on them. Your leadership seeks merely to persuade. It is a weak and ineffective method compared to mine, as you'll soon discover.

There is another reason why we shall enjoy a success that has eluded you, and why my band will grow, while yours will fade. It has to do with human nature; and it is simple. Since the dawn of history, war, pillage and a little light-hearted rape have been what men of spirit most truly enjoy – whether they admit it or not. I shall provide these things to my followers in good measure, and for this reason my band can only grow and prosper.

We shall meet again, probably at gunpoint. I have no real grudge against you, other than the way in which you have disappointed me. But Dalton has insulted me, and has struck me in the face, and for this he must give me satisfaction. We shall pay you a visit, and when we do, I intend to kill him. Inform him of this.

I am, sir,
Yours faithfully,
Roy Griffin

6

Seven streams crossed the district of Glenorchy, coming down from the mountains to join the River Derwent. They ran eastwards across the areas of settlement, providing the water for farms, orchards and flour mills. The district's southern boundary was formed by the New Town Rivulet. Next, moving north, came Humphries Rivulet, where the principal village of O'Brien's Bridge was located. After this came the Islet Rivulet, site of Leyburn Farm. The last of the seven streams was the Black Snake Rivulet: Glenorchy's boundary in the north.

This pleasant and fertile region had been settled early by colonial gentry such as Henry Dixon. Its undulating river flats were bounded in the east by the Derwent. In the west loomed the steep hills of bush that led to the wilderness, while far on the horizon rose those two blue peaks which were nameless to Martin Dixon, but would come to be known as Collins Bonnet and Collins Cap.

The district had been visited by bushrangers since its beginnings, and still kept its windows barred; but that time was felt to be nearing its end. Now that London had been persuaded to stop the transportation of convicts, Glenorchy was enjoying the promise of a peaceful, law-abiding future in a cleansed and renamed Tasmania. Roaming bandits must surely fade into the past, together with the hated name of Van Diemen's Land.

Despite this, however, it was Lucas Wilson's belief that Griffin and his friends would have gone down into the Glenorchy district when they left Nowhere Valley. He pointed out that it was a very short ride away, and that its prosperous farms, little villages and isolated inns would give them plenty of opportunities for the career of plundering they hungered for. It was therefore his intention to comb the district, from Berriedale to the Black Snake Rivulet. He would not give up until he found Griffin.

He and Dalton and McLeod had arrived back in the Valley in the evening as expected. They'd decided not to set out in pursuit until the next morning, however, since there was now no urgency concerning May Bosworth. She had been found, just before dusk.

Bill Bosworth had accepted Joe's proposition that Wilson and Dalton should pursue Griffin, and that he must stay behind; but he hadn't resigned himself to the idea that Griffin had taken May with him. Late in the afternoon, he'd set out to look for her in the vicinity of the farm, and Martin and Joe had accompanied him. They'd come upon her within an hour.

She was walking through the tussock grass on the hilltop behind the settlement. Her only garment was a white petticoat. It was stained with mud, and torn off one shoulder. One of her thin bare arms was scratched and bloody, and there was a bruise on her cheek. Whether she was making for the settlement wasn't clear; she seemed to be wandering aimlessly, not far from that place of stones where Griffin had summoned up spirits. She looked at them, her eyes wide and fixed and her face blank.

Her father gave a shout and ran towards her. He bent and embraced her, murmuring, but her face remained empty, and she made no response. The others couldn't hear what Bosworth was saying; but finally the child answered him.

He hurt me.

She said nothing else, and her voice, like her face, had been empty of expression. Bosworth shook his head as though something invisible tormented him; then he picked May up in his arms and began to carry her down the hill. He looked once over his shoulder at the others. His face was streaked with tears, and his mouth, under his greying moustache, was set in an animal snarl.

Martin begged Wilson and Dalton to allow him to ride with them after Griffin. Wilson at first refused, but Dalton gave Martin his support.

We need him, he told Wilson. Look at how it is, Lucas. We've got to leave McLeod and Bosworth here to look after the women and guard the place. So there's three of those buggers, and only two of us, and they've stolen some of our best weapons. Martin's got plenty of nerve, and he's a bloody good shot. That makes it even. Sure, we'll be glad of him, Lucas.

Wilson looked at Martin, his expression severe.

That's not what I'm thinking of. He may be a good shot, but he has no experience of a fight. And I'm thinking of his parents, who might have to learn that their son is dead. Is that the sort of sorrow you're prepared to risk bringing on them, Martin?

I want to help find Griffin. That's what really matters.

Wilson continued to look at him; then he shrugged his shoulders.

Liam's right: you're a game one. All right: get your gear together. I must hope I won't regret this.

They rode out of Nowhere Valley at eight in the morning and headed down the steep, stony track to the village of Berriedale, five miles below on the Main Road. It was a fine, clear day with scattered cloud and patches of blue sky; but showers could come at any time, and the nights would be cold. All three wore pilot coats and had blanket rolls strapped to their saddles; should they be out for a number of nights, they'd have to find shelter where they could. They were well armed. Wilson carried in his saddle scabbard the prized Colt revolving rifle taken from Leyburn Farm, which he'd currently been keeping in the Lodge. This was fortunate: had it been in the commissariat, it would have been lost to Griffin and his friends. Dalton and Martin both carried Enfield muzzle-loading rifles: highly efficient military weapons obtained from a corrupt gun dealer, together with a good supply of the special military cartridges which made for fast reloading. Martin and Dalton had Colt revolvers in their belts, while Wilson carried Henry Dixon's Adams pistol. They thus had some advantage in the quality of their weapons. Nevertheless, Griffin's group had taken a formidable selection of guns from the commissariat: two double-barrelled shotguns, an Enfield rifle and three Colt revolvers.

It had always been Bill Bosworth's task to go into the village of Berriedale for provisions, since Wilson and Dalton couldn't afford to show themselves there, or in any of the other villages along the highway in the riverland, for fear of recognition. Main Road, running beside the Derwent, was the chief coaching road of the colony, and carried a good deal of traffic. Neither Wilson nor Dalton could risk going on to it, since handbills were up in every post office offering rewards for their capture. Instead, Wilson's plan was to move northwards through the bush some way back from the western side of the highway, while keeping parallel with it. They would not need to cross Main Road to the exposed shores of the Derwent on its eastern side, since Griffin would find no safe haven there. They would search every district between Berriedale and the Black Snake – but they would not go south to the final village of O'Brien's Bridge. As principal settlement of the district, it had two police constables stationed there, so that Griffin would be very unwise to go in that direction. Nor would he venture on to the highway. What he would do, Wilson suggested, was to strike at the isolated farms that lay along the rivulets. After the hamlet of Claremont, near Faulkner's Rivulet, there were no more villages: that would best suit Griffin and his friends, and that was where it would be sensible to search. First, however, Wilson wanted Martin to go into Berriedale and ask people whether any houses had been broken into in the district, or whether anyone had been attacked.

Martin left the others in the bush, leaving his rifle behind, and rode down the track past sloping, autumnal apple orchards whose leaves were turning yellow. It was warmer down below here: the land lay bathed in mild sun, and the sounds of birds and insects and the lowing of cattle seemed to grow louder as the warmth of the morning increased. Emerging on to the edge of the highway, he brought Chief to a halt and stared about him. He took off his hat and ran his fingers through his hair – left uncut since he'd gone up to the Valley – and found himself filled with a curious and unexpected gladness.

He was suddenly buoyed up by a sense of lightness: a sensation of having escaped from an enclosed and constricting dimness into the open air of freedom. It was like coming out of a tunnel. After nearly three months of painless imprisonment – a time which seemed much longer – he'd emerged from the confining valleys and dense, towering forests of the wilderness to find himself suddenly in the riverine flatland of his birth: this open, easy, peaceful region of unobstructed distance, farms and the solid stone houses of civilization. He was home, and it was somehow unreal. Here was busy Main Road, with rattling gigs and the laden spring carts of farmers going by; and they were all like things in a remembered dream. There down the road was the two-storey, stone-built Berriedale Inn, familiar and yet also dreamlike, with the wide silver sweep of the Derwent behind it, and beyond that again, on the eastern shore, the round, grey-blue humps of Mount Direction, and the farther hills. These were the hills of home, known since childhood; and his father's farm was only a few miles to the south. He was surprised to experience a swelling in his throat; and the sudden realization came to him that he could ride off down the road and be home in a very short time, with no-one to stop him. But Wilson and Dalton were waiting, and he shook his head and put on his hat and clicked his tongue to Chief. He rode across the highway to the village's general store, dismounted, and tied his pony's reins to a verandah post in front.

He'd been here before over the years, buying small items that were needed on the farm. It was a very small shop, like all of them out here: a shingle-roofed cottage built of weatherboard, with a miniature front verandah and multi-paned display windows on each side of a narrow entrance door. A wooden sign above the verandah awning read: *H. Turner, General Provisions*, and a coloured placard fixed to one of the windows read: *Smoke Golden Eagle Tobacco.* Both signs were faded by the sun, unlike those in the busy commercial centre of Hobart Town. Out here in the Glenorchy district, many things were allowed to become bleached and faded – commercial signs, the unpainted wood of sheds and barns, little weatherboard houses – and somehow this fadedness of things, on the sleepy edges of the country, formed part of the meaning of home in Martin's mind, and reawakened his feelings of fondness and elation, as though he were here to stay. But then he remembered the mission he was involved in, and a hollow opened in his belly.

He went in, and made his way between crowded wooden shelves. Legs of ham, sides of bacon and pots and pans hung from rafters overhead, and he inhaled the familiar odours of smoked meats and coffee and cheese with something of the gladness he'd felt beside the highway: the pleasure of being enclosed by the humble and familiar. The shop was empty of customers, and silent except for the humming of flies, many of whose corpses blackened a flypaper hung from a beam. Mr Turner was standing behind the counter: a thin, clean-shaven man in his forties with a pale freckled face and red hair. He was wearing a white apron as he always did, arms extended to lean on the counter with both hands, and he smiled with easy friendliness as Martin came up to him. He had always been easy and friendly, and this easiness seemed another part of the pattern that welcomed Martin home.

Good morning to you, sir. It's Mr Dixon, ain't it?

It is. Hello, Mr Turner.

Martin began to order some victuals. Wilson had suggested that he get a small supply of food to carry with them, and he asked for cheese, ham, bread and tea and pushed coins across the counter. As Turner put the supplies into a sack, Martin asked him whether there had been any prowlers in the neighbourhood, or any burglaries. Turner stared at him in surprise.

You ain't heard, Mr Dixon? Yesterday the Berriedale Inn was held up. Three nasty vagabonds came into the taproom and held everyone there at gunpoint. They got away with a good deal of money and valuables. Mr Ball keeps a very nice house – it's a pity. Like the bad old days, ain't it?

Martin asked if the police were out.

Yes, Turner told him. Mounted constables had come from O'Brien's Bridge and were searching the district. More were expected from Hobart Town, because reports had come down the road today of another attack by the three men. He leaned further over the counter.

A farm near Claremont, he said. They beat the owner and hurt him bad – and they insulted his wife. You understand me, Mr Dixon? We don't know all the details yet – but these are really wicked villains. I hope the police get them, afore there's a murder. We don't want scum like those out here, do we?

No we don't. Thank you, Mr Turner, and take care.

I will, Mr Dixon. Thankee.

They rode north towards Faulkner's Rivulet, which entered the Derwent just below Claremont. It was now half-past nine. They kept to a rough bridle track through the bush, riding in single file, well back from the highway. Now they had to keep watch for the police as well as the Griffin gang, and Martin had a permanent knot in his stomach. Dalton was softly humming 'Old Folks at Home', and showed no sign of tension; but Martin noticed that he glanced about him constantly. Wilson's face showed nothing. He sat his horse easily, apparently relaxed, but he'd spoken very little since they'd left the Valley.

After half an hour they came out of the bush on to an empty green stretch of grass, studded here and there with cow dung. On its far side was a post-and-rail fence, enclosing a field where a small herd of dairy cattle was grazing. Wilson reined in his chestnut mare, and the others followed suit. He looked at Dalton.

You know where we are?

I think so. This is the Clements farm, on Faulkner's Rivulet.

Yes, and old Clements is a friend to us. We did business with him a good while ago, remember?

Aye. But how far would you trust him?

I don't intend to. It's his servant I want to find. Old Jim Banks, the pass-holder. Remember him? We brought him clothes and supplies when Clements was having hard times.

I remember: he was grateful. He won't grass on us to the traps. So what are you thinkin, Lucas?

We're not far here from the farm that Griffin visited. Maybe he's been here too, and Banks can tell us something.

They rode across the grass to a leaning gate in the fence. Martin jumped down and opened it, and the others rode in. He led his horse through, closed the gate and mounted again. On the other side of the field was a long slab-built cowshed, where a grey-haired, bent old man was raking up dung in the fenced-off yard in front of it.

Sure, that's Banks all right, Dalton said, and they rode across the paddock towards him. The old man looked up, put aside his rake, and watched them come. Wilson and Dalton dismounted and tied their horses to the fence, and Banks came out of the yard and greeted them. He had a broken nose and crooked yellow teeth and the lined and weathered face of so many old convicts: a face whose worn flesh seemed almost to be metamorphosing into stone. His cotton shirt was ragged, and his moleskin trousers stained and derelict. Wilson spoke to him at some length, questioning him. Martin, who'd chosen to wait in the saddle at a little distance, could not hear much of what Wilson said, though he gathered that he spoke about the raid at Claremont. Banks answered at some length; then he gestured towards the west. His voice was hoarse and his speech indistinct, and Martin could make out nothing of what he said. By the time Banks had finished speaking Wilson was frowning. He spoke sharply, his words now audible to Martin.

Do you realize what you've done?

The old man drew back a step, his face showing alarm. When he replied, still inaudibly, he did so with a sound of guilty protest; then he hung his head, looking from Wilson to Dalton from under his brows as though awaiting punishment.

The two men looked at each other, and shook their heads. They turned away and mounted their horses again and headed back across the paddock. Coming up to Martin, Wilson jerked his head.

Come on. Griffin's up on Mount Faulkner.

He guided his mare to a trough by the fence and let her drink, and Dalton and Martin followed his example. Then they rode out through the gate, while Banks stood watching them go. Martin couldn't imagine what the old man might have said to anger Wilson, and he felt a sudden pity for him. Like many another aged convict out here in the country, Banks would spend the rest of his life a bachelor, and die alone in his crude bush hut. Closing the gate, Martin looked back at him, and the old man raised his hand in a forlorn wave.

They now rode directly west across the area of open grassland outside the property, making for the bush and Mount

Faulkner. It was cloudy but still fine. The mountain rose above the trees and stood out against the sky: a grey-green, bush-covered hump with cloud shadows on it; not much more than a hill. It seemed quite close. Martin and Wilson were riding side by side, with Dalton in front; after a time Wilson began to speak, and told Martin what he'd learned from Banks. He spoke unemotionally, almost mechanically, glancing at Martin seldom, his face remaining expressionless, as it had done since they'd left the Valley.

Griffin and his men had come to the Clements property very early this morning, he said, but they hadn't gone near the main house. Instead they'd visited Banks, who'd been milking the cows in their shed. Banks had known better than to be hostile; instead, he'd made himself agreeable, and had given his visitors some provisions from his store. What they'd wanted from him were directions on how to get to the top of the mountain. They'd apparently learned that there was a property up there called Cloud Farm, owned by a man called Evans and his wife, and that a rough track led up to it: but they didn't know the location of the track, which had to be reached through thick bush. They wanted Banks to describe where it was and how to get there.

They threatened to get nasty if he didn't tell them, Wilson said. There's a bridle path close to here, running south-west through the bush, that leads to the track – and a big stringybark marks the entrance to the bridle path. Instead of giving them false information, Banks told them the truth. The old fool has condemned those people up at Cloud Farm to being robbed and abused – or worse. Griffin has about two hours' start on us, so it's all over by now. That creature's going to commit murder soon, just for the pleasure of it.

Do you think so?

I know it. I know what he's made of, now. Liam knew it long ago. I should have listened to Liam.

You think he'll still be up there?

Wilson said that he thought so. The reason they hadn't robbed the Clements farm, he said, was probably that they were much too close to the last place they'd raided, and knew that the police might arrive here at any time. So they'd needed to move on quickly. Cloud Farm no doubt sounded ideal, in its isolation. They might well dig in there.

They'll feel they're on top of the world, Wilson said. They'll have the advantage over anyone approaching – including us. They might even make it their headquarters.

But surely the police will go up there?

Perhaps – eventually. But it's a hard climb, and most of the constabulary are too damned idle to relish the idea – and too white-livered to want to risk being picked off.

He ceased to speak, and the only sounds were the slow thudding of hooves and bird-calls from the trees in front of them. Soon they'd enter the gum forest, and would have to ride in single file. Before this happened, Martin wanted to talk to Wilson further; but something in Wilson's face made him reluctant to try. Lucas's former affability was gone; ever since the discovery of what Griffin had done to May Bosworth, his face had become a wooden mask.

Suddenly, though, he spoke again. He didn't look at Martin but stared straight ahead, sitting very straight in the saddle.

This is all my fault, Martin.

No, Lucas, surely that's not true.

Oh yes, it's true. I encouraged Griffin out of foolish curiosity, and I wouldn't see what he was. Frances saw it, and Liam saw it – but I didn't listen. Now that poor child is ruined.

You couldn't have known what he'd do.

He thinks he has supernatural powers. He claims he can dominate the minds of others. But he can only dominate feeble minds, and those that wish to be dominated. Griffin is merely a foul devil: I should have seen that.

His mouth worked, and his eyes glittered with anger. He drew a deep breath, and straightened his shoulders. All we can do now is stop him, he said. Stop all three of them.

What's your plan when we reach them, Lucas?

The question sounded foolish in his own ears. And yet it had needed to be asked, Martin thought.

Plan? Wilson turned his head and looked at him. Plan? They must die: all three of them.

A chill went through Martin's bowels. He'd known that this would be Lucas's intention; and yet he'd hoped that there might be an alternative: capturing and securing them, perhaps, and leaving them somewhere for the police to find. Now such thoughts seemed foolish. Griffin and his henchmen would be executed because Wilson had decided they'd be executed – unless they managed to gain the upper hand. And in that case, Martin thought, his own death waited at the top of the humped green mountain.

The track, when they came to it, was rough and stony and very steep, but wide enough for them to have taken all three horses abreast, had they wished. On either side was a forest of giant stringybarks with shaggy, peeling brown trunks; among these were occasional blue-green clumps of wattle. They rode upwards for two hours, stopping occasionally to rest their sweating, panting horses, and to drink from their water bottles. Martin drew out some of the bread and cheese he'd bought in Berriedale, and they ate in the saddle. The trees hid most of the view from up here; but occasionally, looking back to the east, they caught glimpses of the countryside below, with distant bends of the Derwent gleaming like metal. It grew cooler, and a wind sprang up, roaring through the tops of the stringybarks like a river in flood.

It was after one o'clock when the track levelled out a little, and they sensed that they were near the summit, though the view ahead of them was hidden by trees. A little later they came to a gate that spanned the track, with a post-and-rail fence running off on each side. It leaned half open, and a painted legend on its top bar read: *Cloud Farm.* Inside the fence the stringybarks continued, but they were sparser here, with stretches of grass in between: stumps could be seen, and it was evident that the forest was being cleared. Dalton wiped his mouth with the back of his hand and studied the scene.

I believe we're here, Lucas.

I believe we are.

No sign of the farm, though.

No, and just as well. We don't want them to see us coming.

Nor hear us.

Nor hear us. But that won't be so easy.

You want to leave the horses?

Not yet.

Wilson rode through the gate, and the others followed. They rode on up the track a short distance, and it levelled out completely. They were on the top of the mountain here, and the trees grew even fewer. Soon they had a belt of grass and ferns on either side, studded with lichen-covered boulders. The forest now stood some fifty yards off, and they began to be somewhat exposed. The wind had dropped to a breeze, and it made little sound now that the trees were at a distance. The soft thudding of the horses' hooves and the clinking of their bridle bits seemed dangerously loud, and Martin surveyed the track ahead. It ran to a point where it evidently began to run downhill, since all that showed there was sky, and distant treetops. Chief shook his head from side to side as though sensing something, and Martin patted his neck.

Wilson tilted his hat over his eyes, studying the situation. He reined in his horse, and the others did the same.

The farmhouse could be over that rise, Wilson said. I think it's time to go on foot. What's your opinion, Liam?

Sure, I think you're right.

Martin's mouth was dry, and his heart began to race in a way that made him feel faintly sick. Sitting astride his pony, he watched the others dismount, and knew he should do the same. But he found it difficult to move: he seemed to be frozen in the saddle. He watched Wilson and Dalton take their rifles from their saddle scabbards. There was no need for them to carry shot and powder flasks on foot: all their guns were loaded and capped, and they had filled the pockets of their pilot coats with cartridges, caps, and spare loaded cylinders for their revolvers. Wilson half cocked the hammer of his rifle, and hung the gun by its sling over his shoulder. Then he looked up at Martin.

I think you should wait here, Martin. This isn't an easy situation. We may not have much cover, and I tell you again: I don't want to risk your being killed.

I'll come, Martin said.

It's your choice, and I appreciate your grit. But I'm not easy about it.

Martin dismounted, drew the Enfield from its scabbard, and half-cocked the hammer as the others had done. He looked up to find Wilson and Dalton both watching him.

I agree with Lucas, Dalton said. You should think again. It's a game young fella you are, and no doubt of it – but it's little you know of what this sort of scrap is like. Leave it to Lucas and me.

I'll come, Martin said again. He could summon up no other words, and every small action he performed required a conscious effort.

Dalton shook his head, and turned away. He and Wilson led their horses a few yards off the track to a group of blue gum saplings, and Martin followed. They tethered the horses to the trunks of the young trees; then they set off westwards down the track, walking with as little sound as possible, and ceasing to talk. The breeze had dropped altogether, and the afternoon was fine and cool. When they came to the point where the track sloped downwards, they found themselves looking into a shallow valley. Wilson dropped on his belly in the grass beside the track, and Dalton and Martin did the same. Peering from the edge of the slope, they examined the valley in silence.

It was little more than a hollow which had been mostly cleared of trees, and the Evans farmhouse sat at its centre, about a hundred yards away. It was a simple, slab-built cottage with a wood-shingled roof, a small front verandah, and a stone chimney at one end. A little way south of the house was a long set of stables, also slab-built, where horses could be seen tethered in their stalls. There appeared to be an unusual number: four riding horses, and two big Clydesdales for ploughing. On the northern side was a cowshed and an extensive green pasture where some half dozen cows were grazing; behind it were fields that had recently been ploughed. Beyond that, on the western side of the mountain, the eucalyptus forest continued, with the final blue of the ranges visible above the treetops. The farm was an island in the wilderness.

The place seemed unnaturally quiet, and looked deserted. There were no signs of human activity, and no sound came up to them but the murmuring of domestic hens, wandering free in the yard. No dogs barked; there were none to be seen. Wilson pointed to the stables, looking sideways at Dalton, and now Martin recognized Wilson's black stallion and the mare and the gelding that had been brought from Richmond. Dalton, staring down at them, spoke under his breath.

So Griffin's here, right enough.

But where. Inside the house?

Maybe. Maybe nearby. But one thing sure: they must have heard us comin. They're lyin low. And they'll have taken those people prisoner, I'm thinkin.

We'll have to go down there.

Aye. But we'll be needin cover, if we're goin to get near.

Wilson pointed again. Just below to their right, between them and the house, was a weatherboard barn.

That might do.

We may have trouble reachin it. The sods have one of our Enfields, remember – and that has a range of four hundred yards.

He'd have to be a very good shot. I doubt that any of them are.

They looked at each other, and then at the barn. After some moments, the Irishman nodded. Even now, Martin saw, there was a glint of humour in his eyes, as though what was happening touched some secret source of amusement in him.

May all the saints be with us, he said. He crossed himself, then set his hat more securely on his head.

Listen to me, Martin, Wilson said. You're going to stay here. I want you to cover us. You can easily reach the house with that Enfield. If you see one of them get behind us, shoot him – and do it very fast. Have you got the stomach for that?

I believe so.

Wilson nodded. He reached out his hand and lightly squeezed Martin's shoulder. Keep your head down, he said, and Martin experienced a surge of affection for him, as though Lucas had wished him a final farewell.

Wilson stood up and began to run down the gentle green slope towards the barn, weaving as he ran. Dalton followed. Almost instantly, the report of one of the stolen double-barrelled shotguns sounded from the southern side of the house, and Martin saw a cloud of gunsmoke rising from behind a heap of sawn logs there. Its smell carried across to him, pungent in the cool air. A second shot followed, but Wilson and Dalton had reached the barn untouched. They were visible there to Martin, but could not be seen from the house, and Martin calculated that their position was at least eighty yards distant from it. The shotgun had a range of only fifty yards, which was why its pellets had fallen short. Whoever was targeting Wilson and Dalton from the woodheap had no hope of hitting them; but whichever one of the three men below had the Enfield could do so easily. That would probably be Griffin, Martin thought.

The man behind the woodheap was no doubt reloading, and silence fell again. It was now very still, and the calls of magpies from the gum forest came sharply across the hollow. No other sounds: the drawling of the hens had ceased; they'd vanished from the yard. Martin took advantage of the lull to settle himself against a boulder in the grass and rest the barrel of his Enfield on top of it. He had cocked the hammer in the firing position, and sighted along the barrel at the woodheap. There was now a pause in time which seemed to have no dimension, while Martin lay motionless, and Wilson and Dalton crouched against the wall of the barn. He saw everything now with great clarity, and felt everything to be miraculous. The green lichen on the rock where his gun was balanced. The small black ants that scurried there. An expanse of blue sky in the west. His life until now had been pleasant but banal, it seemed; this was its highest point, for better or worse. He'd wanted adventure with Wilson: but was this adventure? If so, it was mingled with dread, and didn't resemble any adventure he'd read about. It was a vast uncertainty; a frowning threat, a singing in the air that was worrying, while the world at its edges remained changeless and quite unremarkable.

Wilson had moved, down at the barn. He was peering around the corner towards the woodheap, his Colt revolving rifle tucked into his shoulder in the firing position. He too must have realized that the man with the shotgun couldn't hit him, and was hoping to lure him out; but Martin wondered if he'd remembered the Enfield. And now, for the second time that day, it seemed to him that what he saw had its existence in the dimension of dream, so that the figures he watched were no longer real, but part of an animated frieze. This didn't prevent him from remaining alert; nor did it cause the tension that stretched his nerves to be in any way eased.

The man behind the woodheap suddenly appeared in full view, aiming his shotgun at Wilson. Even at this distance, Martin recognized the hemp-coloured hair and dough-like face. Henry Hand fired, and the shot fell short again. Wilson fired back, but Hand had dropped back quickly behind the logs. At the same time a second shotgun was fired at Wilson, this time from behind the nearby stables. Gunsmoke rose there, a horse whinnied loudly, and Isaac Smallshaw edged into the open, firing his second barrel. Dalton, who had come from behind the barn to stand next to Wilson, immediately shot Smallshaw with his Enfield. The stocky man threw up his hands and dropped without a sound, his gun falling beside him. Henry Hand stood up from behind the woodheap, aiming at Wilson again. Wilson shot him before he could fire, and Hand crumpled sideways beside the logs, his top half visible from where Martin lay. A dark stain of blood was spreading on his shirt below his chest; but he wasn't dead. He twitched, and Martin heard him groan.

Now a deeper silence fell, broken only by Hand's distant groaning and by alarm calls from the magpies, who were wheeling above the trees on the northern side of the house. Inside his trance, Martin wondered why Hand had exposed himself to fire so recklessly. Then it came to him: when Wilson had fired his gun, Hand had assumed that it would only have a single shot in it, like the Enfield and other rifles, and that Wilson would need a minute or more to reload. Like most people in the colony, Hand probably had no knowledge of the Colt revolving rifle. Martin's thoughts now turned to Griffin. He searched for a sign of him, examining every point around the hollow, but found nothing. Wilson and Dalton, he saw, had retreated behind the barn again, where Dalton was kneeling to reload, biting the paper off a cartridge to free up the powder and using his ramrod to force powder and ball down the barrel of his gun.

Hand's groans continued in the stillness, and Wilson and Dalton stood motionless as sentries, holding their guns and seeming to wait for something. Nothing happened; then Wilson moved to the corner of the barn and looked down at Hand. He called out, giving his voice its full resonance.

Tell us, Hand: where is Roy Griffin?

The voice that replied was weak and moaning and only just audible.

Not here. Gone.

Gone where?

Gone into the bush. You won't find him now.

Martin saw Wilson and Dalton look at each other, and confer inaudibly. Then Wilson called out again.

You'd better not be lying, or you'll die. And you'll die if you reach for that gun.

There was silence for a moment. Then Hand called out in a weak, pleading voice that was only just audible.

Help me. Please help me.

You'll get no help until you answer my questions. Where are the people who own this farm?

Inside.

Are they alive?

There was no answer, only another groan: weaker, this time. Wilson and Dalton conferred again; then Wilson looked up to where Martin lay, and called out to him.

Martin, we're going down. Keep a good look out.

Martin raised a hand in acknowledgement, and shifted his grip on his gun.

Wilson and Dalton moved out from behind the barn and started down the hill, their rifles in the firing position. Wilson walked in the lead with Dalton only a few yards behind, and Martin scanned every part of the hollow, moving his gaze from the south to the north. He knew what was going to happen: knew and yet did not know. His body was cold as though encased in ice, but he found that his hands didn't tremble.

He saw Griffin before Griffin fired: the grey wideawake hat and white face. He'd appeared on top of the pitched roof, lying on the far side, and was peering over the central ridge. His rifle was balanced on the ridge, pointed at Wilson. Martin aimed with great care, and fired. As he squeezed the trigger, he saw the puff of smoke from Griffin's gun, and heard the report. He'd aimed at Griffin's forehead: he saw a hole appear there and a thin stream of blood run down. Even at this distance, Griffin's eyes could be seen to widen; then he fell backwards, vanishing down the far side of the roof.

Only then did Martin look down at Wilson, hoping to find him unhurt. Instead he was lying on his back, his hat flung off, with Dalton kneeling beside him.

When Martin came up to them, having run down the slope, he was panting and trembling. Dalton was still kneeling in the same position, on Wilson's left. He'd taken off his pilot coat and rolled it up and made a pillow for Wilson's head, and he was holding Wilson's hand. There was a small stain of blood at the base of Lucas's chest, soaking through his pale blue blouse.

Martin knelt down opposite Dalton, on Wilson's right.

How bad is it?

Dalton looked up at him, his mouth bent crooked as though from pain. Can you not see? We're losin him. I've checked the wound. It's right near the heart.

Now Martin looked down at Wilson. Lucas looked back at him with a steady gaze, the singular blue of his eyes more vivid than ever. But the bronze of his face had changed to a parchment colour, his lips were pale as well, and only his mane of chestnut hair shone with a life of its own. When he spoke his voice was weak, so that Martin had to bend over him.

Liam's right, Martin. I'm finished.

But there isn't much blood. We could get you below to a doctor.

Wilson closed his eyes.

I'm bleeding inside. Don't try and move me.

Martin looked at Dalton, and Dalton shook his head and frowned. His eyes were full of tears, which he made no attempt to brush away. He still held Wilson's hand.

He and Martin continued to kneel without speaking. Lucas's eyes remained closed, but his chest still rose and fell. Martin glanced across to the woodheap where Hand lay: his groaning had stopped, and Martin assumed he was dead. Silence continued for perhaps three minutes; then Wilson grimaced. He opened his eyes and looked at the sky, and his lips moved. His voice now was little more than a whisper.

Take care of the Valley, Liam. Look after Frances.

I will, Lucas, I will.

Wilson turned his eyes to Martin. Their blue now was clouded, and his voice was so faint that Martin could only just hear it.

Keep faith with the hills, Martin.

His eyes closed, and Martin and Dalton knelt in silence again. How long it lasted this time, Martin could not be sure, since Time seemed to be suspended. Suddenly Wilson drew a deep, harsh breath through his mouth. After he'd let it out, his breathing had apparently stopped. But then he drew another deep breath, as though fighting for air. There was a pause; then he drew another. His eyes opened, and he stared above him with an expression of fierce urgency. But now he drew no more breaths, and his look became stern and fixed.

Dalton bent close to his lips and listened for his breath. Then he closed Wilson's eyes with his finger and thumb.

He's gone.

He crossed himself, and said something under his breath that Martin couldn't hear. He stood up, and his face was empty of expression, but the tears were still wet on his cheeks.

You wait here with him. I'm goin inside the house.

Martin got to his feet, watching Dalton walk to the verandah. The silence seemed more complete than before: it was as though this little hollow had waited for Wilson's death. He stood by Wilson's body for perhaps five minutes; then Dalton came back. His mouth was twisted, and his face was set in an expression that Martin at first read as anger, but then saw as a fury beyond anger.

Don't go in that house, Dalton said.

He walked across to the woodheap, and Martin followed him. Hand was still lying in the same position on his side. The blood on his shirt had spread to cover most of the area of his stomach, and a dark pool of it shone dully on the worn patch of grass beside him. His pallid, sullen face had a yellow colour now, and at first Martin thought he was dead; but his dull eyes were watching them. He spoke in a low voice, repeating his plea of before.

Help me.

I've seen what you've done to those people, Dalton said.

No. It was Griffin. He made us.

You raped that poor woman. All three of you.

No. Please help me.

Help you, is it? I'll help you to Hell.

Dalton pulled his revolver from his belt, aimed carefully, and shot Hand through the head, causing blood to spring out in a small jet, spattering on the grass. Hand jerked and then was still, and Martin turned away, fighting down an impulse to vomit.

When he looked around again Dalton was standing watching him, the revolver back in his belt.

Come with me. We'll make certain sure that other piece of scum is dead as well.

He walked away towards the corner of the house, and Martin followed him. Around at the back of the house they found Griffin's body in long grass and weeds that grew there, the Enfield beside him. He lay on his back, his bulging green eyes looking at the sky, and his lips were parted in what looked like a grin. Martin glanced at him once, and turned away.

You took care of that creature, sure, Dalton said. And what a fine shot it was.

But too late, Martin said.

Not your fault, young Martin. Never think that.

He put a hand briefly on Martin's shoulder. Then he walked on around the house in the direction of the stables. Martin followed him, and they passed the corpses of two dogs. In front, next to the woodheap, Isaac Smallshaw lay on his back, his dark eyes open and staring, the shotgun beside him. Dalton paused only for a moment to study the body; then he turned and went on. Just in front of the stables lay the trunk of a big grey eucalypt, probably left to be cut up for firewood. Dalton sat down on it and put his head in his hands. Martin sat beside him, saying nothing, and the rays of the mild afternoon sun shone down on them like a consolation.

After a time Dalton looked up and took a deep breath.

May God forgive me. I never shot a man in cold blood before.

Martin said nothing, and Dalton spat in the dust at his feet, and wiped his mouth with the back of his hand.

I told you not to go into that house because it's better that way, he said.

How many people are in there?

Just the two: Mr and Mrs Evans. A young couple – no children, and no farmhands. They were leadin a hard life here.

Are they dead?

Evans is dead. He was sittin tied in a chair when I came in. They'd cut most of his fingers off, and destroyed his face, and killed him. Tryin to get him to tell them where his money was, no doubt. And how much money would he be havin, poor young fella?

And his wife?

Dalton put his hands on his knees, studying the dust at his feet as though in search of something. He frowned, his long upper lip drawn down.

I found her in the bedroom. She was tied to the bed, and she was naked. I took a blanket from the bed and put it over her. Then I untied her and brought her some brandy to drink that I found. All three of them raped her, she told me. At first she couldn't say much else, so I left her to dress and recover herself. I went back in the other room, and I took poor Evans's body off the chair and laid it down and covered it with a blanket that I brought from the bedroom. When I told his wife he was dead, she broke down weepin as though never to stop, and I left her so. We're goin to have to look after her, Martin.

Yes. Of course.

I'll tell you how it is: I've thought it out. We must get her down the track to the Clements place. She can no doubt ride a horse: if she can't, I'll take her on mine. I'll get old Clements and his wife to look after her, then. They'll do what I ask, or I'll know the reason why. Dave Clements can take her in to O'Brien's Bridge tomorrow. She'll be attended to there, and can tell her story to the police. We'll sleep tonight in Clements' barn, unless the traps are nosin about.

And what about Griffin and the other two? And Evans? What are we to do about them?

Do? We'll do nothin. Mrs Evans will tell the traps that these buggers up here are destroyed, and why. The traps can come and attend to them how they like – and they can take Evans down below for decent burial.

And Lucas?

They'll not find Lucas. They never found him in life, and they'll not find him in death. You and I will bury him here, and give him the best grave we can. He once said he'd be buried in these hills – and he will be, God rest him.

Suddenly, tears filled Dalton's eyes again, and he clenched his fists on his knees, staring in front of him. The Celtic cadences in his speech, never far away, had become much stronger.

He was my chief, and the best friend I had. There'll be no-one else like him, and now that he's gone my life's empty. They called him nothin but a bushranger, but he was somethin much more than that. You saw that, young Martin.

He could have been anything he wanted, Martin said. I think he was meant to be a poet.

Dalton sniffed, and rubbed his nose with the back of his

hand, blinking away his tears. That may be, he said. He could make you see things.

He could. He changed my life.

Did he, so? Well, he had great hopes for you. He thought you'd help him with his high aims for the Valley. He was a man who had noble dreams – and who might have made them come true, if the people around him had been better. What he didn't understand was the wickedness in particular men, and that those kinds of men love evil. No matter what we do to make the world right, there'll always be devils like Griffin.

He fell silent, staring into some inward distance. His bleak grey eyes were empty of hope, and the small white scar beside his mouth seemed more prominent than usual. Martin felt a rush of compassion that almost resembled tenderness; but he could find no way to express it. Finally Dalton turned and looked at him.

The Valley might not have worked as it should, but it was the only real home I ever had, since leavin Connemara. I was happy there. I thought of bringin that little woman of mine up there, and startin a family. Well, it's over now. We must all shift for ourselves.

Won't you stay in the Valley? Won't you carry on Lucas's work ?

I will not. I couldn't do it. I lied to him, may I be forgiven, to give him comfort. How could a simple man like me carry on what he was doin? No, it's over. You and I must ride up there tomorrow and tell the people that. Bill Bosworth will be all right: he can carry on farmin, and there's no price on his head. McLeod and Jarvis must find a way to go somewhere else, and keep their heads down. And I must take Frances Lambert down to Berriedale and set her on her way to Hobart Town. She has friends there, poor creature, and I hope they'll look after her.

He looked at Martin.

And you must pick up your belongins and go home, young fella. It was time anyway. No police will be lookin for you. And no-one will ever know that you shot Roy Griffin.

Why? I'm not ashamed of it.

And neither you should be. But a thing like that could cause you trouble, people bein what they are. I told Mrs Evans that Lucas Wilson and I shot them all – and that's what she'll tell the authorities. Let it be so, squire. It's best that way.

And what about you, Liam? What will you do?

Dalton bent forward and picked up a twig from the dust. He bent it to and fro, and then snapped it.

I'm thinkin of givin myself up.

Oh, Christ, Liam, don't do that.

Dalton held up his hand. Listen to me. The outlaw days are over – I've told you that. There's nowhere left to hide, and I've no stomach to keep on runnin. My hope was to lead a peaceful life in the Valley, the way that Lucas and I planned, shut away from the world. That won't happen now. So I think I'll go down and serve out my sentence. It might be one that's not too long, if I'm lucky. I've killed no-one until now – and these creatures would have swung if I hadn't killed them. If I were a free citizen, they'd give me a reward.

Maybe they'll give you a pardon.

Dalton smiled. I doubt that. A sentence that leaves me a few years at the end, to live as a free man – that's the best I can expect.

I'll testify in court, Liam. That might help you get a pardon.

Dalton shook his head.

You've a generous heart, squire, but I doubt they'd pay much heed. And now let's be goin, and do what we have to do for Lucas.

At a little after two o'clock, Dalton and Martin Dixon buried Lucas Wilson.

They found a barrow, and lifted him into it, under a blanket. They also found a pick and two shovels. Then, with Martin carrying the tools, Dalton wheeled his chief up the slope out of the hollow, and on to the track. He was very strong: despite Wilson's size, it seemed to give him little effort. Having reached the track, he set down the barrow and they both looked around them. On the northern side of the track the trees grew well apart, almost like those of a park, leaving stretches of grass in between.

Dalton pointed. Over there, he said.

He wheeled the barrow onto the grass, and continued in a northerly direction, weaving among the trees until the track was out of sight. One of Wilson's arms hung out of the barrow. As the vehicle went over the bumps, his long, elegantly-shaped hand swung about as though he gestured, expounding his dream of a promised country. Seeing this brought tears to Martin's eyes for the first time.

Dalton now moved west for a short way, and they came to a place where the mountain sloped sharply downwards, and the virgin bush receded in front of them for miles. Here Dalton set the barrow down, on a level of yellow grass surrounded by slender eucalypts, their white trunks shining in the sun. From here the farthest ranges were visible. Their colour was a deep grey-blue in the cool light, and an autumn haze lay over them: pale and fragile, with a hint of gold, they had the appearance of silk. It gave them the beauty of mirage, and brought to Martin's mind his walks with Lucas.

This should be the right place, Dalton said.

They set to work with the pick and shovels. The soil here was not too hard at first, but then they came to clay, and it took them some time to get the grave dug deep enough, and the shadows of the gums began to lengthen. When they were ready to lower Wilson into his grave, Dalton took his arms and Martin his legs, with the blanket still over him. Grimly, swiftly, they covered him with earth.

Now we'll make a marker of rocks, Dalton said.

There were plenty of well-shaped rocks among the grass, and they built a little cairn. They stood beside it and removed their hats.

I'll be sayin a prayer, Dalton said. I've gone to many a burial in Connemara, and listened to the priest sayin the prayers for the dead. I believe I can remember some words. I hope you won't mind, you bein a Protestant?

I'll be glad for you to do it, Liam.

Dalton closed his eyes and recited.

O God we humbly entreat you for the soul of your servant Lucas Wilson, whom you have summoned today from this world. Deliver him not into the hands of the enemy, but bid your holy angels receive him in paradise. Amen.

Amen, Martin said.

Dalton crossed himself, and Martin said:

This is a good place, Liam. He's where he would have liked to be.

Aye. That's what I thought.

They stood without further speech, and Martin's eyes turned towards the hills: borders of that land outside reality that had summoned Wilson's spirit.

Time to go, he heard Dalton say. We need to get down that track before darkness comes.

BOOK THREE

*

Hugh Dixon

1

When Bob Wall was charged with murder, I was able to persuade my great-uncle Walter to defend him. At the time, Bob and I both saw this as a stroke of luck; but these days I'm inclined to think differently. As I see it now, two unmatched pieces in the pattern of my life came together, just when this was needed.

This took place in 1953: the year I began work as an artist on *The Tasmanian Mail.* Over the years, I'd thought about Bob only seldom, though I'd never forgotten him. He'd ridden out of my life forever on the stolen Malvern Star: he'd become a lost boy, existing only in childhood memory. But in 1953, he suddenly reappeared.

If we live long enough, the people and places belonging to our youth begin to take on the quality of fiction. This is how it is in my case. When I look back to 1953, reveries and actuality are mingled. Glass-thin, sunny visions of joy and the inexpressible are blurred and interwoven with the ordinary, and the people of that far-off decade inhabit another life: a life in which I took part, but where I almost seem to be someone else. My native city has changed since then as well. These days, its penal origins are receding into a final dimness; but in the 1950s, the nineteenth century of its birth still hung on in the central areas of Hobart, like an ancient, ineradicable stench. This wasn't so of the suburbs – whose houses and streets, mostly on the edges of the country, had an untroubled innocence about them – but the city itself remained a dwarf child of London: the sombre, gimcrack London of Dickens and Henry Mayhew. Derelict figures out of Dickens still passed one by in the poorer parts of town, and phantoms of wickedness lurked in the laneways, and bubbled up out of the drains. Serious crime was rare; but when it took place, it seemed to reach out from that old, hard-knuckled century that was gone.

That March, when I was twenty, I started work at the *Mail.*

The position had come to me without my looking for it, through a man called Tom Thorpe. He was a part-time student at Art School: a man in his late thirties who'd enrolled in the black-and-white drawing class. He worked at night on the *Mail,* the city's daily newspaper. He was a lean, cheerful man who wore glasses and a collar and tie, looking rather like a clerk, in contrast to our fellow students. The men tended to wear berets and cravats, while many of the women wore loose, brightly-coloured smocks: signals of membership of an archaic Bohemia, preserved in amber in this European province in the Southern Ocean. (My own gesture towards this culture was a pair of suede boots: unconventional footwear I'd first seen on Walter Dixon.) Tom's drawing was clean and professional, I thought, if a little prosaic. He told me that he was a compositor, which meant that he made up the newspaper's pages for printing. He had an unassuming friendliness, and we got on well. He wanted to become a commercial artist, he told me; when he felt confident that he was skilled enough, he intended to leave the *Mail* and try to get work in a commercial studio, either here or on the mainland.

We would talk in low voices as we sketched, and discuss the work of some of our favourite black-and-white artists of the past: Tenniel's illustrations for the *Alice* books; the caricatures and cartoons of the nineteenth-century German artist Wilhelm Busch; Phil May's work in the old Sydney *Bulletin*; David Low's brilliant wartime cartoons; Norman Lindsay's erotic classical fantasies, whose improbably ripe nymphs and goddesses belonged more to a sunny Sydney of the 'twenties than to the groves of ancient Greece, their knowing smiles those of compliant barmaids. 'Norm's wet dreams', Tom called these; but we acknowledged Lindsay's technical mastery. Occasionally Tom would walk around to my desk and inspect my work; he seemed genuinely impressed, and would always compliment me. I thought he was just being polite; but I'd discover otherwise. One afternoon, as we walked up the street together after class, he made me a surprising offer.

Would you be interested in a job, Hugh?

I asked him what kind of job, and he smiled. He had the air of a man with agreeable news.

A job on the *Mail*, he said. As an apprentice press artist.

I stared at him. I didn't know what a press artist was, and said so.

Tom explained. There were only two such artists on the *Mail*: the chief press artist and his assistant. Their duties were mainly to retouch the photographs that went in the paper, and to prepare the layouts for the social pages and the Saturday magazine section. In addition, I might expect to contribute an occasional political cartoon – although this was mainly the prerogative of the chief press artist, Gordon Carter. Gordon's assistant had recently resigned, and they were looking for a replacement. It wasn't easy to find a black-and-white artist, and Tom was prepared to recommend me. Gordon and he were friendly, and he felt sure that Gordon would be satisfied with the quality of my work.

I was gratified by Tom's confidence in me, and half interested in his proposal; and yet I hesitated. I wasn't sure that this was the kind of work I wanted to do, I told him. My aim was to become an illustrator, and I was currently sending samples of my drawings to the book publishers and magazines on the mainland, hoping to be given commissions. So far I hadn't been successful, but I intended to persevere. Also, I should probably finish my diploma before looking for full-time work.

But Tom persuaded me to think again. There were very few jobs for artists in a small town like ours, he said, and they didn't come up often. I could always finish my diploma part-time; but I should bear in mind that nobody got taken on as a commercial artist on the strength of the diploma: samples of work were what employers based their decisions on.

It'd be a real start for you, Tom said. You'd eventually be doing some of the political cartoons – and being able to show published work like that ought to impress those book publishers. Am I right?

I agreed that he was; and all of a sudden, I made up my mind. I'd be happy for him to speak to Gordon Carter, I said, and thanked him for his help.

Having done so, I began to consider certain other factors that such a swerve in my future might bring. I'd turn twenty-one this year, but I was still living at home, dependent on my father's small allowance. It was an amount that gave me very little to spend on the most ordinary pleasures, and I'd begun to grow restive. I wanted to leave home, and rent a place of my own. I got on well enough with my parents; but I craved freedom. With a proper wage, freedom ought to be possible: freedom, and the possibility of setting up a proper studio for myself: one where I could seriously pursue my real aim in life – which was no longer to become a commercial illustrator, but a painter.

I'd come to this decision in my first year at Art School; but I hadn't lied to Tom Thorpe. I still intended to try and earn my living as an illustrator, but my ultimate ambition was to paint. I'd spoken about this to no-one except Walter Dixon, and didn't intend to declare it to anyone else or to try and exhibit until I had reason to be confident of my talent. Meanwhile, my final aim remained secret.

The way in which I'd recognized my true vocation had been sudden but natural, since I hadn't discarded my love of illustration, but had simply stepped through a door that led beyond it. It was great-uncle Walter, indirectly, who had opened the door. He subscribed to a glossy magazine on contemporary art, and passed copies on to me. In one of these, some six months ago, I'd found an article on the American painter Andrew Wyeth, accompanied by a reproduction of his well-known painting, *Wind from the Sea.* It wouldn't be an exaggeration to say that this single work was a revelation to me. I studied the lightly billowing, transparent curtains and the temperate summer landscape framed by the window in a sort of ecstasy. Here was an image as realistic and meticulous in its detail as any by my favourite illustrators – but one which went far beyond simple illustration. It was an opening onto a world behind appearances which could never be described in words, and I realized in an instant that this was what I'd always unconsciously searched for, and had wanted to depict from my earliest years. The empty room and the quiet, enigmatic New England landscape outside, with its vacant blond meadow and glimpse of water and low, dark border of pines, was magically familiar, since it could have been a scene in the island of my birth, whose cold winters and evanescent summers were surely similar to New England's. Transformed into a landscape in a dream, the scene in this picture was deeply familiar to me, and the warm and fugitive breeze that stirred these curtains and worn holland blind was surely the same sort of breeze as the one that stirred our curtains here – while the sun-warmed wooden frame of the window would no doubt have the same hot, dry odour as the window frames in my parents' house in summer: an odour I'd inhaled as a child, kneeling on the sill in the sitting-room, absorbing through that smell the special bliss that summer can bring to inhabitants of a cold climate. And behind all these things lay a mystery which could only be glimpsed: never finally grasped.

There were a number of reasons why I'd not imagined I'd be a painter until that moment. Although I'd been trained at Art School in oil painting as well as watercolour, I had no wish to work in oils. Most of the people at Art School saw oils as the medium a truly serious painter would adopt; but watercolour proved to be the medium I most loved, while landscape was the subject I most cared for. I'd taken moderate pleasure in working in oils, but it couldn't compare with the sheer excitement that watercolour gave me. You could make mistakes in an oil painting, and make readjustments as much as you liked; but there was only one chance with a watercolour. When you ran a wash, it either worked or it didn't; if you got it wrong, you must start again. Beginning a watercolour was like jumping off a cliff, and in this lay its excitement. Even more important was that watercolour offered an ideal method for painting light: and light, in my mind, was the ultimate source of joy; the ultimate elixir that made the spirit soar. The secret of this luminosity lay simply in the fact that you worked on white paper, and the greater the painter's skill in allowing the whiteness of the paper to show through the wash, the greater his ability to trap light. My skill was at this stage imperfect, but I was prepared to spend a lifetime improving it, like an alchemist in search of gold; and this gave me great happiness. I'd studied the work of such early masters as Claude Lorrain and Turner, and had seen what they could do with watercolour; but it was encountering Andrew Wyeth that changed my life's direction. Until I was confronted with *Wind from the Sea*, I had not really seen myself as a painter, and had resigned myself to being a modest illustrator. This was partly because of my lack of interest in oils, but also because most of the more vocal students at Art School despised realism. Abstract Expressionism was the new vogue, in that era, and this was seen as the ultimate artistic height to be scaled. But I had no interest in the abstract, or in anything but realism as a mode of expression. Now I'd discovered a great contemporary painter who was a realist in technique, and who worked with awe-inspiring mastery in watercolour. I felt fairly sure that my fellow art students would despise Wyeth for his realism, and dismiss it as mere illustration (as some New York critics did then), but I knew better: I'd found my guiding star, unfashionable though he might be. Any success I've subsequently had as a painter – and I've had my fair share – traces back to that first meeting with Wyeth's work, and the image of that empty summer room in Maine.

Some time after this, great-uncle Walter's glossy art magazine introduced me to another American realist who inspired me as much as Wyeth, and did just as much to confirm me in the direction I had to take. This was Edward Hopper, in whose work light was also the central source of inspiration, who also painted New England houses and landscapes, but who painted scenes in New York City as well, often at night. These night studies had a loneliness and strangeness about them, like the celebrated *Nighthawks*, in which the two men and the woman at the late-night drugstore counter seem marooned and without hope. And yet it was not depressing, this painting; the way it was rendered gave it a dark undercurrent of excitement, like the current black-and-white American crime films I was fond of: films like *Dark Passage* and *Out of the Past* – that genre now called *cinema noir*, though nobody called it that then. These films, which had perhaps been influenced in their visual techniques by *Terry and the Pirates*, had possibly been influenced by Hopper's work too, since he'd begun to make his name in the 1920s. And here I see another significant strand in my life's pattern. Milton Caniff's drawings had done something to start me in boyhood down a path which had brought me to this point: to Edward Hopper's pictures, and to a full understanding of the way I had to go.

Two paintings of Hopper's did most to influence me. One was *Gas*, in which a lone man stands by a row of petrol pumps on an empty road; the other was *Early Sunday Morning*, in which some modest brick two-storey shop buildings are lit by early sun in a deserted New York avenue. These images filled me with joy. The petrol pumps were more than petrol pumps, and the shop buildings were more than they seemed, being touched by a light which was the light of dream. They came close to surrealism, these images, and yet they were utterly real; and in this lay their alchemy. They set me on my way; they made me see what I could do, as is often the case with young painters who study the work of masters they admire. And I came to see something then that has stayed with me all my life: that the depiction of reality need not be limiting; that it's only through reality transformed that we truly experience magic. Fantasy and distortion are mere substitutes, empty of genuine wonder, since they're outside the realm of the possible, and we're only moved by the possible.

Once I'd realized this, the apparently ordinary scenes in which I'd grown up – the streets and railway tracks and little shops and factories of the Glenorchy district, for which I'd retained great fondness – became my subjects. I began to go out into those districts and make sketches – one of which became my first serious watercolour. This was a picture of Dickenson's Arcade, on Main Road in Moonah, where I used to meet Bob Wall – and which caused me to think of him whenever I passed. And here too, threads in the pattern asserted themselves. The yellow stucco building that housed the arcade, with its awning above the footpath and its row of tall, multi-paned windows on the upper storey, resembled the urban American buildings that Hopper painted. It dated from the 1920s – the era of those *Felix* comics which had given Bob refuge from his father's violence – and it seemed only natural to place Bob in the doorway in my picture: Bob at eleven years old, a lone, white-haired figure, waiting.

2

This account is a memoir, rather than an autobiography. By this I mean that I'm not attempting a detailed narrative of my own life. Rather, my main focus will remain on two people: on Bob Wall, and on my great-uncle Walter Dixon. For this reason, I'll continue to concentrate almost entirely on the way in which my inner and outer life intersected with theirs. The reader is thus spared details of other youthful friendships, my time at Art School, and my first erotic adventures with girls: exchanges, like so many in the 1950s, which led to much sensual pleasure and moist frustration, and usually fell short of consummation.

The period of my job on *The Tasmanian Mail*, however, is central to this narrative, since this was when Bob Wall appeared in my life again.

The newspaper where I started work as a press artist already belongs to an era of printing as archaic as the stage coach and the oil lamp. Recalling my time at the *Mail* calls up smells and sounds from a technology that's vanished: hot metal and printer's ink, the clatter of the giant linotype machines, glaring blue lights, and the late-night thundering of the presses in the lower depths of the building, making it resound like a drum.

The building stood in the centre of town: in Macquarie Street, next to the GPO. In a town where most business buildings dated from the last century, the *Mail*'s white art deco front, dating from the 1930s, looked stylishly modern to me, and I went up the steps when I first arrived there with a certain degree of awe, inhaling the odour of printer's ink in the foyer as though encountering the incense of an alien temple.

I would find myself working in a very small room on the second floor which I shared with my boss Gordon Carter, the chief press artist. The second floor was the level where those in command of the paper had a series of offices looking out on to Macquarie Street: the Editor, the Associate Editor, the News Editor, and the Chief of Staff. Their doors stood open on to a long corridor that ran the width of the building, its dense, tea-coloured linoleum gleaming and soundless. The newsroom where the reporters sat hammering on their portable typewriters was at the western end of this corridor. The press artists' little room was at the eastern end, facing the back of the building and looking onto nothing: the big windows were of frosted glass, so that it was almost like working underground. Next door, an even smaller room housed the teletype machine, which noisily spewed out stories from Reuters and other international news agencies, as well as stock exchange reports.

Gordon Carter was a good-humoured man who looked nothing like my notion of an artist. Always dressed in a suit, business shirt and tie, his stiff black hair cut extremely short back and sides, he was tall and thin, with a badly set broken nose. The suit and the haircut somehow failed to make him look respectable: his laconic jauntiness, the broken nose, and his sly grin when he cracked jokes put me in mind of my father's one-time friends of the race track – and in fact, Gordon was a dedicated punter. Before he sat down at his desk, with its sloping drawing-board, he would take off his suit coat and hang it behind the door, pull on a shapeless grey cardigan and stand rolling the first of his handmade cigarettes. He sat on an office chair facing the frosted glass windows, a big glass ashtray at his right hand and an internal phone at his left. I was perched on a high stool at a desk resembling a counter, running along a wall at right angles to Gordon's position of command. I would have felt rather like a nineteenth-century clerk, except that I was also equipped with a drawing-board, covered with sheets of butcher's paper. Fluorescent lights fizzed in the ceiling, and angled desk lamps with green shades and powerful bulbs burned day and night on our desks.

My first interview with Gordon had been brief. He'd looked through my portfolio of drawings in silence, squinting through the smoke of his cigarette. Then he took the cigarette from his mouth and grinned at me.

Right. Your work's pretty good, mate. When can you start?

I learned from Gordon how to retouch the photographs that went in the paper, using black and white paint and watercolour brushes of various sizes with the purpose of creating highlights and contrasts, and making chosen figures stand out. In my first week I found myself working on photographs of Soviet Premier Joseph Stalin, whose death had just been reported, and of Georgy Malenkov, his overweight successor. My knowledge of international affairs was sketchy then, but as I worked on the glossy black-and-white prints I began to feel myself connected to the world of great events. I also lettered headings for the Saturday magazine section. In those days it was thought elegant to use hand-lettered headings rather than type for special features, and I had to master the skills that commercial artists used for ticket writing. Gordon gave me a book of fancy types to use as models, whose style dated from the 1930s, and equipped me with a drawing pen, a battery of lettering nibs, and Indian ink. He looked at my first efforts with a critical eye, and it was some time before he allowed a heading of mine into the paper. He could suddenly grow sharp if he wasn't satisfied, his good humour disappearing, and I wasn't always able to feel relaxed with him. He was the master, I was the apprentice, and he proved to be exacting where work was concerned. On the whole, however, Gordon was amiable with me.

Our hours were unusual, because of the production schedule of the paper: four-thirty in the afternoon until one in the morning. I would then walk home to New Town, or else take a cab, as the trams had ceased running by then. We had Saturdays off, since there was no Sunday paper, and we also had Sunday afternoons free; but we worked on Sunday evenings to prepare copy for Monday. To compensate, we each took a day off during the week. Explaining the hours to me when I began, Gordon said:

You don't get out in the evenings much, in this job. We used to have an editor who'd say, 'The heart of the paper beats at night.' Romantic sort of bloke, old Brooks was.

He grinned; there was clearly nothing romantic about Gordon. But when I listened to the muffled, late-night throbbing from the floor below ground level, I understood the old editor's aphorism. During the evening, the tempo generated from the bowels of the building seemed to increase, as deadlines approached and the giant machines demanded to be fed. What they waited for from Gordon and me were the prints brought to us for retouching, carried along the corridor by Vernon the copy boy, or else by one of the photographers. When we'd done our work, the pictures went down to the printing floor, where they were subject to a number of transformations. A photoprinting process transferred them to zinc blocks; then engraving was carried out that made them ready for further metamorphosis, to emerge finally as the pliable stereotypes that went on the rotary presses. As the evening wore on, Gordon's phone would begin to ring: it was nearly always Pat Lynch, the short-tempered head of the Block Department, impatient for pictures that were late. When Vernon the copy boy wasn't about, I would hurry down with these myself, taking the lift to the basement and finding myself in the subterranean, blue-lit caverns where the paper was produced.

At the age of twenty, I still retained enough childishness to be entranced by the strangeness of the printing floor, and to be awed by the roar of the presses: so loud, at close quarters, that it was necessary to shout to be heard above them. It was as though I'd entered the halls of a legendary dwarf kingdom under ground, whose mysteries and industry were entirely alien to the ordinary world above. I'd linger to make quick sketches of the linotype operators in their tennis shades and dust coats, typing away at their giant machines, and the hurrying technicians attending to the presses. Out in the middle of the floor, Tom Thorpe would be standing by a set of raised tables, together with other compositors, arranging the metal slugs of type. I would wave to him and then hurry on to the Block Department, where short, square-built Pat Lynch would look up with fierce brown eyes, his blue-shadowed jaw pugnaciously out-thrust. It was Pat's barely-concealed notion that our job was unnecessary, and that he and his experts could do all that was needed to improve the pictures through the engraving process.

At last. That bloody copy. What have you blokes been doing? Oil paintings?

Some weeks after I began work, Pat's abilities were called in to avert a disaster: one that was caused by a joke of Gordon's. Gordon and I had begun to grow used to each other, and he seemed to be relaxed now about my ability to cope with the job. As the evening wore on, he would tell me stories concerning some of his reckless racing friends, or relate scandal that the journalists had passed on to him about some of our prominent citizens, or Members of Parliament. He would also tell me occasional off-colour jokes, most of which leaned towards wit rather than obscenity; he observed the sort of boundaries that most men did then. In quiet moments early in the evening we would sometimes amuse ourselves by adding temporary additions to the photographs: moustaches or beards were given to clean-shaven men in the social pages, and smiling society women lost teeth, or were turned into hags. These touches were later erased with twists of cotton wool that were spat on or dipped in a bowl of water. Every Saturday in the summer, the paper featured 'Bathing Beauty of the Week', and one Friday night Gordon dealt lewdly with Miss Sandy Bay: a smiling young woman in a one piece swimsuit, seated on a rock. He painted a highly realistic used condom lying next to her, and we had our laugh and forgot about it. But then, late in the evening, Gordon clapped his hand to his forehead and shouted.

*Je*sus!

What?

I left the Frenchy on the rock!

He jumped up and ran for the door, headed for those caverns of thundering machines which even now might be rolling off hundreds of copies of Miss Sandy Bay and the condom. Some time later he reappeared, visibly paler, and threw himself into his chair. He took out his pouch of tobacco and papers and rolled a cigarette with shaking fingers, saying nothing.

What happened? I said. Were you too late?

He looked at me, blowing out smoke, and shook his head.

Pat scraped it off on the block, he said. He was spitting chips.

He began to grin, and I laughed. Soon we were both laughing, pointing at each other and bending double. From that time on, I felt I was his associate, rather than his apprentice.

When I'd entered Art School in 1951, I'd continued my weekly visits to Walter Dixon. I did this partly out of duty, since I knew my visits were important to him, but also because I saw him not just as my benefactor but as a mentor. My gratitude had deepened into a kind of affection, as far as affection was possible in regard to such a prickly and unpredictable old man, and my respect for his intellect continued to grow.

His understanding of painting – or rather, of the sort of painting that I cared about – seemed to me more subtle than that of my teachers at Art School. His strongly-held views no doubt put limits on his appreciation of contemporary art; but since these views largely coincided with my own, they didn't inhibit our discussions. Like me, he had no interest in the abstract, and his enjoyment of the modern more or less stopped with the French Post-Impressionists; he had a particular passion for Cezanne. However, he made certain exceptions among the moderns, such as the Australian Russell Drysdale; and when I expressed enthusiasm for Wyeth and Hopper, I found him in agreement with me, though he didn't quite share my degree of excitement with them.

One afternoon, soon after I'd started at Art School, I confessed that I'd decided to paint seriously, rather than limiting myself to illustration; and I tried to convey to him the way in which Wyeth and Hopper had made me see my way as a painter. His first response was to sit back in his chair in silence, staring at me with an expression of surprise. Then he smiled. It was a smile that was different from usual; not ironical, not guarded, not faintly mocking, but unaffectedly warm and delighted.

I knew it, he said. I knew you had more in you than to be a mere commercial artist.

I'd brought with me my painting of Bob Wall in front of Dickenson's Arcade, and now laid it in front of him. He pored over it for some moments, his eyes narrowed. Then he looked up and nodded.

It's good, he said. I see the influence of Hopper – but there's something in it of your own. You're a fine draughtsman, Hugh, and you'll get better still.

He grew increasingly animated, waving his hands.

You must look again at some of the masters, now that you know where you're going. Look at Flemish naturalism: look at Van Eyck, who takes the commonplace and transfigures it.

You remember his Saint Francis? A saint, yet a real man. Look at how the great Velazquez transforms reality. And above all look at Cezanne, and his wonderful juxtapositions of colour in landscape: far better compositions than those of any damned abstractionist, because they have *life* at their centre. Look at *The House with Cracked Walls,* standing among the cool green pines and warm pink rocks of the South. That house has a meaning beyond mere speech. And his wonderful paintings of Mont Sainte-Victoire – the mountain that obsessed him in old age; the guardian of his native Aix-en-Provence. Those studies have the divine in them. *There's* the sort of mark you must aim for.

We talked for a long time, that afternoon. There could be little doubt that Walter was a thwarted artist, and that he saw in me the bearer of the talent he'd been denied. As I left, he did something he'd never done before: to my embarrassment, he suddenly embraced me. Then he turned hastily away, and banged the big front door.

Soon after that, he made a room in the house available to me to work in as a studio, since I had no suitable space at home. It had once been a spare bedroom, on the northern side of the house, and had good natural light. He had the bed removed and stored away by the man who did his gardening, and provided me with an easel. From then on, my Sundays at Leyburn were divided between conversations with Walter over afternoon tea, and work in my studio. He would sometimes visit me there and inspect my work, and I sensed that this gave him pleasure.

The arrangement suited Walter, since on Saturdays he continued to go to his club. It also suited me, since Saturday was when I spent time with my friends, or else went out with the girls I met at dances or at Art School. In the winter of that year, however, the outings with girls ended. This was when my friendship with Mrs Doran began.

*

It began in that July, not long after my nineteenth birthday. A time of low grey skies and rain; of clear, freezing air and sharp lights at night. Short days, early dark, and snow on Mount Wellington.

I now had a driver's licence, and my father would usually lend me his car to get out to Leyburn Farm. On this particular Sunday, I parked the Hillman in the drive at my usual time – three in the afternoon – and knocked on the front door. Mrs Doran opened it. This wasn't unusual, and I expected her to see me into the dining-room, where Walter would be waiting to take tea with me. Instead, she halted in the dimness of the hall.

I'm afraid Mr Dixon's not well, she said. He's had a bad cold, and an attack of bronchitis. It got worse this afternoon, and he's in bed asleep – so he won't be able to have afternoon tea with you. He asked me to apologize.

That's all right, I said. I'll just get to work in my studio. I'm sorry to hear that Walter's sick.

He's asked me to have afternoon tea with you, she said. He didn't want you to miss out. That's if you don't mind putting up with my company, Hugh.

She smiled, and her smile elated me. This was my first opportunity for a conversation with her since our brief talk in the hall some six months ago. Ever since, I'd hoped to find myself alone with her again; but she seemed to avoid it, merely making a few pleasant remarks when she opened the front door for me. I'd finally given up hope, telling myself that my interest in her was foolish.

I expected her to take me to the dining-room; but instead, she led me down the hall to the drawing room: that museum-like chamber which Walter seemed to avoid – at least, when he spent time with me. On the way, we passed a small room with an open door that I guessed to be Mrs Doran's office; I glimpsed a desk with a typewriter on it, an office chair and a filing cabinet. It was a cold day, and I was pleased to find that a wood fire was burning under the marble mantlepiece in the drawing room, which looked exactly as I remembered it, and still seemed to smell of furniture oil and flowers and dead air. A vase of fresh red camellias stood on the small round table in the centre, and Mrs Doran gestured at one of the balloon-backed chairs there.

Please sit down, Hugh. The tea's ready; I'll be back in a moment.

She hurried out and I sat and waited, in this capsule from the 1870s whose chill the fire was struggling to dissipate. Soon she reappeared, carrying a tray loaded with tea things, a plate of scones, and bowls containing the jam and cream Walter was so fond of. She set all this out on the table as though in accordance with some special design, her eyes lowered in concentration. Then she sat down on one of the chairs opposite me, and began pouring tea. As always, she was dressed as though for an outing, in a long-sleeved, close-fitting navy-blue dress, belted at the waist, with a narrow skirt. Like many dresses in the fifties aimed at mature women, its aim was to emphasize an hourglass figure. It certainly succeeded in Mrs Doran's case; I still remember that dress. First love (or first infatuation, if you like) stamps such things on the mind forever; and I was already in love with her, even though I scarcely knew her.

She finished pouring the tea, giving it her full attention; and still she didn't look up at me. I began to be slightly nervous, and the high-ceilinged, formal room seemed to take on a silence that grew increasingly dense. She held out my cup and saucer, her arm extended across the table, her lips slightly parted. They were quite full lips – something I hadn't noticed before, since she usually kept them closed. She wore bright red lipstick, which emphasized their disturbing look of ripeness.

I thanked her, and passed her the milk jug. When she'd added milk to her tea she passed the jug back to me and looked at me. Her wide-set eyes were of an unusually deep blue that kept drawing my attention. Like her fair complexion, they made an arresting contrast with the straight black hair that curved just below her ears, and her gaze seemed both wondering and insistent – as though she were trying to communicate something remarkable to me, without the use of words. Whether this was intended or unconscious I couldn't tell; but it caused my pulse to race.

She sipped from her cup, set it down, and smiled at me.

I hope the tea's strong enough.

I told her it was. As I sipped from my own cup, I was searching my mind for a polite way to frame one of the many questions I wanted to ask her. She was still mysterious to me, in the way that only an older woman can be to a youth.

I remember you very well now, I said. From the time when I was at Moonah Primary, I mean. I used to see you in the playground. Did you teach there for long after that?

Her smile faded, and I saw that her eyes had become sad. It was a sadness, I realized, that had always been an element in her gaze, despite her pleasant composure; now all other elements had drained away, allowing the sadness to flood in.

No, she said. I left teaching early in 1945. That was when my husband was killed.

I'm sorry, I said.

I was suddenly embarrassed and awkward. Walter had told me that she'd lost her husband in the war in New Guinea and had left teaching afterwards, and I felt that I should have kept it in mind, and not reminded her of it. She was looking away from me now, staring across at the fire, her cup suspended in her hand, her eyes wider than usual, as though studying something in the flames.

He was a sergeant in the AIF, she said. The Third Division. They'd been fighting the Japanese in New Guinea for two years. They were brought home for a rest in 1944, and he and I had some time together. But late in the year the Division was sent back, to fight on Bougainville. Everyone knew that the Japanese were beaten by then – but still they wouldn't give in, and a lot of our men died, on Bougainville. I was told Brian was killed in battle at a place called Slater's Knoll, in March 1945. Slater's Knoll. I hate that name.

She put down her cup, still looking into the fire.

Some people say that what the AIF was made to do on Bougainville was pointless, she said. They only had to wait for the Japanese to surrender. That came a few months later, in August. But by then I'd lost my husband – and he never saw his little daughter.

Now she turned back to me. I was afraid that she might weep, but she didn't; instead, her sad stare remained steady.

But you don't want to hear about this, Hugh.

Yes, I do. I'm really sorry.

Never mind, she said.

She paused, looking into her lap. Then she began talking at some length, for the first time since I'd met her. Her voice was low but clear, and pleasant to listen to.

I was lucky that I met your uncle. I couldn't have gone on teaching, after I had a baby, and it would have been hard to survive on a war widow's pension. My husband had made his will with Dixon and Dixon, and that's how Walter and I met. He offered me part-time secretarial work in the office – but Catherine was just an infant, and I wasn't going to leave her with anyone: not even my parents. So Walter suggested I do his secretarial work here in the house instead. Later on he asked me if I'd cook his evening meal for him if he paid me an extra wage, and I agreed. I also come up here and give him afternoon tea on a Sunday – as you know. He likes my company then, but he doesn't keep me for long.

That's an unusual combination, I said. Secretary and cook.

I quite like to cook, she said, and it's no trouble. When I cook our dinner at home, I put aside some ingredients for Walter as well, and bring them up here in the car to prepare. He eats late, and I'm only a few minutes away, down the road. Walter pays me very well – the equivalent of two salaries, in fact. Almost nobody will employ a woman with a young child, and let her work the odd hours I do. I used to bring Catherine here, when she was still a baby. Now that she's six, I go home in the late afternoon to be with her when she comes home from school. Walter goes in to the office twice a week – more, when he has a case on – but I still keep on with my work here, even if it only takes me a few hours. Walter and I have worked out a situation that suits us both.

I noticed her use of my uncle's first name. They were clearly closer than I'd thought; yet when Walter and I were together, she always addressed him as 'Mr Dixon'.

You and he must work well together, I said. He must rely on you.

She looked at me quickly and paused for a moment, as though deciding what to say.

It's more than just secretarial work, she said. I'm a sort of companion to him. Your uncle has a number of friends in the city, but none out here – and there are times when he gets lonely.

I thought he might.

I bit into a scone, and waited to see if she'd say more. She'd eaten nothing; she toyed with her teaspoon, and looked down into her cup.

Yes, she said. Of course, he's chosen the way he lives – you must know that, Hugh. He doesn't always want other people about. But when there's not much work to do, he likes to talk with me. I'm happy to do it; he's such an interesting man. When he gets sick, as he is now, there's no-one to be with him. So I sometimes come up here in the evenings for a while, and keep him company. He's very private and self-sufficient; he won't let me act as a nurse in any way. All he wants is to chat, and for me to sit by his bed and read to him. Novels, mostly. Or the newspapers.

Really? You read to him?

Oh, yes. When he's tired, he loves to be read to. Some are authors that I know – P.G. Wodehouse, for instance, and Somerset Maugham. Others are rather strange – like

D.H. Lawrence. Lawrence does write well, but some of it's very erotic, isn't it? Walter laughs at me, and says I'm a prude – but I do enjoy Lawrence, even so. He understands women.

Does any man understand women?

She looked amused.

I think Lawrence does.

Walter can't always be easy, though. I know he sometimes makes me nervous.

Her small, private smile gave nothing away in response to this, and I saw that she wouldn't be led into speaking about Walter in any way that showed disrespect.

I understand his temperament, she said. He's impatient with people he thinks are foolish – but he can also be very generous. He sometimes defends people who are poor without charging a fee. And he's been generous to me in ways I can never repay – especially in the time after my husband was killed. I wasn't much good for anything, then, and Walter helped me through it.

He's been generous to me too, I said.

I'm sure he has. He believes in your talent, Hugh, you must know that. You're almost like a son to him – he's told me so.

Sipping her tea, she watched me over the rim of her cup; and now it was my turn to look away into the fire, partly touched and partly embarrassed. I wasn't sure that I wanted to be a son to Walter, and I wasn't yet confident that I'd fulfil the old man's exalted expectations.

You've brought some of your drawings, she said.

She was looking at a small portfolio I'd brought with me, and which now lay on the chair next to me.

Just the one, I said. I was going to show it to Walter.

Would you show it to me? I've never seen one of your drawings, Hugh – you always take them away with you. But perhaps I shouldn't ask.

Her eyes had widened now, fixed on me with an expression that seemed to mingle solemnity with a sort of flirtatiousness.

Even though I told myself that I must be mistaken in reading it in this way, the effect this look had on me was disquieting: a flickering of desire, and a sudden absurd longing to take her in my arms. I say absurd because I still had the common sense at that stage to know that although these feelings would have been perfectly natural had Mrs Doran been a girl of my own age, they were quite inappropriate in relation to a matron in her mid-thirties, however much she might be attractive to me. Later I'd abandon common sense, and enter into a state of self-delusion; but on that afternoon I had no expectation that I might actually begin any sort of involvement with her, and I kept what I hoped was a neutral expression.

Of course, I said. I'd be happy to show it to you. It's a portrait of Walter, actually. He let me do a pencil sketch of him last time I was here, and I've worked it up into a watercolour.

Really? I'd like to see it. I hope he won't mind.

I'm sure he won't.

I opened the portfolio, and handed the painting over the table. It was of medium size, and she was able to hold it out in front of her and study it from that position. I'd painted Walter from the waist up, seated in a chair, three-quarter face. He was wearing a blue linen shirt with an ochre-coloured cravat knotted at his throat: contrasting colours that appealed to me. He was looking away to the right, out of the picture, and had a pensive expression.

She studied it for some time before speaking. Then, still looking at the picture, she said:

I can see why Walter says you have a talent. It's a wonderful likeness – and it sees your uncle's real character. It shows his contradictions. His mouth's severe and hard, but his eyes are dreaming and soft. You've seen that, haven't you, Hugh?

For a moment I could say nothing. Her words had affected me as much as her glance had done. Such a subtle response to my work seemed to me miraculous; and now I told myself that

I was certainly in love with her, and a sort of intoxication began which was not going to release me. When I spoke, it was without thought, and without answering her question.

You call me Hugh, but I don't even know your first name.

She looked up at me swiftly, with a sudden light in her eyes that I thought might be annoyance. But when she answered, her voice was soft, as though she were speaking to a child.

It's Moira.

May I call you that?

If you want. But perhaps not in front of Walter.

When I spoke again, I seemed to hear my own voice from a distance.

I'm very glad you like my work, Moira. I'd like to do your portrait too. Would you sit for me?

She stared at me for some moments in silence. I grew nervous, concerned that I might have overturned whatever good will she had for me. But her eyes now mingled cautious sympathy with the sadness that was always there; and when she finally spoke it was in a low murmur.

I might. I'll think about it.

The following Sunday I had afternoon tea with Walter as usual. When Moira Doran brought in the tray and set it down on the table, she smiled and greeted me pleasantly, just as she always did, but with no sign that we'd begun to know each other better. She was wearing a smart grey suit-dress today, with a narrow skirt and a belted jacket. Perhaps it was at Walter's request, I thought, that she always dressed in a style that suited a secretary in an office. During these afternoon teas, however, she and Walter seemed to indulge in some sort of game where she behaved like a housekeeper. Perhaps it was for my benefit.

Thank you, Mrs Doran, he said. That looks delicious.

Do you need anything else, Mr Dixon?

No, no. Thank you for looking after us, Mrs Doran.

All through my subsequent conversation with Walter I was in a state of tension, wondering how I could find an opportunity to ask Moira whether she'd decided to sit for me. I didn't feel easy about hiding my new familiarity with her from Walter; yet she'd somehow given me the impression that this was what I must do – if only because she'd asked me not to use her first name in front of him. So I decided, somewhat guiltily, that I must wait for an opportunity to speak with her alone.

I need not have worried: when she was clearing away the tea things, it was she who introduced the topic. Walter had gone out of the room, probably to ease his bladder, and she spoke to me quickly, in a lower voice than usual, as she stacked our cups on the tray.

I've been thinking, Hugh: I'd be happy to sit for you, if you want. But I'd rather not do it here. I'd sooner Walter didn't know about it until it's done. I'll explain why later. Can you agree to that?

I said that I could, though elation mingled with unease about our hiding this from Walter.

But my studio's here, I said. Where else could you sit for me?

She glanced once over her shoulder at the door, which added to my tension; Walter could come back at any moment. Then she moved across to my chair, drew a piece of paper from her jacket pocket, and handed it to me.

At my place, she said. Here's the address.

When? I said. I could hear Walter's footsteps in the passage.

Next Saturday, she said. Two-thirty.

She picked up the tray without another glance at me, and was moving towards the door when Walter came in.

The derangement that was about to enclose us both would do so for over two years. It was a derangement where what I wanted to be true magically became so; where Time and fact were put to flight; where the love of a youth just out of adolescence for a woman in her thirties was its own justification, and would surely have a happy ending. It was a place outside reality, in the district called Montrose: that semi-rural area – long since swallowed by a suburb – where little farms and orchards began, and where the first suburban houses had wandered in from Glenorchy, straggling up Montrose Road towards Leyburn Farm. Moira Doran's house was one of these.

I was drawn and obsessed by such districts, at that time: places where the town ended, and the countryside began. They contained a mystery for me, and had done since the days when Bob Wall and I walked up Main Road to school together. At the time when Moira agreed to sit for her portrait, I'd already begun my sketching expeditions about the Glenorchy district, a knapsack of drawing materials and a small folding stool slung over my shoulder, seeking out scenes which I saw as vessels of the mystery: one whose meaning could never be expressed in words; one which tantalized me without ever being resolved, but whose promise I might capture in my pictures. Images of what I called *the last suburb* were a constant theme in my work – and one of these was a final house on a rise at twilight, its glowing, lit windows promising a whole secret life. In most young men's dreams in those days, the image of the Girl hovered: the ultimate love we'd been schooled to expect by that fatal romantic tradition which today has finally expired. At nineteen, I half-believed love might be found in such a house: behind those glowing windows, in that last spellbound suburb where an unknown land waited behind the hills.

My father needed his car that Saturday, so I went out to Montrose as I'd often done in the past, taking the tram to Glenorchy and then walking along Main Road, the knapsack containing my drawing materials hung from my shoulder. It wasn't raining but it was cold, with an ice-blue midwinter sky and masses of low cloud. Anticipation made me more than usually aware of the stillness out here: the humming of cars on the road was the only sound, and few people walked beside the highway.

I turned into Montrose Road. Moira had written clear directions on the piece of paper which was in my raincoat pocket. I'd studied it many times, as though it were a love letter. It told me that her house was one of two on the left-hand side, a short way up from the corner of Main Road. I'd passed these houses often, on my way to Leyburn Farm, but had taken little notice of them: they, and three more on the opposite side, were the only houses here before the farming properties began. First came a small brown weatherboard place with a red roof. Next to it was a vacant field. Then came Moira Doran's house – also quite small – on the other side of which was an apple orchard. From their style, both these modest houses had been built in the 1920s, like my parents' home. Moira's was a typical American bungalow of its time, faced with rough cream stucco, with a green-tiled roof, green-painted window frames and trimmings, and a clinker-brick chimney in its centre. Across the roofs of the three houses opposite, the hills to the north could be seen. In its style and location, Moira's home resembled the last house of my imaginings, and I went up the steps to the porch with a lift of the heart, but also with a formless apprehension. A certain kind of love is often entered through those double doors.

She opened the front door quite quickly after I rang the bell: almost as though she'd been waiting in the hall. Her smile seemed pleased and welcoming, though perhaps a little tense. She waved me inside, told me to take off my raincoat, and took it from me. She hung it on a hallstand and then turned to me.

I didn't hear a car. Did you walk here from Glenorchy?

I told her I had done, and she pursed her lips in mock-sympathy, her eyes glinting with humour.

You're lucky it didn't rain. Come on, then – come and get warm by the fire.

The little hallway we stood in ran through the centre of the house, with doors on either side. Moira led me through a door on our left, and I found myself in a sitting-room that was served by the chimney at the front, its lead-light windows looking out on the hills. It felt cosy, as rooms in the 1920s were designed to do, and was very clean and neat. A wood fire burned in a brick fireplace under a dark-stained mantelpiece with a chiming clock set in its centre and two framed photographs at one end. There were dark-stained wooden beams in the ceiling, and bookshelves of the same timber built into one of the walls. The usual stuffed armchairs and couch, with light-coloured floral covers. Wall-to-wall green carpet. On a low coffee table in the centre stood a vase of the same winter-flowering camellias I'd seen at Walter Dixon's: perhaps she grew them in her garden.

Please – sit down, she said.

I sat in one of the armchairs, and she took another opposite me, on the other side of the coffee table. I put my knapsack beside me, and she looked at it.

I see you've come equipped, she said. Her tone was light, and she maintained her pleasant smile; but I still sensed a kind of nervousness in her. I decided to address this immediately.

Yes, I said. But if you've had second thoughts, I'll understand.

No. No second thoughts – but I do have to ask you, Hugh, not to let Walter know that I'm sitting for you. Not now, at least. Perhaps later.

If you say so. But I don't see why he'd mind.

She was sitting very straight in the armchair, twisting a white pocket handkerchief in her fingers; and now I saw that I hadn't imagined her tension.

It's difficult, she said. To tell you why, I mean. I can only say, knowing your uncle as I do, that I think he might not like it.

But you did agree, even so.

She leaned forward.

Of course I agreed, Hugh. Now that I've seen your wonderful portrait of Walter, I'd be very pleased to have my own portrait done. I'm just asking that we keep it to ourselves, for the present. Maybe I shouldn't ask that – but I am. So now it's up to you. Do you want to go ahead?

I said I did, feeling confused. I was half flattered that she'd been prepared to enter into what amounted to a secret assignation with me, and half uneasy at the way in which we were hiding this from Walter. I picked up the knapsack and began to pull out my sketchbook and pencils, aware that her gaze was still on me. Then she spoke again.

Will this room be all right?

It's fine, I said. There's good natural light through those windows.

We won't be disturbed, she said. My daughter's visiting friends across the road. Shall I sit in this chair?

Yes, if you're comfortable there.

And what about my clothes?

I looked up, startled, and found her blue gaze fixed on me quizzically, and her parted lips smiling. She laughed softly.

I didn't mean should I take them off, she said. I'm only sitting for a portrait, I know. But if what I have on doesn't suit you, I could change.

She was wearing a dark green polo-necked sweater and a brown skirt. She looked attractive, as she did in anything she wore, but I decided to take her up on her offer.

I wouldn't want to put you to any trouble, I said. But I liked that navy-blue dress you wore when Walter was sick.

Fancy you remembering. It *is* a nice dress.

The humorous look had come back into her eyes now, and yet it wasn't mocking; rather, it seemed almost fond, filling me with a glad expectancy, even though reason told me I had nothing to expect.

I won't be a moment, she said. I'll go and change.

When she'd gone from the room, I sat staring in front of me. I could think of nothing else but the fact that somewhere, in another room in the house, Moira was undressing on my behalf, putting on the dress that I thought emphasized her beauty. I must have waited for no more than five minutes, but it seemed longer. She came back into the sitting-room very softly, her feet making no sound on the carpet, and caught me unawares.

Will this do?

She was standing in the middle of the room in the navy-blue dress, her hands raised in front of her as though supporting some fragile, invisible object, and she looked at me now with that expression women sometimes adopt when they hope for approval but are not entirely certain of it: half smiling, her eyes questioning. I studied the dress with the same objectivity that accompanied my planning of any picture: the way it clung to her figure almost like a swimsuit, making me fairly certain that she wore a girdle underneath; the way it plunged in a V to expose her white throat; the narrow, belted waist and long, pencil-style skirt. I loved the look of her in this dress: lately, when she came into my mind, she always wore it, and what I liked about it for my portrait was that its dark blue added to the contrasts in her own colouring: her black hair, white skin and blue eyes. I could do things with those harmonies, I thought.

It's perfect, I said. It suits you so well.

My words had been innocuous, but I knew that my eyes were probably telling her much more. If she noticed, she didn't show it; or perhaps she was simply unaware of it.

Good, she said. Shall I sit down? How shall I sit?

However you feel comfortable, I said.

She sat as before, hands folded in her lap, straight-backed, looking across at me.

It's better if you look away, I said. Out the window, perhaps.

I knew that if her gaze was on me, it would make me self-conscious. Once she was staring out the window, I began to sketch. Now she'd become simply a subject, presenting me with technical challenges, and I was able to concentrate.

You're working in pencil, she said. Won't you do a painting?

Yes, I said, but not today. I like to do a number of sketches first, and think about them. Then I hope you'll sit for me again, and I'll do the painting. Will that be all right?

I waited, not looking up at her. There was a pause; then she said:

Yes. That will be all right.

The warm little sitting-room was silent after that, except when the clock on the mantelpiece chimed three. Time went by without my being aware of it, as always happened when I was drawing. Detached now, focussed almost entirely on capturing Moira Doran's likeness, I was able to study without embarrassment the face of this woman I believed I was in love with. It was a flawless face: shield-shaped, with a moderately wide jaw, but tapering to a small, firm chin. She wore only a touch of lipstick today, and her full lips could have been a young girl's. It seemed to me that she could be in her mid-twenties, rather than some ten years older. Her fair skin was unblemished, and there was little sign of ageing, except for a single line across her forehead, and a few lines under her eyes. I knew little about the use of make-up, but the faint flush in her cheeks (perhaps from the heat of the fire) seemed natural. I was glad that I'd asked her to look out the window, since her eyes now reflected the daylight out there, and their deep and mesmeric blue was made translucent. To reproduce their colour would be difficult enough; but more difficult still would be to capture their expression: one which seemed to contemplate a secret. Only a great talent could do that, I thought, since the secret, the object of her contemplation, remained unknown. Despite the fact that we'd begun to become acquainted, I sensed that it would probably remain unknown, and that all I'd be able to do would be to hint at its existence. Its nature, I thought, was somehow reflected in the calm of her face: a calm that appeared to stem from a pleasant contentment, but which sometimes resembled melancholy. It caused her to recall to mind those women in the Renaissance paintings that Walter used to show me. I was thinking in particular of Crivelli's Mary Magdalene.

Only a very young man, as I was then, could have seen such mystery in a woman – and perhaps only a very young man who was infatuated with an older woman. It's easy to dismiss this as callow illusion. But perhaps it's not. perhaps men lose the capacity to see a woman's mystery, just as they lose the capacity to experience many other revelations: visions that fade under the flat glare of reality.

When I'd finished two sketches, I studied them for some time and knew I had to do at least one more. These images were Moira and yet they weren't: I hadn't really captured her. While I was still dissecting this in my mind, looking for what I'd missed, I heard her voice.

You concentrate very hard, Hugh.

I looked up from the black-and-white creatures in my sketchbook, and met the eyes of the real woman.

I'm sorry, I said. It's been nearly an hour, and I haven't given you a break.

That's okay. Are you done?

Almost, but I'm not really satisfied. Will you let me do one more sketch, after you've relaxed?

She stood up.

Of course. I'll get us some coffee.

When she came back, I was standing by one of the windows next to the fireplace, looking out between the curtains. It was nearly four o'clock now, and the early winter twilight was already gathering, draining the colour from the houses and the hills out there, turning the sky a silver grey. She poured our coffees and handed me my cup and saucer. Then she remained standing, sipping from her cup, holding the saucer below her chin. I did the same.

I needed a break from sitting down, she said.

I won't keep you much longer, I promise.

There's plenty of time. Catherine won't come home until five-thirty.

I was standing close to the mantelpiece, and found myself looking at the two framed portrait photographs there. One was of a fair-haired infant girl in a party frock; the other was of a soldier, in the slouch hat of the AIF. He was somewhere in his late twenties, and was smiling at the camera with his lips closed. It was hard to see what lay behind his smile: he seemed to be questioning something. His future, perhaps. His eyes were thoughtful, and he looked like the sort of man you'd trust.

I turned to Moira, and saw that she'd followed my gaze.

That must be your husband, I said.

Yes. That's Brian.

Her tone was without expression, but the sadness that waited in her face had now become dominant.

He looks a good man, I said.

He was, she said. He was the best sort of man.

I felt awkward, but her silence compelled me to say something more, rather than leaving the subject.

What did he do, before the War?

Brian was an electrical engineer. He only got his degree a year before the War came. He'd just started a job with the Hydro when he got called up.

You've never thought of remarrying?

She looked at me quickly, and there was something defensive in this look.

No. Brian and I were both Catholics. There's no second marriage for a Catholic.

But you're a widow. The Church doesn't forbid remarriage then, does it?

No, of course not. But I still feel it's wrong for me. Silly, perhaps, but there's nothing to be done about it.

Abruptly, she drank off her coffee; then she turned away from the mantelpiece and looked through the window at the twilight.

This is a sad time of day, isn't it? Especially in winter. And this is a sad subject, Hugh. Time for you to get back to work.

She smiled: a small, firm smile that told me the subject was closed.

I took something like half an hour over the final sketch. While I worked, the room began to grow dim, and Moira asked me if I needed a lamp turned on. But I rejected this; there was still enough light from the fire, and through the windows behind me. As well as that, I secretly enjoyed the fact that the twilight was enclosing us, creating an ambiguous intimacy. Neither of us spoke again; we were cocooned in warm quiet, and in the sober promise of evening. Finally, at somewhere past four-thirty, I told her I was finished, and closed my sketchbook. I was much more satisfied with this final drawing; in fact, it came somewhere near capturing her in the way that I wanted.

Are you happier this time?

I think so. It's still only rough, though.

Will you show it to me, Hugh? Not if you don't want to, of course.

I stood up, opened the sketchbook to the final drawing, and put it down on the coffee table. Moira came around to my side of the table and stood bent over the drawing, her brows slightly raised, her face blank. Then she turned to face me, smiling but saying nothing.

You don't like it, I said.

Of course I like it. It's beautifully done. But it's strange to see yourself in a drawing. Quite different from a photograph. You've made me far more attractive than I really am.

No. It's nothing like as beautiful as you really are.

My tone was more fervent than I'd intended, and I felt myself flush; this time I'd openly declared my feeling. We were standing quite close together, facing each other in the same position as before, between the window and the fireplace; and I was reminded of the time when she'd first talked to me alone, standing by Walter Dixon's front door. Once again I could smell her perfume, and sense her body's warmth. Her nearness made my breath come quicker, and I wondered if she knew this. When she finally answered, her voice was very soft, and she looked up into my face with an expression that seemed wondering and almost tender, as though she spoke to a child.

You shouldn't say such a thing.

But I do say it. You're beautiful.

I'd only just managed to speak again, and to control my voice.

You imagine it, she said. You imagine it because you're young, Hugh.

She reached out and touched my cheek with the tips of her fingers. The wondering, tender expression hadn't left her face, and I summoned up my courage and put both arms around her and drew her against me and kissed her, my hands on her back, feeling her live, startling warmth through the fine wool of her dress. Everything then changed: in that moment, and in my life. I'd half expected her to push me away; instead she came willingly closer, prolonging the kiss, her arms around my neck, one hand on the back of my head, her open lips seeming fuller and softer than those of any girl I'd known. A woman's lips.

But then she broke away, and spoke in a whisper.

No! This has to stop.

The room had grown dark now, except for the light from the fire. Between the black wings of her hair, her face had become a white mask. Her expression seemed dauntingly severe; but it was difficult to tell, in the dimness. Out the window, the twilight was almost complete: the houses over the road were mere outlines, and only a band of cold yellow light circled the rim of the horizon.

Moira followed my gaze.

It's dark now, she said. This would never have happened if it hadn't got dark. It's my fault.

No it's not. I wanted it to happen. I've always wanted it to happen.

I tried to kiss her again, but she pushed me away.

No. No. It's time for you to go, Hugh. I'll see you out.

With a leaden feeling in my stomach I gathered my things together, followed her out into the hall, and put on my raincoat. She stood looking up at me.

Do you still want to finish your painting?

Of course I do. But will you let me?

Come next Saturday.

She reached up and straightened the collar of my raincoat. As she did so I put a tentative hand on her shoulder. Her response was to kiss me lightly on the cheek.

Goodbye, she said. I'll see you on Saturday.

I opened the front door and she stood beside me as I paused there.

It looks like rain, she said. You'll get wet through.

It's okay. I often walk in the rain.

Don't be silly. You need an umbrella. Take this.

She bent and drew an umbrella from the hallstand and handed it to me.

I thanked her, and hesitated on the doorstep. She was smiling again, now: a small, thoughtful smile I couldn't read.

I'll look forward to seeing the finished painting, she said.

I went down the steps into the extending night of the country. When I looked back from the gate she was watching me go, framed in the light of the hallway. She waved, and gladness flooded out despair with that speed and completeness we only know in youth.

I plodded through the rain along the highway, conjuring up many foolish hopes.

During the week I was swung between such hopes and a deep despair. In my more lucid moments I told myself that it was foolish to imagine that she might ever love me; doubly foolish to hope for any serious involvement with her. And yet I could think of little else. I would stare at my sketches of her, these poor inadequate images, and recite a mantra to myself, trying to make myself believe it. *It's not really foolish. She's young. She's like a girl. She's not too old for me; not too old.*

How old was she? Thirty-two? Thirty-four? I didn't know, at that stage, but I saw her as young. I willed her to be young.

By the time Saturday came common sense prevailed; I was drained of hope, and walked along the highway to Montrose in a state of resignation. It was a day of piercing cold, which matched my mood. When I rang her doorbell, there was no immediate response. She'd decided not to see me, I thought, because of what had happened. I'd ring once more, and then I'd go.

But before I could ring, she opened the door. She was wearing the navy dress again, ready to sit for me, and seeing this gave me a rush of tenderness. She raised her brows, her expression pleasantly neutral. She said nothing, but opened the door wider and stood aside to let me in. She shut it behind me, and I turned to her. As I did, she surged against me, sliding her arms around my neck and drawing my face down to hers.

This time there was a wildness about the way she kissed me, and her arms held me with a desperate tightness. When we broke away, she put her mouth close to my ear, whispering.

I thought about you all the week. I tried not to, but it was no use.

Now the life of derangement began: the dream that would hold us both.

That it held us for as long as it did was because it took place in a compartment that was hidden from the world: her cream and green cottage in Montrose. That was where I must go to her: there, and nowhere else. I belonged to the night and her bed, and remained entirely faithful to her; girls my own age were a thing of the past, and I went to no more dances. The only other place where we met was in Walter Dixon's house, where we pretended, with Walter's eyes on us, that we were still purely formal acquaintances. She would not go out with me in public; would not consider our appearing together as a couple. The critical eyes of the world must never be on us, she said: in this way, the world could never snigger at the young art student and his lover the older woman. We were safe in our haven on the edge of the country; and although I sometimes resented this covert arrangement, she was adamant: if we declared ourselves, she said, if we went out together as a couple, everything would be spoiled.

I see us there, in that house from the 1920s. It's one night and yet many: dream and memory mingle, so that I'm no longer sure where they divide. Dreamlike, that long-lost reality: a dream where we had our being, each of us knowing it to be dream, each of us denying it. There are very few times in any life when such a thing happens – and in many lives, I suppose, it never happens at all. When it does, we have the subterranean knowledge that it isn't intended to last; and yet we deny this until the final minutes; deny it until we wake to desolation.

I see us there, in the cold winter night of Glenorchy, where darkness unfolds across the hills: safe in her immaculate bedroom. It's the first night, yet many nights. The room is half-lit by a bedside lamp with an orange parchment shade, and the air carries scents of powder, cosmetics and furniture polish. The typical bedroom of a fastidious woman of the suburbs, into which I've come like an invader: wall-to-wall cream carpet, polished cedar dressing table with a central mirror and wing mirrors on each side; matching cedar wardrobe. On one of the yellow walls is a framed print of Hobbema's *The Avenue*. The bed we lie in is covered by a big patchwork quilt that Moira made herself. Next to the lamp on the bedside table is a cream bakelite radio, turned down low. Drifting together late at night, we listen to a strange, novel tune called 'How High the Moon', and Les Paul's electric guitar is the sound of an unknown future. New and old pop tunes, soft and half-heard, weave through the night of the world: Bing Crosby sings 'Just One More Chance'; The Ink Spots sing 'If I Didn't Care'; Webb Pierce sings 'Back Street Affair'.

I love that song, she says. Maybe it's about us. She laughs to show she's not serious, raised on one elbow above me.

The curtains are drawn back from the bedroom window. It faces north-east, framing black night, looking across the paddock next door. Beyond the roof of a house over the road the hills begin, dim and limitless under a white half-moon. A number of very far lights glimmer and dance there, making me alive with joy. How high the moon.

I'm here, I say, *in the place I've always searched for: in the last suburb.*

I went to her on my two free nights each week, usually in my father's car. Sometimes she would give me dinner; more usually I came well after she'd eaten, when her six-year-old daughter was in bed.

Catherine was a fair-haired, pretty little girl who mainly resembled her father, the soldier in the photograph. She would study me solemnly with Brian Doran's grey eyes, and say very little; I could tell that my presence puzzled her. Moira had told her that I was Walter Dixon's nephew, and a friend. She also explained that I was a painter, and showed Catherine my finished portrait of her, which I'd given to her as a present. It was crucially important to her that the child should not suspect any intimacy between us, and should never see me entering her bedroom. We were probably successful in this, since six-year-old children in that era had only the vaguest idea of what sexual relationships between adults were about – especially small girls as sheltered as Moira's daughter was. I respected her wishes about this, but it made for an atmosphere of guilt, where I moved about the house on tiptoe. And guilt, I discovered, was strongly present in Moira's nature.

In all the years that she'd been a widow, she had never been involved with a man. She had taken a sort of vow, it seemed, to be faithful to her husband's memory, never to re-marry, and to devote herself entirely to raising her daughter. The vow was broken on that night when she kissed me in the hall; and when I discovered this, her wild hunger was explained. It took me some time to understand something else: something which she was perhaps only half-conscious of herself: that in choosing me as a lover, she was in some way remaining faithful to her vow, and was safe from breaking it. I was too young ever to be considered as a husband – little more than a boy – and I could be kept hidden: an illicit pleasure.

Once understood, this was a key to the rituals of passion that established themselves from the beginning, on that night when we clung to each other inside the front door. She veered between passion and resistance: a sort of ritual, last-minute attempt to escape our inevitable destination. Head flung back, throat gleaming white in the dark, eyes half-closed, she repeated a guilty incantation.

No. No. This is wrong, Hugh. We have to stop.

But her body did not draw back, and I soon understood that ritual words were all that these were: words that created the peculiar spice of guilt which must always accompany our feeling. It was a feeling beyond anything I'd experienced, and took me out of my depth. I was now in love to a degree that consumed my life; and after six months I proposed to her. We must marry, I said, as soon as I'd finished my course and found a job. She smiled, and ran her fingers through my hair as though I were a child.

Darling, I love you too, but it's impossible. I'm almost middle-aged. You'll find a nice young girl, eventually.

You're not *old! Thirty-four's not old. There'll never be anyone else for me.*

But however frantic my protests, her smile remained unaltered: the same calm smile I'd tried to capture in my painting: the smile that contemplated the secret, whose nature I'd still not plumbed.

There'll be the right girl some day – you'll see. Let's be happy with what we have.

This was the pattern of our relationship for the rest of that year, and all through 1952. This was how things stood in 1953, when I joined the *Mail*, and when Bob Wall came back into my life.

3

I'm going on leave, Gordon said. I'll be off for a fortnight.

He had swung around on his swivel chair, legs outstretched, hands behind his head. It was an early afternoon in June, and we weren't yet very busy. I put down my brush and pushed aside the photograph I was working on: American troops carrying their wounded through the bleak, rocky landscape of Korea.

Don't worry, Gordon said. You won't have to manage on your own – there's a fella coming in to replace me. Name of Max Fell.

The name sounded familiar, but I couldn't place it.

Is he a newspaper artist?

He's a bit of everything. Runs a commercial studio in Liverpool Street. Photography, fashion advertizements – that sort of thing. We run some of his ads for women's clothing in the paper. He draws a comic strip that's in some of the mainland papers. *Rod Callaghan, Private Eye.* He offered it to us, but the editor said it was a bit too spicy for a family newspaper.

Gordon's grin was sardonic now, and I understood why. I'd seen the strip in *The Herald*, a Melbourne evening paper: it was clearly an imitation of the classic American detective strip *Dick Tracy*, and featured half-clad women and a kind of sadistic violence that went close to the boundaries of what was then tolerated in popular entertainment. I was impressed that an Australian artist had managed to sell a strip to the big dailies, but I didn't find *Rod Callaghan* attractive. There was something vaguely repellent about it: a brutality that seemed to be there for its own sake, rather than being simply an aspect of that realism employed by overseas masters of the genre.

Now I remember the name, I said. He's pretty successful, isn't he? Why would he need to fill in here?

He's glad of the extra money. Freelance artists don't do as well as you might think. Max is always moaning about it. He's got overheads as well, of course: rent of the studio, materials, pay for casual staff – it's like any other business.

What's he like?

What's he like?

Gordon took his hands from behind his head, pulled his tobacco pouch from the pocket of his cardigan and began to roll a cigarette. He seemed to ponder.

You've got no worry about him pulling his weight, he said. He's a pro. Odd sort of bloke, though.

Odd in what way?

Gordon lit his cigarette, and squinted at me through the smoke.

Hard to say. Different. Looks a bit like a Frenchman, or some other kind of Continental. You'll find him amusing – but there's something about Max that's hard to put your finger on. The sort of fella that might have a dodgy past. I probably shouldn't say that – it's just a feeling. He came here from Melbourne a few years ago, and not much is known about him. In his forties, but he's got no family: a loner. I met a bloke once who claimed Max got into trouble in Melbourne, and that's why he came here. But when I asked what sort of trouble, the bloke closed up. So forget I said this, Hugh: you'll find he's easy to work with, and he'll do a good job. That's all you have to care about, mate.

*

It was strange to see Max Fell sitting in Gordon's chair. He was very efficient, retouching the photos quickly and deftly, and producing headings for the Saturday magazine section that somehow looked more modern and stylish than Gordon's efforts or mine. As Gordon had said, there was something foreign-looking about him: he somewhat resembled one of those European migrants who'd begun to appear on our Anglo-Saxon streets since the War. And yet, as far as I was able to discover, he was simply a native-born Australian from Melbourne.

We worked mostly in silence on the afternoon of his arrival, and I sneaked occasional glances at him from my stool. He was thin, of medium height, with hunched shoulders – no doubt from many years crouched over a drawing-board. One thing that was immediately odd about him was that he wore a cap indoors: a navy cloth cap with a peak, making him look like a seaman. He added to this marine look by wearing a crew-necked sweater and a pea jacket. Once he took the cap off to scratch his head, and I discovered that he had spiky dark hair cut very short, in what was then called a crew cut. Another oddity about him – and this was probably the one that made him look foreign – was that he wore blue-tinted glasses, through which it was difficult to see his eyes clearly. They appeared to be very pale, and I assumed he was sensitive to strong light. His other features were ordinary enough: a somewhat snub nose, and a wide mouth.

He swung around suddenly and spoke to me. He had a jerky delivery, and a faint stammer that came and went.

C-can you let me have a number four brush?

I passed him the brush and he sat with it in his fingers, continuing to look at me – or rather, in my direction, since his blue-screened eyes seemed to look past you rather than at you.

So, mate: you're Gordon's apprentice. But maybe you've got other ambitions than staying on the dear old *Mail*, a young bloke like you. What are your plans for the future?

I told him I hoped to be an illustrator.

Is that so? Kids' books are the thing – they do very well. Have you had any luck yet?

I told him I hadn't, but was approaching a number of publishers.

You'll need to go over to the mainland, and get yourself around. I might be able to help you, if you let me see some samples. I've got contacts at Ross and MacDonald, the Melbourne publishers.

I warmed to him at this, and began to feel that I liked him. And over the week that followed, as we worked through the evenings under our hot, green-shaded lamps, he turned out to be an entertaining companion, with a quirky sense of humour. I got on well enough with Gordon Carter, but I was always conscious that he was my boss; whereas Max made me feel that we two were working together unsupervised, like schoolboys whose master had been called away. He was a man of moods. Mostly he was brimming with liveliness, his stutter somewhat pronounced, his hands gesticulating, his wide mouth smiling. At other times he was silent and withdrawn, concentrating on his work. He had little regard for the *Mail*, which he dismissed as a country newspaper, and remarked that he was doing the paper a favour by bringing his talents here. He clearly had a big ego.

As we went into the second week, I began to ask him about his career before coming to Hobart. He said nothing about his origins, and I felt that any questions about these would be discouraged; but he gave me a mainly humorous summary of the way in which he'd become a commercial artist. He hadn't served in the War, because he'd been found to have a dicky heart – or at least, he said, that was what the doctors thought he had; and I was almost certain that he winked, through the blue lens of his glasses. When he was young, he'd worked as a window dresser in a big Melbourne department store; but he and a co-worker had been fired for molesting the dummies.

I stared at him, not comprehending.

It was around C-Christmas, he said. We both got pissed, and we went into a window to work on a display. There were two female dummies there that were *nude*, see? So we started groping them and pretending to shag them. It attracted quite a crowd, out in Bourke Street. The management took a dim view. We were out on our ears that night.

He gave a high, falsetto laugh, his darting glance inviting me to join in.

After that, he told me, he took a commercial art course at night, and was eventually hired by an advertizing agency. There he illustrated advertizements for women's underwear, among other things. These appeared in the brochures put out by the big department stores, and in the newspapers. Now that he had his own studio here in Hobart, he used his skill in this genre as a good source of income, together with advertizements for women's dresses. He also went in for portrait photography, which he'd mastered as a sideline. Two of the big stores employed him to supply illustrations for their brochures on women's wear, and his work often appeared in the advertizing section of the *Mail*.

There's quite a demand for the underwear illustrations, he said. That's because there's some kind of ban on using photographs in those ads – did you know that? The powers-that-be think that real live ladies in their bras and girdles would excite people too much. Maybe they're right, eh, Hugh? If they s-saw some of my models in their Maidenform bras and girdles, I reckon a lot of blokes would get the horn. Tits pointing at the ceiling: Lana Turner and Jane Russell ain't in it.

He looked at me sideways with a salacious leer. This seemed oddly adolescent in a man of middle age – especially a professional artist – and it made me briefly uncomfortable with him. But then he went on in a satirical vein, his voice deepening to imitate that of a commercial radio announcer.

So I'm an expert in the field of underwear, mate. I can tell you all about the Nu-Vu bra with its special new underwires for *uplift*. I can give you all the details about the Roussel Corselette, with the cleavage gap for low-cut *decolletage*, and the Illa Knina strapless Marquise with the deep *plunge*, and the Berlei two-way stretch *foundation*.

I began to find him amusing again, and joined in his high, falsetto laughter. Then I went back to working on a photograph of young Queen Elizabeth's coronation.

The system of censorship that held sway in the fifties over all matters sexual seems alien and remarkable now as that of some foreign culture. Demurely tantalizing underwear advertizements of the type that Max Fell produced were one of the few sources of erotic imagery in the mainstream media, and many a youth was led into early onanism through perusing his mother's fashion magazines. Max made several crude references to this as the second week went on.

We discussed a range of other topics, but there could be no doubt that sexual themes preoccupied him in a special way. A sort of extra alertness would appear when these were introduced, and his wide mouth would grin suggestively. Once he asked me whether I'd attended life classes at the Art School, and had worked from the nude. When I told him I had, an expression of distaste crossed his face.

Hopeless models they use, he said. I tried a few: no good to me. They're bags.

Well, they're not meant to be glamorous, I said. So you use models for your underwear ads?

Of course. I photograph them, then do drawings from the photos.

Where do you hire them from?

They're amateurs. I have my ways of getting them interested. All s-sorts of women like to show off their figures – you'd be surprised. They love to be admired.

We passed on to other things. I was interested in his comic strip, *Rod Callaghan*, and flattered him by saying how professional it was: as good as any of the American strips.

Nice of you to say so, he said. It wasn't easy, selling it to the metropolitan papers. All they want usually are the syndicated strips from overseas.

I asked him how he got his story ideas, and he told me that when he'd devised the strip in Melbourne he'd drunk in a hotel frequented by petty criminals, and had picked up material through talking to them. He also struck up a friendship with a police detective who had helped him a good deal. Here in Hobart, he'd discovered a similar source of stories: a hotel down on the wharves which was a haunt of criminals and prostitutes. He'd also made friends with a number of detectives, who were flattered to contribute to *Rod Callaghan*.

I began to buy the Melbourne *Herald* in the evenings, and studied *Rod Callaghan* closely. Like Dick Tracy, Rod was square-jawed, and wore the kind of narrow-brimmed felt hat that was almost a required uniform for men of my father's generation. When he took it off, he revealed bristly dark hair in a crew cut, similar to Max's. He seemed to derive also from Raymond Chandler's Philip Marlowe: he had a seedy office like Marlowe's. He flirted with most of the pretty women he encountered, and it was hinted that he bedded some of them – though this was never shown. He had a masterful and jocular manner with women that wouldn't be popular with editors today: but what is now called male chauvinism had yet to be challenged. He pursued various criminals who'd evaded detection by the police, and always succeeded in bringing them to justice. Most of the women in the strip were victims, at the mercy of various grotesque and brutish criminals. Some were murdered; others were rescued by Rod; but before this eventuated they were tormented and beaten and ill-used in a variety of ways, resulting in images which I found repellent, but which must have been satisfying to any sado-masochists among Max's readers. Clad in the varieties of underwear that Max was so expert in drawing, they were tied to posts or hung by their wrists from rafters; or else, clad only in their slips, they were beaten and lay on the floor looking up pleadingly at their tormentors, the torn garment hanging as low as the unwritten rules allowed.

I asked Max if he'd modelled Rod on anyone, and he looked up with a small, diffident smile.

Nobody in particular, he said. But maybe he's got things in common with *me*, the old Rod. He looks a b-bit like me, have you noticed?

This was hard to see, except for the bristle-cut dark hair. But perhaps Rod was Max's fantasy self, I thought, in some private world of his wishes where all the desirable women in distress were his for the asking.

We had many more conversations after this, as we laboured under our lamps, but I've forgotten most of them. He was given to brief discourses – no doubt offered as wisdom from which a young man like me might benefit. Two of these come back to me: dissertations I'd eventually wish I'd thought about more carefully in forming a judgement of him. The first concerned women: his favourite topic.

He asked me if I had a regular girlfriend, and I said that I didn't: I'd no intention of discussing Moira Doran with him.

If you do get involved, he said, remember one thing. A woman has to be shown who's boss – even if you have to slap her around a bit. A lot of people disapprove of that, but they're wrong. L-let a woman see you're weak, and she'll lead you by the nose. And I'll let you in on a secret, son: underneath, women *enjoy* a bit of rough stuff.

He was looking at me now with an insistence that made me uncomfortable. I wasn't inclined to discuss this notion, let alone agree with it, so I merely nodded, and changed the subject.

The second discourse that remains in my memory is an excursion into philosophy. I'd brought in a book I was currently reading, and had been glancing at it during our tea break. Max was pacing restlessly about the room, cup of tea in hand, and paused beside me to peer at the book's jacket. It was Balzac's *Old Goriot*, borrowed from Walter Dixon's library.

Ball-zac, Max said. What kind of a name's that?

It's French, I said.

So you r-read French writers. Have you read anything by this bloke Jean Paul Sartre? (He pronounced it 'Sartray'.)

No, I said. All I knew was that he wrote about a philosophy called existentialism.

That's it, Max said. Ex-existentialism. I read about it in a magazine. It's a new way of thinking, and I reckon there's a lot in it. What S-Sartray says is: there's no God, so we're on our own. This is a new time we're going into, and we have to m-make our own judgements. No-one can tell us what to do any more: no-one can lay down rules of right or wrong for everybody. So if I decide s-something's right for me, then that's what I must do – n-no matter what anyone else thinks about it.

He was smiling with an air of triumph, and I stared at him.

But that would mean people could commit any crime, I said. Provided they thought it was the right choice for them.

He'd begun to laugh under his breath now, and his eyes were gleaming in the way that they did when he spoke of women.

Th-that's right, he said. Any c-crime!

His laughter had become a sort of sniggering, and he pointed at me as though to emphasize a joke. But was all this just a joke to him? I remember suspecting that it wasn't – but then I forgot about it.

*

At the end of the week, on Max's last day at the paper before Gordon returned, I brought in some of my illustrations to show him, in the hope that he'd put in a word for me at the Melbourne publishing firm he'd mentioned. He spread the drawings out under his lamp and studied them. He took off his glasses and bent lower, continuing to scrutinize the material in silence. Then he turned to me. I found his naked eyes very strange, without the glasses: large and pale grey, with dark lashes, they were difficult to meet and yet difficult to look away from. He wasn't wearing his cap tonight, and I seemed to have him in focus for the first time.

You're good, he said. You're a b-bloody good draughtsman, aren't you? I'll be glad to write to my friend and tell him they should look at your work.

I thanked him and he held up his hand, replacing his glasses.

It's no problem. I wouldn't do it if you didn't have the goods.

He sat looking at me in silence for a moment, as though turning something over in his mind; then he reached into a pocket of his jacket, drew out his wallet and produced a card, which he held out to me.

Here's my phone number at the studio. I've got a proposition for you: think it over, Hugh, and give me a call if you're interested. I've got more work than I can handle, and I'm looking for an assistant. If I had an assistant, I could take on more work, and not have to stretch myself like old rubber bands. W-would you be interested?

I was startled, and must have shown it. I began to tell him cautiously that I appreciated the offer, but he stopped me.

Don't give me an answer now; there's no rush. But I reckon you'd get more experience with me than you do here. For instance, I need someone to ghost *Rod Callaghan* – or at least share the load. Turning it out in addition to everything else is getting too much for me. You might enjoy that.

I told him I'd think about it, knowing I was unlikely to accept. I had the feeling that life with Max would be uncertain, and I was happy for now to stay on the *Mail*, until I tried to launch myself as a painter. This was an ambition I'd continued to keep secret – from Max, from Gordon Carter and from everyone except Walter Dixon and Moira Doran.

Good, Max said. You think about it, mate.

He smiled and shook hands with me, as though we already had a deal, making me feel somewhat guilty.

When I came in the following afternoon, Gordon Carter was back in his chair. He looked up and smiled.

Well, son: how was life with the dodgy comic strip artist?

I told him I'd got on well with Max, and we went to work without further discussion. Soon it was as though Max Fell had never been here. But dodgy or not, he'd certainly been unusual.

Over a month later, on a Saturday evening in July, I called in for a drink in the Green Room: the lounge bar of the Duke of Norfolk Hotel.

The Duke was in Bathurst Street, opposite the Hobart Repertory Theatre, and was patronized by Hobart's actors and broadcasting people. The actors were few in number and mostly amateur, since no full-time living could be made in theatre or radio in Hobart; but the Duke's proprietor was a member of the Repertory Society, and had set out to make the hotel attractive to his fellow drama enthusiasts, as well as to the small group of Hobart citizens with artistic aspirations. Like other Australian hotels in the fifties, the Duke had two bars: the stark and noisy public bar, inhabited only by men, and the lounge bar, catering for women and couples. Lounge bars generally resembled funeral parlours, and were sunk in a funereal quiet; but the Green Room was different. You came in from the hall through a frosted-glass door that was lettered with its name. It was quiet and well-carpeted, and its decor was tasteful, with a theatrical motif. Soft light came from red-shaded lamps that were set in niches around pale green walls hung with prints by Toulouse Lautrec, and with sketches for theatre sets. The twin masks of comedy and tragedy were fixed above the fireplace. Occasionally a customer from the public bar would look inside the door and then retreat, probably imagining that the Green Room was a private club. Certainly it resembled one.

Tom Thorpe had first brought me here, and had introduced me to some friends he drank with. They were here every Saturday night, and would stay until closing time. I usually only stayed for an hour, before going out to visit Moira. Saturday was my night off, and being with Moira then was precious to me. Tonight, though, she was taking her daughter to a school function, so I planned to spend the evening here, for something to do – even though the company was mostly middle-aged.

It was cold tonight, and foggy: when I came in I was grateful for the warmth of the open fire. Herbert the barman smiled at me, polishing a glass in front of a display of coloured lights: shelves of spirits and liqueurs, lit from some secret source and reflected in a mirror along the back wall. Plump, elderly and pink-faced, Herbert wore a gleaming white jacket to match his sculptured white hair, and was more like a club steward than a barman. He knew nearly all the regulars here, addressing them deferentially by their surnames, and offered unusual little courtesies. When he sold cigarettes to the smokers, he would open the packet, shake out the first cigarette and extend his lighter.

Tom was here, drinking with Nigel Carmichael. They were seated on stools at the bar with glasses of rum in front of them – the city's favourite winter drink.

Hugh, me boy, Tom said. Let me buy you a Captain Morgan, to thaw you out.

I took a stool next to Carmichael, who turned and looked at me with wide, faded eyes, his dreamy, absent-minded smile that of a man who was almost permanently drunk. Carmichael was a drama producer with the local branch of ABS, the national broadcaster. Always addressed as Carmo, he was large and handsome in a florid, fleshy way, with thinning black hair arranged in strips across the top of his large head.

Ah, Hugh, he said. Are they treating you well at Tasmania's leading daily?

I told him they were.

Splendid. I've just been telling Tom here, my play's developing well. That third act is coming together now. Everything's beginning to cohere.

That sounds good, Carmo, I said.

Carmichael always talked about his play, which he'd been writing for years; it seemed that nobody expected him ever to finish it, and it was part of the pattern of Saturday evening that he'd bring his friends up to date with its progress. This bored me slightly, but it was impossible not to like Carmo, who showed a bemused benevolence towards everything and everyone.

Coheres, does it Carmo? Tom said. He adjusted his glasses, looking severely at Carmichael and then winking quickly at me. About time, I would have thought, mate, he said. How many drafts have you done now?

Carmichael looked vague.

I've rather lost count. The thing is to get it to work, Tom.

Tom relented, and smiled.

Of course it is, Carmo. It takes pains, to produce quality.

True. Not everyone realizes that.

Carmichael picked up his packet of cigarettes from the bar and drew one out. Before he could light it, pink and smiling Herbert had materialized and leaned across the bar, extending a flaming lighter.

Thank you, Herbert. And perhaps we need three more Captain Morgans.

Of course, Mr Carmichael.

Herbert swayed off, and Carmo drew deeply on his cigarette. He wrenched it from his lips with a theatrical flourish and released a long stream of smoke, staring above our heads with a visionary fixity, at the same time touching his strands of hair, reassuring himself that they were all in place.

That third act's immensely improved, he murmured. It really is, Tom. I'd value your opinion, if you'd care to read it.

The evening wore on: a set pattern with minor variations. One of the amateur actors came in who was in a play running at the Repertory, and Carmichael engaged him in an extended conversation. Tom and I exchanged gossip about the *Mail*, and Tom told me of his latest efforts to get a job with a commercial studio in Melbourne. So far he'd had no luck, but he continued to hope, he said. We all lived in hope, it seemed, harbouring dreams of the glamour and success that lay beyond the island.

At about nine o'clock, when I'd begun to think of leaving, the frosted-glass door opened and a young man in his early twenties paused there. He looked about him in the muted light as strangers often did – as though wondering whether the Green Room was open to the public. Then he came on into the bar. He was stocky and broad-shouldered, with thick blond hair.

We all glanced at him briefly as he moved past us. He took up a position at the far end of the bar, looking at no-one. Herbert hurried along there to take his order, elbows and eyebrows raised, and Tom and Carmo continued their conversation. After a time I glanced at the man again. Certainly he wasn't the type most commonly seen in the Green Room, and he wasn't dressed like an office worker. But nor did he look like one of the labourers who filled the public bar on a Friday night, most of them still in their dusty and grease-stained working gear. He wore a leather jacket and roll-neck sweater, and his boots were well polished. I had a vague feeling that I'd seen him somewhere before. At that moment, having drained a beer and set it down on the counter, he felt my gaze and turned to look at me, his eyes holding mine with a challenging expression. They were set under low eyebrows, which made their blue appear dark, and he looked out from under these brows with his head slightly lowered, like a bull about to charge. Embarrassed at having been caught studying him, I looked away quickly, and turned my attention back to the group.

Some time later, Tom moved over to the fire to talk to some people he knew there, and I was left with Carmichael, who began to deliver a discourse on the plays of Terence Rattigan. I encouraged him in this, since I feared he might otherwise return to the subject of his own play. We were drinking beer now, and I was no longer very clear-headed; my mind drifted, and I stared at the radiant, many-coloured bottles that stood ranked in front of the mirror behind the bar. Suspended for what seemed a timeless interval, I was hypnotized by the bottles and their reflections, while Carmichael's gentle, meditative voice rambled on near my ear.

The Deep Blue Sea must surely be Rattigan's masterpiece, he said.

Another voice spoke on my left: a voice that was slow and unfamiliar.

Excuse me, mate – don't I know you from somewhere?

The man from the end of the bar was standing next to me, looking down into my face. His low-set eyebrows gave his eyes an intent, severe expression.

I don't know, I said. My name's Hugh Dixon.

For some seconds he continued to stare at me. Then he began to smile.

Fritz! he said. It's me: Hans.

For a moment I looked back at him without comprehension. Then he came into focus: the remnants of the boy could still be seen, inside the man. He looked older than twenty-one, and the hair that had once been almost white was a darker shade, now; but the eyes were the same: the eyes that had challenged me to hand over my homework.

Bob, I said. Of course.

We shook hands, staring at each other in elated disbelief.

Hello *dummkopf*, Bob said.

We both laughed, while Carmichael watched us in muzzy bemusement. I introduced them, and Carmichael spoke to Bob with the same dreamy pleasantness he showed towards everyone, asking him if he was an artist, like me.

No, Bob said. I'm a carpenter.

Carmo's benevolent smile remained in place, and he nodded approval.

Ah. A craftsman, he said. Good for you, matey.

Bob sat down on the stool next to mine, and we began to talk. Soon Carmichael got up and drifted off to join Tom and his group by the fire. He probably did so out of boredom, since Bob and I had begun a conversation that was focussed on our lives at the age of eleven: reminiscences which caused us to burst into disproportionate laughter over puerile things, such as snatches of dialogue from *The Captain and the Kids.*

I asked him how it was that we'd never run into each other before.

I've been away a bit since I left school. Went to the mainland – worked on building sites in Melbourne; went fruit picking in Mildura. Lots of knocking around. I came back here a while ago, when my mother got sick. She died soon afterwards.

I'm sorry.

Yeah. Well. She never had much of a life, and she did her best for me.

What about your father?

His face went blank.

He died a long time ago – while I was in the Boys' Home. The grog got him.

I asked him what life had been like at Hillcrest. I did this with some diffidence, since this was the first time he'd touched on what had happened to him after he ran away, and I didn't know whether he'd want to discuss it or not. But he answered me in an even tone, staring at the bottles behind the bar.

It wasn't much fun there. The screws in charge were big tough bastards in black uniforms, like bloody crows. They used the strap a lot – but I soon got the hang of avoiding it. They didn't teach us much: just gave us stuff from the Correspondence School to work on. Some of the little blokes there couldn't read or write, so *that* wasn't much good to them, was it? We slept four in a room, and there was never any time to yourself: that's what mainly gave me the shits. Mostly we worked in the vegetable gardens, and looked after the animals. I didn't mind that – I liked looking after the chickens.

Now that he'd begun to talk he seemed happy to continue, and I listened attentively to the new, deep voice that had replaced the boy's. He'd been at Hillcrest for two years, he told me; then his mother had successfully appealed to the Child Welfare Department to release him, on the grounds that his violent father was dead, and he now had a safe home to come to. He went to the Technical College for his secondary schooling, where boys were given a basic education, as well as being taught trades. He'd emerged with a good grounding in carpentry, and had been taken on as an apprentice by a carpenter in Hobart. Now that he was back here, he was working for a building firm.

He drained his latest beer and turned to me, suddenly solemn, his mouth a straight line.

I shouldn't have pinched that bike, Fritz. That was a big mistake.

I searched for an adequate reply, not feeling sure what kind of answer he wanted.

You always told me you were going to run away. I thought I was going with you, remember? Comrades, we said.

He laughed softly, and shook his head.

Yeah: comrades. But just as well you didn't come, Hans – you didn't have any reason. I had to get out because I couldn't stand the old man's beltings any more. But I shouldn't have done it on Donald Grant's bike.

He paused, half-turned towards me, his gaze fixed on my face, seeming to wait for some further response that was important to him.

You were only a kid, I said. Your old man's the one who should have been arrested. They were pretty hard on you, sending you to Hillcrest.

He smiled.

It's great to see you, Hughie.

It's good to see you too. What made you come in here, tonight?

The blokes I was drinking with in the front bar went home, and I got sick of the noise there. Thought I'd have a quiet beer, before I pushed off. Didn't intend to stay long – it's not my sort of bar. Mostly arty people in here, aren't they? And that old bloke Carmichael said *you* were an artist – is that true, mate?

I'm just a newspaper artist. I've got a job on the *Mail.* I retouch the photos that go in the paper. Now and then I'm allowed to do caricatures of politicians. One of them wrote to the paper and objected – said I'd made him look like a rhino. Well, he does look like a rhino.

Bob leaned back and laughed.

But that's great, Hughie. You made it. I always reckoned you would.

You were better at drawing than I was, Bob. Did you ever think of going on with it?

He looked down into his empty glass. He seemed reluctant to answer; but when he did, he spoke rapidly, in a toneless voice that I suspected hid frustration. He'd thought about it often, he told me, and he still worked at drawing in his spare time. It was what he really wanted to do – not carpentry. He'd once hoped to be an illustrator of some kind, or a commercial artist. He shrugged.

Fat chance, he said. I've never had your training. And I've got no bloody idea how to get into the game.

Well, it's not easy, I said, and he nodded, plainly confirmed in his pessimism, and ready to leave the subject. But then I said:

I've got an idea. I might be able to help you.

*

The guilt I'd eventually feel over recommending Bob to Max Fell has dwindled now, as even our most searing emotions dwindle with the years. The guilt was never really justified, of course: after all, I'd acted as Bob's sponsor with the best of motives – and at first it had worked out well. Sometimes I'd tell myself that I should have suspected what Fell was; but that wasn't reasonable either. No-one could have suspected what Fell was.

I hadn't seen any more of Max Fell after he'd worked with me on the *Mail*. He hadn't got in touch with me about his offer to recommend me to a Melbourne publishing firm, and nor had I phoned him about his offer of a job – although I still had his card. Since I wasn't interested, I hadn't seen further contact as necessary; but now I decided to telephone him and recommend Bob in my place.

First, though, I wanted to see some samples of Bob's work. I asked him if he had anything I could look at: examples that could be shown to convince Fell of his ability. It was a long shot, but I thought it might work; and I could only hope that Bob's precocious childhood talent had developed as it had promised to do. Privately, of course, I feared that it mightn't have done; that he might have nothing substantial to show. I'd already met such people, in the Green Room and at Art School. They came from the tribe to which Nigel Carmichael belonged, their great works of art and literature stalled in their minds, their dreams remaining dreams. But something about Bob's response gave me confidence. The only way I can define it is to say that his fearless stare remained fearless, and that his expression grew even more serious. He'd always been serious; he hadn't changed since boyhood, and he seemed unlikely to let any sort of obstacle intimidate him. His face had remained impassive when I'd outlined my plan; only a shine in his eyes and a drawing together of his brows hinting at inner excitement – and perhaps at a mixture of hope and disbelief. He'd been particularly impressed with the fact that Max was the artist who drew *Rod Callaghan*, and he examined me with an attention that was almost menacing.

You reckon he'd take it seriously? Just from looking at my stuff?

I can't be sure. He's an odd sort of guy – but there's a chance, if your work impresses him. It's worth a try, don't you reckon?

He agreed it was worth a try, and asked me to come out to visit him at the place where he lived in Moonah the following Saturday. He had plenty of drawings stored away, he said.

Saturday being my day off from the *Mail*, I'd arranged to have dinner with Moira at Montrose. But I agreed to go out in the morning to the address Bob gave me. When he'd returned to Tasmania from the mainland, he'd come to roost in the district where he'd grown up – although not in his childhood home. That house hadn't belonged to his parents, and it had passed into other hands when his mother died. Bob hadn't wanted to rent it: too many bad memories, he said. Instead, he rented a place from a carpenter he worked with called Fred Tyson, an older man who apparently took a fatherly interest in him. Fred and his wife lived in a house in West Moonah, an area where the suburb began to climb towards the hills. There was a separate dwelling in the garden: a miniature bungalow, or garden house, that Fred had built for his son. Now the son had married and moved away, and Fred had let the place to Bob.

I came there at about ten o'clock. The bungalow was reached by a driveway from the front gate. It stood on the edge of a sloping stretch of lawn, shaded by a pine tree: a small, cream, weatherboard structure of the plain and basic kind often put together by men like Fred Tyson, somewhat resembling a stranded railway carriage. But basic though it was, I envied Bob. It was a place all his own – not some cramped bed-sitting-room in someone else's house. Raised on small brick pillars, it had a flat, red-painted iron roof, a door in the centre with a wooden awning over it, two wooden steps leading up to it, and small windows on each side. A little further on stood the Tyson home: a rambling old weatherboard place with a glassed-in verandah and an iron hipped roof. The garden had a view to the east, looking out over the roofs of Moonah to the river and the hills. In the west, Mount Wellington could be seen beyond the hilltop, capped with winter snow.

I knocked on Bob's door with a certain amount of curiosity. Young men of our age weren't usually very fastidious in their personal habits, and I didn't expect that Bob would be; in fact, I anticipated a fair amount of disorder. Instead, when he brought me inside, I found the place neat to an unusual degree. Here was a clue to his adult character, I thought: a discipline that perhaps did something to explain how it was that he'd survived his harsh childhood and his detention in the Boys' Home, to become a qualified tradesman. He might easily have become a petty criminal instead, filled with an incurable rage against the world. And yet – though I'm ashamed to recall this – I couldn't forget that he'd been a thief, and I'd catch myself wondering whether the theft of the bicycle had been an isolated incident, or whether other thefts had followed, at some stage. I didn't want to think so, and tried to dismiss it from my mind; but still the question persisted. I understood why he'd run away, of course – but not why he'd stolen. For me, this was a line that couldn't be crossed; and I didn't want to think that Bob somehow justified it to himself. He'd said that it had been a mistake; but that wasn't the same as having said it was wrong. He hadn't discussed it again, though, and I didn't expect that he would.

Sit down, Hughie, Bob said. I'll make us a coffee.

I sat in one of two upright chairs that were placed at an old cedar dining table in the centre of the room. The bungalow seemed to consist of three rooms: the large living area where I was now sitting, and a small bedroom with adjoining bathroom, visible through a door at one end. There were basic kitchen facilities at the other end of the living room: a bench with a portable stove and an electric jug on it; a sink; a small refrigerator. Bob had switched on the jug, and was spooning instant coffee into two cups, his back turned to me. Under one of the windows was a drawing-board on trestles: a sight which encouraged me. All around the walls were broad pine shelves. Stacks of drawing paper, magazines, and large numbers of old gramophone records were set out there, arranged with an almost geometrical precision: further evidence of Bob's surprising attention to order.

I stood up to inspect the shelves more closely, and saw Bob look over his shoulder at me.

There's some books there that might interest you, Hughie. Just near those records.

I bent over. I could see no books – but next to the gramophone records I found the antique American comics he'd shared with me in the playground, all those years ago. (He'd always called his comics 'books'.) They were still in mint condition, and stacked in such neat piles that not one was crooked. I made some exclamation, and began to look through them; and as I handled these artefacts from a lost decade, with their strange, dry odour of the past, I was oddly moved. Here was a clue to Bob's adult spirit: a spirit that was hidden by his phlegmatic exterior. He'd somehow hoarded these comic books through all his trials: in that house I'd never seen, where he'd been terrorized by his violent father, and through all the years since. And this suddenly spoke to me of the pathos of his life. No doubt his mother had kept the comics in safekeeping for him, in the time when he'd been in the Boys' Home, and later in the period when he was roaming on the mainland. She'd known what they meant to him: that abused, frightened woman who'd read *Felix the Cat* to him in his childhood, giving him consolation after one of his father's beatings. These strip cartoons, which most people outgrew and came to dismiss as dross, were more than just comic books to Bob. He'd been given little contact with literature or art; instead, the comics were his literature and his art, and I guessed that he saw in them things that their creators had never intended, or even imagined.

I cleared my throat.

So. You've still got them, Fritz.

He came across to the table, carrying our cups and saucers.

Right. I've still got them. Even those Katzenjammer Kids.

I looked at him in puzzlement: I didn't recall this title.

There were two different comics, he said. See? I've got examples of both. *The Captain and the Kids*, started by Rudolph Dirks, and *The Katzenjammer Kids,* by Harold Knerr. Both of those guys were German-Americans. Knerr took over from Dirks when Dirks took a break from the strip, way back in the Great War period. Same characters, but carried on by Knerr. Then the two strips ran in competition, for about fifty years. Knerr was the best, in my opinion.

His eyes gleamed: this was a subject that clearly stirred his enthusiasm. He raised a big hand and pointed at me across the table, his fingers loose.

Tell you something that might surprise you. The Kids are based on two boys called Max and Moritz, drawn by the German artist Wilhelm Busch, in the nineteenth century. Did you know that, Hughie?

No. You've really studied it, Bob.

I can tell you the names of the original artists for every Yank comic strip that matters. The people who ghost those old strips today are never as good: look at the Katzenjammers, for instance. And *The Phantom*. Absolute crap. The magic's gone. The skill's not there.

I guess that's true. But tell me: how would you feel about ghosting a strip yourself?

You mean Max Fell's strip? *Rod Callaghan*? You serious?

I told him that this was what Max had wanted me to do, when he offered me the job. So he'd probably expect Bob to do the same. Would he be interested?

He slowly put down his cup, staring at me.

Of course I'd be interested. I'd do anything to get into the game.

I asked him then what he could take to Fell as proof of his ability. Instead of answering, he went over to one of the shelves and pulled out a number of large, semi-stiff sheets of drawing paper. He brought these over to the table and laid them down, sitting opposite me. They were the good-quality pasteboard known as Bristol board: the kind that Gordon and I used at the office. The first two sheets that he pushed across to me – still in silence – were samples of an original adventure strip whose hero was a pilot for an air rescue service in northern Australia. Its professionalism exceeded my hopes: it was crisp, accomplished black-and-white work of a quality I thought superior to Max Fell's. I exclaimed, and made complimentary remarks; but still he said nothing, watching me, his mouth compressed into a thin line: a habit with him, it seemed, whenever he was tense or concentrated. What he pushed over next were samples of advertizing work: pictures of late-model cars; ads for men's and women's clothing; smiling women in kitchens displaying the latest refrigerators and washing machines.

It's all first-rate, I said. It really is. I can't believe you were never trained.

Still looking at me intently, as though trying to read his future in my face, he sat back, running his fingers through his thick thatch of hair.

You really think so? No bullshit?

I'll phone Max on Monday and ask him to see us, I said. I'll take you to the studio.

He smiled for the first time, his face lighting up with a gladness I'd never seen there before.

That's good of you, Hughie. You're a real mate.

I was glad to do it, I told him. But then I warned him that he mustn't count on anything: after all, I said, I hardly knew Max Fell.

Something more than the usual caution compelled me to utter this warning: one which would come to have a much darker resonance later on. There are things we anticipate without being conscious of them.

When I phoned Fell's studio, a woman's voice answered. I asked to speak to Max, and she told me to wait. I hung on for some time; then she came back on the phone again.

Max wants to know who's speaking.

I gave her my name, and she told me to wait again. Then Fell came on.

Hello, young Hugh. Do you want that job?

I'd decided for now to stay on the *Mail*, I told him. But I wanted to introduce a friend who was a talented black-and-white artist. He'd be very interested in the job, and had plenty of samples of his work that Max could look at.

What's his background? Who does he work for?

The thing is, Max, he's working as a carpenter at present.

A high, sniggering laugh came over the phone.

You're joking. A carpenter?

I now set out to be persuasive. I explained that Bob was my age, wanted to become a commercial artist, but had never had a chance to become a professional. He hadn't had any formal training, but if Max would only look at his work, he'd realize that this didn't matter: Bob had such natural talent that his work was already of professional standard. He was especially interested in becoming a comic strip artist, and was a great admirer of *Rod Callaghan*.

Max grunted. There was a pause; then he said:

Normally I wouldn't even look at him. But since you've given him such a wrap-up, maybe I should. I'm flat out all this week – no time to see him. Bring him in around ten o'clock next

Tuesday. Tell him to have plenty of samples with him. Can he be free then?

I'll make sure he is, I said.

That evening, I called Bob on the phone at Fred Tyson's house and gave him the news. The week's wait could be an advantage, I said: it would give him time to get his best work together. He agreed, and asked me to come out on Saturday afternoon and look at it.

We spent only a short time that Saturday going through the samples in his garden shack. Then we drank beer, and talked about our likes and dislikes, cementing the adult friendship that had replaced that of childhood. I found that Bob liked the same Hollywood crime films as I did – those *cinema noir* vehicles featuring actors like Humphrey Bogart and Robert Mitchum – and that we both had a particular fondness for an early Mitchum film called *Out of the Past*, which we'd seen a number of times.

That Mitchum, Bob said. What a cool character.

After that we listened to some of his record collection – old wax 78s, played on a wind-up gramophone – and found that we also shared a liking for traditional jazz. The first disc Bob put on was Fats Waller's 'Basin Street Blues'. I'd first heard this recording on the radio when I was no more than thirteen years old, and its effect on me had been electric. I'd never heard anything like it, since the jazz of the 1930s was rarely played on the air. I scarcely knew then what jazz was, but I was spellbound by Fats Waller's blithe and masterly piano – the light, flamboyant treble notes filling the world with sunlight, the deep bass chords from his striding left hand swinging me along, casting a spell of happiness that was close to bliss. The vintage recording surfaced on the radio only a few times after that, and it would be many years before I came across it in a music store, and began to collect other Fats Waller records – but I'd never forgotten it, storing the melody in my memory. And 'Basin Street Blues' contained a vision: one that I came to think of as *the Fats Waller road*. I saw a sunny

American highway, lined with shops and little cafes, stretching into the distance. A set of petrol pumps stood in the foreground, completing a picture that might have been painted by Edward Hopper: a uniquely happy, promising place where I yearned to go.

Old Fats, Bob said. You like the fat man?

He's a genius, I said. There's no-one like him.

True, Bob said. He's not just any old jazzman. A genius: you got that right, Fritz.

I nodded, and we smiled at each other. Then, on an impulse, as though cementing an important agreement, we leaned across the table and shook hands, as Fats played on.

Even now, after so many years, that moment of affinity and elation is still vivid in my mind. We'd been friends as boys, drawn together by our childhood love of drawing, and by the Katzenjammer Kids. Meeting again as adults, we'd been strangers to each other, seemingly with little in common. Now we were confirmed as friends again, linked by *Out of the Past*, and the Fats Waller road.

4

Max Fell's studio was at the top end of Liverpool Street, between Harrington and Barrack streets. Here, just beyond the central business district, Liverpool began its slow ascent towards the heights of West Hobart, beyond which rose the extinct volcanic cone of Mount Wellington, frowning over the town. The studio was on the first floor of a two-storey Georgian building on the eastern side of the street, dating from the 1830s. Built of the orange hand-made bricks of colonial days, it had a rusty iron roof in which two skylights were set. These gave natural light to the studio. In the ground floor was a dim secondhand shop, run by a large old woman who seldom seemed to move, sitting in an armchair in front of her catacomb of goods.

A number of these plain Georgian buildings survived along Liverpool Street, both here and in the centre of town. There, where the prosperous Quaker emporiums and enterprising Jewish warehouses of the nineteenth century had once supplied the colony with luxuries, some of the old buildings housed department stores and other successful businesses. At the top end, though, none of them did. Once you crossed Harrington Street a creeping shabbiness began; a melancholy emptiness. It was a territory of mournful little grocery stores, secondhand clothing shops whose ranks of grim garments had survived owners long dead, and tall, gloomy rooming houses which had once been brothels, catering for the redcoats and whalers of old Hobart Town.

Behind the buildings on the eastern side of the street ran the Hobart Rivulet, on its journey from Mount Wellington to the harbour: sometimes open to the sky, often disappearing under ground. A hundred years ago it had carried a reeking broth of effluents, and a maze of wooden hovels had squatted along its banks: hidden, unofficial villages of beggars, prostitutes and unregenerate criminals, beached in Van Diemen's Land by the penal system. Those warrens were gone now: gone with the cook-shops, flour mills, bakehouses, tanneries, booksellers and dancing-halls of nineteenth-century Liverpool Street; gone with its whorehouses and brawling taverns. And yet, as I led Bob Wall to the address on Max Fell's card on the Tuesday morning of our appointment, and we stood in front of the building at number 216, I was visited by a feeling that an invisible miasma of vice and despair still hung here, drifting from the Rivulet to enclose Fell's studio like a warning.

I won't call this a premonition: that would be an exaggeration springing from hindsight. The fact is that I carried in my mind what amounted to a personal map, dividing the town into good zones and bad; and the top end of Liverpool Street was a bad zone. This private geography wasn't simply a product of prejudice, but of old rumours, old stories that had been passed down in the town for generations. My father had told them; my mother and aunts had told them; the parents of my friends had told them. In the 1850s, half of Hobart Town's inhabitants had been felons or ex-felons, and what accompanied these stories were memories of ancient suffering; ancient crime. They'd grown very faint now and were fading away, like the remaining whiff of gas when a pipe has been leaking; but still they lingered. They lingered here at number 216, where a lane at the side of the building ran towards the Rivulet. Bob and I made our way down this lane and arrived at a doorway with a signboard fixed above it: *Max Fell, Commercial Artist and Photographer. First Floor.* We went in, and I led the way up the narrow set of stairs that led to the studio.

That visit was the only one I ever paid there. I stayed only long enough to introduce Bob to Max Fell, and I took my leave as Bob put down his portfolio and began to pull out samples of his work. That afternoon he rang me at the *Mail*, his slow, deliberate voice full of a rare enthusiasm. Fell had hired him, he told me. The wage he was offering was less than Bob earned as a carpenter, but that didn't matter, he said; he'd got his start as a commercial artist. He began to thank me, but I told him I needed no thanks; it had put me to no trouble, and Max was lucky to get him.

We arranged to meet for a drink in the Green Room on the following Saturday afternoon. This would be the first of a number of such meetings, in which he'd describe his progress as Fell's assistant.

Bob was never eloquent; he hadn't learned how to be eloquent. But he chose his words carefully, giving thought to what he said; and I found he had a strong imagination. When he described something, he made me see it, so that even after all these years it's as though I was there with him. His actual words are lost, of course, except for odd snatches. What I'll be attempting now is a faithful reconstruction, colouring it with details he sometimes merely touched on, but which still live in my mind.

He'd never been in an artist's studio before, he said. He found it an odd sort of place.

It ran the full width of the building, and resembled a storeroom – which was probably what it had been, in the old days. On the street side, the ceiling followed the slope of the roof, and the two skylights there added to the light from three tall front windows. An inner wall divided the studio from Max Fell's flat. The flat occupied the rest of this floor at the back, Bob told me, and could be entered from the landing outside or else through a door connecting it to the studio. But that door was kept locked, and Fell made it clear that his flat was off-limits. Bob had the use of a washroom on the landing outside.

The studio had a bare wooden floor and its furnishings were sparse. In the centre was a large pine table covered with an array of drawing materials, newspapers, tea cups and an electric kettle. A number of tungsten lights on tall tripod stands stood about, together with a white reflector board, also on a stand. These were for Max's photographic sessions. A low wooden dais was set against the inner wall for his models to pose on. Next to it was a folding Chinese screen decorated with a bird in a blossoming tree, and a little further along was a faded, chintz-covered sofa of nineteenth-century vintage. Two wooden cupboards stood at a far end of the room – one of them padlocked. A gas fire provided heating. Under one of the skylights was a big, sloping, purpose-built desk: Max's workplace. A drawing-board on trestles stood under the other skylight, and Bob was told that this would be his.

On the morning when he first reported for work, Max greeted him briefly and asked him to wait a few minutes. He then went over to his desk, sat down on an office chair, and began to rummage through some brochures. A phone rang on a little table next to him and he picked it up and spoke for some minutes. Meanwhile, Bob paced about the room and studied the wall decorations. These, he told me, were all framed enlargements of Max's black-and-white advertizements for women's dresses and underwear. He paused in front of a seductively smiling, full-busted woman in a challenging uplift brassiere resembling armour. She reminded him, he said, of those Amazonian women encountered on other planets in old *Buck Rogers* comics. The legend below it read: *Nu-Vu. The underwire bra that makes the most of YOU.*

Suddenly Fell was standing next to him, the peaked cap he constantly wore tilted at an angle. He'd come up very quietly, and Bob started. Fell said nothing; he looked sideways with what might have been an enquiring expression. But Bob couldn't be sure of this, he said, since he was still becoming accustomed to Max's blue-tinted glasses: he found it difficult to see his eyes, and thus to judge his mood. Finally Max spoke to him.

This one gives you a horn, does she, son?

Bob wasn't amused by this, he told me; bar-room chaffing was something he hadn't been expecting from his new employer. Nevertheless, it was important to him to get on well with Fell, and he summoned up a suitable reply.

I like your work. She looks pretty glamorous.

Fell continued to look sideways at him; then he ran his tongue across his lips and grinned. The grin might have been lecherous or it might have been mocking, Bob said; because of the blue-screened eyes it was impossible to be certain.

You might well say so, son. That lady's one of my best models. A forty-inch bust: tits as big as Jane Russell's. B-but don't get any ideas. Drawing those luscious pieces won't be your job: that's my department. Come and sit down. We need to talk about *Rod Callaghan.*

Fell now explained what he wanted at this stage. Because of the volume of fashion work he had to do, he was finding it more and more difficult to get time to work on the strip. This was where Bob could give him most help. To begin with, Bob would simply letter the dialogue in the balloons of some of the episodes that were already drawn. Then he'd draw some test episodes of his own, working to Max's storyline and dialogue. If these proved satisfactory, Bob could begin to contribute episodes for publication, still working to Fell's script and taking week about with him. Ultimately, Max said, Bob might take over the strip for most of the time.

He sat back and lit a cigarette, looking at Bob through the smoke with narrowed eyes.

How does that sit with you, matey?

Bob was delighted, and must have shown it. Max smiled: perhaps with gratification, perhaps with sardonic amusement. It was difficult to tell: he never held your gaze for long, Bob said.

The month that followed was deeply satisfying for him. It seemed that at one stroke, he'd been granted something he'd never believed could become reality, and his reports to me were full of low key excitement. His usual guarded manner was gone, and I shared his pleasure – taking, I must admit, a certain satisfaction at having played a part in his life's transformation. I followed with interest every fresh development that he reported, as Fell allowed him more and more responsibility. I also took an interest in all Bob had to tell me about Max himself.

Despite Fell's jocularity and wryly friendly manner, there was something about him that made Bob mistrust him. 'Creepy' was a word that he applied to him. But since he was grateful for what Max was doing for him, he was prepared to dwell on the artist's good qualities, in that first month: among them his quirky sense of humour, and his mastery of his craft. Nevertheless, as we drank together in the Green Room each week, Bob began to make some critical judgements that I found surprisingly penetrating. Although he and I were the same age, he was already much more worldly than I was. He would talk to me about his roaming days on the mainland, and I saw that they'd toughened him, and given him a kind of precocious wisdom. Roughing it around the country and sharing workplaces with a variety of men had given him insights into their natures that had made him realistic to the point of being cynical. 'That bloke had a grudge against life,' he would say. Or: 'He was a weak self-pitying bastard.' His life on the road and in Melbourne had largely been a male one – that being the way it was for young single men in Australia at that time. Women he knew less about, despite having had a number of brief affairs; but certainly he wasn't cynical about them. In spite of his rough life, he seemed to idealize them, in fact. He was romantic, I suppose, as so many of us were then, and he'd once confessed to me that he was looking for the right girl.

Working alone with Fell for the hours that he did, Bob began to get to know him better than I'd done. Although Max was certainly professional where his fashion work was concerned, his boasting about the vicarious sexual pleasure it provided for him was something Bob didn't find amusing, in a man so much older than himself – though he had to pretend that it did. Years ago, Max had been married, he told Bob; but the marriage had broken up. The circumstances weren't made clear, but Fell attached all the blame to his wife, referring to her always as 'the bitch'.

He often calls women bitches, Bob said. That's the way he seems to see most of them. Maybe they're all taking the blame for whatever his wife did – but I'll bet old Max was more to blame than she was. He's got a lot of hate in him, I reckon, even though he laughs a lot. You've got to be careful of blokes like that.

I'm setting out those judgements of Bob's that have stayed in my mind, mainly because of their relevance to what eventually happened. But at that stage such judgements didn't affect his attitude to the job: he was still well disposed towards Max as an employer, and impressed by the artist's skills.

Fell's illustrations for women's fashions were featured in the brochures the department stores mailed out, as well as in the *Mail* and some small suburban papers. The two big stores that employed him would send him the promotional literature supplied to them by the manufacturers, together with samples of the dresses and underwear they wanted advertized, so that Max could work from live models.

In those days, all such fashion illustrations were in black and white, and drawings of the latest women's dresses were often preferred to photographs: they had better definition, and were thought to be more elegant. In the case of the ads for underwear, there was no choice in the matter; as Max had told me, there was an unofficial ban on the publication of photographs of models in brassieres and corsets. Max's drawings, however, were in some ways more provocative than photographs, and I remember Gordon Carter studying some in the *Mail*, grinning and shaking his head.

I dunno how he gets away with it. Close to being spicy, this stuff is.

For a time, Bob didn't encounter any of Fell's models, since Bob worked only by day, and Max did most of his photographic sessions at night. But in Bob's fourth week at the studio, close to the end of August, Max brought in a model to pose for a sequence in *Rod Callaghan.* He'd pronounced himself satisfied with Bob's test episodes of the strip, and now Bob was working on some episodes for publication. Max had supplied him with a script scribbled on notepaper, incorporating dialogue for the balloons.

I often use models for scenes in *Callaghan*, he said. There's a scene in this episode where we might set up a photo for you to work from – the one where that c-crim beats up his girlfriend. I'll see if I can get Madge in for you. She's f-fairly new, and the right type.

There were no professional fashion models in Hobart. The town was too small to support such an occupation, and Max's studio was the only one carrying out fashion work. Even the life-class models at the Art School were merely part-time amateurs: mostly middle aged, and scarcely attractive enough for fashion modelling. In that era of extreme sexual modesty, any sort of public nakedness other than life-class modelling was taboo, and the only nude photographs of women to be found were in nudist publications and what were called 'men's magazines' – and these were posed with the pubic zone painted out, imitating the chaste white deltas of classical statuary. Very few young women would have considered posing in the nude, which was regarded as little better than prostitution; nor would many have agreed to pose in their underwear. So Bob was curious to know where Max got his models from. When he asked him, Fell's voice took on a confiding note.

I've got my ways. There are two sorts. First, there are the ones some of my mates put me on to. L-little girls who are fairly easy, and who want to earn some money. They're the ones who mostly model the underwear ads.

You mean prostitutes?

No, no. Whores don't have the looks – they're too clapped out. Just little girls who aren't too proud, who work in places like factories and who like to feel I'll make them into p-pinup girls. I make the little bitches feel like bathing beauties; I tell them they've got film-star looks. And when they see my d-drawings in the paper, they get a real thrill knowing it's really them.

He drew on a cigarette, screwing up his eyes with a canny expression.

The second sort are not so easy. Women in their twenties or early thirties – usually married with kids. Respectable. I need them for the dress ads, but also for the underwear fashions for mature women. The big sizes in bras and corsets.

Bob said he could see that this wouldn't be easy. Wouldn't their husbands be opposed to it? And how did Max find such women?

Fell grinned.

I prowl around. I talk to women working in shops, for instance. When I go into the department stores to discuss my work with the buyers, I get into conversation with likely-looking saleswomen there. And quite a few turn out to be interested to model for the dress ads. I pay well, and they're flattered to do it. It's p-perfectly respectable – and they're happy for their husbands to know about it. The underwear's another matter, of course. Not so many want to do that.

Bob asked him how he persuaded them. Fell winked at him, slowly releasing smoke: at least he seemed to wink, through his pale blue lenses.

Vanity, he said. Female vanity. Flatter a woman, tell her she's got a beautiful figure, and you'll often get them to pose – even the ones that seem s-strait-laced. You'd be surprised how many women want their bodies to be admired – even some of those pure married ladies who've never stepped out of line. D-deep down, they'd like the whole world to appreciate them, before their figures have gone. They look at themselves in the mirror in the nude and think: some day this will all be gone; I'll be old and wrinkled and fat. But a painting or a photograph preserves it forever – see? That's why women posed for the g-great artists – and that's why they pose for me. *I'm* an artist – the best there is at what I do. I make them look like goddesses. I'm the best thing that ever happened to them.

He raised his chin, his eyes half-closed behind their glasses, and smiled, wearing a look of triumphant pride. He was clearly serious in these claims; and at this point Bob began to entertain a doubt about Fell's mental balance. He thought Max might be a little bit mad, he told me. But he nodded, and tried to remain expressionless.

A woman starts by modelling dresses for me, Fell said, and then I ask her to model undergarments. At first she says no – but when I tell her what a m-magnificent figure she has, and that no-one but me will ever see the photo, she begins to think again. 'My husband mustn't know,' she says, and I agree. Sometimes she wants a copy of the photo for herself – and that gives me a sort of power over her, doesn't it? She's always available to model again, after that.

He gave a sudden high giggle.

The one I'm getting in to pose for the *Callaghan* sequence is that kind of woman, he said. Works part-time in a store. A respectable married lady with two kids. Quite g-genteel. Madge has only done a couple of dress ads so far. Hasn't agreed to do underwear ads – not yet. But she will. She l-loves to be admired, I can tell. Lovely full figure: the matronly type. I'm going to get her to pose in her slip, for *Callaghan*. If she'll do that, it's only a s-step to underwear ads in the future. That's for sure. You see, matey?

Bob's essential respect for women was making him feel an increasing dislike of these work methods of Fell's. But clearly it wouldn't have been sensible to question them – especially at a time when Bob's contribution to *Callaghan* was about to be published in two interstate newspapers. His first published work. He was very excited about that, so he nodded and said nothing.

The episode in *Rod Callaghan* for which Fell wanted a model was one concerning a criminal who believed his girlfriend had betrayed him to the police. He would beat her up to try and make her confess to it; but in the final frame, Rod Callaghan would crash in and rescue her. It would be good for Bob to work from photographs for this sequence, Max said; it would make it especially lifelike.

There was one problem. Although a number of Max's male acquaintances were willing to pose in such sequences for a small fee, there weren't any that were currently available during the day – and Madge Gregson didn't want to come in at night. So Bob would have to take the part of the criminal when Fell took his shots.

Madge arrived at somewhere around three in the afternoon. When Fell had ushered her inside, she paused by the littered table in the centre of the room, carefully removing her felt hat with both hands and looking from Fell to Bob with a hesitant smile.

As Max had told him, she was pretty, Bob said – but not in a way that was particularly striking. Somewhere in her late twenties, she seemed essentially ordinary: the sort of married woman you might see on the tram, or out shopping. In fact, she was the last kind of woman Bob had expected to find posing for Fell's photographs, he told me; and knowing the attitudes that Max brought to these sessions made him uneasy for her. Max helped her off with her heavy woollen overcoat, and she thanked him.

It's freezing outside, she said. Snow right down the mountain. I'm glad you've got the fire on.

We want you to be warm, Max said.

He introduced her to Bob, using only her first name. Her smile now became one of eager friendliness: the smile of a woman who'd seldom encountered anything but goodwill. She had wavy brown hair, a fair complexion, large eyes, and an open, guileless face: one that seemed to Bob to be almost naive, despite her maturity. 'A bit like a schoolgirl,' was how he summed her up.

Bob's my assistant, Max told her. He'll be doing the drawings from these shots. He'll be posing with you today.

That's nice, she said. But I don't quite understand what we'll be doing, Max. Can you tell me a bit more about it?

You've seen my strip in the Melbourne *Herald*, Max said. Haven't you, darling?

I think so. My husband gets that paper now and then. It's about a detective, isn't it?

That's him: that's Rod. And for some scenes we like to use models and take pictures the artist can work from. This scene is about a bad guy who beats up his girlfriend. Bob will be the bad guy; you're the girlfriend.

She looked doubtful, and then gave a little laugh.

I hope he won't beat *me* up.

Max echoed her laugh with his high giggle.

Not to worry: it's all make-believe, Madge. I'll explain it to you.

He explained. Bob would be standing over her, his fist raised. She would be lying on the floor in her slip, cowering away from him. As he spoke, doubt crept into the woman's face and her brows drew together in a questioning frown – so that she looked, Bob said, like a child who was beginning to be dubious about some adult demand.

In my slip? I don't know, Max. I wasn't expecting –

She broke off, while he waited.

I told you: I don't want to pose in my underwear.

Instead of being decisive, her voice was now imploring; but Max said nothing. Instead he took a step closer to her and took off his glasses, peering into her face, his pale, naked eyes appearing unnaturally large, like those of a nocturnal bird. The woman stared back at him, her smile returning like a ghost of itself, while the sound of a car horn floated up from outside. All this took place in only a few seconds, Bob said, but it seemed much longer. Finally Max put his glasses back on again and spoke in a low, throaty voice.

Listen to me, darling. There's no harm in this: you'll be well covered up in your slip. Bob and I are professionals, and we're used to women posing in all sorts of ways. No-one but us will ever know you were the model – but I can tell you, you're ideal for the girl in this story. She's very beautiful and seductive, with a superb figure. And that's a description of *you*, Madge. No-one else would do. Won't you help me out?

During this speech, Madge had continued to hold Fell's gaze as though compelled in some way. At the end, however, she looked down at the floor, breaking the connection with what seemed a visible effort, her full lower lip drawn under her teeth. She was silent for a moment; then she nodded, and Max grinned triumphantly.

Does that mean yes, Madge?

She raised her head.

Yes. All right. As long as it's just in my slip.

Her smile had returned like a flickering light: faint and doubtful, and yet with a suggestion of gratification in it. Max's flattery had succeeded, it seemed.

Good, Max said. Good.

He rubbed his hands and gestured towards the Chinese screen, with its bird on the blossoming bough.

You g-go over there and change, while Bob and I get prepared.

She turned away obediently and walked towards the screen. When she'd gone behind it, Max turned to Bob.

Okay. Let me get my camera and we'll be ready to go. Take off that jacket, mate. You'll look more like a thug in your shirt-sleeves.

He hurried away down the room, opened one of the cupboards there and came back with his big Rolleiflex, which he placed on the table.

I'm loaded and ready, he said, and grinned as though he'd made a suggestive joke. He went over to a tripod stand which was placed on the left of the dais, supporting a tungsten lamp. He switched the lamp on, and the dais was flooded in a white radiance. It was a grey day outside, with only a weak winter light coming through the skylights and tall windows, and the sudden brilliance was startling. The white reflector board stood on the other side of the dais, also supported on a tripod, and Max paced around to it and began to adjust its position. As he did so, the woman emerged from behind the screen and walked towards the dais, still in her stockings and shoes, but now clad only in a pink nylon slip with a V neck. She stepped on to the dais in the glare of the light and waited, squinting, her eyes avoiding both Fell and Bob. Her cheeks were slightly flushed, and her hands were crossed protectively in front of her bosom. She didn't speak, and the room was silent.

Fell went across to the windows and drew their heavy curtains, dimming the room. The dais was now an island of pitiless white light where the woman stood isolated, as though trapped in another dimension. Fell came back and adjusted the reflector board again. This done, he studied Madge with dispassionate care, as though he were intending to dissect her.

Now then Madge, the bad guy's just knocked you to the floor. Bob's the bad guy, and he'll be standing over you with his fist raised. You're frightened, and you're begging him to stop, looking up at him. You understand?

I think so.

Her voice held an uncertain note, and her gaze had become in some way anxious. She was still standing to attention, her hands still crossed in front of her bosom.

All right then, Fell said. Get rid of those shoes and lie on your right side, facing me. Bob, get up there and stand over her. Crouch a bit. Fist raised.

Bob did as he was told, while the woman kicked off her shoes, knelt carefully on the floor, and then lay down awkwardly in the position that Max had asked for, propping herself on her right elbow. Her eyes, shining in the glare, remained on Fell, whose appearance now captured Bob's attention. He stood, entirely focussed on the woman, bent a little as though at the start of a race and seeming to vibrate with electric energy. His lips were parted in a fixed grin, and his expression was eager, as though in anticipation of some vastly fulfilling event. He rubbed his hand briefly across his mouth, and his hand seemed to tremble, Bob said.

Good. Good. You're looking up at the bad guy, Fell said. The guy who's going to hurt you. I want to see that scared look on your face.

Madge looked up at Bob. Her expression didn't change very much; but it didn't need to, Bob said. The anxious look in her eyes had deepened.

All right, Fell said. Now we need to do something to show that you've been roughed up.

He stepped on to the dais, squatted next to Madge, and reached toward her left shoulder. She looked up at him with a dawning expression of protest, beginning to raise her hand. But he'd moved quickly, grasping both the strap of her slip and the bra strap underneath, jerking them off her shoulder in a single violent movement, exposing her left breast almost completely. She shook her head, one hand still ineffectually raised; but Fell had already left the platform and had picked up his camera.

That's perfect, he said. Perfect. Drop the hand, darling. Just look at Bob, and hold the position.

He raised his camera and began to take shots. The woman remained still, looking at Bob now with an expression of shock.

Obeying Fell's order, she'd lowered her hand, and made no attempt to cover her breast. The colour had left her face, its whiteness made whiter by the glare of the lamp.

I nearly stepped forward and pulled the bastard away from her, Bob said.

We were sitting over beers in the Green Room on the following Saturday evening. Carmichael wasn't in yet, and Tom Thorpe was talking to a group of people over by the fire. There was no-one to hear our conversation.

But you didn't, I said.

No. I didn't. It had all happened so bloody quickly. When he did it, I started to move – but then I saw that he'd got down off the platform again, and wasn't going to do any more to her. But she wasn't the sort of woman who should have been treated like that – you understand what I'm saying, mate? Someone's wife. A woman with kids. I felt bad for her. She didn't seem to like what he did, but she didn't object, either. Didn't do anything to cover herself – just let Max take his bloody pictures.

I looked at him. He was breathing hard, and I saw that he was gripped by a kind of outrage. Fell's behaviour certainly sounded crude, and I understood Bob's response to it; but his anger seemed disproportionate, and I wondered why. Then I remembered his mother, and how as a child he'd tried to protect her from his father's beatings.

Look, there was nothing you could do about it, I said. And maybe the woman didn't really mind. In which case, it's all right.

I don't think so. I think she was scared of him. If she'd agreed to the pose, maybe it would have been all right. But Max assaulted her – that's what it amounts to. The bastard's kinky. He did it because he got a kick out of it.

I finished my beer and thought for a moment, studying our reflections in the mirror behind the bar. Bathed in lemon light among the bottles, we looked an unusually serious pair: an inconsequential image that somehow persists in memory. Hans and Fritz: fair hair and brown.

Assaulted her? Maybe that's a slight exaggeration, I said.

My concern was to see Bob put the incident behind him, and not come into conflict with Max, so I tried now to analyse what had happened in a way that would reduce its seriousness. After all, I said, Madge had gone on with the session; and according to Bob, she'd even agreed to pose for Fell again. So although Max might be kinky, the woman felt flattered enough to go on modelling for him. Unless he actually hurt her, surely it wasn't Bob's problem. What mattered was to stay with the job, and to avoid having a run-in with Max.

Next week, you've got your own episodes of *Rod Callaghan* appearing in the big mainland papers, I said. That's really something, Hans. Do you want to throw the job away right at this point?

He shook his head, and spoke softly.

No Fritz. You're right.

For the following month or so, Bob did as I advised, working hard at his contribution to *Rod Callaghan*, and trying to avoid more contact with Fell than was necessary. This wasn't difficult. Now that Fell had come to have confidence in Bob's abilities, he'd handed over the *Callaghan* strip to him almost completely, and was concentrating on his fashion work. This meant that their hours coincided less than they had done, since Max did most of his photography at night, and a good deal of his artwork then as well. Bob suspected that he often slept late; he would emerge through the door from his flat at mid-morning, pale and unshaven, carrying a cup of coffee and blinking in the light through the windows.

This was a time of elation and high achievement for Bob: a time of great happiness. Here he was, at just twenty-one, producing a daily adventure strip for two interstate newspapers read by many thousands of people around the country. It continued to be signed by Max Fell, since Bob was simply his ghost; but at present that didn't bother him. Some day, he said, he'd have a strip of his own. I'd often visit him at his garden house on a Saturday, and he'd show me a week's episodes of *Callaghan*, clipped from *The Herald*. And just as he'd surprised me as a boy with his talent, he continued to surprise me now. As far as possible, he was imitating Fell's style for the sake of continuity; but in spite of this the difference was marked. He couldn't help himself. He was simply a better draughtsman than Fell, competent though Max was: a more talented artist in every way. The drawings in Fell's frames were often cluttered, with little effective use of contrast; and his renderings of the figures were sometimes clumsy. Bob's work was stylish and impeccable, with a deceptive simplicity. He used light and shadow to maximum effect, and I saw the influence of Milton Caniff – an influence he acknowledged. He was born to be a black-and-white artist; I told him so, and he grinned with pleasure.

But this time of happy fulfilment was short in duration. On a Saturday evening near the end of September, Bob arrived in the Green Room with a set, unsmiling face. This, and the fact that he had little to say, brooding over his beer, began to concern me, and I asked him what the matter was. But I'd already guessed: it would be something to do with Max Fell. And although I may be investing memory with far more foresight than it had, I seem to recall a hollow premonition that Bob's flight into success was ending.

At first what he had to tell me, bizarre though it was, hardly seemed to justify such a fear.

I found something in the studio I don't like, he said.

Something to do with Max?

Right. I tell you, the bastard's sick in the head, mate.

He ran his hand through his hair, and a sheaf of it fell across his forehead. His mouth had taken on its thinnest line, and his big hand closed into a fist. He looked like a man about to get into a fight, and I remembered his telling me that when he was knocking around he'd learned how to handle himself. I could believe this now, as he stared towards the mirror behind the bar; I sensed in him a need for violent action of some kind. I waited for him to explain, while he sipped his beer. He put it down, and looked at me.

I'm on my own in the studio quite a lot now, he said. Max is either in his flat, or off around town. Yesterday he spent a bit of time with me, discussing his script for the strip; then he went off into the city. After a while, when I was almost ready to knock off for lunch, I did something I shouldn't have. I wish I hadn't.

He was curious about one of the big cupboards at the end of the room, he said: the one that Max kept padlocked. Yesterday he'd noticed the padlock dangling loose: Max must have forgotten to close it. Bob was having an easy day, with most of his current work on *Callaghan* almost done, and he had some time on his hands. He wandered across to the cupboard and stared at it. The fact that Max kept it locked undoubtedly meant that it was private, and he knew that he shouldn't open it, he said. Yet he did. He didn't try to justify this; he simply told me he was curious. Perhaps had he respected Fell he wouldn't have done it. But he didn't respect him now: not since the incident with Madge. And simply glancing inside the cupboard didn't seem a serious offence; after all, he was supposed to have the run of the studio.

I wish I hadn't done it, he said again, and paused. He released a long breath, blowing out his cheeks and looking at me.

There's a second *Rod Callaghan*, he said.

I stared at him.

He's got stacks of episodes of *Callaghan* in that cupboard, he said. But not a version that could ever get printed. One that's really pornographic.

In spite of his seriousness, I couldn't help laughing.

Well, well, I said. Just for his own consumption. Or maybe to get printed as dirty books. But you shouldn't be surprised: you know Max has a dirty mind.

It's worse than that. You don't understand Hughie. This is really bad.

I don't see what you're so concerned about. So he's got a secret obscene version of the strip. Why is that anything to be so worried about?

He told me. Female nudity – and there was a good deal of that – was the least worrying thing about the strip. The primary preoccupation of the secret *Rod Callaghan* was not eroticism, but sadism.

And that was where it began to come to an end: his strange apprenticeship, and his brief entry into that cherished dream surviving from his boyhood. Since sado-masochism for mass audiences didn't exist in our youth, Bob had no previous acquaintance with sadistic fantasies, any more than I had: so these images of women being raped, tortured and brutalized were not just novel to him, but sickening. Even today (from my memory of what he described to me), I believe that Fell's efforts would immediately be banned. His depictions of men inflicting suffering on women – repeated in various forms and contexts, with the ultimate tedium that's always the hallmark of evil – were both lovingly drawn and atrocious. Bob went into a good deal of detail in describing them, as though this might purge the images from his mind. It didn't, so far as I could tell. One figure in particular seemed to haunt him: a gaunt, saturnine individual who was more prominent than any other as a vicious tormentor of crying and pleading women. He wore an outfit similar to a stage magician's: dark suit, bow tie and opera cloak.

He looked like a bloody demon, Bob said. He also looked like Fell. I dreamed about him, last night. I'm going to tell Max I'm quitting the job tomorrow.

But even now, I set out to dissuade him – or rather, to get him to postpone his decision for a week or so. He reluctantly agreed to this; but when we met in the Green Room again it was evident that his mind was made up: he'd resign immediately, he said. He hated *Rod Callaghan* now, and got no pleasure from working on it: those other images kept rising in his mind. And since his discovery, even the old building at number 216 had begun to depress him; had begun to get into his dreams, together with Max's images of cruelty. This had something to do with the place's age, he believed, and that past it seemed to store like a container: the penal nineteenth century, with its miseries and crimes. The gloom of a hundred years permeated the building, and he associated this gloom with a smell: a kind of dank mustiness that hung on the stairs, and lurked in the corners of Max's studio. He couldn't get it out of his nostrils, he said. It hung as well in the laneway at the back, where the Rivulet flowed past between greasy stone walls: a pure mountain spring degraded into a drain. Number 216 was just the place for Max Fell; but it wasn't the place for him, Bob said.

And if the building oppressed his spirits, Max's presence did so still more.

I hate being in the same room with the bastard, Bob said. He took off those bloody glasses the other day and looked straight at me. Did you ever notice his eyes? It's like there's nothing behind them. I've got to leave, Fritz.

But still I persisted in asking him to think again. He might never have another chance like this one, I said – and it might be very difficult to find any sort of job as an artist.

He stared ahead of him grimly. Then I'll go back to carpentry, he said.

But now I became determined. He was succeeding against all the odds, in a specialized niche that was perfect for his talent, and I couldn't bear to see him walk away: it was almost like losing a cherished opportunity of my own. Finally I got him to change his mind by making him a promise: one that hinged on a plan I had for my own future.

I'm planning to quit the *Mail* pretty soon, I said. I want to paint full-time. When I go, I'll recommend that Gordon take you on. You can't fail, with the background you've got now. I've already shown him your work on the strip, and he thinks you're bloody good. Just promise me you'll stay on with Max until then.

Swinging around on his stool, he looked at me hard from under his brows: a look that seemed almost threatening.

You'll do that for me? In that case I'd better hang on.

My promise had been sincere, and I intended to carry it out. At the same time, it was something of a delaying tactic at present, rather than a solution I could deliver immediately. I hadn't lied to Bob: my plan to leave the *Mail* and paint was genuine; but I didn't really think it would evolve quickly. It was a plan that had two stages. The first was to begin to exhibit, when I naturally hoped that my paintings would sell – though I wasn't foolish enough to see them doing so in a big way immediately; I had more common sense than that. Only when they did sell well would I be able to quit my job. That was the second stage. Meanwhile, I'd yet to sell a single picture.

Two weeks after my talk with Bob, however, as though guided by some extraordinary intuition, Walter Dixon made me an offer of help: one that seemed likely to make the first stage of my plan possible. Such harmonious coincidences happen more often in life than one might think, I've found; but they usually come with a price attached. This was the case with Walter's offer; and the price was one I was bitterly opposed to paying.

Our meeting took place on a Sunday afternoon. My visits to Walter and the studio continued to take place then, since I was free until the evening, when I had to go in to the *Mail*. It was early; I'd only arrived about half an hour ago, and was sitting at my easel looking through one of my sketchbooks and planning the start of a painting. On the easel, the white paper waited, stretched and immaculate on its board. It was now October, and the tall north-facing window framed a scene that was full of the signs of spring: a bright day with patches of blue sky; daffodils in full bloom in one of the garden beds; the orchard erupting in a burst of white blossom.

Do I intrude on inspiration?

It was Walter's usual greeting. I always left the door ajar, and he leaned half inside the room, holding the doorknob, his eyebrows raised enquiringly. He was very considerate; if he saw that I was busy, he'd retreat, and we'd meet at afternoon tea.

I told him no, I'd not yet started work, and he sat down in a small brocade-upholstered armchair he'd donated to the room – I suspected for his use on these visits. He leaned back and folded his hands on his stomach, looking at me with a benevolent air. Today he was casually dressed in a light cotton golf jacket and baggy cord trousers, as though in acknowledgement of the end of winter and the arrival of the brisk, sunny days that were raising all our spirits. I'd seen him through the window a short time ago, walking through his orchard, his face upturned as though in prayer, his white hair catching the sun like the blossom.

You'll have no shortage of outdoor subjects in this weather, he said. The orchard looks wonderful, have you noticed? A painting by Bonnard.

I agreed, and we talked of the Impressionists for a time; a topic he never tired of. After a time he got up and moved over to a small table under the window where I'd put a stack of my finished watercolours.

I'll leave you in peace in a moment. But may I just glance through these?

Of course, I said. But then, having said it, alarm ran through me; I'd forgotten that this group of paintings included a study of Moira. Having given her the first one I'd done to keep, I'd worked from my sketchbook to produce one for myself: a far more ambitious picture. I called it *The Last Suburb*, and it showed Moira standing on Montrose Road with the hills behind her, entirely alone in the landscape, looking directly at the viewer with an expression of mingled calm and sadness. Now, in a few minutes, Walter would discover this painting, and the secret she and I had kept from him all this time would be out. There was nothing I could do about it, and I sat and watched him, trying to formulate some innocent-sounding story to explain how it was that she'd sat for me.

He'd resumed his place in the armchair and had pulled out his glasses from a shirt pocket, perching them far down on his nose, his head thrown back, carefully studying each painting. I was half afraid, and half ashamed: afraid of losing his friendship and support – though I no longer depended on him in any way, and had recently paid back every penny of my Art School fees – and ashamed that Moira and I had deceived him by hiding our love affair. Meanwhile, his painfully slow examination went on, as he commented on almost every painting, giving a respectful amount of time to each one. From where I sat, I couldn't see the paintings themselves; but when he came to Moira, I knew it instantly. He frowned, sitting absolutely still, and studied it for what seemed an interminable time, saying nothing. Then, still without speaking, and showing no expression, he held it up so that I could see it, gripping the sheet firmly on each side.

This is Moira, of course. You've seen into her soul, haven't you? Did you do this from memory – or did she sit for you?

Mostly from memory. I made a quick sketch of her a long time ago – on the day that you were sick.

I'd formulated this lie in the last few seconds, and hoped that it would work. But for some moments, his face still expressionless, Walter held my gaze and said nothing, as though waiting for more information.

There are not many people who'll sit for me, I said. And Moira's a wonderful subject. A very expressive face.

Still he said nothing, and waited. I knew then that my lie hadn't worked, and decided to say nothing more. The silence deepened, and finally Walter returned the painting to its place among the others and sat holding them on his knee. He cleared his throat, and now he wore that severe expression which made him formidable, and which even now had the power to intimidate me. His judicial look.

You really mustn't take me for a fool, young fellow. You forget that it's been my business over a lifetime to see through people's little lies and deceptions. I've noticed the way you two look at each other – but I've tended to dismiss it from my mind as a superficial flirtation. I didn't dream that the pair of you might be acting on it. Even now I hope that's not so – but this portrait is the work of a lover.

Perhaps it is, I said.

I'd decided suddenly to be truthful with him. He saw this, and his expression changed. I'd expected him to become angry; but instead he closed his eyes, and his expression became pained.

Oh dear, he said. Oh dear oh dear.

He stood up and carried my pictures over to the table, replaced them, and came back to the armchair. Seated, he studied me again in silence. Then he said:

This is perhaps forgivable on your part, since you're young and foolish. But I'm very surprised at Moira. I've always had the greatest respect for her.

So you should, I said. She's a very good person.

His voice hardened again.

And since that's so, how do you justify this dalliance?

The old-fashioned word half amused and half annoyed me, and I said:

It's not a dalliance, Walter. I'm in love with her. I want to marry her.

Oh good God.

He sat back in the chair, shaking his head.

You silly young bugger. You can't be serious.

I *am* serious.

I'd begun to be angry as well as defensive, and had raised my voice. He looked at me quickly.

And Moira? What does she say?

She says it can't happen. She thinks I'm too young.

I see. So she has *that* much sense left. And how far has this gone?

We love each other, I said.

Hearing myself say this, I was embarrassed to find I was flushing. Walter studied me, opening his eyes wide as though he found the phenomenon interesting. What was more likely was that he wanted me to taste my discomfiture to the full. When he spoke next, however, his voice was low, and his tone had perhaps softened.

Lovers. I see. And I also see that I should explain a few things to you. I wonder how much you know about Moira Doran? She's someone I care for a great deal. She's not just an assistant to me in my work, but in many ways a companion: a woman of intelligence and taste.

I realize that.

He held up his hand.

Yes. But I very much doubt that you realize everything. Perhaps she hasn't told you how close our friendship is – or perhaps she has. But leave that aside. Let's just say that we've been a solace to each other, and that I know what sort of suffering she's been through. What you need to understand is that there are people who take a long time to recover from grief, and that Moira is one of those people. She had a breakdown after her husband was killed, and although she recovered, her grief has never released her: that grief your painting shows in her face. She mourns inwardly, always. She's withdrawn from the world. That's why she's preferred the haven I've been able to give her. She's an attractive woman; yet she's never re-married, and I'd feel sure she's never taken a lover – until now. Why? Because of her loyalty to her husband's memory, and the guilt she'd feel if she replaced him. Moira is a Catholic, and very devout. She has a capacity for guilt that an Anglican like me can scarcely comprehend – and nor can an Anglican like *you*.

Perhaps. I know all this. But I can help her get over it.

Walter shook his head.

Somebody has to, eventually. But it won't be you, young fellow. She's refused to marry you, you say. Instead, she took you for a lover, in secret. Yes. I can understand that, even though it saddens me. She'd denied herself for so long – then this attractive and talented young man appears, here in the cocoon where she spends her days; here, where nobody needs to know – and she succumbs. Don't you see? The truth is that she's been living in this cocoon with me for years – and now she's sharing it with you. You two don't go out anywhere, I'm sure. You're not a couple, are you?

I said nothing, but my expression told him he was right.

No, he said. Of course not. But eventually, she has to break out of the cocoon. When she does, it will be with a man who's her own age or older: probably a man who's a Catholic, and certainly one who can help her provide security for her daughter.

I shook my head. No, I said. *No.* She can break out of it with me.

My tone had become strident, and Walter's expression seemed to soften still more; and yet it was an expression that held pity rather than sympathy: a pity I hated. He shook his head.

You aren't that kind of man, I'm afraid. You're an artist, and artists can't be relied on, especially young ones. They're flighty and unpredictable and self-centred. It's the nature of the beast. She'll have realized that, of course. And for heaven's sake, Hugh, consider: when you're thirty-one, she'll be forty-six. When you're forty-five, she'll be an old woman. You're standing on the verge of life, and she's not. You must leave this island soon, and discover the world; you must paint full-time. You'll do it, and you'll succeed. But not with her.

It must be with her.

Walter sighed. He got up from his chair and crossed to the window where he stood with his back to me, staring out over the orchard with its joyous, teeming spring blossoms. For a time he was silent; then he turned back to me.

With the light behind him he was no longer distinct; but his large eyes seemed to gleam, though I couldn't read their expression.

You're in the grip of the madness of Eros. Be careful, Hugh: the condition created by the winged child is something to be resisted.

His voice had taken on that tone of portentous gravity with which I was familiar, its faint tremor more pronounced. But I wasn't in the mood for Walter's classical allusions; his predictions had frozen me inwardly and threatened me with despair, and part of me feared that they might be true. For the first time, I resented him; I wanted to get away from him; and yet I had little choice but to stay and listen.

Eros can lead you down bypaths to chaos, he said. He can lure you into illusions that will enslave you; he can cost you a normal life, and bring you great grief. I know about this, Hugh: it happened to *me*, long ago.

You mean a love affair.

He looked at me without answering for a moment, and at first I thought he'd ignore or dismiss what I'd said. In all the time I'd known him, he'd never gone in for personal confidences, and I began to be curious in spite of my animosity.

I mean my marriage, he said. I lost it because I gave my love somewhere else: somewhere unsuitable. Since then I've become one of a dying breed: a monkish bachelor. But no more of that. *You're* my concern at present; you and Moira.

Suddenly he hauled himself up again, gripping the arms of the chair. He came across to where I sat at the easel and stood beside me and placed a hand on my shoulder, squeezing it quite hard.

You and Moira are the two people I care about most in the world. I love you both.

I was made uncomfortable by this, and could not look up at him.

I don't want to see either of you hurt, he said. But one of you must be, and it has to be you, I'm afraid. You're young, and can afford wrong turnings – Moira Doran can't. The next turn she makes must be the right one. She knows that, or she wouldn't have refused you.

I won't give her up. I love her.

His hand fell away, and I glanced up at him. He was contemplating me now with an expression of weary regret, and he suddenly looked very old. When he spoke, it was under his breath.

Love. Love. How we misuse that word. Perhaps only Christ ever used it correctly.

He turned and moved away a few paces; then he swung around.

The time is well overdue for you to exhibit your work.

This sudden change of topic startled me, and I stared at him.

You're ready, he said. More than ready. You've a fine body of paintings, and I think you should have an exhibition in Melbourne. They'll have a chance of attracting serious attention over there, and perhaps starting to give you a name.

And how would that be possible?

I'll arrange it.

He saw my expression, and nodded.

Yes, I believe I can do that. I know a dealer who's sold me a number of good things, and who takes me seriously. He has a small but influential gallery in South Yarra. I'll take a trip over there shortly, and show him some samples. He'll need to like them, of course. If he does, then you'll get your exhibition. There'll be some expenses – framing and so on – but I imagine you can cover those. Let me do this for you: I'm sure you'll succeed.

And the price I have to pay?

I beg your pardon?

That I give up Moira – that's it, isn't it?

I believe this might help you to get through losing her, and to set you on your true course.

I appreciate it, Walter – but the price is too high.

As soon as I'd spoken, I realized how crass this sounded; but it was too late. Walter's eyes became entirely cold, and his mouth bent down to form its cruellest line.

You're a bloody young fool. And as stubborn as your father.

He turned and went out, closing the door behind him with a click that was more final than a slam.

I don't intend to give too detailed an account of love lost. Even after so long, a faint, residual echo of pain remains, together with wisdom's verdict that the loss was both inevitable and beneficial. But what have Eros and Athena ever had in common? Walter was right about that.

The end came quickly, two weeks after my argument with Walter. I hadn't visited Leyburn Farm during that time, since I assumed that Walter would no longer welcome my visits. Nor did I say anything to Moira about his knowledge of our affair, or his advice to me to end it. I intended to, but I held off. I'm not quite sure why I did; perhaps because I unconsciously dreaded the outcome. When Moira asked me why I hadn't appeared at afternoon tea for two Sundays in succession, I simply made some excuse about having extra work to do at the *Mail.* And if Walter had spoken to her about his discovery of our secret, she didn't tell me.

Part of me knew that Walter was right: the difference in our ages was too great, and I was in no way ready for marriage; what I was ready for was the life of youth and freedom. Part of me knew too that Moira would never relent; would never marry me. Only derangement made me stubbornly dismiss this, and prevented me from seeing how foolish the idea was. Instead, I told myself that her refusal was no more final than that erotic ritual of resistance that often preceded our lovemaking. Eventually she'd accept me, and the world would accept us both.

I was addicted to her body, of course. Ready to receive me every week in the sweet-smelling bedroom in her cottage in Montrose, she had reached that ripe perfection which in some women in their mid-thirties far surpasses the beauty of first youth. There was a fierce yearning in our lovemaking, as though we strove for some sublime goal that could never be reached; but I dimly realized that this addiction might pass. What I believed had enthralled me permanently was her spirit: a spirit I found constantly subtle and surprising. We would talk for hours, often about books and paintings, sometimes about trivia I've forgotten: talk that was rather rarefied, I suppose, since we had no acquaintances in common except Walter, and no shared past except for that brief passage in my childhood when Moira was already a young woman. She would talk a little about her own childhood, and the time when she was a student; but she never spoke of her marriage, and I knew better than to ask.

I showed her nearly every painting I did, and the way she responded to my work was what did most to deepen my feeling for her. She seemed to see what was behind the images I produced, and to be able to express it in words. Some of our words come back.

Your pictures are very real – and yet they're like dreams. Are they dreams you've actually had?

Yes, but they're waking dreams.

The strange thing is, some of them seem like dreams I've had myself.

You have. We dream the same dreams.

Her eyes filled with tears at this, I remember. She looked at me as though something had come to her mind that she couldn't voice; and she stayed silent.

Walter was right again, of course: all artists are egotists, and this was the type of empathy that no artist could fail to delight in – especially at the age I was then. It had come to a point where I couldn't imagine my life without her. Very soon though, I'd have to do so.

She gave me no warning. Perhaps she wanted to reduce the pain of severance by making the process brief.

It was a Saturday late in October. I'd made my usual visit; she'd given me dinner, which we'd eaten with Catherine, sitting at the dining-room table like a family. She told me over dinner that she was going away with Catherine on a fortnight's holiday, leaving in the morning; they'd go to a guesthouse on the east coast. Later, in bed, nothing seemed different, except that she clung to me with a lingering persistence that felt like sadness.

Because of Catherine, I never slept at the house overnight. Somewhere around eleven, I dressed to drive home as usual, and Moira came with me to the front gate. Usually she said goodbye to me at the door, but it was a mild spring night. She closed the low gate after me and stood behind it, unusually erect, her face very white in the dark. Then, without preamble, she told me that she wouldn't be seeing me again.

Most of the exchange that followed is lost to memory. Perhaps I want it to be. I know I spoke to her with a desperate urgency, convinced that I could will her to change her mind: that hopeless belief with which so many delude themselves, as love's final lights dwindle off into the darkness. I recall that I questioned her wildly, always revolving around the same question: why?

Because it has to end – for all the reasons we've talked about so often. I still love you, but I have to be sensible. I'm doing this for both of us. Please, Hugh – let's end it quickly.

It's Walter, isn't it? He's been talking to you.

Yes – but this isn't his doing. It's my decision. You won't see me at Walter's any more either – I'm going to look for other work, and make a clean break. This is what I want, Hugh. I have to be fair to us both – and to Catherine. You've got a whole wonderful life in front of you. You'll soon realize this is right.

Never.

I'm going in now, darling. God bless you and keep you.

She turned away and walked quickly up the path, while I watched her. Halfway to the porch she stumbled, and I thought she'd turn back. But she went on up the steps and onto the porch and was gone.

I headed towards the innocent shape of my father's car. I felt half paralysed, and found walking difficult. The darkness looked denser to me, and I seemed to be walking in my sleep. The blow that had fallen on me was both inevitable and necessary, of course; but I didn't believe that then. Like many another young man, I was sure that my pain was unique.

Two days later, a letter from Walter Dixon arrived for me at my parents' home. I've kept it all these years; its pages lie in front of me now. Executed with a fountain pen in sky-blue ink, its elegant, old-fashioned calligraphy and stiff, high-quality writing paper make it an artefact from another time.

> *Dear Hugh,*
>
> *Have you conceived the notion that I don't wish to see you again? Or that you're not still welcome to work in your studio here at Leyburn? Your absence after our last discussion – and following what I know has taken place between you and Moira – make me suspect so. I'm therefore writing to assure you that such a notion would be nonsense. This remains your second home.*
>
> *The disagreement we had was distressing to me. It was never my intention that it should cause any final rift in our friendship. I hope you'll agree that a friendship is what it is, and one which has been given extra depth by our tie of blood. Being deprived of watching the future development of*

your work, and of offering what help I can, would be deeply painful to me.

As to Moira Doran: you probably imagine that I urged her to end the affair between you, and blame me for it. I assure you I did not. We discussed the matter, as she and I discuss most things, but I did not press her to a decision. In fact, when she came to me, she'd already made her decision – and told me at the same time that she'd no longer work for me as my secretary. Certainly I don't blame you for that, though I'll miss her badly. She's decided that it was time to make a new life – and of course she's right. We must both do without Moira now, and I'll value your company more than ever.

Yours sincerely,

Your fond uncle Walter

This letter had an ambiguous effect on me. The sincerity of its feeling was something I didn't doubt; but I was too bitter to be sympathetic to it. For some days I postponed sending a reply – and during that time I continued to suspect that Walter had in some way influenced Moira in her decision. But then, as I replayed in my mind her responses to my pleas for commitment, I could no longer fail to see that the decision had been her own, and had waited at the heart of our relationship from the beginning, like a cancer. She'd given me enough hints, after all, and even open warnings.

Once I'd admitted this to myself, I replied to Walter. I haven't a clear memory of my note, which was brief, and no doubt rather cold and pompous. I told him that I bore him no ill will, and would call on him soon. But I gave no indication of when that would be, since I didn't know when I'd be able to face going out there again.

Over the week that followed, I continued to be held by the inward paralysis that had gripped me at Moira's front gate. I was dealing with that particular grief which has the same intensity as first love: grief which is the penalty we pay when first love is lost. I moved about automatically; I went to the *Mail* and did my work as well as I could, and I spoke to no-one about what had happened, since no-one except Bob Wall had known of the affair – and even he knew very little. I was like an invalid who believes that his illness isn't curable – a condition I probably indulged deliberately, with the tender self-pity we're prone to at that age – and I found it difficult to respond when people spoke to me. But in my moments of honest clarity (which were few), I recognized that another feeling altogether lay below my surface emotion, like water underground.

That feeling was relief. In the moments when I recognized this, I was appalled, and detested myself; but its reality couldn't be denied. For some time, I'd entertained certain longings: longings that were incompatible with my dream of marriage to Moira: a marriage which would have had to mean stability, and being tied to a particular place – if only because of Catherine, for whom I'd have become partly responsible. These longings were for a life that I could only pursue alone. I saw waiting for me the big cities on the mainland, and cities far beyond that, in the other, ancestral hemisphere: in Europe, where I'd paint, and study the works of the masters, and plunge into experiences of a kind I knew only from works of fiction. Reveries of youth, in other words: reveries that had nothing to do with marriage to a mature and serious woman.

The longings had troubled me, when Moira and I were together. I'd wrestled with them, but had found no answer to my conflict. Now, at one stroke, the answer had been provided: I was free, through no action of my own, and need feel no guilt. But I must pay for it with grief.

At the end of that week, on a Saturday night, Bob Wall and I went on a pub crawl, starting at the Duke of Norfolk and going on to other pubs around town. He'd just bought a big three-year-old Studebaker which he was paying off in instalments, and had promised to drive me home. It was my aim to get drunk, and Bob knew why. We confided in each other about most things, but until now I'd told him only the bare essentials about Moira Doran: that she was fifteen years older than me; that I loved her; that she wouldn't agree to marry. I hadn't wanted to say more than that, and he'd sensed it and had asked me no questions; he had a natural tact in such things. Now, without elaborating, I told him it was over, and he looked at me quickly and touched me once on the shoulder.

She was too old for you, mate, and she knew it. I guess it's not easy for you, but it's better to move on.

We spoke no more about it; but a little later, when we were both half drunk, he said suddenly:

It's probably a bad time to tell you this, Fritz, but I've just got engaged. My girlfriend's agreed to marry me.

I looked at him in disbelief. He'd mentioned once that he had a girlfriend, but had not even told me her name.

Jesus. You said *I* was too young to get married. So what about you?

I'm different, mate. I'm ready to settle down – you're not. You want to go abroad, don't you? Besides, I don't want to lose her. She's –

He stopped and looked at me sternly from under his brows, glass of beer suspended, his eyelids drooping from the drink.

She's the right one, he said. I'd never want anyone else. I met her one day in Moonah, and we remembered each other. You might remember her too: she was at school with us when we were kids. Her name's June Leaman.

I remember her.

I'd like you to meet her. Come out to my place tomorrow afternoon. She'll be there.

I recall that October as one of fine spring weather: the sort of season that can never be counted on in the island, since the

Roaring Forties can often deliver wind and rain until Christmas. The blossoms on the fruit trees and hawthorn sparkled like snow in the thin bright sun; shrubs in suburban gardens were budding or putting out infant leaves, and the dry grass on the hills had turned green from the winter rains.

That was how the world looked when I took the tram out to Moonah to visit Bob Wall, on Sunday afternoon. My grief had receded today: sitting in the rocking tram, enfolded by a dreamlike calm, I was carried through the soundless explosions of spring like a convalescent. Out the tram window, houses and gardens and traffic all appeared unreal, as though passing on a screen, and I thought about Bob Wall and June Leaman. That they'd met wasn't very surprising to me. Ours was a small town, and most people then stayed in their home districts, spending their whole lives there; so when Bob came back to Moonah, he and June Leaman had been likely to encounter each other eventually. But now, just when love was lost to me, Bob had fallen in love with this girl I'd loved as a child, whom I'd carried in my memory, whom I'd pictured in her adulthood as Flora; and this gave me mixed feelings. Above the whining of the tram, I could hear her clear child's voice reciting 'Meg Merrilies', and exquisite pangs ran through me. What were these pangs? Envy? No, I said, of course not. The two children I'd loved in a remote time had fallen in love with each other: how could I resent that, or envy Bob? He deserved June, I said, and my feeling was simply one of wistfulness.

As I came up the driveway of Fred Tyson's place, I could see two figures sitting in the sun on a bench in front of Bob's garden house: Bob, and a slim young woman with pale blonde hair, in a short-sleeved floral dress with the big spreading skirt that was currently in fashion, its pink and green pattern matching the colours of the spring. Fred, whom I'd met a few times, was standing there talking to them, and Bob's big bullet-nosed Studebaker was parked nearby. When Bob caught sight of me he stood up and waved, Fred turned to look at me and grinned, and the young woman sat still, her hands folded in her lap. As I came nearer, I looked for some resemblance to little June Leaman. I couldn't see any, unless it was the wavy, light blonde hair. She looked very young and fresh – not much more than a girl, though she must have been twenty or twenty-one.

June, this is Hugh Dixon, Bob said. You remember him?

Of course I remember you, June said to me. You've grown up a lot though, Hugh.

She smiled, looking up at me. It was the open, happy smile I remembered – the child's, still intact – and now she became June Leaman, who'd grown into a pretty young woman: somewhat Danish-looking, but otherwise no different from other pretty young women: quite unremarkable, in fact, and hardly Botticelli's Flora. Yet memory hadn't entirely misled me: her narrow, light blue eyes were Flora's – though unlike Flora's, their expression wasn't enigmatic. Instead, they shone with delight at the world, just as the child's had done. And the sight of her suddenly brought back all that had been special to me at eleven years old: the sunny flatland by the river with its little weatherboard shops and bungalows; the sun-warmed fadedness of things; the whitened grass that smelled like warm bread, and the train's lone cry as it rattled north.

Come and sit down, mate, Bob said to me. He waved at a garden chair near the bench, and then turned to Fred Tyson.

Tell Hugh what you just told us, Fred. About your escape from death.

Standing, Fred looked down at me with an expression of sly amusement. He was a lean, balding man in his early sixties, clad in clean khaki overalls, slightly stooped, with small, friendly eyes and large carpenter's hands that seemed to belong to someone bigger.

I was up on top of a long ladder, see. Yesterday, on a buildin site in South Hobart. All of a sudden, she began to tip backwards. I was losin her.

Bob and June began to laugh, and Bob said:

But you kept your presence of mind, Fred. You didn't jump ship.

No, I stayed with her. It's the only thing to do. *I rode her down.*

He said this with satisfied emphasis, and Bob started laughing. He slapped his knee, his face growing pink, his hair falling across his forehead.

You rode her down, he said, and glanced at me with an expression of glee. You hear that, Fritz? He stayed with her all the way.

Fred grinned with satisfaction, looking around at us all, and repeated his incantation.

Yes, I *rode her down* – and hopped off a second before she hit. It's the only thing to do. Jump off higher up, and you could end with a broken back.

You're not wrong, Fred, Bob said. I'll remember that, if I go back to the old trade.

I don't reckon you'll do that, Bob. You're an *artist* now, like Hugh here. But if you ever want to come back, I'll always find you a place.

He looked at me.

Bob's a real good carpenter, he said. He could get a job anywhere. Takes a pride in his craft.

I wouldn't doubt it, I said.

I saw that Fred was fond of Bob, and it pleased me: his kindliness and contentment were soothing, dispelling life's pain and complications. And June Leaman, though I scarcely knew her yet, any more than I'd done as a child, seemed to me already to have the same kind of contentment; the same unquestioning certainty that life would be generous. Everything assured me of this, as we sat in the sun in Fred's garden, and I suddenly found myself happy. Nothing was painful or complicated; grief was a receding darkness.

After Fred went on up to his house, Bob and June and I talked. Our conversation was easy, with placid pauses, and the scene that stretched in front of us remains vivid, even after so long, together with its scents and small noises. On the other side of the drive, a garden bed where Fred's roses and daisies had come out. On the lawn, a cherry tree spreading its arms, flaring with pink blossom. Beyond and below the garden, the roofs and streets of Moonah, small with distance. Little white smokes going up, almost static in the stillness. A clean smell in the air like wood shavings. The distance filled with small whirring sounds, the way it was when Bob and I walked to school, in that time when I believed in the presence of a magical, unknown race.

As we talked, the elfin June Leaman of childhood faded away, and I began to be acquainted with the ordinary young woman she'd become. Her father ran an electrical business in Glenorchy. She had a younger brother. She'd gone to the Commercial High School and had learned typing and shorthand; now she worked as a secretary in an insurance company in the city. Yet despite the manner in which she shared these prosaic details, and despite her easy friendliness, I sensed that in some indefinable way, June was one of those people who could never fully be known. She was both open and elusive; and in this she resembled Bob. They were meant to be together, I saw: they even resembled each other, and belonged to a special breed of people who were suited to no other kind; who would only tantalize others, and perhaps make them unhappy.

You used to recite poetry very well, I said to June. Do you remember?

She laughed and ducked her head and looked up again.

My parents sent me for elocution lessons. They were keen about that sort of thing.

You had good parents, Bob said. Your father and mother wanted the best for you.

She took his hand and held it. But your father didn't, she said softly.

She turned back to me.

Dad remembered that Bob ran away on that bike as a little kid – and he knew he'd been in Hillcrest. So he and Mum didn't want us to get serious, at first. But now they know that Bob had to run away. I got them to see that.

As she spoke, Bob had been staring into the distance. Now he looked back at June, still with his hand linked to hers. Instead of the guarded look that had always been in his face, I saw a kind of trust that was new.

I wanted that bloody bike so that I could get away as far as possible, he said. Also because I'd never had one. But I told your father I've never stolen anything since, and never will again.

I asked them when they planned to marry.

Bob laughed. Not so fast, Fritz. We've got to save a bit of money. We want to buy a house. And I'd like to know first that I've got that job on the *Mail.*

It's yours when I go. You just have to wait a bit.

June leaned forward.

You're a really good friend, Hugh. I know Bob appreciates it.

Bob winked at me. You see how it is? She's already speaking for me. But it's true what she says, Fritz.

We grew silent, and watched the afternoon light thicken and turn wheat-coloured over the roofs and the river and the hills; over the district that contained the mysteries of childhood, and that hidden joy at the heart of things that Bob and I had run after as boys, holding out our hands.

I'd decided to seal my reconciliation with Walter Dixon by presenting him with a painting: one that I hoped would have a special appeal for him. Entitled 'The Outlaw's Vision', it was a portrait of Lucas Wilson. In the last couple of decades, thanks to its purchase by a state gallery and its inclusion in a number of books on Australian painting, it's become quite well-known.

Walter knew I'd been working on it, since I'd borrowed the photograph of Wilson some time ago with the painting in mind;

but I'd taken some time to complete it. In order to create its background I'd driven up to Collinsvale, a small village in that valley in the mountains which I judged to be the site of Wilson's Utopia: the place he'd called Nowhere Valley. The region had finally been settled and farmed in the 1870s by German and Danish immigrants; but most of it was still virgin forest. I made a series of sketches of the hills and valleys, and of the mountains called Collins Bonnet and Collins Cap; and from these I created a landscape extending around the figure of Wilson. He stood poised with his rifle on a rocky hillslope, looking with fanatic concentration towards the mirage-like peaks, as though his dream had become manifest there.

I didn't phone Walter to warn him of my coming; instead, on a Sunday near the end of the month, I arrived at the front door on the assumption that he'd be at home as usual. An echo of sorrow went through me as I rang the doorbell, knowing that Moira would no longer answer it. I expected Walter to appear, but instead a strange woman in an apron confronted me: plump, with grey hair in a bun and a round, impassive face. I told her who I was, and she looked doubtful.

He's out in the orchard, she said. Do you know the way?

I said I did, and went around to the northern side of the house and through a small gate in the aged post-and-rail fence that surrounded the orchard. I walked along one of the rows between the apple trees, carrying my rolled-up painting in a cloth; it was the largest I'd ever done, and too big for my portfolio. I hoped that Walter would like it as much as he'd done my portrait of him, which now hung in the dining-room beside his Russell Drysdale drawing.

The trees were out in leaf but not yet bearing, and there were fresh damp smells from their leaves and from the earth. It had rained this morning, but the afternoon was fine, and everything was drying out. Walter appeared unexpectedly, coming out of another row up ahead of me. He was more casually dressed than usual, in a battered felt hat, a belted brown corduroy jacket and work boots. Seeing me, he started visibly and halted, waiting for me to come up to him. He didn't smile.

So. You're finally here, he said.

Yes. I hope your offer still stands. I'd like to use the studio again, if I may.

Of course you may Hugh, you know that. You've been neglecting your work, I imagine.

Not really. I've brought this to show you.

I held up the cloth-covered painting.

It looks very large. We'll have to take it up to the house, and you can show me there. Come along, then.

We walked side by side along the row, towards the little gate.

You've met Mrs Anderson?

Yes. Who is she?

I decided I needed a housekeeper. She comes most days and looks after the house and cooks my evening meals. She'll give us some afternoon tea. She's a reliable woman. Divorced and lives alone somewhere in Glenorchy.

He trudged, head down, not looking at me, and Moira's name hung unspoken in the air. It was possible he was embarrassed, as far as he could ever be embarrassed.

The trees are looking healthy, I said.

Yes. Old Dave always does a fine job of pruning. We should have a good crop of apples this year. When that happens, it's like a wonderful gift. I never tire of this orchard. Some of these trees are a hundred years old: they were here in my grandfather's day. They were here when Liam Dalton first called. I met Dalton once, you know – here in the orchard.

I looked at him in disbelief.

You met him? Surely you're not old enough, Walter.

Come now: that time isn't as long ago as you think. Dalton lived to a good old age, after he served his reduced sentence. He married, and ran his little orchard at Berriedale – and he was always grateful to my father for testifying on his behalf. They stayed friends, and he used to visit here now and then, until he died. I remember just one of those visits. I was about six years of age.

He rubbed his chin, looking above the trees.

Let me see. I was born in 1880 – so this meeting would have been around 1886. Dalton would then have been about sixty-four. I was playing here in the orchard on my own, and I saw a big man in a broad-brimmed hat coming towards me through the trees. He looked somehow dangerous, and I was rather frightened at first. He stopped, and said: 'You must be young Walter.' I said I was, and he spoke to me for a time. I've forgotten what he said, except for one thing: as he went, he said: 'You be a straight shooter, Walter – like your father.' Well, I've tried to be so, in the way I practise Law.

He was silent for a moment, looking down at his feet as he walked.

His face doesn't come back very clearly, he said. But I remember he had a twinkle in his eye. My father told me he always had that twinkle – even in the midst of trouble. Sometimes I almost expect to see him coming through the orchard again. I'm glad that I met him – but how I wish it had been Lucas Wilson. I might have glimpsed the mystery of his soul: children have that power.

His gaze had become distant, and he seemed to talk to himself, rather than me. We went on to the verandah, and he led me through one of the French doors into the dining-room, where he asked me to wait while he washed, and changed his boots. While he was gone, I spread the painting out on the table and weighed the paper down at each end with some books I found on the sideboard. When Walter returned, I gestured at the picture and stood back.

It's for you, Walter. A present.

He looked at me quickly – a serious, questioning look. Then he moved close to the table, putting on his glasses and bending over the painting. His eyes widened.

Wilson, he said softly. So. And this is a present?

Yes – if you like it.

Like it? It's the best thing you've ever done.

Suddenly he held out his hand. In some bewilderment, I took it, and he smiled at me with great warmth, squeezing my hand with surprising strength.

It's a wonderful peace offering, dear boy. Thank you – and let us be friends again.

He turned back to the picture, animated as a young man, his movements quick and excited.

You've captured his soul; his obsession. And this is the land of his obsession: real, and yet beyond the normal. I told you once that you must aim for the divine, and now you have. When I look at these hills, I recall Goethe's words: that Nature is the visible garment of God.

You're very kind, Walter.

His tone sharpened at this, in the way that it did when something I'd said didn't satisfy him.

Kind? Don't be silly, Hugh. I never speak to you out of some sort of soapy sentiment, and I'm not being kind. Let me just say that you must never aim lower than you've aimed here. And now let's talk about your Melbourne exhibition. This picture will be its centrepiece.

I went to bed that night in a state of some hope and contentment, and had a vivid dream. I was in the orchard again, and Walter Dixon was coming towards me, in his old felt hat. But when he reached me, it was no longer Walter who looked at me from under the hat, but a younger man, a stranger, with high, knob-like cheekbones, tanned skin and unnaturally pale eyes. He smiled, and slowly raised his hand.

I'd met him before; I was unsure where. I knew that he had some sort of claim on me, and tried to remember what it was; but I found I couldn't. I was gripped by a mixture of alarm and elation, as though a different life was about to receive me: a life not my own. But I woke before this could happen.

5

Bob was washing his car when the two detectives came for him. This was on a Tuesday in the first week of November, close to midday.

He'd worked on his own in Max Fell's studio the evening before, he told me, instead of working there during the day, and he intended to go in again that Tuesday at seven o'clock. Max had asked him to work these hours because of a special photographic session he'd arranged on the Monday with a model who would pose for him only in the daytime: one who was so sensitive that she wanted no-one else present in the studio. Fell hadn't said who the model was, but Bob suspected that it had been Madge Gregson.

The Studebaker was parked as usual in front of Bob's shack, and he was using a hose on it that was attached to a garden tap. When he saw the two men coming up the drive he took little notice of them and went on hosing, since he assumed they were going to see Fred Tyson. But they stopped in front of him, staring at him with an intentness that began to annoy him. He put the hose down in the grass beside the drive, straightened, and stared back. Both were big men; both wore felt hats and three-piece suits and had well-shined shoes, and he thought they might be salesmen of some kind. One was middle-aged and heavily built, with a florid face; the other was young and bony-faced, with prominent ears that appeared to be supporting his hat. The middle-aged man spoke first.

Are you Robert Wall?

Who wants to know?

The man frowned and took a step closer, pulling a badge from his pocket and briefly holding it up.

I want to know. I'm Detective Sergeant Parsons, and this is Detective Constable Webster. Now I'll ask you again: are you Robert Wall?

Yes. Why?

You'll find out why soon enough, the younger detective said.

Parsons looked at him, and then turned to Bob again.

We'd like you to come in to the CIB in Liverpool Street for a chat. Our car's out on the road. There are some questions we'd like to ask you.

What's this about?

We'll tell you when we get in there. Now are you going to co-operate, Mr Wall, or do we have to cuff you?

Bob looked around him. The day had suddenly become unreal to him, he told me, and the roofs of Moonah below seemed to belong in another country. The hose was still running in the grass, and he began to walk over to the tap. The two men followed him, one on each side, and watched him turn off the water.

I'll need to change my clothes, Bob said.

Make it quick, Parsons said.

The room they took him to in Police Headquarters in the city had no outlook, since the single tall window was of frosted glass. It reminded Bob of similar rooms in the Boys' Home, he said: brown linoleum, and walls painted the dingy institutional yellow that dispelled all hope. An electric bulb hung from the ceiling under a white china shade in the shape of a coolie hat: ubiquitous light-shade of poverty, and the cheap rented rooms he'd known in his roaming days. The only furniture here was a long wooden table and three upright chairs, all varnished the muddy, yellow-brown colour he also remembered from Hillcrest. It was a room that seemed to wait to reclaim him, and he began to feel now that he was in serious trouble, without any notion of what the trouble might be.

The table was entirely bare except for a large typewriter and a stack of paper at one end, a telephone and a directory set close by, and two glass ashtrays. Detective Constable Webster sat down immediately and began to feed paper into the typewriter, having dropped his hat in the middle of the table. His ears became even more prominent without the hat, since his hair was shaven at the sides. Detective Sergeant Parsons placed his own hat next to the younger man's, and the two hats sat in the empty expanse like objects intended for the opening move in some obscure game. Parsons remained standing, looking at Bob. He gestured towards a chair at the other end of the table.

Sit down.

Bob obeyed, saying nothing. Neither of the detectives had spoken on the ride in, and he'd decided to wait for one of them to make the first move. He'd expected Parsons to sit down on the third chair, halfway down the table, but instead the detective came and stood over him, looking down on him. In order to look back, Bob had to tilt his head. He didn't like the look of Parsons. His ill-tempered face was a drinker's, with muddy hazel eyes whose whites were yellowish, and a net of broken veins in the nose. He had a powerful build but was running to fat, with a heavy jowl.

Let me explain something, Bob, Parsons said. Can I call you Bob? Right. I'm going to ask you some questions, and Detective Constable Webster is going to type them out, together with your replies. We call this a Record of Interview. Do you understand that?

Yes. But I'd like to know why I'm here.

Parsons looked up the table at Webster and raised his eyebrows.

He wants to know why he's here, he said. They both laughed under their breath, and Parsons turned back to Bob.

We want to ask you about the murder of Mrs Madge Gregson, he said. Her body was found at eight o'clock this morning. She was dumped at the edge of the Rivulet, at the back of the building where you work. What can you tell us about that?

She's dead? How did she die?

She was choked to death. But we think you already know that, Bob.

For some moments Bob found it difficult to speak. When he did, his own voice sounded strangled and distant to him.

Why would you think that? I don't know anything about it.

Parsons looked up the table at Webster again.

I'm now commencing to question Mr Wall for the Record. I'll begin by answering his question to me.

He bent low over Bob, one hand holding the back of the chair.

We think it because your own employer, Mr Max Fell, accuses you of murdering her.

He what?

He says that you did it. What do you say to that, Bob?

I say he's a bloody liar. It's likely that he did it himself.

Webster was now hammering hard on the big typewriter, the sound of its carriage loud and grating as he slammed it across for each new line. Parsons straightened up and waited for him to finish.

Mr Wall denies the charge that his employer Mr Fell makes against him. He denies raping and killing Mrs Gregson. He accuses Mr Fell of being guilty. Have you got that?

Got it.

Parsons walked some paces away and then turned back, facing Bob.

You're an *artist*, is that right?

Webster sniggered. His bulging blue eyes looked elated, as though at the commencement of a pleasing entertainment.

Yes. I'm a commercial artist, Bob said.

And you work as an assistant to Max Fell.

Yes.

Do you deny knowing Mrs Madge Gregson, who's done modelling work at the studio?

I met her there once a couple of months ago.

And you haven't seen her since?

No.

The typewriter was hammering again, and Parsons waited and then went on.

Let me explain the situation to you, Bob. We were called to 216 Liverpool Street at eight o'clock this morning, to find Madge Gregson's body lying on the edge of the Rivulet. She'd been stripped naked and strangled. A preliminary report from the pathologist tells us that she was almost certainly raped. We've interviewed her husband, who told us she'd been missing since early yesterday afternoon. She leaves two young children.

Jesus.

Parsons stared at him in silence, his mouth slightly open. He shook his head, and his look was one of amazement; or perhaps a simulation of amazement. Suddenly he began to shout, his hoarse voice echoing off the walls.

Is that all you've got to say, you bloody animal? This is what *you* did to her. Right?

No. No.

Parsons walked back to Bob's chair and leaned over him again.

Where were you yesterday evening from six o'clock onwards?

I worked in the studio from about seven. Before that I was at home.

And Madge Gregson was with you in the studio – *posing* for you, half-naked. You got carried away and raped her – then, so she couldn't accuse you, you throttled her, using your bare hands. I see you've got big hands, just right for the job. Isn't that so?

No. She wasn't with me. She was posing for Max during the day.

How do you know that?

He told me he was working with a model on his own. I believe it was Madge.

You believe.

Yes. He didn't tell me her name, but I know Madge could only pose during the day.

You're making this up as you go, sonny. I know Max Fell – I've known him for years, and I believe him to be an honest man. He says that you were working with Mrs Gregson yesterday evening, that he didn't see her yesterday at all, and that he was out with friends all that evening – friends who'll confirm that. You understand?

The typewriter hammered on, its little bell ringing at intervals with a festive sound. Parsons leaned down and brought his face close to Bob's, his open mouth stretched in a grin. He had ill-made false teeth, and Bob smelled whisky and smoke on his breath.

And guess what, you rapist bastard? It was Max Fell who reported the discovery of the body to us this morning. Now why would he do that, if he was the one who did it?

Bob said nothing. He was struggling against a swimming in his head.

Parsons sighed and straightened up and pulled out a packet of cigarettes. He lit one and inhaled, throwing back his head as he released the smoke. He waited until Webster had finished typing.

The suspect makes no reply, he said, and embarked on a long, wheezing cough.

There's nothing he can say, Webster said. The bastard's guilty.

He stood up and came down the table to stand beside Parsons, and they both stood looking down at Bob.

You should admit it now, squire, and save yourself a lot of trouble, Webster said. The case against you is open and shut, so don't waste our time. I'll type your admission into the record, you'll sign it, and then we'll be done.

I'll admit no such bloody thing. I want a lawyer.

Webster smiled at Parsons.

He wants a lawyer, he said. He's a smart bugger.

Parsons put his cigarette down carefully in one of the ashtrays. Hold his arms, he said, and walked away down the table.

Webster came around the back of Bob's chair and pinned both his arms from behind. Bob struggled, but couldn't get free. Parsons walked back carrying the phone book, which he placed against the side of Bob's head. His muddy eyes looked sorrowful.

Let's get this over with, he said. Will you sign?

No.

Parsons punched him with full force through the phone book, and Bob's head jerked sideways. He found that the room was spinning, and the air was filled with little sparks.

Now then, Parsons said. Sign.

Bob shook his head.

Tell your mate to let me loose, he said. Try fighting fair, you fat bastard. I'll knock the shit out of you.

He didn't see the next punch coming. Something seemed to explode in his head, and the room went half dark. After that, he told me, things became vague. He was pulled out of the chair and held upright, and punched through the phone book about the head and body. Finally he was dragged to the end of the table where the typewriter was. Webster pulled out the sheet that was in it, spread it in front of him and held out a ballpoint pen.

Sign there. Sign it.

Bob shook his head again.

Get fucked, he said.

After that they beat him some more through the phone book, but he still refused to sign. He was unable to focus very well at that stage, and didn't look at them. Eventually, after cursing him once more, they walked out the door and slammed it.

He sat down in the chair again, trying to bring things back into focus, and after some minutes two uniformed constables came in. Bob asked them whether he was free to go, but one of them shook his head.

You're off to a remand cell in Campbell Street, sport. Let's get you going.

He hauled Bob to his feet, pulled his hands behind his back, and locked a pair of handcuffs on his wrists.

If I hadn't been working on a newspaper, it might have been quite some time before I found out what had happened to Bob. As it was, I learned about it on the day he was arrested, in the middle of the afternoon. The news was brought to Gordon Carter by one of the senior reporters: a lanky red-haired man called Pat Dwyer, who did the police rounds.

The door of our little office stood open, and Dwyer paused there to pass on a racing tip to Gordon. Like Gordon he was a keen punter, and their racing talk went on for some time, while I got on with retouching an early batch of overseas news photographs. Then I became aware that Dwyer was discussing a murder, and turned on my stool to listen. His voice had dropped, and had become unusually sober. He'd just come from the CIB office, he said, and what they'd passed on to him would make a front page story.

A young woman, he said. Strangled. Dumped by the Rivulet up Liverpool Street, probably during the night. Naked. They think she was raped, as well.

Nasty, said Gordon. Have they made an arrest?

They have, as a matter of fact. A suspect is 'helping them with their enquiries' – you know the drill. Quite a young bloke: name of Bob Wall. That's all they'd tell me, at this stage. I must press on, mate, and get it typed up.

When he'd disappeared from the doorway, I got up from my stool and stood fixed, the brush I'd been using still between my fingers. Gordon swivelled his chair around and stared at me.

Something the matter, son? You look a bit off colour.

I told him that Bob Wall was a friend of mine, and that he couldn't possibly be guilty. The words came out in a rush, as Gordon continued to stare at me. I said that Bob would need a lawyer, and that I wanted to contact an uncle of mine who might represent him. Then I asked for an hour or so off.

Gordon studied me, drawing on his cigarette. I thought he might refuse; but when he answered, his tone was considerate.

Okay – off you go then, if it's that important to you. Let's hope they've got the wrong bloke.

The firm of Dixon and Dixon was in Murray Street, five minutes' walk from the *Mail*, occupying a two-storey Edwardian building of red brick and sandstone. Its big arched windows were framed by stone architraves, and a green wrought iron fence ran along the pavement in front. Walter and my late grandfather Charles had begun leasing the property when they first set up practice in the early years of the century, and Walter and my uncle George now owned it. It was a fashionable address: directly opposite the neo-classical Public Buildings that were the city's official hub, and just around the corner from the Supreme Court.

I'd never visited Walter at his office, and nor had he ever suggested I come there. Now, as I hurried up Macquarie Street, numb with fear for Bob, I tried to summon up what I'd say to persuade Walter to represent him. Walter spent more time at the firm now that Moira Doran was no longer his home-based secretary, and I hoped against hope that he'd be there today. To find out, I stopped at a public phone in the GPO and spoke to the firm's receptionist, who said that Walter was in. I told her who I was, and that I was calling to see him in a few minutes.

She said that he might not have time for me immediately. I told her to tell him the matter was urgent, and hung up.

Walter stood up when a male clerk showed me into his office, and gestured at one of a pair of green-upholstered bridge chairs set in front of his large mahogany desk. It was a hard chair, no doubt intended to discourage his clients from lounging. Walter sat down at his desk again and smiled at me; but his gaze was questioning, as though I were a client. Here in his place of business, he looked different from the Walter Dixon I'd known until now. It wasn't just his well-tailored pinstripe suit and starched white collar and dark tie; it was something more subtle than that. His place of work transformed him, giving an extra keenness to his glance: a sharpness that I found almost intimidating.

So: a surprise visit, he said. You told Miss Harding it was urgent. It must be, for you to beard me in my den.

Yes, it's very urgent. I hope you don't mind, Walter.

Not at all. In fact, I should have invited you to call here long ago, and taken you for lunch at the Club. Now tell me, what's this about? Nothing too bad, I hope?

I said it was very bad, and recited what the police roundsman had just let drop about Bob Wall's arrest. I told Walter how I'd got Bob his job as an artist with Max Fell, and that I guessed that the murdered woman had been found somewhere in the vicinity of Fell's studio. This was a crime Bob couldn't possibly have committed, I said. I reminded Walter of my painting of Dickenson's Arcade, with the small boy standing in front of it: that was Bob, I told him. Bob and I had been friends since childhood, and I knew his character: there was no way he could have committed a murder.

My own voice in my ears had begun to sound strained and vehement, and it was causing Walter to look at me with a dubious expression. He was leaning back now in his antique-looking swivel chair, his hands locked under his chin, his joined index fingers raised to touch his lips.

You're fond of this young fellow, he said.

He's my best friend.

And you want me to represent him.

Yes I do. I'd be very grateful.

A phone on Walter's desk rang, and he picked it up and listened.

Tell them I've been unexpectedly delayed, he said. They can either wait or make another appointment.

He listened again, and I could hear the voice at the other end speaking rapidly. To distract myself from my anxiety, I glanced about the room: this chamber where Walter led his other life. Everything had a look of sober, slightly shabby Edwardian solidity, and seemed to be pickled in time: the worn Persian carpet; the tall mahogany bookshelves filled with leather-bound English and Commonwealth Law Reports; an aged Genoa velvet armchair in a corner. One of the arched windows looked out on to the broad expanse of Murray Street, framing the stone Public Buildings and a plane tree putting out pale green leaves.

Very well, Walter said into the phone. That will be satisfactory.

He put the receiver down and looked at me.

I can see you feel very strongly about this, he said. I'd like to help, Hugh, but I need to know more. First of all, can your friend afford my fees? I'm rather expensive, in a case like this.

I'm sure he'll have a bit saved, I said. I have too, and I'll put in what I can.

That's all very well – but you probably have no idea what sort of costs will be involved in a murder trial. However, let's leave that aside for the moment. You say the young man's being held by the police for questioning. In other words, he's on remand, prior to being charged. By now they'll have him in the Hobart Gaol in Campbell Street.

I was filled with horror, and exclaimed. Walter held up his hand and went on, and his tone disheartened me: it was measured and pitiless, and I began to think he wouldn't even consider representing Bob.

He'll next appear in the Magistrates' Court. When he does, he'll be told that he's charged with the murder, and asked how he pleads. At that point, he'll need a lawyer to represent him who'll ensure that he doesn't plead, and that the matter is adjourned and ultimately tried in the Criminal Court. He'll then be returned to the gaol.

But Walter, he can't stay in the bloody gaol. Can't he be bailed out?

Walter spread both hands and slowly shook his head.

Impossible I'm afraid, Hugh. In this state, no-one is ever bailed who's chief suspect in a murder. He'll stay in gaol until he's tried.

How long will that take?

Three months, perhaps. There are quite a number of steps before the actual trial. It might only take two months, if things go smoothly.

I sat back and closed my eyes. Christ, I said.

I understand how you feel about your friend, Walter said. The Hobart Gaol isn't a pleasant place. No better than Port Arthur used to be, I'm afraid. But let's forget about that for a moment. Tell me more about Wall, and why you're so sure he's innocent.

I told Walter that the police suspected the woman had been raped as well as murdered; that she'd been found naked. I told him that Max Fell hired young women as models for his underwear advertizements, and that it seemed to me likely that she'd been one of them, and that she'd been raped and murdered by Fell.

Oh? And why would you think that?

I gave him an outline of Fell's behaviour towards women as Bob had described it to me, and I included an account of Bob's discovery of Fell's secret cartoon strip, and what sort of things it portrayed. Walter's face remained expressionless, but his eyebrows were raised. In the centre of his desk was a leather-bound blotting-paper holder fitted with a clean white sheet; he'd picked up a pencil and had begun to doodle there. Now he looked up at me.

Interesting. It would be useful to produce those drawings as evidence – but I don't see how we could ever get hold of them. And don't get carried away, Hugh: none of this amounts to proof of Fell's guilt. I must also ask you: why do you feel so sure that your friend Wall is incapable of rape? What could I tell a court about his character in that regard?

I spoke of Bob's respect for women, his contempt for Fell's attitudes towards them, and of how he'd been planning to leave the job because of it. I told Walter of his recent engagement to June Leaman – the sort of girl who would never have fallen in love with him if his character had been that of a rapist. I told him of Bob's harsh childhood, and of how he'd gone on from those beginnings and learned a trade and done well, despite his spell in the Boys' Home.

Walter had produced a spiral notebook and had been taking notes; now he put down his fountain pen and looked up at me sharply.

The Boys' Home? The Prosecution may try and use that against him. But I think I could argue that it was prejudicial, and shouldn't be admitted.

I leaned forward. Does this mean you'll take his case?

I might do. It certainly presents interesting challenges. First though, I'll visit him at the gaol.

That's wonderful, Walter. Thank you.

He looked at his wristwatch, and stood up.

I'll go around to Police Headquarters now. I'm well known to them there. I'll inform them that I'm considering acting for Wall, that I need to interview him, and that I want him taken before a magistrate tomorrow morning. That's the first step. That will at least get things moving.

I can't thank you enough. This is the second big favour you've done me.

Walter was straightening his tie and patting his pockets, not looking at me. When he answered, it was in a dry, offhand tone.

Both the favours you've asked for have been for other people – not for yourself. That has a certain appeal, Hugh. And now I must be off, and you must go back to your newspaper.

The old Hobart Gaol stood in Campbell Street, a drab thoroughfare running along the eastern edge of the town. Campbell Street crosses the bottom end of Liverpool Street, and the prison in those days was located only two blocks north of this, conveniently close to Police Headquarters. In the 1960s, the authorities decided to build a new prison out of town, and demolished much of the old gaol's original structure, including the outer wall that reared above the street. In doing so, they also removed a reminder (perhaps with intent) of the island's days as a penal settlement, since the gaol had originally been the Prisoners' Barracks: a penitentiary for newly arrived transportees, and a dormitory for convicts working for the Government. This was where Lucas Wilson and Roy Griffin had both served time, as convict clerks.

Walking up Campbell Street past the towering sandstone walls, I would sometimes try to imagine what might lie behind them. This was difficult, since not even the prison buildings were visible above the walls, and very few people other than offenders and those connected with the penal system ever got inside. Now, on the night of Bob's incarceration, I lay awake in bed and tried to picture his situation. At first I imagined a grim stone cell, bare and dark as those of the last century; but then I thought this might be wrong. These days, surely, they'd have the better-appointed cells you saw in films. People were still hanged for murder in the gaol though. If Bob were convicted, would this happen to him? My thoughts quailed away; I refused to believe that such a thing could take place. It had been some time since there'd been a hanging in Hobart, but I'd heard they still had the facilities for it in the gaol: the platform with its trapdoor; the beams and the ropes. I saw them in my mind, and went cold.

To turn my thoughts from this, I recalled the only attractive feature of the prison complex: Trinity Church, the old penitentiary chapel, standing at the northern end of the gaol behind two English oaks. Of all the Regency buildings in Hobart, I thought the tower of this church the most charming. Built in the early 1830s, it showed the influence of Christopher Wren; I'd once made a sketch of it. Its warm red brick was trimmed with stone, and it was topped by a small dual-faced clock tower. The clock, brought out from London, struck every quarter hour, the chimes floating through the green clouds of oak leaves and out across the hills and hollows of the town. Lucas Wilson would have listened to these chimes, and so would his dark alter ego, Griffin. Now I pictured my friend Bob Wall doing the same, and told myself that the sound might bring him hope, as it measured the passing hours. Help would come soon; he must surely tell himself that.

My assumption that twentieth-century cells would have been installed in the prison turned out to be naive. The gaol remained frozen in that old, hard century of the convict transports, and what lay behind the sandstone walls in Campbell Street was the same bitter territory in which the felons of a hundred years ago had spent their days. Clad in his prison uniform of shirt, trousers and coarse black jacket, Bob found himself in a windowless, brick-walled cell with a domed roof and two doors: one of wood, the other an iron grille. Lit by a bare electric bulb, the cell was approximately five feet deep by four and a half feet wide, and its only furnishings were a crude wooden bed that filled the length of the cell, a small shelf with a billycan of water and a mug on it, and a bucket with a lid for a lavatory. There were no facilities for washing, he told me; prisoners washed in the yard outside, in cut-down forty-four gallon drums.

What were called the visitors' rooms, where Walter Dixon came to interview him, were housed in a little weatherboard lean-to set against the wall of the Gaoler's office, in an entrance yard leading to the gates of the gaol proper. There were two of these rooms – if they could be called that. Each was a small cubicle, somewhat resembling a Confession box in a Catholic church, with space for only one visitor at a time. The prisoner was conducted to a similar cubicle on the other side, and spoke to his visitor through an opening covered with wire mesh. Bob was led there by a guard late on Tuesday afternoon. All he'd been told at that stage was that a barrister was coming to see him; he didn't know who it was or who'd arranged it. He sat down on a bench close to the wire mesh with the guard standing behind him, and waited. Presently Walter Dixon came through the visitors' door, carrying a briefcase. He looked about the cubicle with an expression of distaste, took out a large white handkerchief and flicked it over the bench provided and sat down. Then he peered through the mesh at Bob. In those first few moments, Bob told me, he was somewhat taken aback by the appearance of this aged man with his long white hair and bald pate, immaculately dressed though he was; he'd imagined a younger lawyer.

Good afternoon Mr Wall, Walter said. I'm Walter Dixon. Your friend Hugh Dixon has asked me to represent you. Hugh's my nephew, as you may know.

Yes. He's talked about you.

Hugh speaks highly of you, Robert – may I call you that?

It's Bob.

Bob, then. He's convinced that you're innocent. *I* don't have to be convinced of it, but I do need to have a case that will impress the jury. That's what I need to talk to you about, before I decide to defend you.

I'm innocent. I hope you'll believe that. I shouldn't be here.

Let me explain, Bob. Under the Law, I simply assume you're innocent unless proved otherwise. That's the way it works. So if you're guilty, you mustn't say so. I don't want to know that. If I did, I couldn't defend you.

I told you, Mr Dixon – I'm innocent. I didn't kill that woman.

Many a guilty man has said that to me. I'm not setting out to doubt you, Bob – I just want you to understand the system. And what I want you to do today is to give me some facts that I can work with: facts that will convince the court that you didn't rape and murder Mrs Gregson. Do you see?

Bob sat frowning at Walter, trying not to grow angry. Finally he said he understood.

Good. Now one thing that will work for us – and there aren't many – is that apparently you didn't sign the Record of Interview the detectives wanted you to sign.

No. I didn't trust them.

Walter smiled faintly. Very wise. You must be quite tough. I know all about those interviews of theirs. They're quite capable of falsifying the record, to make it into a confession. Did they get out the phone book?

Yeah. And Detective Parsons seems to be friendly with Max Fell. So he believes what Fell's told him.

Walter looked at him intently, his head on one side. Indeed? That's interesting.

He drew a notebook and a fountain pen from his briefcase and wrote for some moments. Then he looked up again, and Bob began to notice his large, youthfully clear eyes and air of alertness. He decided that Walter's age might not prevent him from being a capable lawyer.

I'm going to be frank with you, Bob, Walter said. At present the case against you seems very convincing, and will be hard to disprove. Let me summarize what I know from the police. This man Max Fell has told them that Madge Gregson was modelling for you in the studio last night, when he was away. There was nobody else in the building. The adjacent businesses would be closed for the night, and that part of Liverpool Street would be pretty much deserted, except for some passers-by. During that time, according to Fell, you must have murdered Mrs Gregson.

He's lying.

Walter held up his hand.

Don't interrupt me at this stage. Instead, just answer a question. Is there a back door in the building opening on to the edge of the Rivulet? One that could be reached by stairs from the studio?

Yes.

And at that time of night, could anyone view that area from windows in the other buildings?

Probably not. They'd be all closed up then. There aren't many windows there anyway.

I see. So according to Fell, after you killed Mrs Gregson, you would have been able to carry her body downstairs and leave it by the Rivulet, with no-one to see you.

Except that I didn't. I've told you, Mr Dixon: he's lying.

He may be – or he may not. Let's look at it from a jury's point of view. Mr Fell phoned the police early this morning and reported his discovery of the body. Not what you'd think he'd do if he was guilty. Why wouldn't he hide the body, instead? What's your answer to that?

Walter's expression now was so severe, Bob told me, that he began to fear that my great-uncle might not take his case. A feeling of enormous hopelessness came over him.

He wants to frame me, and it's working. He's doing it so that I'm the one who's convicted, not him.

Come now, young man: you'll have to be more convincing than that. Why should I believe you? Why should anyone believe you? I've no doubt the police arrested you and put you in here on remand because they were convinced you're guilty – and I can see why.

Bob had clenched his fists on his knees, conscious of the guard standing behind him. No doubt he was listening, and smirking at what Walter was saying. He wanted to hit out at someone; he wanted to shout with rage; but he did neither. He sat still, staring at Walter, and finally he answered in a tight, low voice.

The first lie he's telling is that Madge was modelling for me on Monday evening. But she wasn't.

She wasn't.

No. She wasn't. I don't do the fashion work – Max does. My job is to draw episodes of the comic strip that Max puts out. That's what I was doing that evening, working in the studio on my own. Max had told me to take the day off and get my work done in the evening instead. He arranged it because he wanted to take photographs of a model that afternoon, and he didn't want me there. I believe the model was Madge Gregson. She was very modest. She didn't want to pose for underwear ads with anyone else around.

You *believe* it was Madge Gregson. But you don't know it.

Max didn't say so, but I know it must have been. She was the only model who wouldn't work at night like the other models did. And she hadn't posed for that kind of ad before: she was very shy about doing it. Max had been trying to talk her into it for quite a while. I figured he'd finally succeeded. Poor woman. I wish to Christ she hadn't listened.

He looked down into his lap, gripping his hands together and frowning, while Walter said nothing.

I had the feeling that bastard would do something bad, Bob said. But not this. They should stop him, before he does it again.

Listen to me carefully. Hugh has already told me some of this, but I wanted to hear your account of it. And I've tried to give you a taste of what we'll face in court. Do you understand?

Does this mean you'll defend me?

I believe so. And I'll say this much: you don't seem to me like a young man who's capable of anything vile – even if you do look a bit like James Cagney.

Walter smiled faintly, and Bob returned his smile, though he didn't feel like smiling.

You'd better tell me about your fees, he said.

We can discuss those later. Don't worry about them.

No, we ought to talk about them. I might not be able to afford them.

Very likely not. I don't imagine Fell paid you very much. Have you got any money put by?

A bit. Not much.

No. Well, let me put this to you. When it's all over, and you see my bill, you can pay me whatever you can afford.

Why would you do that for me?

Hugh believes in your innocence, and I'm inclined to think he may be right. Let's leave it at that, and get our business over with. Hugh says you're engaged. Would your fiancée testify to your good character?

I won't have June involved.

Well, we'll leave that for now. What we must concentrate on is finding evidence that can be used against Fell. I'm interested to hear about the secret comic strip Hugh mentioned to me. And also about the way Fell behaved towards his models – in particular, Mrs Gregson.

Bob described the strip, giving examples, and Walter listened carefully, frowning and making small humming noises which seemed to indicate surprise, or perhaps distaste. Bob then gave an account of the first photographic session with Madge Gregson, when he'd witnessed Max's pantomime assault.

During this, Walter made notes. Finally he picked up his briefcase, pushed his notebook into it and sat back. When he spoke, it was so softly that Bob could only just hear him.

'I do not like thee, Doctor Fell.'

What? Bob said.

Just an old nursery rhyme, Walter said. He was looking through the mesh at a point above Bob's head. He wore a musing expression, as though he entertained some sort of daydream.

We may be in the presence of genuine evil here, he said. That's a rather rare thing.

His voice had remained soft, as though he hadn't been speaking to Bob at all; but now he seemed to return from his daydream, looking back at Bob with his former alertness.

I must go, he said, and stood up. But I hope to have you before a magistrate tomorrow morning.

As Walter had predicted, it took over two months for Bob to be brought to trial in the Criminal Court. Those two months of waiting are not a period I like to recall.

What pervaded them was my fear concerning Bob's fate and my outrage at what was happening to him; and what comes back to me most vividly are my visits to him at the gaol, sitting in that wretched, dank-smelling wooden cubicle they called a visitors' room, and looking at him through the wire mesh. From behind it, he looked back at me as though through a grey mist: pale and solemn, his occasional smile like a wince. He'd always kept part of himself withdrawn; now he'd retreated still further inside himself.

Because of my hours at the *Mail*, I was able to visit him most mornings. When I saw him on my first visit, everything in me protested at the sight. There he sat, in khaki prison shirt and trousers and a shapeless black jacket with a number below the collar; behind him, standing to attention, an expressionless, dull-faced guard in blue uniform looked over our heads and pretended not to listen. Prisoners were allowed small comforts from their visitors, and I'd brought him magazines and fruit – checked by the guard to be handed over later. I asked him how he was managing.

I'm getting by. There were some shitheads in the yard wanting a punch-up, but I thumped one of them and they haven't tried it on since.

Good. Don't get low, Hans. You'll be out of here sooner than you think. We'll drink beer and listen to Fats Waller.

It's nice to think so, Fritz, but I reckon I'll have to be lucky. I got myself into trouble all those years ago – but this time trouble found me. I'm not sure I'll get out of this one.

You will, Bob. They'll see you're innocent.

Maybe. But that filthy bastard Fell's framed me up properly, hasn't he?

He's tried to. But Walter Dixon's the best barrister in town, and I know he's working hard on it. He'll get Fell on the witness stand and take him apart.

I hope you're right, mate. You and June are what keep me going. She's here nearly every evening. She's wonderful.

The goodness I'd seen in June Leaman hadn't been illusory. Pat Dwyer's front page story in the *Mail* naming Bob as chief suspect had caused most people to decide he was guilty, and June's parents were among them: they'd begged her to break the engagement. She'd refused to do so, and apparently never doubted his innocence. She came to him almost every evening after work, and I knew that this was mainly what got him through his days. He had no-one else to visit him. With his parents dead, there were no living relatives except for his father's brother – and he was a drunk whom Bob hadn't seen for years. He had only June, me and Walter.

During the two months of his imprisonment, three legal rituals took place before the trial itself. In each case, Bob made an appearance before a magistrate, in the Magistrates' Court in Liverpool Street.

On the day after his arrest, Walter had appeared for him as he'd promised to do, and had told the magistrate that no plea was being entered at that stage. The matter was then adjourned. Two weeks later came the Plea Proceedings; at these, Walter announced that his client was pleading not guilty, and requested Committal Proceedings.

I attended these proceedings, which took place a month later. Their purpose was to decide whether Bob had a case to answer, or else must be committed for trial. This time, witnesses were called, including Max Fell. Fell was questioned by the Counsel for the Prosecution and cross-examined by Walter, as Counsel for the Defence. Fell told the Crown Prosecutor how he'd discovered the body by the Rivulet. He then went on to say that everything pointed to the fact that only Bob Wall could have killed Mrs Gregson, and gave his reasons. Mournfully shaking his head, he said how talented Bob was, and what a tragedy it was that he must have lost all control, and been carried away by lust. When Walter cross-questioned him, he made similar answers. During all of this, Fell never looked across at Bob in the dock.

At the end of the hearing, the magistrate announced his decision: Robert John Wall was committed for trial by jury in the Hobart Criminal Court in a month's time: on the 6th of January, 1954.

Walter's cross-examination of Fell had worried and disappointed me. It seemed to me that his questions had been neither hostile nor probing: he'd simply gone over Fell's testimony, and had asked him to enlarge on some factual details which were apparently innocuous. When I asked him why he'd taken this direction, he simply said that he was keeping his powder dry.

This conversation took place in Walter's office. I sat on one of the green-upholstered bridge chairs and Walter leaned back behind his desk, toying with a paper-knife and sometimes glancing at a little gold clock placed beside his blotter. I was discovering once again that the Walter Dixon of the office had an entirely different persona from the one who enthused about painting at Leyburn Farm, and I began to get the impression that he didn't want to discuss the case with me any further. He listened to my questions with a stony expression, and answered them in a way that told me little or nothing. Despite this, I decided to press him once more, before giving up.

Everything seems to be against Bob, I said. It's his word against Fell's, and the police believe Fell. How can you possibly show that Fell's lying?

I believe I can. But you really must leave this to me from now on, Hugh. Once I begin on a case, I don't discuss details with anybody except my legal colleagues.

I'm sorry. It just seems so hopeless. To Bob as well as to me.

He'd been looking at me sternly, but now I saw a slight softening in his face.

I'll simply tell you this. It's a matter of finding evidence to disprove Fell's story. I've already begun on that, with the help of a private investigator I've used in the past. A somewhat seedy fellow, but good at his work. I've also defended a number of low-life characters in this town who've helped me before and are doing so again: some of them know Fell, and what they're telling me is useful. It's a small town, and not many things can be hidden. That's all I'll tell you at present – and now you must excuse me, Hugh. I've a good deal to do.

The past is a dimension that can't be escaped, however hard we try. Old Van Diemen's Land had claimed Bob Wall: that past which most people here preferred not to think about, just as they preferred to forget their convict ancestors. Only the present was thought to be clean and harmless: modern was good. But when Bob entered the Hobart Gaol, the bland and transient present was dissolved. He was locked not just in prison, but in the nineteenth century. It had never gone away, that sombre old century; instead it was hidden and preserved behind the high sandstone walls in Campbell Street, waiting for recruits from outside.

The past was preserved as well in the Criminal Court in Campbell Street, which was part of the prison complex. I came there, together with June Leaman, on Wednesday the 6th of January: the first day of the trial. The clock was striking ten in the tower of the penitentiary chapel as we went in, and the sound no longer appealed to me as it used to do; instead, it seemed ominous. The anxiety in June's face – that face which had always been serenely and enigmatically happy – filled me with concern, and I spoke to her softly, doing all I could to calm her fears, and pretending a confidence I didn't feel.

We sat in the crowded public gallery at the back, behind a low picket fence of aged cedar that separated us from the court. Waiting for proceedings to begin, we looked around us. The place chilled me. Back in the 1850s, when the Prisoners' Barracks had become the Hobart Gaol, part of the penitentiary chapel had been converted to build this court, and the pews and other fittings were turned into court furniture. It was all still here, the dark cedar benches and boxes and panelling; no modifications had been made for a hundred years. The room was very plain, with bleak blue walls and an immensely high ceiling. Despite the bright summer morning outside it was cold, and gave no glimpse of the outside world, since the tall windows stared down from a height of some twenty feet above the floor.

At the head of the room was the Judge's Bench, empty at present, with a cedar canopy suspended above it. On its right was the witness box and the press gallery, and on its left was the jury box, where the all-male jury sat waiting to be empanelled. Four journalists were sitting in the press gallery, notebooks at the ready, and I recognized Pat Dwyer. Below the Bench was a long table at which the Judge's Associate and the Court Clerk were sitting. Then came the Bar table, closer to our place in the public gallery. Walter was already sitting there, imposing in his wig and gown and looking like a Roman senator. Opposite him sat the Crown Prosecutor, Hubert Maxwell: a tall, heavy man with a large pale face who wore thick-lensed, black-framed glasses and an ill-humoured expression.

Just in front of where June and I sat was the dock: a box-like structure enclosed by another picket fence. Bob was already sitting there, staring in front of him, with a blue-uniformed guard standing behind him. A few minutes ago he and the guard had appeared there in a theatrical manner, by coming up out of the floor. Later Bob would tell me that he'd been held in an underground cell, and had been conducted to the dock through narrow stone-built tunnels and then up tight, winding stairs. He'd blinked in the courtroom's sudden light when he'd appeared, his fair hair tousled, and hadn't looked in our direction. I'd half expected him to be in his prison suit, but he was wearing his own clothes: his leather jacket, and a shirt and tie. Seeing him there, I grew colder than before, and I heard June draw in a breath.

The Court Clerk called for us to stand. Justice McPherson came on to the Bench, and the classical liturgies of the system of British justice were set in motion: that system transported here by the military founders and administrators of the colony, and by those who'd organized the building of the complex we sat in: gaol, chapel and courtroom.

The Judge's Associate stood facing towards the dock.

Are you Robert John Wall?

Yes.

The Prosecutor then stood and faced the judge.

I appear for the Crown.

Walter stood.

I appear for the accused, if it please the court.

The Judge then told the Associate to read the indictment, and the Associate looked towards Bob again.

Robert John Wall, you are charged with murder, in that on Monday the 2nd of November 1953, you did murder Madge Patricia Gregson. How say you? Are you guilty or not guilty?

Not guilty, Bob said. His voice was low but firm.

After this, the jury was empanelled. The Counsel for the Defence had the right to challenge any juror he wished; but Walter didn't do so. The Prosecutor then began his opening address to the jury. He had a relentless, grating voice which I still hear in my mind.

Gentlemen of the jury, the accused is charged with an extremely brutal murder. We intend to produce evidence which should convince you of his guilt not only in this, but also of raping his victim, Mrs Madge Gregson.

I glanced at June. Her light blue eyes, empty of their usual happiness, were squinting as though she tried to discern something at a remote distance, and her right hand was clenched on her knee. I still see her small white fist resting on her tartan skirt: one of those images that persist in the mind for decades, when memories of more apparent significance are lost. *None of this should be happening to you,* I thought. *Your spirit was only made for joy.*

The trial lasted for a surprisingly short time: only three days. This was partly because of the small number of witnesses. June and I attended every day, meeting outside the Court. She'd taken time off from her job in order to do this, and I'd taken a week of my annual leave.

On the first day, after his opening address, the Prosecutor began to take his witnesses through their evidence. In each case, Walter cross-examined them afterwards. Bob didn't give evidence at that stage, since the rules forbade it. He could only be called by the Defence, and then the Prosecutor would be able to cross-examine him.

The first of the witnesses was Max Fell. When he entered the box, I studied him with a mixture of loathing and fascination. He wasn't in his usual casual dress and nor did he wear his cap, which made his spiky dark head look somehow stunted. He wore a grey lounge suit with a collar and tie, and this gave him a certain gravity. Having taken the oath, he looked about the courtroom and then at Maxwell with a confident stare, both hands resting on the rim of the witness box. At the Committal Proceedings, he'd appeared rather solemn; now he had an expression which almost approached good humour. I say almost, because those blue-tinted glasses of his made it as difficult as ever to read his expression accurately: the only clue was in the set of his wide mouth. Perhaps my new knowledge of what he was influenced me, but I noticed now that it was an ugly mouth, constantly working and changing, the lips often loosely parted. I looked at Bob, in the dock. He was staring at Fell with an expression I can only describe as concentrated. As usual, his face showed little emotion. Fell didn't look back at him, and nor would he do so throughout his appearance.

The Prosecutor guided Fell through much the same testimony as he'd given at the Committal Proceedings. At eight-thirty in the morning, Fell said, he'd come downstairs from his flat at 216 Liverpool Street and had gone out to the back of the building in order to put some rubbish in a bin. Then he'd caught sight of a body, lying next to the Rivulet.

And you've told me that you recognized Mrs Gregson, Maxwell said. A woman who'd modelled for you. She was quite naked, was she not?

Yes.

Maxwell allowed a pause to develop at this point, and looked towards the jury. The thick lenses of his glasses magnified his eyes, giving him an appearance of frog-like belligerence. He turned back to Fell, lowering his harsh voice.

Yes. A young wife and mother, killed and stripped and dumped among the rubbish by the Rivulet. And were there marks on the body?

Fell looked down at his hands for a moment, where they still rested on the rim of the box.

Yes. Marks around the throat.

And what did you imagine had happened to her?

I thought she'd been murdered.

The Pathologist will testify that she'd also been raped. Did you see anyone in the vicinity you suspect might have done this?

No. Bob Wall had worked with Madge the previous evening, while I was out. There was nobody else in the b-building. I left at six o'clock to spend time with friends in a hotel on Salamanca Place. I didn't come back until t-ten o'clock, when the studio was empty. Bob and Madge had been alone together most of that time. Nobody else could have killed her.

Walter rose to his feet.

Objection. This is simply opinion, your Honour.

I agree, the Judge said. As opinion, this is inadmissible. The jury will ignore it.

The Prosecutor turned to Fell again.

You'd employed Robert Wall for some time. What was your estimate of his character?

I thought him a promising young fellow, but I'd noticed that when some of our m-models posed for underwear ads, he took the wrong sort of interest. I noticed him p-paying special attention to Madge Gregson.

What do you mean by that?

Fell grinned, and licked his lips. I found the grin shocking, in the circumstances.

Meaning she excited him. I could tell by the way he looked at her. He must have got carried away when she posed for him, and tried to rape her. She p-put up a fight and he killed her.

Maxwell thanked him, and then Walter began his cross-examination.

He did so in the same low-key style that he'd adopted at the Committal Proceedings. His voice, in contrast to Maxwell's aggressive tones, was elaborately courteous, and its just-perceptible tremor made him seem the kind of genteel, aged man who was too frail to represent a threat to anybody. Because of this, I was gripped in those first few minutes by a worrying doubt. Walter was now seventy-three; in spite of his reputation, was it possible that he was simply too old to mount the formidable defence that was needed?

You say that you worked at the studio in the afternoon, Mr Fell. You worked alone there?

Yes.

You're quite sure of that? You weren't working with Mrs Gregson, by any chance?

Walter had moved closer to the witness box, and was looking at Fell now with an expression of bland enquiry. Fell stared back at him. Even through his glasses, I was able to see his eyes widen. Before he could reply, the Prosecutor rose to his feet.

I object.

The Judge looked at him. On what basis?

Unfounded supposition, your Honour. Mr Fell has already testified that it was Robert Wall who worked with her – and that was in the evening.

Walter turned to the Judge.

Your Honour, my client Robert Wall will claim that it was Mr Fell, not he, who worked with Mrs Gregson that day. I should like to hear Mr Fell's reply to that accusation.

I'll allow it, the Judge said.

Walter turned back to Fell, and his demeanour had suddenly changed. He now wore his most severe and penetrating expression, and his large Roman nose, pointing at Fell, reminded me more than ever of the beak of a predator. His voice remained courteous, but it had hardened.

Let me put this to you, Mr Fell. Mr Wall will claim that he worked *alone* that evening – not with Mrs Gregson – and that he did so because you asked him to leave the studio clear for you in the afternoon. And why did you ask for this arrangement? You asked for it because you said you'd be working with a model who was to pose for an underwear advertizement – one who wanted privacy. I put it to you that the model was Mrs Madge Gregson. What do you say to that?

During this speech, Fell's mouth had been working spasmodically, and he was frowning. When he answered, his voice was no longer even: it had a strident note.

It's rubbish. Bob's lying. M-Madge Gregson was never there in the afternoon. She modelled for Bob that night.

Walter looked towards the jury with an air of surprise, his substantial white eyebrows raised to their ultimate height; then he looked back at Fell.

This is all quite a dilemma for the jury. It seems that they must either believe what *you* say, Mr Fell, or believe Mr Wall. One or the other of you almost certainly committed this crime, but there are no witnesses that we know of to give us guidance on the matter – though who knows? Perhaps somebody might be found. That's what it comes down to, doesn't it?

Fell had regained his air of certainty and looked back at Walter with a sardonic expression.

Yes. I suppose it does.

The Judge leaned forward.

Mr Dixon, have you any more questions for this witness?

I have, if it please your Honour. Quite important questions.

In that case, I will adjourn the court until two-fifteen.

In the afternoon, as soon as Fell had entered the witness box, Walter moved close to him again, carrying a sheaf of papers. He studied them for some moments; then he looked up at Fell. When he spoke, his voice was sharp and penetrating, reaching easily to the back of the court, like that of a seasoned actor.

I have a question for you, Mr Fell, concerning your past. You may want to think carefully before replying. Have you ever been convicted of indecently assaulting a woman?

Fell's face became entirely blank

No.

No? I want to suggest that in fact you've assaulted a number of women. You've made quite a habit of it, in fact.

That's not true!

Fell's voice was suddenly loud, and his mouth was working as though he were afflicted with some nervous ailment. The Prosecutor rose and addressed the Judge.

Your Honour, I can't see where this is leading. I hope my

learned friend can substantiate these accusations, and has a reason for making them.

The Judge looked at Walter. Mr Dixon? Have you some evidence for what you're saying?

I have, your Honour, and I shall produce it in a moment. My purpose is to demonstrate that Mr Fell has a background that will show that he's entirely capable of having committed the crime with which Robert Wall is falsely charged.

You may proceed.

Walter turned back to Fell, who had removed his hands from the edge of the box and was standing in a stooped posture, watching him with a guarded air.

Mr Fell, Walter said, I'll put my question again and will be more specific. Have you ever been convicted of assaulting a woman in any state of the Commonwealth?

No. This is rubbish. You shouldn't be asking these questions.

I believe I should, and I'll put another question to you. Have you ever lived in Victoria?

Yes. I come from Melbourne.

And were you not convicted in the Supreme Court of Victoria, sitting at Melbourne on the 9th of April 1948, of indecently assaulting a woman?

There was a stirring and murmuring in the courtroom, and the Judge ordered the gallery to be silent. Then he looked at Fell.

Please answer the question, Mr Fell.

Fell looked at the Judge, then at Walter, and then at the court, his head moving jerkily, like that of a badly manipulated puppet. Suddenly he began to shout, his voice strained and unnatural, echoing from the high ceiling.

No! That's all bloody lies. W-what you've got hold of is a pack of lies.

I looked at the faces of the men in the jury box. All of them appeared shocked or else profoundly interested, like spectators at a road accident.

Mr Fell, the Judge said. You will moderate your tone and your language.

Walter bowed to the Judge with eighteenth-century courtesy. Thank you your Honour. I will now show the witness a document which I'd like him to read.

He stepped closer to the witness box and handed a sheet of paper to Fell, who took it, peering first at Walter and then at the page.

Walter waited; then he said: Have you read the document, Mr Fell?

Yes.

And is that not a record of your conviction of assault upon Mary Gillian Dawson on April 9th, 1948, by tearing open her clothing and striking her repeatedly in the face?

For a moment Fell was silent, staring at the document.

The Judge leaned towards him. You must answer the question, Mr Fell.

Yes, Fell said. His voice now was only just audible.

Walter remained near to the witness box, his gaze remaining on Fell.

So you now admit, Mr Fell, that your previous answer was untrue?

I suppose so. But –

Yes or no, Mr Fell.

Yes.

I've been in touch with the Victorian police, Mr Fell, so please don't trouble to lie to the court. You've had previous convictions for assaulting women, have you not?

Fell looked up; his voice rose again, and his stutter became more pronounced. Yes. But b-based on the women's *lies.* W-women who wanted to get me into trouble.

And you managed to avoid serious punishment on those occasions. But on this occasion you were sentenced to twelve months' gaol, which you served in Pentridge, did you not?

Yes. Wrongly. Unjustly.

Fell looked around the court with an air of defiance, his hands gripping the edge of the box.

So you say, Walter said. But you've just admitted that you lied to the court when you denied these convictions, and I suggest that you are also lying when you deny that it was you who worked with Mrs Gregson on the afternoon of November the 2nd. I suggest that she posed for you, and during that session you were possessed by lust, raped her and then strangled her.

No.

I further suggest that you then hid the body in the flat adjoining your studio and went out for the evening. So when Robert Wall worked alone there that night, he did so quite unaware that the body of that violated woman was just next door. I suggest that once he'd gone home you came back, and somewhere during the night you carried the body down the stairs that lead from your flat to a door at the back of the building, where the Rivulet flows past. Isn't that so?

No, Fell said, and shook his head violently.

At that time of night there would have been no-one in the adjoining buildings to see you, and no-one in the laneways. I put it to you that you left the body there, in that deserted, wretched place, planning to phone the police in the morning and put Robert Wall in the frame. Which you did. Isn't that the case, Mr Fell?

No. No. You've g-got it all wrong.

No more questions, your Honour, Walter said, and turned away.

When Fell left the witness box there was a loud murmuring in the courtroom, and the Judge called again for the gallery to be silent. I wasn't sure what the mood of this murmuring was; simple surprise, perhaps. But I felt sure of one thing: the evidence Walter had produced concerning Fell's past marked a turning point in the trial right at the outset. It had come as a shock to me, just as it had done to Fell and the court, since Walter had told me nothing of his private investigations; but it had also filled me with hope. Walter had gone to the Bar table now, and sat talking to his Junior. I studied him with a mixture of regard and puzzlement. Was this remorseless barrister the true Walter Dixon? Or was his true self the semi-recluse and cultivated lover of art who'd been so important in my life? It puzzled me then, but I believe I know the answer now, long after his death. My great-uncle was one of those individuals who harbour two opposite spirits inside themselves: spirits never to be reconciled. In this lay both his complexity and his sadness.

The next witness the Prosecutor called was Detective Sergeant Parsons. Parsons told how he and his partner had gone to the crime scene immediately after Max Fell had telephoned him. They had interviewed people in the surrounding businesses but had learned nothing, since all the businesses there were closed by six pm, and the area at the back of the buildings was deserted at night. After that, having interviewed Madge Gregson's husband, they'd gone out to Moonah and arrested Bob Wall. Parsons concluded by giving his reasons for believing that Bob had committed the crime, and Walter then began his cross-examination.

Detective Sergeant Parsons, you say that you based your assumption that my client was guilty on Mr Fell's say-so. Is that correct?

I wouldn't put it like that. I formed my own conclusions. The fact that Mr Fell phoned and reported discovering the body made it very unlikely that he'd done it. And it could only have been done by him or by Wall, as I see it. Mr Fell is known to me, and I believe him to be telling the truth.

Yes, you know Mr Fell quite well, don't you? You might almost be said to be cronies.

Parsons' red face went redder, and his heavy jaw jutted.

I don't know what you mean by that.

I put it to you that you are a friend of Mr Fell's. I have reports that you are often seen at the races together, and that in your off-hours you are also seen with Mr Fell in hotels at night, in the company of women.

The Prosecutor rose, and objected on the grounds of relevance.

I'll think I'll allow it, Mr Maxwell, the Judge said. Mr Fell's relationship with Detective Sergeant Parsons may have a bearing on the case. You will answer the question, Detective Sergeant.

Parsons looked at the Judge with an air of frustration; then he turned back to Walter.

I run into Mr Fell occasionally in off-hours, that's all. I know nothing about any women. I've also given him professional advice on the comic strip he draws: a crime thriller.

Ah yes. *Rod Callaghan*, is it not? We've all seen it in the newspapers. A comic strip which is not at all comical, and in which half-nude women suffer constant violence – is that the one?

Parsons looked sullen.

I wouldn't describe it like that.

Would you not? Many would, I imagine. Well, let's pass on. Let me say that I agree with you on one point that matters, Sergeant: the murder could only have been committed by Wall or by Fell. A third party is unlikely. But it appears you have no witness to the crime, and no direct evidence that Robert Wall committed it – a young man with no history of violence or molestation of women. So would you not agree that Mr Fell can't be ruled out? And would it not have been your professional duty to look closely at Mr Fell's background and character before you decided to accuse Robert Wall of the crime?

Mr Fell is well known in Hobart, Parsons said. He's run a successful business here for some years, he has a good character, and has no convictions here of any kind. That's how I formed my judgement. And as I've said, he reported the murder immediately. If he was the perpetrator, surely he'd have hidden the body.

Hiding a body is difficult, Detective Sergeant. Framing someone else for the crime is much simpler. But whatever the case, let me ask you this. You have now heard the evidence that I've obtained from the Victorian police in regard to Fell's history of assaults on women, and his gaol term. How is it you knew nothing of that? Did you not check on the mainland for any prior offences?

Parsons now looked at Walter with open hostility.

I saw no reason, at the time.

Really? And if you *had* checked, and if you'd learned of Fell's term in Pentridge, might you not have approached this case in a different way?

I suppose I might have done.

Is that a yes, or a no, Detective Sergeant?

Parsons appeared visibly to clench his teeth. Yes, he said.

No more questions, your Honour.

After that, the Judge adjourned the court for the day.

In retrospect, the climax of Bob's ordeal will always seem to me to be that first day of the trial, when Walter's cross-examination put the main focus on Max Fell. It certainly had that effect in the town when Thursday's *Mail* came out. As I walked down Liverpool Street towards Campbell Street that morning, on the trial's second day, I passed a banner for the *Mail* outside a newsagent's doorway.

COMMERCIAL ARTIST HAS HISTORY OF VIOLENCE WITH WOMEN.

Pat Dwyer's report dominated the front page, accompanied by pictures of 216 Liverpool Street, of Madge Gregson, and of Fell leaving the court, his tinted glasses giving him a furtive air. The story's revelations concerning Fell made clear to the public that the trial had now changed course. Until now, most people in Hobart had probably assumed that Bob was guilty, in the absence of any other suspect; now their attention seemed more likely to be fixed on Fell. Pat's story led with the fact that Fell now had to be regarded as an alternative suspect, and made much of the Defence's suggestion that he was lying, and that he and not Bob had been with Madge Gregson on the day she was murdered. It then reported without comment Fell's record of assaults on women, and Walter Dixon's revelation of his conviction and imprisonment in Victoria.

Although in my memory much of what followed in court on Thursday seems almost like an anticlimax, it actually wasn't so at the time. Walter had yet to produce hard evidence that would cement his case against Fell, and I dared not be certain at that stage that he'd achieve this; but as June and I sat in the public gallery waiting for proceedings to begin, I did everything I could to make her confident that Bob would be found innocent. I looked about the gallery to see whether Fell had dared to attend; he wasn't there, and I was never to see him again.

Everyone will realize that Fell's guilty, I told June. You can be sure of it. It's all changed now.

She looked at me doubtfully. I hope so, she said. But we can't count on it, can we? And if they *do* find Bob guilty –

She broke off, and bit her lip. He can appeal, she said. Can't he?

Of course, I said. But I wasn't sure of that.

I looked across at Bob in the dock, as June was doing. She had brought some of his clothes to him at the gaol, and today he wore a blue pinstripe suit. I'd never seen him in a suit before; he looked stiff and uneasy in it. Sensing June's gaze he turned and looked at her, and smiled for the first time: a faint smile, but one that had evident feeling in it. She smiled back, sitting very straight.

The final witness for the Prosecution was the Government Pathologist. He testified that Mrs Gregson had been throttled – probably by a man with large hands, from the bruising on the throat. There was also bruising to the chest and arms, indicating that she'd been violently handled: probably punched. She had also been raped. Asked for details, he spoke of vaginal bruising and internal scratches from digital penetration.

Walter then cross-examined him, and asked whether it was possible to set the approximate time of death. The Pathologist said that it was, and spoke of the drop in the body's core temperature, and the degree of *rigor mortis.* His estimate was that death had taken place in the late afternoon.

Walter looked from the Pathologist to the jury.

Let me have this clear. In the late afternoon? Not in the evening, which is when Mr Fell says Mrs Gregson must have died?

No. My estimate, as I've said, is that the victim died in the afternoon.

No more questions, your Honour.

It was now Walter's turn, as Counsel for the Defence, to give his opening address before examining his witnesses. He began by stating that the crime under consideration had almost certainly been committed by one of two men: either by Robert Wall, who was accused of it, or by his employer Max Fell. The task of the jury was to decide whether Robert Wall was the one who was guilty of it. He then increased the intensity of his voice, so that it reverberated to the back of the courtroom.

Gentlemen of the jury, Robert Wall has been charged with rape and murder largely on the word of Max Fell. Mr Wall is a young man who has committed no previous offences of this kind. The Defence will maintain that the charge against him is outrageous, for a very simple reason. Mr Fell, who made the charge against Wall to the police, has a very different record, as we have shown the court: a record that surely makes him the more obvious suspect. You have learned that Mr Fell has actually been in prison for indecent assault on a woman – the very type of crime with which Mr Wall has been charged. You might well consider that Mr Fell would have been on trial here, had the police investigated him more thoroughly – but leave that aside.

What the Defence will now do is to produce evidence proving that Mr Wall could not have committed this crime: that in fact, he was not with the victim in the studio that evening, or at any other time that day. We will show that when Mr Wall went to the studio that evening, Mrs Gregson was already dead.

There was a prolonged murmur of voices at this, and the Judge called for silence. He then adjourned the court until two-fifteen.

Walter's first witness was Bob Wall. Standing in front of the dock, he took Bob through the statements of the various other witnesses, asking for his comments. Bob's answers were terse, and nothing new emerged from them. Recently, since he'd been with June Leaman, I'd begun to see a new softening in his face; but now his expression had reverted to the way it had been in the time when we were boys, and had first walked up Main Road together. His mouth was set in the same tight line, his dark blue gaze was fixed and defiant, and I heard his eleven-year-old voice again. *There's no fucken peace.* I knew he was simply trying to endure, as he'd done as a boy, and he had a look of stubborn honesty; but he must have seemed a hard type to the members of the jury. I glanced about me at the faces in the public gallery, wondering what they made of him. All of them were looking at him with intense curiosity; but their opinions were impossible to judge.

The only time that Bob showed emotion was when Walter asked him to comment on Max Fell's evidence against him.

He's lying. I wasn't there that afternoon. Max Fell was, and Madge Gregson was modelling for him. I believe Max killed her. He was always likely to do it.

And why do you say that?

Maxwell objected, and the Judge asked him on what basis he did so.

Mr Wall is being asked to speculate in an area beyond his scope, Maxwell said. One for which he has no hard evidence.

Walter turned to the Judge.

Your honour, my client will quote certain facts about Mr Fell which make it seem likely that Mr Fell was capable of this crime. I ask that Mr Wall be heard.

I'll allow it, the Judge said. Mr Wall, you will confine yourself to facts, not speculation. Proceed.

Bob then related the incident that had taken place when Max first persuaded Madge Gregson to model in her underclothes, and had torn down her slip.

You felt uneasy about this incident, Walter said. Is that the case?

Yes. It made me feel very bad for her.

Did you think of intervening?

Yes. I would have, if it had gone any further. After that he always had his models alone with him.

Had you any other reason for thinking him capable of violence towards women?

Yes. It was the way he talked about them. And the way he always wanted to show women being beaten up in *Rod Callaghan.*

Ah yes, the so-called comic strip. Did you see any unpublished drawings of his of the same kind?

Yes. They showed women being raped and tortured. Drawings that could never be published. Drawings that made you sick to look at them.

Maxwell objected again, and the Judge asked him for his reason.

We have no evidence of these drawings, Maxwell said. Only Mr Wall's statement, which could be a fabrication.

I must agree with the Prosecutor, Mr Dixon. The jury will disregard Mr Wall's last statement.

The Prosecutor's cross-examination followed. He attempted without success to find weaknesses in Bob's testimony, and I felt that his heart wasn't in it.

The next witness that Walter called was an elderly woman named Mrs Harris, who turned out to be the proprietor of the secondhand shop on the ground floor of the building at 216 Liverpool Street. I'd often passed her shop over the years. Ever since I could remember, she'd been sitting in the doorway in her armchair, perfectly immobile, watching the street and apparently undisturbed by any customers: a large, shapeless woman in a felt hat, wearing a dark, high-necked, long-sleeved cotton dress whose style appeared to date from the last century. Now, as she came into the witness box, she seemed to be wearing the same dress; but no doubt she had a succession of them, very likely drawn from her stock. She also wore her hat, from beneath which some strands of dyed red hair had escaped and hung down. She sat and stared across the court, immediately assuming her customary immobility: a petrified figure from another era, her fleshy, pallid face with its large double chin expressionless and composed.

Once she'd been sworn in, Walter approached the witness box.

Good afternoon, Mrs Harris. You own a shop on the ground floor of 216 Liverpool Street: the building where Mr Fell runs his studio, on the upper floor. Is that correct?

That's right, Mrs Harris said. She had a slow, deep voice that carried well, and seemed in no way awed by the court.

And you generally sit in your shop doorway, watching the street. Is that so?

Yes. I look out for customers, and I keep an eye on anyone leaving the shop. Some of them has light fingers.

No doubt. And were you there all day on Monday the 2nd of November last: that is, on the day when it's alleged Mrs Gregson was murdered by Robert Wall?

That's right. I'm there every day except Sundays.

And how can you recall that particular date?

It was the date of my late husband's birthday. That's how.

And did you see Mrs Gregson enter the studio that afternoon?

Maxwell rose and objected, and the Judge asked him on what basis he did so.

How would Mrs Harris know that it was Mrs Gregson? I assume they weren't acquainted.

The Judge turned towards Mrs Harris.

Will you tell the court, Mrs Harris, how you knew the victim by sight?

I didn't *know* her. Not to speak to. Didn't even know her name. But now I've seen her picture in the paper, and I'm sure that's the young woman I often seen goin down the lane at the side, to the door of Max's studio. She came there that afternoon; I'm pretty sure of that. Nice-lookin, she was. It's a real shame.

It is, Mrs Harris, Walter said. And now will you tell the court roughly what time she arrived?

I'd say about three o'clock.

And when did she leave?

I never seen her leave. And I thought that was a bit funny. She's generally only there for an hour or two.

You didn't see her leave. I see. Thank you, Mrs Harris. No more questions, your Honour.

The Prosecutor's cross-examination of Mrs Harris was brief. For some moments before he spoke, Maxwell examined the old woman with a dubious expression, lower lip out-thrust. Motionless, Mrs Harris stared calmly back at him, like an image in a shrine.

November the second, nineteen-fifty-three, Maxwell said slowly. Over two months ago. And yet you recall seeing Mrs Gregson, whom you didn't even know, arriving at the studio on that particular day: a day like any other. How can you be so sure?

Mrs Harris cocked her head very slightly to the left. She gazed at the Prosecutor with wise placidity before replying: a Sybil of the realm of secondhand.

I've said. It wasn't an ordinary day. It was my late husband's birthday.

Yes. But do you observe his birthdays with such care that you can recall what happens on those days – even though he's not there?

He's there in spirit. And I light a candle for him. I'd lit one that day, I remember. At the back of the shop.

The Prosecutor's face grew resigned, and he closed his eyes for a moment.

Thank you, Mrs Harris. No more questions, your Honour.

The Judge then adjourned the court, and fixed the next hearing for ten o'clock the following day.

Walter's final witness surprised me. He called Fred Tyson.

Like Bob, Fred had put on a suit and white shirt and tie to appear in court. Like Bob he looked uncomfortable in a suit; he probably only wore it for weddings or funerals. It appeared somewhat large for his thin frame, and he gave the impression of being encased in some hard material like tin. His sparse, greying, straw-coloured hair had been oiled and combed close to his head. He stood stiffly in the dock, with stooped shoulders. As he took the oath, he licked his lips nervously, and I guessed that he'd never been in a court before.

Mr Tyson, Walter said. I understand you worked with Bob Wall before he left the building trade to become a commercial artist. Is that so?

Yes. He's a carpenter and joiner, like me. He's a first-rate tradesman.

He also rents a bungalow on your property at Moonah, is that so?

Yes.

So you know him fairly well. Can you give the court an estimate of his character?

He's a fine young bloke. I'd trust him in every way. We're friends.

Mr Tyson, Bob Wall is charged with a capital offence. A hanging offence. From what you know of him, could he be capable of that offence?

Fred looked closely at Walter, then at the Judge.

No. He could never have done this filthy thing he's accused of. He's not that kind of man.

Why do you say that?

My wife and I know him, and we're fond of him. I know the young lady he's engaged to, and she's stuck by him all through what's happening. She's real quality: not the sort of girl who'd stick to a rapist and a murderer.

Thank you, Mr Tyson. One more thing. It's been stated that Mr Fell worked in his studio on the afternoon of November 2nd last year, and went out at six o'clock. Bob Wall says he went in to the studio at about seven. Now it might be alleged that he actually went there at six, just after Mr Fell had gone, and that for some reason Mrs Gregson was still there. Upon which, Mr Wall raped and murdered her. Do you follow me?

Yes. But –

Good. So tell me, Mr Tyson: are you able to tell the Court whether Bob left your place when he said he did?

Yes – I seen him go. I went out in the garden at seven o'clock, and I seen him get in his car and leave. I remember because the news had just come on the radio.

Thank you, Mr Tyson. No more questions.

The Prosecutor walked across to the witness box. He surveyed Fred Tyson with a smile I thought patronizing.

Mr Tyson, may I ask your age?

I'm sixty-two.

Getting along in years. No offence meant, Mr Tyson, but you're at an age when some people become forgetful, isn't that so?

Some might do. I ain't forgetful.

No? But after all these months, isn't it possible that you may have forgotten what times Mr Wall came and borrowed the milk, and afterwards left for town? Or confused it with another day?

Fred's mouth set.

No. That ain't possible. The day after, the police came on to my property and took him away. I ain't likely to forget that.

I see. I get the impression that Mr Wall is almost like family to you. Is it possible you're not quite as sure of these facts as you say you are? That you perhaps don't *want* to be sure, for his sake?

Fred's eyes narrowed; he pursed his lips, his large hands gripped the top of the witness box, and his wiry frame seemed to expand. He looked from Maxwell to the Judge and back again.

I believe you're callin me a liar. Let me tell you somethin. I'm a Baptist, and I've just sworn on the Good Book to tell the truth. That's a thing I take seriously. When I take an oath on that book, I don't lie.

For a moment, the Prosecutor didn't answer; he seemed disconcerted by the vehemence in Fred's voice. I looked across at the jury. Most of them, at a guess, were men very like Fred Tyson, and they were studying him with expressions I read as sympathetic. Justice McPherson was also studying Fred, his head cocked. His narrow, sober face, framed by his big wig, gave little away; I could only read his expression as speculative.

No more questions your Honour, said the Prosecutor. His voice had a resigned tone.

It was now time for Walter's final address to the jury, which is still vivid in my mind.

He began by summarizing the facts that had emerged to bring the case against Bob into question. Then he paused, adjusting his gown more securely about his shoulders, surveying the jury and the court. When he began to speak again, it was with the controlled passion and measured cadences of an orator. The faint tremor in his voice had become more marked, and seemed to be a symptom of the intensity of his feeling. Up to this point, I'd tended to see Walter as something of an actor, like so many successful barristers; but now I didn't believe he was acting.

Gentlemen of the jury, my client Robert Wall has been accused of the vicious crime of rape and murder, he said. The Defence contends that this accusation is false. Mr Wall's character has been vilified, and he's been subjected to an ordeal very few of us would care to undergo. He's been held in gaol for months, and now finds himself on trial for his life. All this purely on the word of his employer, Mr Max Fell.

He paused and drew closer to the jury box, scanning the faces there.

You must now consider what Fell's word is worth. Fell is the man whom the Defence has shown to be a liar, a lecher, and a sadistic hater of women: a man who has served a prison sentence in Victoria for assault and attempted rape: exactly the type of crime we are dealing with here. In other words, an evil man. Yet this is the man on whose evidence you are being asked to find Robert Wall guilty. I submit to you that Mr Fell is lying again, that his evidence is false, and that he is doing this in order to escape being charged with the murder himself. This is the obvious conclusion the Defence believes you must come to – and I put it to you that were it not for the negligence of the police, who failed to discover Fell's past conviction for violence against a woman, Fell would not have succeeded in his plan, and the charge against Mr Wall could not have been made. I submit that Max Fell has emerged as the likely perpetrator of this crime.

He paused again, and I became aware of a more intense silence than usual in the court. Nobody coughed or moved.

The Defence has now shown you that Robert Wall could not have committed this crime, since Madge Gregson was not modelling for him that evening. She was modelling for Max Fell, in the afternoon. Mr Fell denies this; but you have heard the evidence given by Mrs Harris, the lady who runs the secondhand shop downstairs, that she saw Mrs Gregson arrive there that afternoon – and, most significantly, did not see her leave. She did not see her leave, we suggest, because Max Fell had murdered her. You have also heard the statement by the Government Pathologist that Mrs Gregson was not murdered in the evening, since his tests show that she died in the afternoon.

He broke off, wiping his face with a large white handkerchief and looking about the courtroom. Then he looked across at the jury again.

What you must do now, gentlemen of the jury, is to consider the facts that point to Robert Wall's innocence, and consider the injustice that's been done to a decent and honest young man. The Defence submits that you are bound to declare him not guilty.

Walter turned away, and there was a sudden and startling burst of clapping in the public gallery. I felt something touch my hand where it rested on the bench; I looked down, and was surprised to see that June had taken my hand in hers. She'd never done such a thing before. She turned and looked into my face: her eyes were filled with tears but she was smiling, and the light in her eyes made my head swim.

The Judge called for the gallery to be silent, and the clapping died away. Meanwhile Walter had reached the Bar table, and it seemed to me that his tall, stooped figure swayed a little before he sat down. Suddenly he looked frail, and paler than usual. This was odd and unexpected after his forceful presence of a few moments ago, and I felt a fleeting concern.

It was now time for the Prosecutor's closing address. It was measured and authoritative, but it seemed to have little conviction in it. His case had collapsed, I felt sure, and Maxwell must have known it. When he'd done, I turned to look at June again.

Don't worry, I said. You've got Bob back.

6

A narrative of youth has no final ending; it must simply be broken off at a point that seems natural. I've now come close to that point.

At the age I've reached, memories of conflict, setbacks or success tend to remain with more distinctness than those of happiness. Being bathed in happiness is like being bathed in sunlight: everything is intense, yet nothing stands out sharply. For this reason, my memories of what took place after the jury declared Bob innocent float in a pleasant haze.

On that Friday, when the trial was concluded and the jury was still out, June and I waited outside the tall old doors of the Court in the stone-floored vestibule, together with a group of other spectators. Most people had drifted off, since there was no telling how long it would take for the jury to come to a verdict. Walter had warned me that they might not even reach it that day; but June refused to leave the building, and I had no wish to do so either. As it turned out, only a little over half an hour went by before the Court Crier emerged through the doors and called out that the Court was sitting. Everything then moved with confusing rapidity, and with a feeling of anticlimax.

After the foreman of the jury had announced their verdict, the Judge looked down the courtroom at the dock.

Discharge the prisoner. You may go, Mr Wall.

Bob, looking bewildered, came out through a gate in the fence around the dock, leaving his guard behind. He walked slowly across the courtroom to the Bar table, where Walter was standing and beckoning to him. I watched Bob shake his hand; then I took June by the arm and led her out of the public gallery and across to Walter and Bob. I too shook Walter's hand and congratulated him. He acknowledged this briefly, but he seemed preoccupied and was still very pale. He was looking at a group of journalists who were moving towards us with eager expressions, led by Pat Dwyer. Bob and June were unaware of them, and of everything else; they stood looking at each other as though at some vision that was not to be trusted. Walter tapped Bob on the shoulder.

You'd better follow me, he said. You don't want to be badgered by the press. You can come with me to my Robing Room: I'm not supposed to share it with the public, but this is a special day. Come along: all of you.

We followed him out through a back door of the courtroom and down a passageway to a bare, dim chamber lined with lockers, set aside for the Defence Counsels to change into their wigs and gowns. Bob and June were walking ahead of me, and I saw that they were holding hands. As soon as we were inside the room and the door was closed, Bob put his arms around June and she buried her head in his shoulder. When they broke away they searched each other's faces without speaking; then they both looked at Walter, suddenly growing self-conscious.

But Walter wasn't looking at them. He'd removed his wig, and I saw that the bald white dome of his head was perspiring. He seemed even more pallid than he'd done in court, and I said:

You look pale, Walter. Are you all right?

Of course I'm all right. Perhaps I'm a little tired: it's been a fairly demanding case.

His tone had been impatient and dismissive, and I tried to mollify him.

I know it has. You've been superb.

He waved his hand in dismissal, and began to remove his gown.

No need for the compliments. It did go well, and McPherson's summing-up was very fair. And now let's be out of here.

Before I could answer, Bob stepped close to Walter. His expression was serious: so serious it appeared almost aggressive.

Maybe you don't want to hear this, Mr Dixon, but I have to say it. You've saved my life, and I'll never forget it. We'll always remember you, June and me.

Yes, we will, June said.

Walter looked at them both with an air of faint surprise. Then he put his hand on Bob's shoulder and smiled briefly at June.

I did my job, that's all. This is a good young man, Miss Leaman: I saw that straight away. Otherwise I wouldn't have defended him.

Perhaps because my work is painting, some of the most significant moments in my life persist in memory purely as images: vivid, static and immutable as pictures by a master, and entirely without sound. Even after fifty years, these images hang in my mind with the freshness they had when they first came into being, and no words are needed to define them. Yet words are what I must reach for now.

One of these images is of Bob Wall and June Leaman, just as they were when they embraced in the gloomy Robing Room, afterwards leaning away from each other to look at Walter Dixon, their expressions mingling joy and faint embarrassment: Bob in his unaccustomed blue suit, June in one of the light, short-sleeved dresses she seemed nearly always to wear that summer, this one in a pattern of blues and greens, with a large bow at the neck. It's the joy in their faces that comes back with such clarity, and will never leave my mind. Bob's joy is guarded, as everything is with him; but it's joy nevertheless, making him smile like a distrustful child who's suddenly glimpsed happiness. June Leaman's joy is of another dimension. It has no reserve, and no unease lurks behind it; it springs from the same delight that's been inherent in her nature since she sat in front of me in Grade Six: a delight that shines in her narrow Danish eyes in the way it did on that sunny afternoon when the three of us sat in Fred Tyson's garden, lapped by a mindless happiness. I saw her as Flora then, and she was Flora in Bob's arms in the Robing Room, her freshness and youth seeming to create an aura in the room's dimness. She and Bob are grandparents now; but it's this image from their youth that tells the final truth about them, and not what Time has done – though Time has been kind enough.

Contemplating that image, that reunion of theirs in a back room of the Criminal Court, I was filled with gladness for them, mingled with the wistfulness I'd been gripped by when I learned of their engagement, since I had enough insight even then to be aware that a girl like June could never have been for me: we were too different. During the trial, I'd met her every day outside the Court in Campbell Street, and afterwards had walked with her to her tram. I still see her clearly, walking through the January heat beside me, cool in her summer dress and a wide-brimmed straw hat with a green band around the crown. What did we talk about? Of nothing very much, except Bob and the trial; we had so little in common. June was uncomplicated and ordinary, while I was afflicted with the kind of sensibility which is the source of art, but which hardly ever makes for serenity. Yes, she was ordinary; but I don't use this word condescendingly. She was one of those special beings in whom another quality exists: one which adds spice to the ordinary. For want of a better word, I'll call this her mystery; but it was a different kind of mystery from Moira Doran's: something far simpler and yet more elusive. It was the mainspring of her charm for me, since I was beguiled by the ordinary when it combined with mystery: a fixation that would continue all my life, and form the main subject of my work.

So what was the reason for my sadness? I suppose it lay in the fact that in spite of my nature, *I wanted to be one of them*, that special kind like June and Bob; that kind who were so alike, even in their fair-haired looks, that they might have been brother and sister, and who were suited only to each other. I wanted – knowing it could never happen – to be one of those fair-haired chosen ones who were ordinary yet always enigmatic, and who took life's gifts for granted. The longing for it filled my being, in that time when Moira Doran was gone from my life.

The day after the trial I spent at home, working on a sketch I'd done of the courtroom, the Judge and the jury, and of Fell in the witness box. The next day, Sunday, I went out to visit Walter as I always did.

Mrs Anderson answered the doorbell, and told me that Walter was sitting on the verandah, outside the dining-room. She looked solemn.

He hasn't been all that well, she said. But he's expecting you.

I found him lying on a cane reclining chair with his feet up, casually yet sprucely dressed in a white short-sleeved summer shirt and tan slacks. There was a book on the round bamboo table beside him, but his glasses lay beside it and he wasn't reading; he was gazing out at the orchard, his head on a cushion, blinking in the sun that flowed through the verandah. A carafe of water and a glass also stood on the table, together with a bottle of pills and a small brass bell. When I came up, he greeted me with a gentle air, his voice rather low. His edginess of Friday was gone, but his head was dewed with perspiration again. It was a hot day, which might have been the reason for this, I thought; but it wasn't the kind of intense heat that would normally have caused perspiration.

He gestured at a cane armchair on the other side of the table and told me to sit down. I asked him how he was feeling.

Mrs Anderson's been talking has she? It's nothing to fuss about, he said. I had a little turn, and my doctor came to see me.

A turn? What sort of turn?

I must have looked worried, because he shook his head impatiently.

You're as bad as Mrs Anderson, Hugh – a slight indisposition, and you fuss. I had chest pains yesterday after dinner, which I thought were indigestion, and pains in my arm. I imagined they'd pass off, but they got worse: rather oppressive, in fact. So I called Doctor Duncan. He informed me that it was an attack of angina, and prescribed these Anginine pills.

He waved at the bottle on the table, and I stared at him with increased concern.

But Walter, that's a kind of heart attack isn't it?

He frowned, and wiped away perspiration with his handkerchief.

That's being over-dramatic. Lots of people have small bouts of angina – it doesn't mean they're about to be felled by a full-blown heart attack.

Is that the way the doctor sees it?

Doctor Duncan is inclined to look at the worst possibilities. That's what doctors have to do, no doubt, but he fusses as much as Mrs Anderson does. He's told me to keep the pills by me, in case of another attack, and to ring this silly little bell for Mrs Anderson and ask her to call him if the pain gets worse.

He pointed to the bell, which I suddenly saw as a rather ominous object; I began to realize that the situation was more serious than Walter wanted to acknowledge.

Duncan says my heart's not as strong as it was, Walter said. He's told me to rest. I don't like being idle, but I'm inclined to do what he says for a bit. I'm somewhat tired since the trial.

That's natural. You were magnificent, Walter. You're a hero to Bob and June.

Tut, he said, and waved his hand; but I saw that this had pleased him. He drew himself up higher in his chair; then he turned to look at me more directly, and his voice grew stronger.

I have two pieces of news for you. One of them is rather grisly; the other I hope will please you. The first news concerns Max Fell. He's dead.

Dead?

This is not known to the public. They'll no doubt learn of it in the *Mail* on Monday. I have a friend in the police – not Detective Sergeant Parsons, I may say, who now hates me with a passion – and my friend telephoned me yesterday. He gave me some information that they won't release to the press until tomorrow. It seems that as soon as the jury gave their verdict on Friday, the police obtained a warrant for Fell's arrest, and intended to charge him with the murder. They went up to Liverpool Street on Saturday and found him dead in his flat. An overdose of sleeping pills, apparently. When he read the newspaper reports of the trial, he must have decided that this was his best option. The alternative was almost certainly the noose. I imagine he did the deed on Saturday morning.

I made some sort of exclamation, and sat digesting what he'd told me.

I hope you'll find my next piece of news more savoury, Walter said. It concerns the exhibition of your paintings in Melbourne. It's all arranged. It will open in the Hallmark Gallery in South Yarra on Saturday the 23rd – subject to their being happy with what you send them – and will run for four days.

I stared at him with what must have been a stupid expression.

That's in two weeks. I'm not ready.

Of course you're ready. You've got a fine body of work, and you've prevaricated long enough. All you have to do is get it framed and shipped over.

But I don't understand. They haven't seen an example of my work. How could they decide to exhibit me?

Ah, but they *have* seen a sample. I'd been negotiating this by telephone for some weeks, before the trial devoured everything. Nigel Cuthbertson, who runs the gallery, is something of a friend of mine, as I told you. I sent him on loan the picture of Lucas Wilson you gave me, and he was immediately convinced: he admires it greatly. So get cracking, Hugh – get your best work together. Unless of course you think it not worthwhile.

He looked at me coldly, and I quickly assured him of my appreciation. The news had been very sudden, I said, and I'd needed to absorb it. Of course I wanted to exhibit, but I feared what the public might think of my sort of work. It had all been a private activity until now, and the leap into the public eye was daunting. But I'd do all I could to get a group of pictures together during the week, and I'd be grateful for his opinion of the selection.

Walter's face softened, and he smiled. Of course, he said. I understand. It's like leaping off a springboard. An artist of your kind lives in a private world, and when he opens a door on it to the public, his privacy is invaded. But consciously or not, you're making your pictures to be *seen* – and have no fear, Hugh: if Cuthbertson's any indication, they'll like it. I hope to come over to Melbourne with you, and give you moral support – but that's not yet certain.

I do hope you can come, Walter.

So do I, but Doctor Duncan's being a tyrant. It depends on my passing muster with him: on whether my health's improved by then. And now let's have tea. I'll ring this bloody bell for Mrs Anderson.

The housekeeper brought us the usual tea and scones on a tray, and set them on the table. Eating our scones, we were quiet for a while. Then Walter said:

Moira Doran came and saw me yesterday. She's getting married, and brought her prospective husband to meet me. He seemed a nice fellow. Middle-aged; an accountant. I found him a little tedious, but I imagine he'll be good to her.

A vivid pang went through me. I said nothing, and looked out over the garden. When Walter spoke again, his voice was softer.

It was bound to happen, Hugh. She needs the security. I doubt that she loves him, but that's not what matters at this stage of her life: she likes him and trusts him.

Still I sat in silence, and Walter's voice came to me from a distance.

She loved you, Hugh – not much doubt of that. I also believe she was the right kind of woman for you. That might surprise you, considering what I said to you at the time. But Moira was too old, and for you it was too soon. No remedy for that. No remedy. It's a pain you must endure.

I know, I said. I continued to look out towards the orchard. The bright green leaves of the apple trees were shimmering in the heat, and their multitude of shadows seemed to dance in the light breeze. There was a smell of woodsmoke from somewhere.

Moira and I had some interesting conversations, Walter said. She changed my thinking in certain ways – and not many people can do that, at my age. As you know, she's a Catholic, and she made me consider the possibility that the Devil really exists. Have you thought much about him, Hugh?

Not much. I suppose I consider him a superstition.

Yes. So did I. Now I'm tending to change my mind. You're an Anglican of course, like me. Do you go to church much?

Not for years. My parents only go at Christmas and Easter.

Many of us Anglicans drift away, don't we? I've tended to do so, and seldom go to church either – though I've never lost my belief in the divine. As you know, I believe it to be the source of the greatest art – even though belief has declined so much since the Enlightenment. But I dismissed the medieval horned figure with the pitchfork, as so many do. I saw Catholic belief in him as Mediterranean superstition, until my talks with Moira. What she made me consider is that disbelief in Satan suits him very well, since it's made his work easy – and that Satan is nothing like the caricatures. All we can know is that he's a force – and so are the many demons who seek to possess people. I read my New Testament again, and I was surprised to find how often Christ was casting out demons. Do you remember the incident in Saint Mark, about the man possessed by an unclean spirit? When Christ ordered it out and asked its name, it said: 'My name is Legion, for we are many.'

I looked at Walter in surprise, wondering if his attack, with its serious implications, had brought about this interest in religion. He read my expression, and smiled.

You think I've had some sort of conversion to fundamentalism. Far from it. But I've never dismissed the world of the spirit, even at my most sceptical; I simply look at the possibilities. What has set me thinking about this more than anything else is my contact with our friend Fell. His was no ordinary wickedness. At times one encounters people who seem genuinely possessed by a demon. I believe Fell may have been one of them; and he confirms a suspicion I've had for some time: that the minor demons, if they exist, are squalid, and not very intelligent.

It's an interesting theory, I said.

I remained rather dubious about such things, but had no wish to debate them with him now. We sat quietly for a time; then I asked him if I could bring my paintings out during the week. I wanted him to have the final word on the selection, I said.

I'd be delighted. Let's say Wednesday, Hugh.

His voice seemed to have grown weaker; almost languid. He was clearly tiring, and I stood up to go and asked if I could get him anything.

No, no, he said. Mrs Anderson will look after me. I have my little bell. She's going to live in for a time, after tomorrow. I'm providing her with a pleasant room, and all she asks is to bring her cat with her. I've no objection to a cat.

*

Walter remained too weak to come to Melbourne. I managed to get leave from the *Mail* for the duration of my exhibition, and stayed for the four days in a hotel in the city. As soon as I got back, I telephoned Leyburn Farm. Mrs Anderson answered.

He can't come to the phone, I'm afraid. He's had another attack, and he's not well at all. The doctor said he mustn't move from his bed.

I'll come out there tomorrow, I said. That's if he'll see me.

I'm sure he will – he keeps asking if you're back. But you'll have to be quiet with him.

When I arrived the next morning, Mrs Anderson answered the door. She had the distracted expression that simple people display when they feel that events are getting beyond their control.

He's in the library, she said, and led the way down the hall.

The library? I thought he was in bed.

He *is* in bed. But he wanted to be in the library, so he got the gardener and his mate to move the bed in there. He can get to the bathroom, but otherwise he's not supposed to move. He's that wilful: Doctor Duncan said he should be in hospital, but he refuses to go. He's hired a nurse to come here three or four times a week, and I get him his meals and look after him. Doctor Duncan says he'll come if there's an emergency – but it worries me. Your uncle needs expert attention, I would have thought.

I came into the library to find Walter in a big old-fashioned four-poster bed set up in the middle of the room, walled in on three sides by his books. A black-and-white cat lay asleep on the end of the bed. It was another warm day and the French windows stood open, framing his favourite view to the north: the garden, the orchard and the distant hills. Seeing this, I understood immediately why he'd wanted to be here. He was propped up against a number of pillows, and looked immaculate as ever in dark blue pyjamas of fine cotton. He was well-shaven, and his aesthete's white locks were neatly combed. A small table stood next to the bed with books on it, as well as his carafe of water, his pills and the little bell. He smiled as I approached him, and I saw that he'd changed in some way; at first I wasn't sure how. Then I saw that his alert, stern demeanour had changed to one of peculiar gentleness, and that the combative gleam in his large blue eyes was gone.

I sat down on a chair by the bed, and he put out his hand and took mine, squeezing it for a moment.

So, he said. You see how it is, dear boy. If I have to be confined to bed, I prefer to be here. The bedroom became depressing.

He pointed to the cat.

This is Magpie: he belongs to Mrs Anderson. Since old Jock died, the house has no animals, and I miss their little spirits around me.

You've had a bad attack, she tells me.

I'm afraid she doesn't exaggerate, this time. The pain was really quite bad, and Duncan says I nearly departed this world. He gave me a shot of morphine, and he'll come back and give me more shots if the pain visits me again – which no doubt it will. He's a good man – he'll always come if there's an emergency. I also have an excellent nurse calling in who'll alert him if things get dramatic.

Walter – you should be in hospital, shouldn't you?

His mouth set, and he looked away out the French windows. There was a faint dew of perspiration on his forehead.

I won't have that, Hugh. I won't leave this house. I'll only leave it when I'm carried out feet first.

I saw that it wouldn't do to argue with him, and I said: You got my letter from Melbourne?

He pointed; it was lying on the table by his books. It contained a clipping of the long and favourable review I'd been given in the leading Melbourne daily.

Of course, he said, and I'm proud of you. So enough of my trials; congratulations, Hugh. You've had all the success I said you would. Cuthbertson phoned me, and he was gushing. You're hailed by the Melbourne arts fraternity as a kind of prodigy, apparently. How do they describe you? As a realist? How inadequate – but let them, if it makes them happy. They need their little labels. And how were the pictures selling, when you left?

They've nearly sold out, I said.

Good, good. So now your career begins. And in regard to that, I have some things to tell you. I tire easily now, so I'll make it brief.

He reached out and picked up his glass of water and sipped from it, his hand trembling a little.

Listen to me, Hugh. What you must do now is resign from that silly job and go abroad. Go to Europe, and explore the galleries. I wouldn't advise London as a base. Go to Paris, or better still Florence, where the great works of the Renaissance will be all around you. Then come back and set up a studio in Melbourne or Sydney.

I can't do that. I've no money.

Yes you have. I'm about to give you a sum that will pay your passage on a ship and finance you for a year. I have a cheque here ready for you.

I can't accept it, Walter.

He looked at me now, and some of his old sternness had come back.

You can, and you will. Look here: I'm under doctor's orders not to get upset. If I do get upset, I'm told it could bring on another attack. Do you want to be responsible for that?

It was a kind of blackmail, and I shook my head and sat in silence. He reached out and took my hand again, and this time continued to hold it. His voice sank, and its tremor grew more pronounced.

I refused to accept my condition when I had the first angina attack. We're never ready for death, when he comes calling. But now, thanks to that realistic medico Duncan, I do accept it. This last attack nearly killed me; the next one probably will. Don't look like that Hugh, it's simply a fact. My time is over, and that's why I won't leave this house. This is where I want to die, not in some damned hospital. I've made my final will, and it's lodged at the firm with your uncle George. I've left a small sum of money to you: enough to free you to work for a couple of years and establish yourself. After that it's up to you. Leyburn is left to George: that was always agreed between your grandfather Charles and me. No doubt George will sell it, and he might as well. A tide of little houses will soon come up Montrose Road and surround it, and I'm glad I won't live to see that.

He paused, and lay back on the pillows and closed his eyes. Then he opened them again, and his voice strengthened.

Just regard this bit of money I'm going to give you now as an advance on what's coming to you later. Don't give me any bloody arguments, I beg you. You're my spiritual son, Hugh; why shouldn't you inherit some of my useless money? You'll live the life I wanted to live, and develop the talent I never had. I'm not being generous; this gives me selfish pleasure. Just promise me one thing: go out and discover the world, but never lose touch with your native hills.

That's easy to promise, I said.

He let go of my hand and turned his head towards the French windows, looking out at the orchard.

I'm going to have to sleep in a moment, Hugh. Will you come tomorrow?

Of course. I'll be here by three.

He nodded. His eyes closed, and I soon saw that he was asleep. I got up and moved to the door.

*

When I arrived the following afternoon, the door was answered by a small woman in a belted white uniform with a red cape. She introduced herself as Sister Ford.

Mr Dixon's been asking for you, she said. But you may not be able to talk to him for very long. He's drifting.

She led me down the hall, and I asked her for more details. Walter had taken a turn for the worse during the night, she told me. Doctor Duncan had come and given him some morphine, and had asked her to stay in the house tonight. It was possible that Walter might not live for more than another twenty-four hours.

She left me at the door of the library, and I paused there for some moments before I went in, digesting what she'd said.

I found him lying in bed as before, with the French windows standing open on to the verandah. The cat was still there, at the foot of the bed, but it wasn't sleeping now; it was watching the garden. It was a calm, still day, and the murmuring of bees in the roses outside floated into the room, wavering, fading, and then becoming distinct again. Walter's eyes were closed, and I was shocked by his appearance. His face seemed to have grown thinner, and it was bloodless, like that of a corpse. His hands lay side by side in front of him on the counterpane, as though they'd been arranged there by somebody else. His mouth was agape, and I thought he was asleep; but as I crossed the room, his eyes opened, and he smiled faintly.

Hugh, he said. You're here. His voice was very weak and low.

I'm here, I said, and sat down on the chair by the bed. One of his hands opened, and moved uncertainly across the counterpane towards me. I took it and it clasped mine feebly. Yesterday it had been warm; today it was cold and sweaty.

I'm afraid I may be leaving you sooner than I thought, he said. Then, before I could reply, he said: There's no need for you to comment on that. Don't let's have any sentimentality, for God's sake. Duncan thinks I'll go soon, and it's just as well. I've no wish to protract this. It's come to the point of bedpans, and who wants that sort of wretchedness?

He stopped and closed his eyes; his breathing was shallow, and I saw that he was already tiring.

Don't talk if you're too tired, I said.

I want to talk. We may not talk again. But forgive me if I drift off. One of the few nice things about this is the lovely morphine Duncan provides me with: it gives me interesting dreams. I'm thankful to be here where I wanted to be: I love to look out at my orchard. Once I saw Liam Dalton again, walking through the trees. Probably in one of my morphine dreams, but he seemed very real.

His eyes closed, and his voice became fainter.

A rogue, I suppose; and yet a good man. Such a thing was possible, then. They lived in hard times.

He fell silent again and I continued to hold his hand, wondering if his mind was wandering. But then he began to speak again.

I'd have liked to see Lucas Wilson there; but he never comes. Perhaps I'll see my father, if I watch long enough. Perhaps even an angel. I'm afraid I won't keep awake much longer. I'm very glad you came, Hugh.

I bent closer to hear him if he spoke again. But he'd ceased, it seemed.

I owe you everything, Walter, I said.

His eyelids fluttered open and he looked at me.

You owe me nothing, Hugh. I chose to help you because I believed in you. I've been proved right, haven't I?

He broke off again; his breathing became deeper, and he seemed to have fallen asleep. There was no sound now but the intermittent humming of the bees, and I sat for a long time, not moving. The cat was sitting up, staring at Walter as though it sensed something. Suddenly it sprang to the floor, and glided out on to the verandah.

Something like half an hour went by, and then Sister Ford came in. She came over and took Walter's pulse.

He'll probably sleep for some time, now. He tires very easily. Perhaps you should come back tomorrow, Mr Dixon. Don't worry about him: Doctor Duncan's doing everything he can.

I said I'd wait a short time longer, and then go. I sat for perhaps another quarter hour, and Walter didn't move. But then I noticed that his eyes were open, staring at the ceiling, and that his lips were parted as though he were about to speak.

Walter? I said; but he didn't answer.

He hadn't heard me, yet he seemed to be listening, lying there with his mouth open, his face upturned: listening as he'd no doubt done so often over the years, standing on the verandah and looking towards the hills, conjuring up the thudding of hooves, and waiting perhaps for a visitation from that doomed, misguided visionary who'd seldom left his father's thoughts and had so long invaded his own: not the man that Wilson had actually been, but a spirit of ultimate freedom, coming down from the ranges to liberate his life.

Walter died that night, with Doctor Duncan in attendance.

I only learned this from Sister Ford when I arrived the next morning. She told me that George Dixon had been there last night, just before Walter died, and would be arriving again soon to take charge of the funeral arrangements. I was filled with guilt, even though she told me that Walter had seldom been conscious since I'd left the previous afternoon, and probably could not have spoken with me. He'd had a series of heart attacks, the last of which, at nine in the evening, had been the last. He hadn't suffered, she said; the morphine had seen to that.

I'm seventy-two, as I write this: one year younger than Walter was when he died, nearly fifty years ago. Sometimes I wonder how long it will be before my own turn comes – and perhaps that's part of the reason I embarked on this memoir. I've lost my wife, many of my relatives are dead, and some of my friends have begun to die. What remains of those who've gone? Fading images of their faces – even the face of my wife – growing ever less distinct. Lost voices, repeating a few disjointed words that have lodged in my memory: voices of those I knew, and of others, like Wilson and Dalton and my great-grandfather Martin Dixon, whom I met at one remove. From the perspective of old age, almost everything begins to be marooned in the past, and to take on the same unreality. My friend Bob Wall, June Leaman, Moira Doran and even Walter Dixon have almost the same remoteness now as those figures from that old, lost century of whom Walter spoke so often, and whose voices I hear in my mind.

Keep faith with the hills. I believe I've heeded this appeal of Lucas Wilson's – which was also Walter Dixon's last advice. Though I've lived most of my life outside the island, my native hills have figured very often in my work. Back here again, perhaps to stay, I wander outside the town and study their rhyming outlines: olive-green; deep green; blue. Familiar, unchanging and apparently static, they nevertheless have a look of illusory fluidity, and are constantly renewing themselves. Their enigma is never solved; it continues to beckon me, even now. It's the enigma of distance, and of territories forever beyond reach. Go near to them, and those hills that wove a mystery against the sky dissolve; become mere tree-covered slopes; cease to be themselves. Distance, and only distance is where they have their being; distance makes them into visions.

It's a distance that can never be crossed, since it belongs in another dimension: the dimension of the angelic, and the life beyond this.

Author's Note

All the characters and incidents portrayed in this novel are fictitious.

The outlaws Lucas Wilson and Liam Dalton are both invented, as is their Utopia in the mountains. However, some minor elements concerning them are partially drawn from fact. The episode concerning Wilson's recruitment in the Royal Horse Guards and his transportation for assault on a superior officer owes some of its factual accuracy to a sequence in an autobiography by Charles Cozens: *Adventures of a Guardsman*, published in 1848. And Liam Dalton's escape from Port Arthur is modelled on the achievement of the Irish bushranger Martin Cash – though Dalton's origins in Ireland and his career as an outlaw are quite different.

I wish to thank my editor Jamie Grant and my agent Margaret Connolly for their unfailing encouragement. Thanks are also due to the following friends for their generous help with background detail: Warren Reed, Neville Ludbey, Paul and Gillian Fenton, Piers Laverty, Max Angus and Lucinda Hawkins. For advice on aspects of colonial Van Diemen's Land, my thanks to Tasmanian historians Alison Alexander, Hamish Maxwell-Stewart, Alex Green and Brian Rieusset. I'm indebted to the following legal experts for their advice and information concerning criminal court procedures and police methods in Tasmania in the 1950s: David Gunson, SC; Mary Hodgson, LLB, and Kenneth Read, LLB.